AETHERIAL ANNIHILATION

OVERWORLD CHRONICLES
BOOK ELEVEN

JOHN CORWIN

ISBN- 978-1-942453-02-4

Printed in the U.S.A.

RAVEN
HOUSE

To my wonderful support group:
Alana Rock
Karen Stansbury

My amazing editors:
Annetta Ribken
Jennifer Wingard

My awesome cover artist:
Regina Wamba

Thanks so much for all your help and input!

Books by John Corwin:

The Overworld Chronicles:
Sweet Blood of Mine
Dark Light of Mine
Fallen Angel of Mine
Dread Nemesis of Mine
Twisted Sister of Mine
Dearest Mother of Mine
Infernal Father of Mine
Sinister Seraphim of Mine
Wicked War of Mine
Dire Destiny of Ours
Aetherial Annihilation
Baleful Betrayal

Overworld Underground:
Possessed By You
Demonicus

Overworld Arcanum:
Conrad Edison and the Living Curse
Conrad Edison and the Anchored World

Stand Alone Novels:
No Darker Fate
The Next Thing I Knew
Outsourced
Seventh

For the latest on new releases, free ebooks, and more, join John Corwin's Newsletter at www.johncorwin.net!

THE MAGIC IS GONE

When crystal meteors slam to earth and drain the magical energy from the world, Justin and gang are once more pressed into action.

Confronted with the prospect of a world without magic, they'll face their toughest challenge yet—how to destroy the crystalline threat and discovering who's behind the attack. But the meteors are all over the planet and getting to them without the use of omniarch portals or magical transportation poses a daunting task.

If Justin and his allies can't disable the meteors in time, the world may lose magic for good and the supernatural community will be destroyed.

Chapter 1

I found Nightliss sitting in the war-torn field behind Arcane University a few days after the end of the Second Seraphim War.

Wondering what she was doing out there all alone, I sat down beside her and put an arm on her shoulder. "Are you okay?"

She looked at me, her expression as bleak as the blasted landscape. "No." She wiped tears from her eyes and stood. "I don't think I can go on anymore, Justin."

"But you're the Templar Clarion—their guiding light." I squeezed her small hand in mine. "They need you—we all need you."

She took a deep breath, eyes lost in the distance. "My sister is dead and Eden is safe. Now Ketiss marches to Seraphina and into another war."

"Do you plan to go with him?" I asked.

She shook her head. "Seraphina doesn't feel like home anymore."

I sensed something more to that statement. "And Eden?"

Nightliss blinked and looked up as if waking from a dream. "I don't know where I belong."

"With us, with your family."

She hugged me. "I love you, Justin. You are a true and dear friend."

Dread spread its cold tendrils through my chest. "You're not planning to kill yourself are you?"

Nightliss smiled and stood. "No. But I'm going away for a while." She looked around the destroyed field and over at the blackened ruins of Colossus Stadium. "I have fought too many wars in my life. I want to find peace. I want to find *myself*."

Her statement hit a nerve deep within me. I'd gone from hardcore nerd to supernatural warrior in the space of a year, fought demons, angels, and almost everything in between without a break. How many thousands had died under my watch? How many more would die when Ketiss invaded his homeland to wrest control of the government back from the traitor Cephus? I pushed to my feet as the past swirled through my mind.

"You're haunted by ghosts too, Justin." Nightliss looked at me with intense green eyes. "You just haven't realized it yet." She stood on her tiptoes and kissed me on the cheek. "I will see you again."

Tears stung my eyes. I embraced her petite frame. "Don't pick any fights with stray dogs."

She laughed and cried. "You will always be my hero, the man who saved a little black cat."

"I'm going to miss you so much." I kissed her forehead and reluctantly did what I had to do.

I let her go.

Nightliss wiped her eyes, turned, and walked away.

War is an ugly thing.

Even if you survive, it slowly kills you inside. Nightliss had woken something inside me—a realization that I hadn't made it unscathed through the countless battles I'd fought against Daelissa and her minions. I wasn't ready to embark on a journey to Seraphina to unseat a usurper, much less to fight a long war against more Brightlings.

Maybe Nightliss had the right idea. Maybe I needed some time away from death and destruction.

Ketiss has an army of super-charged Darklings. He won't have any problems beating Cephus.

I called Elyssa.

"What's up, babe?" she asked.

I took a breath to soothe the knot in my throat. "How would you like to see the world?"

A pause. "Right now?"

"The train leaves tomorrow."

She chuckled. "A plane or portal would be a lot faster."

"We're taking a break from the supernatural." I couldn't remember where I'd left my wallet and ID. "Do you have a passport?"

"No."

"Well, I guess we have some nom stuff to take care of."

Elyssa made a thoughtful noise. "You're serious, aren't you?"

I kicked a rock across the mud. "Yeah. I just want to be a normal guy with his normal girlfriend for a while. Is that okay?"

"There are a lot of loose ends around here, Justin." She sighed. "Now isn't really a good time."

"There will never be a good time." The more I thought about fighting in Seraphina, the more desperate I was to run away. "Please."

She spoke in a soft voice. "As you wish."

The tightness in my chest eased. "I love you."

"I love you too."

Three months later, Elyssa and I watched the sun set over the Andaman Sea in Thailand. Splashing in the water and bathing in the sun was nice after our visit to Switzerland and chillier climates. A young woman raced past us and into the water. Her dark hair, petite figure, and olive skin looked so familiar.

Elyssa looked at the woman. "Something wrong?"

I shook my head. "She looks like Nightliss."

"You've seen someone who reminds you of Nightliss in every country we've visited."

"Yeah." I forced a smile. "I hope she's doing okay."

"She's a powerful Seraphim, Justin." Elyssa squeezed my hand. "Of course she's okay."

"Emotionally, I mean." I cleared my throat to ward off the knot forming and changed the subject. "Gorgeous sunset."

"Mhm." She watched me for a moment. "You're feeling guilty again, aren't you?"

I looked down. "Are you?"

"This vacation has been amazing, and my father tells me everything is under control but—"

"You feel like you're shirking your duty?" I said.

She nodded.

3

I blew out a breath. "Maybe I wimped out, I dunno. When Nightliss told me how she felt, it just hit a nerve, you know?"

Elyssa wrapped her arms around my neck. "You have nothing to prove to me. I'll travel the world with you for eternity if that's what you want."

I chuckled. "I'll settle for cuddling for now."

She planted a kiss on my lips. "Maybe once it gets dark and everyone leaves, we can do a little more than cuddling."

"Like stargazing?"

She punched my shoulder. "Yes, that's exactly what I meant."

We leaned against each other and watched the last rays of the sun vanish over the horizon. Before long, it was dark. The lack of sunlight didn't deter many people, and it looked like the privacy we wanted wasn't coming anytime soon.

Elyssa pointed up. "Look, a falling star."

I noticed it as well. In fact, it was hard not to notice the massive glowing ball in the sky growing larger and larger with every passing second. "Holy farting fairies, that thing is huge."

"Shouldn't it have burned up in the atmosphere?" Elyssa asked.

I sat up and watched the massive meteor slam into the ocean just off the coast of another small island a few clicks from ours. The water didn't quench the flames. Instead, the glow grew brighter until it lit the ocean like a massive pool light.

Shouts of alarm rose from the other people on the beach. Those shouts turned to screams as a great glowing mountain of water crested and headed for shore.

A tidal wave.

People ran inland toward the small tourist town. A mountain loomed about a half-mile away, but I didn't see how anyone could possibly make it there in time—anyone except for Elyssa and me.

Despite the uncountable monsters I'd faced, I didn't know how in the world to fight Mother Nature's wrath. I might channel a magical shield to protect Elyssa and me from the wave, but that wouldn't save the stampede of normal people running for their lives.

Think, Justin, think!

4

Seraphim magic came in four different flavors: Murk, Brilliance, Stasis, and Clarity.

Brilliance, the element of destruction, would only turn the water to steam. Stasis might freeze the water temporarily, but channeling it required a great deal more effort. Clarity revealed a soul's deepest inner truths, but water didn't have a soul.

That left Murk, the magical energy of creation. It formed the strongest barriers, but I'd never before attempted a shield so massive.

"You've got that look again," Elyssa said.

"The one where I just ate a lot of spicy Indian food and really regret it?"

"Actually, it does kind of resemble that expression, but in this case, you're not running for the bathroom." She gripped my arm. "You're going to try to stop this thing, aren't you?"

I nodded. "I can't let all these people die."

Elyssa looked at the fleeing crowds and a look of firm resolve erased the fear from her eyes. "Then let's save them."

We raced toward the glowing ocean and the looming tidal wave. In the distance, I saw water crash across the surface of the distant island where the meteor had fallen. I wondered how many lives the ocean had just snuffed out of existence but forced the thought from my mind. I walked to the edge of the water, took a deep breath, and prayed I had it in me to keep this monster at bay.

I drew in aether, the magical energy of the world, and channeled it into Murk. My veins grew icy cold as I flooded myself with the dark ultraviolet energy, letting it build until I felt ready to freeze solid. The air rumbled and a gust of hot wind hit my face as the water loomed like a leviathan from the deep poised to consume me and the island whole.

Despite the power coursing through me, I felt insignificant—like an ant preparing to thwart the advance of an elephant.

"Oh my god," I whispered. "That thing is huge." My confidence melted and my knees buckled. Unfortunately, there wasn't much I could do at this point but try or die. Holding my left hand out before me, I imagined a giant wall forming along the beach and opened the floodgates.

Ultraviolet energy flooded the air, shimmering and crystalizing like black ice. I drew more and more energy from the magical ley lines in the earth, until it felt as though I were nothing more than a conductor discharging aether into the air.

My body could take no more. I felt something pop, like a fuse snapping in my brain. My legs went limp and I fell. Strong arms caught me by the armpits and Elyssa spoke.

"I've got you, babe." She dragged me away from the water.

My body finally regained some strength and I climbed wearily to my feet. My crystalline wall rose fifty feet tall and a hundred yards wide, curving slightly inward. It was by far the largest shield I'd ever conjured, but it might as well have been a picket fence compared to the monstrous beast I hoped to contain.

"It's not enough," I said. "It's nowhere near enough."

Elyssa stared at the oncoming horror, futility in her eyes. "You did your best, Justin. That's all anyone can ask."

With a thunderous roar the tidal wave struck my shield. Water rushed around the sides, filling in the gap behind it while the brunt of the wave pressed against it. Cracks sprouted in the middle and I knew it wasn't going to hold for long.

I ran back to our beach towels and slid on my flip-flops. "We've got to run for it."

Elyssa grabbed her purse and slung it over her shoulder. "Are you strong enough?"

I nodded. "Yeah, I think so." My legs felt wobbly, but my demon aura was already speeding my recovery.

Fangs flashing, violet eyes glowing, Elyssa called upon her supernatural dhampyr strength. Half human, half vampire, and all Templar, she wasn't quite as strong as me, but she made up for it in agility.

My flip-flops flipped and flopped at about a hundred flip-flops per minute for the first fifty yards until I lost one. *I wonder if it's just a flip now, or a flop.* We passed by a parking lot. I saw people atop hotels and houses, their faces hidden in the shadows until the luminescent wave crested close enough to cast the small town in light.

I heard them scream when they realized the wave was far higher than their hotels. Elyssa and I soon caught up to the crowds of fleeing people and it occurred to me that our supernatural speed wouldn't do us a lot of good if we couldn't squeeze through the throng.

Screaming metal, shattering glass, and the crackling of trees rose above the sound of rushing water as the wave crashed through the parking lot a few hundred yards behind us. I glanced back and saw the wall of water quickly gaining on us, preceded by a swell that swallowed the street moments before the wave annihilated everything in its path.

I grabbed Elyssa's waist, aimed a hand at a nearby building, and channeled a web of Murk to swing us over the throng. Nothing happened.

Elyssa raised an eyebrow and urged me to run. "Was that a hug, or did you have something else planned?"

"We need to get around this crowd, but I can't seem to channel magic." Trampled bodies lay in the street and a wall of humanity prevented our escape. I knelt next to a moaning woman on the side of the street. Two children cried over her and a fallen man nearby. Anger, sorrow, and worst of all, futility weighed me down with guilt. My attempt to save this island had failed miserably. Looking up at the nearest hotel buildings, I realized they were probably tall enough to protect people, but how was I supposed to get people up there before the wave hit?

Elyssa wiped tears from her eyes. "Justin, you can't save everyone."

I shook my head. "No, but saving one person is better than just saving myself." Without my magic, there was only one way to do this. I unleashed my inner demon and manifested. Muscles rippled and bulged along my arms and bare chest, making me even stronger than my human form. My body grew taller and wider, and a tail sprouted from my backside. A light blue tone shaded my skin. I ran to the children.

They looked up at me, the demon monster, and screamed.

"I'm here to help," I said, my voice deeper than usual.

7

The boy recovered first. "You're a superhero? Is that why you look so scary?"

"Exactly." The unconscious man next to them moaned. I glanced back at the wave and made a quick decision. I slung the man over a shoulder, took off his belt, and wrapped it loosely around my waist.

"I have something better," Elyssa said, and produced a strand of diamond fiber rope from her purse.

"What *don't* you have in there?" I asked. "Come hug my waist," I told the kids. "I'm going to tie you to me."

The girl, frightened as she looked, followed her brother. I knelt and secured them against my waist. All those bodies hanging encumbered my stride, but there really wasn't a way around it.

Elyssa picked up the woman in the road and placed her over a shoulder. She pointed to the tallest hotel. "That's our best bet."

When we reached the building, I leapt up and caught the railing of the lowest balcony, pulled myself up. Leapt to the next one, wash, rinse, repeat. The boy whooped with excitement. His sister shrieked and buried her face in my ribs. I looked down. Elyssa hung three stories below me, sweat-streaked face grim with determination.

We still had a dozen stories to go before reaching the roof. The rumbling of the wave drew closer and closer. I looked back and saw it tearing up the street less than a hundred yards away. We'd never make it in time. I redoubled my efforts, springing myself as high as possible and skipping balconies in between.

Even with my demon form strength, I was panting by the time I reached the roof. People cried out in shock and fell over themselves in an effort to get away from me. I unbound the kids and put the man on the roof. I looked down and saw Elyssa seven stories away and struggling. Without thinking, I leapt off the roof. When I was only a short distance from her, I pressed my claws into the brick, digging deep gouges, and gained a foothold. I wrapped my tail around the woman and snatched her from Elyssa's back.

"Go," she said weakly.

"Not without you." I grabbed her hand. "Get ready for launch."

She braced her feet on the side of the building and bent her knees. "Go!"

I slung her upward with all my might. She performed a graceful flip, clearing five stories and grabbing the railing. She hung upside down by her legs and held out her arms. "Throw her!"

I dangled the unconscious woman, bent my knees, and whipped her up with my prehensile tail. Elyssa caught her by the arm.

The roar grew deafening. I turned and faced a wall of water.

It's over.

Water slammed me into the side of the building. I tumbled back and forth along the wall as if gravity had suddenly gone sideways. A final breath exploded from my lungs as the incredible pressure forced it out. Something shattered and I flew inside a hotel room, bounced off the bed and plowed through a wall. A torrent of glowing water slammed into my face and sent me spinning over hard bathroom tiles and against a Jacuzzi tub. Pain knifed through me with every tumble.

Sputtering and gasping, I found a moment of respite from the flood. A door hung open to my right. I staggered through it and another door leading into the main hallway, trying to ignore the knifing agony in my ribs. Water flooded from every door on this side of the corridor. I nearly lost my balance to another surge from the room I'd exited. Somehow, I kept my wits and ran to the stairwell door. I wrenched it open and ran. Waterfalls cascaded down the stairs, raining down the center well. I raced up the stairs as fast as I could, my thick toenails aiding my grip on the slick, wet concrete. Every step brought stabbing pain to my guts.

I burst through the door at the top. People yelled and jumped back when they saw me.

"His eyes are on fire!" a woman cried.

"What the hell is that thing?"

A chubby sunburned man pulled a gun from a fanny pack and aimed it at me. "God preserve us, it's a demon! Satan has sent his minions and Armageddon is upon us!"

I was too tired to dodge. Too tired to resist. I braced for impact.

A large ebony-skinned man karate-chopped the gun wielder's wrist.

The other man yelped. "What the hell, man?"

"That demon saved two children and their parents, you moron." My savior picked up the gun and hurled it off the side of the building.

"No, not my gun!" The sunburned man seemed to have completely forgotten about the end of the world as his prized possession vanished.

I groaned and sank to my knees.

"Justin!" Elyssa appeared and hugged me fiercely, eliciting groans through my clenched teeth. "I thought you were dead," she sobbed. "I thought I'd lost you forever."

My savior knelt. "I'm Harley."

"Justin," I gasped. My ribs felt broken in a dozen places, and my right arm hung numbly at my side. "Thanks for the assist."

"I'm Elyssa." Elyssa didn't take time to shake the man's hand, instead inspecting my ribs. "Oh, god, Justin. You have a bone sticking out of your back."

"No wonder I feel like crap."

"Are there any doctors up here?" Harley shouted. "We need medical assistance."

"I'm a doctor!" A young woman pushed through the crowd around us. Her eyes went wide behind her glasses. She flashed the sign of the cross. "What is that?"

"A man who needs help," Harley said. "Now stop gawking and help him!"

She stepped forward uncertainly. Behind her, another woman clasped her hands in prayer.

"Fine, I get it," I said in a strained voice. "If it helps, I'll look more normal." It was a huge relief to shut away my inner demon and let my body shrink back to normal size, though the relief was short lived. Shifting bones wracked my torso with agony.

Gasps rose from all around.

"It's an alien superhero," said a young boy. "Cool!"

Despite her wide-eyed fear, the doctor knelt and felt my ribs. "Does that hurt?"

"Yes," I hissed.

"That?"

"Yes!"

"How about that?"

"Agh! Yes it freaking hurts! All of it hurts like a bitch!" She touched something else and I blacked out.

"I don't think I can do anything," said a faraway voice.

"We need to set that broken rib," Elyssa said. "At least put it into position so it can heal."

"Heal?" The doctor sounded incredulous. "He needs to be in intensive care for weeks."

"He can heal on his own."

"Impossible."

"Lady, you just saw that man morph from a demon into a young man, and you're saying impossible?" Harley barked a laugh.

I wanted to open my eyes, but I felt so damned tired. My demonic senses drifted out and latched onto the doctor, to Elyssa, and to several other female presences. Then it did what it did best—it fed. I barely had the self-control to keep my emotions neutral. Even so, I heard feminine gasps and moans.

"If you feel any strong sexual sensations, try not to act on them," Elyssa said helpfully.

"Oh, my," the doctor said. "What's happening to me?"

Elyssa supplied an answer. "Probably all the adrenalin wearing off."

I wished I could laugh, but even thinking about it hurt. It took nearly an hour before I felt well enough to speak.

"Hi," I croaked.

"He's awake!" Harley shouted. "How you doing, bud?"

"I'm better." I gingerly touched my ribs. They were incredibly sore, but it felt like the badly broken one had shifted back into place.

"The bone—it's gone! The skin is healed." The doctor peeled my eyelids wide and looked into my eyes. "What sort of being are you?"

"Let's just say my genealogy is something of a mixed bag." Telling her I was part demon, part angel would probably push her off the cliff of insanity.

Elyssa stroked my hair. "Can you stand?"

11

I nodded. Despite my rapid healing, I whimpered when she helped me up. By now, the other people had moved away from me and stood in small groups, staring out at the wasteland that had once been a tropical paradise.

Muddy, debris-choked water submerged everything close to the beach. In the distance, I saw the glow fading from the water, and the darkness of night once again began to claim the sky.

"What in God's named happened here?" Harley asked.

The doctor collapsed into his arms and began to sob.

I wondered if the sunburned man had been right.

What if this is the end of the world?

Chapter 2

My conclusion about Armageddon was probably a bit melodramatic and premature, but my sensitive ears overheard a man with a cell phone as he relayed news to others in his group. "Meteors fell all over the place. People say they're nothing like anything they've seen before."

Elyssa took out her arcphone. "Weird, I'm not getting a signal." She messed around with it for a moment. "I had to switch to a nom cell tower." She handed me my phone.

Arcphones integrated technology and magic all into one amazing device and used magical ley lines to transmit voice and data. I fiddled with Nookli—my beloved arcphone, but the aether signal bars fluctuated wildly and the phone couldn't get a lock. It was waterproof and incredibly sturdy, but something wasn't working right.

Elyssa adjusted the settings on her phone. "I've never seen this happen before." Using a nom cell tower, she was finally able to browse to a news website. "Looks like these meteors hit all over the world."

"Atlanta?" I asked.

She nodded. "Yes, but not in the city center." She turned on a live newsfeed.

A female reporter, her professional demeanor fully intact despite the day's calamity, spoke a few hundred yards from a smoking crater in the center of a field. "Speculation is rampant, but scientists believe the Earth may have passed through a meteor storm. Emergency officials haven't arrived on site since the remote impact in Sweetwater Creek State Park caused no casualties."

"Karen, do you think it's safe to approach the crater?" An unseen man, presumably in the newsroom, asked her.

She looked back at a crowd of people moving toward it. "That's anyone's guess, Don. We're going to move in for a closer look."

"Here in the studio we have our science specialist, Bert Mathis," Don said. "Bert, do you think these craters are dangerous?"

"Only if you fall inside and twist your ankle." Bert chuckled. "But seriously, there could be cosmic radiation, deep space viruses, intense, flesh-melting heat, or even some form of alien life involved here."

"That's quite a list," Don said.

The camera wobbled and shook as the cameraperson followed Karen toward the crater. Every time Bert spoke about how dangerous it could be, she cast worried glances back. Death by aliens or not, Karen was apparently determined to do her job.

"To have so many of these hit the Earth all at once strikes me as nothing short of a possible attack by forces unknown," Bert continued. "For all we know, North Korea may have finally created a superweapon capable of reaching all across the world."

"So you don't think this is a natural occurrence; that the Earth simply passed through the tail of a comet or meteor belt?" Don asked.

"At this point, anything is possible." Bert sighed. "I just hope the heat and radiation from that crater isn't enough to melt the flesh off Karen's face."

Karen stopped in her tracks, jaw tight, a few feet from the crater. Her back stiffened, and she took a deep breath. "We're here now, Don. Let's hope Bert is wrong, or the viewers are going to get quite a show."

"Fingers crossed, Karen," Don replied.

"I think she's safe," Bert said. "If there was intense radiation or heat, she'd already be dead, her body bloating as her internal organs swelled—"

"I get the picture, Bert." Karen looked over the crater's edge and shrieked. "My eyes! My eyes!"

"What did I say?" Bert said. "First, her eyes melt—"

14

Karen stopped screaming. "Actually, I'm just pulling one over on you, Bert." She motioned to the camera and it moved toward her. "What's inside this crater is truly spectacular."

The camera view peeked over the edge, revealing an unevenly shaped hunk of crystal the size of a compact car. Black and white shards several feet in length jutted in all directions from the top half, while the rest of it was embedded in the ground.

"It's a crystal meteor," Karen breathed. "Amazing."

Sparks of energy danced along the crystals and the camera jumped back.

"What was that?" Don asked.

She shook her head. "It looks like electricity."

"Probably static charges left from the ionosphere," Bert said. "If they discharge, the jolt could flash-fry Karen like a fish in boiling oil."

"Maybe we should get Bert out here for a first-hand analysis," Karen said. "It might be interesting to see what happens if he touches one of these crystals."

"Interesting," Bert said. "It would seem—"

Elyssa stopped the playback. "I don't think that was electricity running through those crystals. If anything it look like—"

I finished her sentence. "Aether."

She nodded. "We have to get home."

"Let's arrange for a portal," I said, and took out Nookli again. Like Elyssa's, my phone couldn't get a solid aether signal so I had to switch to nom frequencies. I called the number of an omniarch station in Atlanta, but the signal beeped busy. I tried the station at the omniarch near the mansion in Queens Gate, but got the same thing.

"I can't reach anyone," Elyssa said.

I frowned and tried Shelton.

He answered almost immediately. "What in the name of god is going on?" A pause. "Oh, and, how's it going, man? I haven't heard from you in a while."

"I don't know, and it was going great until today." I blew out a breath. "These meteors caused a huge tidal wave. I don't know how many thousands of people probably died because of it."

15

"Is that Justin?" Bella's voice grew closer as if she'd walked next to Shelton. "Hello, Justin! Hello Elyssa!"

"Will you let me talk?" Shelton said. "We can save the happy hellos after we figure out why I can't cast a damned spell to save my life and why the aethernet is off the air."

"Wait a minute, you can't cast any spells?" I remembered my sudden inability to channel Murk. I thought I'd just overextended myself.

"Nope. Whenever I try to aetherate, it feels like I'm sucking in air." He made a thoughtful sound. "It feels like the aether is thinner than usual. I don't know how else to explain it."

"Where are you?" I asked.

"We went for a walk in London." He huffed. "We were about to head back down to the Queens Gate way station when this crap started."

"Hang on." I opened my Arcane senses and tried to draw aether into my well. Instead of the static feeling usually associated with the aether, I felt almost nothing. I flicked on my demon sight. In addition to revealing the auras of the people around me, it also revealed the magical energy in the air and ground. Elyssa's aura shone like a bright cloudy halo around her body. Varying shades of auras hung around the other people.

Harley's was bright and gray. The doctor's was slightly duller and darker. The sunburned man's shimmered weakly. *I'll bet feeding on him would taste like crap.*

My chest felt as though it was filled with lead when I searched for something else I should be seeing. Floating nebulas of dark, white, and gray aether should be all around me. Instead, only a few sparse patches drifted nearby, and those were quickly fading. I looked over the edge of the building, but the ground was flooded, making it impossible to see if the aether lines in the ground were also affected.

"Are you there?" Shelton shouted on the other end of the phone.

"There's no aether," I told him. "I can't see it even with my demon vision."

"Holy rabbit turds in ravioli." He went silent. "It's like someone took the magic out of the world."

16

"If that's the case, how can I still use my demon abilities?"

After a long pause, he posed a theory. "I think it's because those abilities are built into your physique, and they don't use aether. They use soul essence."

"It doesn't take a math genius to put two and two together about those meteors." I gazed out at the faint glow in the roiling ocean where the meteor had landed. "This was a deliberate attack. Whoever did it wants to destroy our ability to use magic."

"Argh! Didn't we just win a damned war?"

"Calm down, Harry," Bella said. "You're going to burst a blood vein."

"It's 'burst a blood vessel', woman." He huffed. "I suppose you want me to open a portal so you can come home. Give us twenty minutes to get down to the way station."

"That'd be great. We need to find a private spot. I'll send you a picture and call you back." I ended the call we gave Shelton the time he needed. Twenty-five minutes later, we headed toward the stairwell door.

Harley stopped us. "Where are you two going?"

"I'm just going to look in the stairwell to see if anyone else needs help," I said.

"I'm coming with you."

"I need to take care of some personal business as well." Elyssa smiled shyly.

Harley cleared his throat. "Ah, well, make sure you aim it down the center." He chuckled.

"That won't be a problem." Elyssa hooked her arm in mine and we went through the door. She removed chalk from her purse and drew a symbol on the wall.

"Why do you have chalk in your purse?" I asked.

"I started carrying it everywhere when you needed to draw circles all the time for magic." She tucked it back inside. "Good memories."

"Back then I could hardly light a candle." I tried to remember what it was like to be bad at magic. Faced with the possibility of no aether, it seemed like heaven. I took a picture of the drawing and sent it to Shelton. A moment later, the air rippled and slowly split vertically.

17

Elyssa and I looked at each other. Opening a portal was usually instantaneous.

Shelton appeared through the hazy gateway. Static and sparks made ominous zapping noises. "I should've known!" His voice sounded muffled. "This aether problem is affecting the omniarches too."

"How is it even operational?" I asked.

"Because we're right over major ley lines." He jabbed a thumb over his shoulder. "None of the pocket dimensions got hit by meteors."

"Since the omniarch is in the Queens Gate control room, shouldn't it work?"

He pursed his lips and put a hand on his chin. "Let me check something." The portal flickered away. Moments later, it reopened just as slowly as before and with the snap, crackle, and pop of static discharge.

"Well?" I asked.

"Opening a portal here works fine. I asked the arch operator here, and the Obsidian Arch network seems mostly functional too." He held up what looked like a sandwich. "Watch out."

Elyssa and I backed away. Shelton tossed the sandwich. The moment it hit the portal, sparks flew and the sandwich burst into a fine mist that washed across our faces.

"Eww!" Elyssa wiped off her face. "What kind of sandwich was that?"

Shelton sighed. "Waste of a perfectly good chicken salad sandwich."

"God, no wonder I smell like eggs now." Elyssa made a face. "Thank you so much."

I didn't much like chicken salad, but I didn't let that stop me from making a conclusion. "We've got to hoof it to the nearest Obsidian Arch if we want to get home."

"Yup."

Bella appeared behind him. "Things have been so quiet around here without you two around."

"I guess the universe decided our vacation was over," Elyssa commented dryly. "Where's the nearest Obsidian Arch?"

"Where are you guys?" Shelton asked.

"An island off the coast of Thailand," I said.

18

"Looking it up." Shelton fiddled with his phone then held it out to show a map. "Bangkok."

"Are you able to use magic in the way station?" I asked.

He waggled his hand. "It works, but it's weaker than usual. I think the arches are still working fine because they use silver circles to trap all the ambient magical energy."

"Makes sense." I looked at Elyssa. "Maybe I'll need that chalk again after all."

"The reason the portal isn't working well on your end is because it doesn't have enough magical energy to fully materialize." Shelton put a hand on his chin. "Maybe drawing a circle to trap aether would work."

"I'll try it." I hesitated. "Deactivate the portal first. I don't want my head to end up like the chicken salad sandwich."

He chuckled. "You got it."

After the portal vanished, I drew a circle around the spot and willed it to close. Using my incubus vision, I saw clouds of aether slowly accumulating, but it was nowhere near the amount that usually gathered in a circle.

The portal reopened, but the results were only marginally better. Shelton's voice was a little clearer at first, but the portal slowly reverted to the hazy window of static as it consumed all the aether in the circle.

"Son of a dirt eater." Shelton slapped his leg. "Looks like you're walking."

"More like swimming," Elyssa said. "Since we're relying on the nom cell towers for reception, it's likely we'll lose contact until we hit the mainland."

"Maybe your dad could send a slider," he suggested.

"I wouldn't want to rely on magical transportation," Elyssa said. "The aether charge wouldn't last, and then it couldn't recharge."

Shelton threw up his hands. "Why do they have to make everything so difficult?"

"Commander Borathen called a meeting," Bella said. "He wants to speak with the heads of the Overworld Conclave factions about the magic outage."

19

I wrinkled my nose. "How many responded?"

"The vampires didn't, but most of the other factions will attend." She sighed. "I don't know if the vampires will ever willingly come back into the fold. I've heard rumors the ancients are once again trying to control them."

A shudder ran through my back. I'd met the ancients. Not only could they fly, but they were far more nimble and powerful than their more modern brethren. "Vampires are intrinsically strong like Daemos, lycans, and so forth. They rely on blood, not aether."

"Yeah, while Arcanes are left out in the cold." Shelton scowled. "That could really give the vamps a chance to shift the balance of power back into their favor."

"Hmm." Elyssa tapped a finger on her lips. "What about Serena? She's an Arcane, but she was also Daelissa's top person when it came to mad inventions. These crystals look like something she'd come up with."

"She escaped the last battle, too." Shelton looked as though he knew where she was going.

"You think some of the factions who fought for Daelissa are looking for revenge?" I asked.

Elyssa nodded. "It makes sense."

"I can tell you right now the battle mages and Arcanes on her side wouldn't go for a plan like this," Shelton said. "Not unless they had a way out."

Shelton held up a finger. "Remember those aether interdictors they used so we couldn't cast or channel spells when we were in their range? Their Arcanes had those tokens that allowed them to cast spells."

"Yeah, but those were highly localized," Elyssa replied. "And they didn't remove the aether, they simply rendered it unusable unless a token filtered it."

Shelton snapped his fingers and shaped them like a gun. "Bingo!"

"I don't know how a token would put more aether in the air," I said. "This seems a lot different."

"But troublingly similar." Bella scrunched her forehead. "I don't believe Serena would do this without a way to keep her own power intact."

"If she's found a way to do it, then we're in big trouble." Shelton rubbed the back of his neck. "Basically, she just crippled more than two-thirds of the army that defeated Daelissa."

"The Seraphim will still have physical strength." I felt somewhat certain on that point even though I couldn't prove it right this moment. "But the Arcanes will be…"

"Yeah, go ahead and say it," Shelton grumbled. "We'll be useless."

"Well, you could play the battle flute," I suggested.

He snorted. "Anyway, we don't have many Seraphim left in these parts. Legiaros Ketiss took his army back to Seraphina." Shelton's forehead wrinkled. "The only Seraphim left in Eden are Justin, his mom, his sister, and Nightliss."

My heart grew heavy. "I don't know if Nightliss will show up to help."

Bella's eyes grew downcast. "The poor dear was really in a depression when she told me goodbye and left."

"Bah." Shelton rolled his eyes. "I don't get why she was so upset about Daelissa. That crazy bitch tried to kill her more times than I can remember."

Bella raised an eyebrow. "Yes, but family is family, Harry."

"There was more to it than that," I said.

"Isn't there always?" Shelton slashed the air with a hand. "All right, enough talk. You need to get your ass to Bangkok. I'll mention our wild theories to Thomas and see what he has to say about it."

I nodded. "We'll see you soon."

Bella blew us a kiss. "Please be careful." She sighed. "It's so frustrating you can't simply step through the portal."

"I just hope the Obsidian Arches aren't the same as this." I motioned to the barely functioning portal. "We'll talk soon."

Shelton sighed and nodded. "Good luck, man."

The gateway winked off.

Elyssa squeezed my hand. "We may have to wait out the flood before we can leave."

"It'll give me time to recover." I touched my ribs and gritted my teeth. "Maybe we can find a boat."

"Let's pray one survived." The look in her eyes didn't hold much hope.

No matter what, it was going to be a long journey home.

Chapter 3

We left the stairwell and went back outside. The hopeless misery on the faces of our trapped comrades dragged my emotions into the mud. We had to get back to Queens Gate or Atlanta as fast as possible, but I couldn't just leave these people behind. I would help them if I could. Unless we figured out how these meteors were destroying aether, it didn't matter how quickly I returned home.

"Let's see if any news organizations have charted the locations of the meteors," I told Elyssa. "I want to see one first hand."

"I wonder if destroying them would stop the effect," she mused.

I nodded. "Same thing I was thinking." My gaze shifted to the glow in the ocean. "I think that one is too far underwater to view."

"Probably." Elyssa stared at it for a long moment. "It's difficult to tell how deep it is from here."

It was hard for me to ignore the eyes of the others watching me. I couldn't blame them. Seeing a blue-skinned demon climb up the side of the building had probably been quite a shock. Then again, they'd probably been in shock already from seeing the asteroid crashing into the ocean.

The breeze should have somewhat cooled the area. Instead, a warm wind swept over us. I wondered if it had something to do with the way the meteor was destroying the aether, or if it was simply a slight change in weather from such a major disturbance. *Well, at least now I know why they call it meteorology.*

Harley walked to the railing and stood beside us. "A lot of people are talking about you, Justin." He cast a look over his right shoulder.

"Are they ready to break out the pitchforks?" I asked.

"If Jay has his way, they'd throw you over the side." He chuckled. "Thankfully, nobody's taking him too seriously, especially after you took his gun."

I looked back at Jay—the sunburned man. He wore a Hawaiian shirt and bright red bikini briefs. "Where do you think he was hiding that gun?"

Elyssa grimaced. "Harley, we don't want any trouble, but if they come at us, we're more than capable of protecting ourselves."

"Considering the show you put on earlier, I think the others know that." He drew in a deep breath and stared at the glowing water offshore. "I've never been one for fairy tales or fantasy, at least not until today. Something otherworldly is going on, and I'd like to know what it is."

Elyssa and I exchanged a glance. She spoke first.

"A supernatural society has existed on Earth since the dawn of mankind. They eventually formed a government called the Overworld Conclave." She gauged Harley's reaction.

He simply nodded. "Okay. What kind of supernatural beings?"

"Vampires, lycans, felycans, Arcanes, Daemos—"

"Daemos—like demons?" Harley glanced at me.

I nodded. "We're humans with a mixed human-demon soul."

"And you can transform into that demon thing?"

"Yep." I crossed my arms and leaned on the railing. "Earth has several realms. The ones we know about are this one, Eden—"

"Like the biblical Eden?" His face betrayed the first signs of surprise.

"The name is the same, but don't get it confused with places from the Bible." Elyssa took over the narrative. "Haedaemos is what most people call Hell, and Seraphina might be analogous to Heaven."

"Yeah, but the Seraphim are anything but angels." I snorted. "In fact, we just won a war against them. There's a faction called the Brightlings who wanted to rule Eden. With the help of the other faction, the Darklings, we stopped them from taking over."

"Maybe I'd better sit down." Harley gripped the railing as if he needed it for support. "How in the world did you fight a war without it ending up on the news?"

"I'm with the Templars," Elyssa explained. "We have a faction called the Custodians who cover up supernatural scandals."

"You know, I expected a simple explanation, like, sure there are vampires and maybe even werewolves, but—" Harley shook his head. "This is almost too much." His eyes widened slightly. "Are you going to kill me now that I know?"

Elyssa chuckled. "No, we have Overworld Orientation for noms who find out about us."

"Noms?" He looked at us. "Oh, wait, kind of like normals, right?"

"And nom-noms," I added, as if he didn't already look disturbed enough. "That's because some factions feed off humans."

"I take it you're not bad people." Harley's voice sounded hopeful.

"I might be half demon, but I'm a nice guy." I grinned. "I'm also part Seraphim, but these meteors seem to have wrecked my magical abilities."

Harley seemed to relax. "You mentioned Arcanes earlier. What do they do?"

"You might also call them sorcerers or wizards." It brought back my first memory of Shelton. I'd called him a sorcerer for quite a while before adapting to the official lingo. "Just don't call them magicians, or they get really peeved."

"Where are you from, Harley?" Elyssa asked in an abrupt change of subject.

"I'm originally from Chicago, but I got tired of the same old crap job and crap life." He closed his eyes as another warm breeze found us. "I sold everything and moved here." He pointed toward the flooded beach. "I have—or had—a little shack where I sold surfboards and other knick-knacks. Just enough to make a living."

"Are you familiar with the mainland?"

"Of course." He grinned. "I travel to Bangkok regularly. The women there are amazing."

"We need to get back to the States." My stomach rumbled and I tried not to think about food. "To do that we need to get to Bangkok. There's an arch there that can instantly transport us back."

Harley's mouth dropped open. "Are you serious?"

I nodded. "Yep. If you want to visit Chicago, I might be able to arrange it."

"I'd love to see my sister. I haven't been back in years." His gaze traveled to the beach. "Looks like I won't be doing business anytime soon."

Jay, flanked by a small group of other men, approached us.

"We want you off our building," Jay said to me. "Get thee behind me Satan!" He and the others held up their fingers in the sign of the cross.

"Ah!" I held up my hands and backed away. "Please, no, the pain! The pain!"

Jay bared his teeth in a grin and advanced. "I told you it would work! This creature is the harbinger of the apocalypse."

I limped backward a few more steps, then couldn't hold it in any longer and burst into laughter. My ribs protested angrily, and a few tears of pain joined the tears of mirth.

Elyssa rolled her eyes and sighed. "Seriously, Justin?"

Jay and his pals looked comically confused, especially as they pushed their crossed fingers toward me to no effect.

I made the cross with my fingers and walked toward them. "Be gone, ye moronic buffoons. Ye harbingers of the idiocracy that will destroy this world."

"You leave us no choice, demon." With that, Jay loosed a roaring battle cry that sounded a lot like a midget trapped in a washing machine. The others in his group ran at me and picked me up.

Despite my supernatural strength, I wasn't much heavier than most other people, even with my extra dense muscles. All those hands grappling my sore body sent pain racing along every nerve fiber.

I heard explosive exhalations, meaty thunks, and the sound of bodies hitting the floor—or as it were, the roof. I landed on my feet as the last hooligan caught the business end of Elyssa's fists and went down hard.

She stood over them, violet eyes glowing with menace. "Stay away from us, or I'll throw you off the roof next time."

"We're doomed!" Jay curled into a ball and wailed. "The Devil himself is here with his succubus whore."

26

Elyssa's fists tightened and every knuckle cracked. I hopped in the way before Jay received a one-way ticket to the Promised Land. "Let's everybody just calm down." Much as I wanted to kick Jay in the stomach a few times, it would only make me a bully. I couldn't pummel the guy just because he was a misguided idiot.

I looked at the rest of the group, some twenty or so people, huddled against the railing. The doctor—I still didn't know her name—stood apart from them, an appraising look in her eyes. She finally walked over to us.

"I've official decided you're not evil." She glanced at Harley who was having a good laugh at Jay's expense. "Can you use your super powers to get us out of here?"

"That's the topic of discussion." I winced and rubbed my right side. The broken bones there still hadn't mended very well despite my supernatural abilities. I had to assume the lack of magical energy might be the cause. Then again, I'd suffered extreme physical trauma. The water had nearly squashed me like a bug.

"I don't suppose you can fly," the doctor said.

"Not at present." Though I'd recently learned how to fly with aether wings, that wasn't going to work with the aether shortage. "By morning I should be healed enough to swim out and look for a boat." The glow of the meteor gave us limited vision, but not enough to see any great details far out from our refuge.

"The water should be receded by the morning," Harley said. "We'll be able to leave the hotel and look around."

"If that's the case, I'm going to bed." I'd planned to just leave and go to a dry bedroom, but looking at the miserable faces nearby, I felt like what they really needed was some sort of leadership, even if they thought I was a demon. I caught Elyssa watching me.

She smiled. "I love you."

"You sound proud of me for some reason."

"That's because you can't ignore suffering. You want to help people." Elyssa leaned her head on my shoulder. "You're a good man with a big heart, and you want to do what's right even if it's a pain in the ass."

"If that's the case, why did I run away from my responsibilities?"

27

"Everyone gets burned out, Justin." She put her hand on my shoulder. "You deserved the time off."

"I guess this is my reward." I took a deep breath. "Here goes." I clapped my hands and winced at the jolt of pain in my ribs and right arm. I raised my left hand to get everyone's attention. Since most people had been keeping an eye on me ever since my dramatic entrance, every gaze was on me in an instant. "Hello, everyone. My name is Justin, and I have a few ideas I'd like to share." Nobody screamed at me, so I continued. "The rooms on the top few levels are probably dry. I suggest everyone find a room and get some sleep. In the morning, I'll try to find a boat. We'll navigate back to the mainland and get everyone safely to Bangkok somehow."

"I'll not follow you," Jay proclaimed. "You're leading us to the branding iron to be marked with the number of the Beast." He staggered to his feet. "He leads you to temptation and damnation."

I let Jay go on for a moment as he shouted all the awful things that would happen to anyone following me.

"Will you kindly shut the hell up?" a large man bellowed. "That guy is strong enough to launch you into orbit. His girlfriend could've torn off your head. Instead, they let you live." He blew out a frustrated breath. "If you'd messed with me or my family, I would've already thrown you off the roof."

"Yeah, just shut your stupid mouth," a woman chimed in. "I want to get home."

Murmurs of agreement rose from the others.

Jay growled, but slunk to the stairwell door. He stopped and faced us. "May God have mercy on your damned foolish souls." He slammed the door behind him.

I sighed. "Alrighty, then. Let's get some rooms, get some sleep, and hopefully in the morning, we'll find a way off this rock."

An older man spoke. "I've been checking the news on my phone and it doesn't sound like the Thai government is sending help anytime soon. The mainland coast suffered some damage too."

Groans rose from the others.

"Is Bangkok still in one piece?" I asked.

He nodded. "From what I've read, nothing happened farther inland."

"Okay, let's go get some sleep." I went to the stairwell door and tugged on it. It opened a fraction before catching on something. I peeked through the crack and saw a fire axe lodged in the handle. "Looks like Jay tried to lock us up here." I motioned to Elyssa. "Will you do the honors?"

"Sure, hon." Elyssa gripped the door handle and tugged hard. Wood cracked. The door flew open and the axe head dinged on the ground.

"That's it," the big man said. "I'm gonna punch that moron in the face."

I held up a restraining arm. "Let's just leave him be for now."

The man growled deep in his chest, but nodded. "All right."

Dim emergency lighting gave us just enough light to see by. I didn't know how much longer the backup batteries would last and figured it didn't matter. We ran into another problem not more than two minutes later.

"The doors are locked," the doctor said.

"What's your name?" I asked. "I'm getting tired of thinking of you as the doctor all the time."

"Elizabeth." She looked at the door. "Can you get it open now?"

Elyssa rammed it open with her shoulder. She and I repeated the procedure down the hallway until everyone had a room.

As Harley entered his room he smiled and said, "I don't suppose you can get the cable working again, can you?"

I chuckled. "I think you've had enough entertainment for the day."

"Yeah, a disaster story, a fantasy adventure, and a drama." He opened the curtains to let in the light from the glowing ocean. "What more could a person ask for?"

I told him goodnight and then went to the room Elyssa had procured for us. She opened the balcony door to let the breeze into the stuffy room and then flopped on the bed. She got up a minute later. "I wonder if the water works."

My throat was already feeling parched.

I heard movement in the hallway and two silhouettes appeared a moment later. The big man was pushing a service cart loaded with candy bars, potato chips, and a variety of beverages. "We raided the vending machines." He motioned to the snacks. "Junk food. The supper of champions."

I was too hungry to be picky and grabbed a handful. "Great thinking."

"Yeah, we thought about going to the kitchen, but the bottom floors are flooded." He shuddered. "There are bodies down there too."

The woman with him gripped his arm. "How many do you think died, Justin?"

I shook my head sadly. "More than I want to count." I looked at the snacks. "Thanks for the food. I'll see you in the morning." I closed the door and latched the top latch since the bottom one was broken.

"The water doesn't work," Elyssa announced as she exited the bathroom. "It worked for a few seconds, but then it turned muddy and clogged."

I dropped our small feast on the bed. "Let's just eat and count our blessings."

Tomorrow was going to be a long, hard day.

Chapter 4

My stomach felt like it was full of rocks when I peeled open my eyes the next morning. My body apparently didn't appreciate all the junk food I'd consumed. Elyssa was already up, standing on the balcony and gazing at the ocean.

I pushed myself up and immediately regretted it as my ribs and joints reminded me of the brutal thrashing I'd taken the day before.

Elyssa sat by my side and checked my bare ribs. "You still have some nasty bruising."

"I don't understand why it's taking so long." I gingerly poked a rib and winced. "Must be the lack of aether."

"Probably." She motioned her head to the window. "I want you to see something."

I followed her outside and immediately saw what she meant. The ocean roiled and swirled where the meteor had landed. "That can't be good."

"Understatement of the year." She sighed. "I hope Shelton and the others find out more by the time we get home."

"Speaking of which..." I scanned the water for boats. Mostly, I just saw wreckage. The flood had receded, leaving behind tons of debris speckled with human bodies, dead fish, and vegetation. I idly wondered where my missing flip-flop had ended up and decided that mystery would never be solved.

"We should go to the roof for a better look." Elyssa grabbed a bottle of water and headed for the door.

My stomach grumbled hungrily then revolted when I looked at the junk food on the dresser. I grabbed bottled water and followed Elyssa. A few people already gathered on the roof. I nodded at them, but

31

didn't much feel like chatting or smiling, for that matter. I needed real food.

The view from the roof offered little hope. The only boat in one piece teetered on the roof of a building down the street. Elyssa and I might possibly dislodge it, but carrying it through the tons of debris blocking the road and beach was out of the question.

"Out there." Elyssa pointed to a boat that would be better described as a yacht. Two stories high and a boatload bigger than a boat, it drifted in the middle of a mound of unidentifiable debris.

"How far of a swim is that?" I asked.

She pursed her lips. "At least a mile."

I didn't like the idea of such a long swim, but we didn't have a choice. "Let's find some food, then we can make the trip."

"I don't think we have the time to spare." Her finger drifted from the ship to the maelstrom forming between our island and the smaller one in the distance. "The yacht is drifting toward that."

It only took a moment for me to confirm her observation. The yacht and its accompanying flotsam, jetsam, or whatever kind of –sam a sailor might call the debris, were definitely headed for the whirlpool. I took a quick glance around and failed to locate any other suitable seaworthy vessels.

"Let's go now." My stomach threw a tantrum of borborygmus when it got the message that there wouldn't be any breakfast this morning. I wholeheartedly agreed with its dire assessment, but if we didn't snag that ship, we'd be stuck in this miserable place a lot longer.

We ran into Harley on the way down. He held up a brown bag. "Hey, someone left a take-home bag of rice cakes in my room's fridge. I was going to have some for breakfast up on the roof if you want to join me."

I told him the situation. "We've got to get that yacht before it gets sucked down the drain." My belly made an awful sucking noise and explained its plight as well.

Harley took out a couple of rice cakes. These weren't the dry crunchy kind found in grocery stores, but the homemade moist ones. The rice didn't smell bad, so I took them and gave one to Elyssa.

"Thanks, Harley." I took a big bite of one. "Wish us luck."

"Can I tag along?" he asked.

"Sure, but you'll have to stay on the beach."

He chuckled. "I like to swim, but not that much."

I saw the big man coming out of his room and told him the plan. "Let everyone know we'll be back unless we die horribly, okay?"

He grimaced. "Man, don't talk like that." He gripped my hand and shook it. "Be safe."

"I will." I bit my lip and thought about what else needed doing. "In the meantime, could you get the others to help look for food, water, and other survivors? I have a feeling we're going to need supplies before taking off."

He nodded. "You got it."

I looked down at my bare feet. "Before we go, daddy needs some new shoes."

Elyssa snorted. "Let's find you something fancy."

We went a couple floors down and raided the rooms. I found a dead man in the hallway on the fourth floor with feet about my size.

"He doesn't have any use for them," Harley said when he noticed how hesitant I was to take them.

Elyssa tugged off the tennis shoes and handed them to me. "No time to be picky, Justin."

The shoes were cold and wet. I tried not to think of the dead flesh that had touched them. "Not to sound trite, but these things have death cooties all over them."

"Better than slicing your feet open on broken glass." Elyssa headed for the stairwell.

The thought of walking with cut and bleeding feet helped me overcome my aversion. I gave the dead man one last look. "Rest in peace, bro."

Harley, Elyssa, and I navigated the treacherous streets, wending our way through a maze of wrecked cars, demolished buildings, broken trees, and the awful sight of the dead. The crash of the waves on the beach and the cacophony of birds squawking and fighting over beached fish were the only sounds. Most of the other buildings in the area had been too low to avoid the flood.

"Hey, over here," Harley called. He pointed to a jumble of wood beneath a pile of bricks. "I found some of the surfboards from my shop."

"If only we had time to surf," I said dryly.

He pulled on one. "You'll be a lot safer if you take one of these instead of straight-up swimming for it."

I hadn't thought of using a flotation device, but his advice made sense. "Good idea."

Elyssa lifted the topmost surfboard and I was able to free two more beneath it. The fins were broken, but the boards looked seaworthy.

The closer we got to the beach, the more waterlogged the ground became. Mud sucked at our feet, and half-dead fish flopped in puddles of water. We reached the edge of the water moments later. Even then, floating debris obstructed our view of the yacht.

"I guess this is where we leave you," I told Harley. "Thanks for the rice cakes."

"Good luck and godspeed." He chuckled. "Sorry about the God part if it offends you."

I snorted. "Like I said, the supernatural world isn't like the Bible." I squeezed Elyssa's hand. "Ready?"

She nodded. "Let's go."

We waded into the filthy water. Jumbled bricks, broken wood, and other debris made footing treacherous. It took us several minutes to get to a place where we could climb atop the surfboards and start paddling. By the time we reached the open water, the yacht was more than halfway to the maelstrom. Though I couldn't see the whirlpool itself, churning water highlighted the boundary.

Elyssa and I kicked and paddled like crazy. My shoes made kicking cumbersome so I took them off and put them on the surfboard. She soon followed suit. By the time we reached the yacht, only a hundred yards remained between it and the mother of all drain holes. The swift current of the turbulent water gripped us and pulled us toward our target.

We swam to the back of the ship where a low dock allowed us to easily slip onboard with our handy surfboards. Broken alcohol bottles and glasses littered the deck so we quickly slipped back into our shoes. A woman in a bikini lay in a tangled mess next to a large tub that had once contained pool water. A rope tied around her waist kept her from going overboard, but it had also broken her back when the tidal wave threw her hard against the end of the tether.

A pair of doors leading to the interior cabins hung open. I saw crimson stains in the hallway and other unidentifiable fluids spattered on the walls and elected not to go inside.

We made our way upstairs to the second deck. Judging from the number of alcohol bottles, there had been quite a party in progress when the meteor hit.

I looked back and saw the whirlpool growing ever closer. "Where's the bridge on this thing?"

Elyssa jogged forward. We entered the cabin area, stepping over bodies and making our way toward the bow—or was it the prow? I really needed to read up on my nautical terms. She found a door leading into a sleek control room that looked as though it belonged in a space ship.

"This ain't no ordinary sea-going vessel," I muttered. "Now, where's the ignition?"

"I don't have the faintest idea, but we don't have much longer." Elyssa didn't have to explain. The roar of the maelstrom sounded like a distant waterfall, and the vibrations running through the ship's hull knotted my guts with anxiety.

I saw a figure in a navy blue uniform on the floor and ran over to it. The man had a cut on his forehead and bruises on his face, but he was breathing ever so slightly.

I slapped him lightly on the face. "Wake up, Captain. We need to start this boat." I was afraid to shake him, but the thundering whirlpool quickly changed my mind. Elyssa found a bottle of water and dumped it on the man's face. He moaned slightly, but didn't wake up.

"Screw this." I left the man where he was and ran up and down the control screens. I finally found a big red button next to a silver handle jutting from the console. I offered up a quick prayer and pressed the button. The LCD screens in front of me lit up, displaying more information than I could easily take in.

Elyssa jabbed a finger at two green bars rising from zero. "I think these are the engines."

Over the roar and vibration of the vortex, I couldn't tell if the engines were on. Elyssa looked through the rear window and her eyes grew huge. "Justin, go."

I didn't even need to look back before jamming the silver lever all the way forward. Then I looked back. The back of the yacht sat on the brink of the void. "Holy crap!" The ship groaned as the turbulent water tore at it. I looked at the countless readouts and didn't know what else to do. *When all else fails, panic.* "Go! Go! Go!" I banged my fists on the large steering wheel. "Do something, you stupid boat!"

I looked back again. *Do we have slightly more room between us and the edge?* I couldn't be sure if my terrified imagination was playing tricks on me. "Get ready to abandon ship," I told Elyssa.

"That sounds like something you've always wanted to say," she said far too calmly for someone in our situation.

"Yeah, I mean, for a spaceship maybe, but not a stupid boat." The steering wheel jerked hard right. I tried to counter it, but the ship began to drift to the side.

"We're caught in the side current." Elyssa pressed her lips together. "I have an idea."

I eagerly let her take the steering wheel. "You're a better driver than me."

Muscles straining on her arms, she twisted the wheel. The ship groaned and lurched. The maelstrom slowly shifted from being behind us to being on our right side. We picked up speed and suddenly hurtled along the outer rim of the death hole.

The ship shook violently. Metal shrieked. A window shattered and a hot gust of wind rushed inside. The entire ship tilted to the side and I saw the crystal meteor glowing brilliantly far below.

"What are you doing?" My butt clenched as tight as a clam.

Elyssa gritted her teeth and fought with the steering wheel. "Saving us."

Round and round we went, gathering speed. Something giant rushed past us. I gawked as a massive spotted whale swam past, engaged in its own furious fight against the tide. A smaller ship appeared on the opposite side of the whirlpool and began its own circuit of the edge. A figure on the deck of the smaller vessel jumped up and down, waving his arms.

"Oh, god." I didn't want to watch.

The other ship twisted and turned, out of control. I realized that within seconds, we'd plow right into it.

"Get ready," Elyssa said in a strained voice. "I can't hold this course much longer."

I remembered the dead woman with the rope and had an idea. "Do what you need to do." I ran to the lower deck and untied the rope from the woman and the railing, then raced to the front of the ship.

We were less than a hundred feet from the spinning boat. Hot wind whipped against my face. The man on the deck of the other boat had given up yelling for help and apparently braced for the inevitable. I leaned over the railing.

"Grab the rope!"

He didn't see or hear me. I shouted again and again, but the deafening din of the swirling water was too much to overcome. I decided to try another tactic and tied the rope to the railing and around my waist then I rappelled down the side of the ship. The yacht abruptly turned and I lost my footing.

The rope played out all the way to the end, jerking me to a halt inches from the rushing water. Agony inflamed my ribs and I shouted in pain. Dangling and twisting in wind and the stinging salt spray, I heard a faint cry. When I rotated toward the front, I saw the man and his boat only feet away. With a yell of surprise, I put out my feet to ward off the blow. The other boat's hull knocked me swinging out over the void. For a moment, I hung over the violent maw, then swung back toward the boat as the yacht crushed through its hull.

The man's face filled with fear. I held out a hand as I swung toward him. "Jump to me! Jump!"

He ran to the edge and leapt just as I swung back into range. He slammed against me, clinging tightly to my ribs. I cried out in agony. He slipped and his weight shifted to my foot. Water foamed around his waist and I knew I'd lose him to the tide unless I did something fast.

Using every bit of supernatural strength, I fought gravity and tried to pull him up with my leg, despite the burning pain in my abdomen. One of the man's arms hung limp by his side and I realized he must have dislocated it.

The fingers of his left hand held my shoe in a white-knuckled grip. My hand reached for his as I pulled up my leg. With one last gasp of pain, I wrapped my fingers around his wrist.

The ship shifted directions and we swung back over the glowing vortex. The other man screamed. I imagined his shoulder hurt as badly as mine did with all his weight and centrifugal force jerking on mine.

The gravitational slingshot threw the yacht out of death's door, past the event horizon of the maelstrom, and into open water.

I heard a man sobbing. At first I wasn't sure if it was me or the guy I'd rescued. It turned out to be both of us. Unfortunately, I was out of juice. There was no way in hell I could get both of us up the rope. I'd be lucky to get up there myself. Elyssa probably had no idea where I was, so that left me little choice. The man's feet were already trailing in the water.

"Can you keep afloat until I untie the rope?" I asked him.

"Yes," he replied.

I released him into the water. The knot had tightened considerably from all the weight on it, but I managed to work it loose and dropped into the water a moment later. I swam to the man and grabbed him under an armpit as the yacht motored past. Just as the rear dock neared, I swam for it, and grabbed the ladder. With a chorus of grunts, groans, and sobs, we heaved ourselves up onto the back deck.

I was in pain and beyond exhausted, but we'd done it.

We had a ride to the mainland.

Chapter 5

I heard Elyssa screaming my name as we neared the bridge.

"I ought to slap you silly, Justin!" She threw herself into my arms, eliciting a yelp from me.

"I think a slap would've been less painful," I groaned.

She jumped back. "Oh, god, I'm sorry." Her lips quirked. "Sort of." She suddenly noticed the man trailing behind me. "Who—what?"

"He was on another boat caught in the whirlpool." I shrugged and instantly regretted it as aches lanced into my shoulders. I motioned toward the space-age console. "Got that figured out?"

She shook her head. "Just the basics." Elyssa's eyes flared and she went over to the unconscious ship captain. "He's still out."

Despite his slumbering state, the man moaned and groaned like someone trapped in a nightmare. "Maybe the doctor can patch him up."

"I hope so. I'm afraid to take the boat too close to shore." She went to the throttle and eased back the lever as we neared the clods of floating debris a few hundred yards off the island. "I don't even know how to drop the anchor on this thing."

The man I'd rescued stepped to the console and regarded the buttons and switches for a moment before pointing to a button that plainly said "Anchor" on it. "This is it."

"Pardon my manners," I said. "I'm Justin, and this is Elyssa."

"Alon," he replied. He touched his dislocated shoulder and winced. "The wave hit my boat last night." Tears gathered in his eyes. "My wife was lost. Somehow, I survived."

"I'm so sorry, Alon." Elyssa placed an arm on his good shoulder. "We're trying to get back to the mainland, but we have a group of people to rescue from the island first. We have a doctor who can probably reset that arm for you."

Tears rolled down his cheeks. He nodded. "I am grateful."

I noticed a small refrigerator tucked into the back corner of the cabin and opened it to find bottled water and soft drinks. "Maybe you should have some water." I handed one to him, and then gulped one down myself.

He sat cross-legged on the floor and forlornly drank his water. "Why did this have to happen here?"

"If you're talking about the meteors, they hit all over the world." I didn't want to dampen his mood further, but I had the feeling he was blaming bad luck or god for killing his wife.

The news obviously surprised him, because his head rocked back as if I'd struck it. "All over the world?"

Elyssa slowed the ship and released the anchor. "Hope it holds."

"What's the best way to get everyone onboard?" I asked.

"There should be inflatable dinghies," Alon said quietly. "Look for the pods on the sides of the yacht."

"You seem pretty experienced." Elyssa knelt next to him. "Can you pilot this boat?"

He nodded slowly. "If I must, though I have never piloted such a large craft."

"That makes you a gazillion times more qualified than us." I rolled my head to ease some of the muscle spasms gripping my neck. "I'll go look for the dinghies."

"I'm coming with you." Elyssa regarded Alon, sympathy softening her eyes. "Will you be okay alone?"

He nodded and leaned against bottom of the console. "I will rest."

We found several rafts and paddles located in compartments all along the length of the ship. We inflated one and put the others inside it. Elyssa grabbed a paddle and pushed us toward shore. Harley stood atop a giant mound of debris and waved when we he spotted us. He carefully made his way down and met us.

"I thought you were dead for sure." He whistled and showed me a video of the yacht on his phone. "This is definitely something you can tell your kids about."

Elyssa grinned. "They'll have no shortage of stories to keep them entertained."

I noticed a crowd of people streaming down the street from the direction of the hotel with the big man in the lead.

Harley whooped and waved at them. "Looks like Reese took care of business."

"Is Reese the big man?" I asked.

He nodded. "Yep. Former special forces, if I had to guess. I see a lot of those types in these parts. I think they figure Thailand is a good place to lose themselves and forget the past."

Elyssa gave me a knowing look. I knew she didn't mean anything by it, but guilt used my guts as a hammock. I'd left behind plenty of loose ends when I ran away from responsibility after the war. If one of Daelissa's former minions caused all this, then I was partly to blame for leaving them free.

Harley seemed to sense my unease and chuckled. "Hey, there's nothing wrong with running away." He flashed his teeth. "While you were gone, I did some research on the internet."

"At least that's still working," I mumbled.

"There were over a hundred reported impacts yesterday." He pulled up a map with red marks. "Some of the impacts were negligible. The meteors fizzled or shattered before reaching the ground." He scrolled along the map. "As you can see, they hit all over the place. I don't think they missed a single country." He switched to pictures from all over the world. All the meteors more or less resembled what we'd seen on the first newscast. "Here's the weird part."

"I think you need to reevaluate how you use that word from now on," I said.

He chuckled. "I see your point. But the oddity here is none of these meteors show burn marks from atmospheric entry."

I hadn't really thought about it, but he was right. "In other words, they were launched inside the atmosphere."

"I suppose." He seemed to have as hard a time wrapping his brain around it as I did. "I just don't see how anyone would be capable of launching so many of these things worldwide, especially in such a short time frame." He looked up. "It would take hundreds of stealth bombers all over the world."

Elyssa showed us her phone. "Look at this video."

A girl taking a selfie video of herself in a small airplane shrieked and flipped the phone around as something the size of a basketball streaked past the nose of the plane.

"What the hell is that?" a male voice asked. "Hang on, I'm gonna follow it." The view through the windshield shifted sharply down.

"Dwayne, what are you doing?" the girl cried.

"I want to see where it lands. Keep videoing, babe. This is our chance to become internet famous!"

Sunlight sparkled off the crystalline object. As it fell, it gathered speed and swelled in size. Before long, it was big as a bus and trailing sparks. The aircraft shook violently.

"N-n-no!" the girl shouted, her words stuttering from the turbulence. "G-g-get us out of here!"

Dwayne cursed and turned the plane from the meteor's trail. The view evened out for a moment and then shook violently as the sound of impact rumbled in the distance. "Holy sh—"

Elyssa stopped the video. "Did you see how small the crystal was at first?"

I blew out a breath. "This must be the work of Serena. Who else could make crystal meteors that grow to the size of an elephant and then suck all the magic from the world?"

"I'll let you two figure that one out." Harley shook his head. "This stuff is crazy."

Reese and the crowd of refugees reached us a moment later.

I shook his hand. "Good work. Did you find many supplies?"

"Yep, but I gotta warn you—I saw Jay and a group of his loonies looting a gun store." His upper lip curled. "Judging from the size of the crates they were pulling out of there, they can't be up to anything good."

My chest tightened. The last thing I needed was Jay trying to kill me. "We've got plenty of inflatable rafts. Let's get everyone loaded onto the yacht."

Reese looked out at the craft and whistled. "She's a beaut."

"Yeah it's okay, I guess." I would have settled for a speedboat, but at least this way we could take a boatload of people with us.

I found Elizabeth and took her aside. "I'd like you to go on the first raft. The ship pilot needs some attention, and there's a French guy named Alon there who needs his arm put back into the socket."

She raised an eyebrow. "You're like a magnet for serious injuries."

"If only you knew." I motioned her toward the shore. "You'll find the rafts up there."

It took an hour to get the first rafts of people onboard the yacht and paddle the inflated rafts back to shore. All the remaining refugees boarded the rafts and piled the supplies inside. We'd just pushed off from shore when I heard an outboard motor revving nearby. Mounds of floating debris blocked my view, so I couldn't tell where it was coming from. We finally reached relatively open water and were about halfway to the boat when the rumbling motor grew louder behind us.

"Oh, crap," Elyssa eloquently stated.

I looked back and saw Jay and his merry band of demon haters riding in a flat-bottomed steel boat and coming straight for us. Every one of them held a rifle of some sort. Elyssa had told me to take it easy, but the sight of those gun-wielding maniacs lit a fire under my ass. I grabbed a paddle and worked it like mad despite the agony in my muscles.

Elyssa growled. "Why can't people like him just go away?"

It was slow going, but thankfully, a lot of unpleasant people weighed down Jay's boat. We reached the yacht just as the other craft caught up to us.

A shot rang out. People cried out and ducked. I turned and glared. Jay grinned smugly and fired another shot into the air.

"Give us the demon," he shouted. "We'll throw him into the fiery inferno in the ocean and rid the world of his evil."

I pumped my fist at him. "You're a grade-A certified lunatic, jackass!"

Another man held up a handful of grenades. "We're going to blow him all to hell."

Bullets spattered the water all around the small boat. Jay and crew nearly crapped their britches.

"I've got a better idea," Reese said, the butt of a sleek black automatic rifle pressed against his shoulder. "Why don't you go away and stay away?"

One of Jay's men whipped a pistol out of a holster. Before he could aim it, a bullet pinged off the handle and sent the gun flying into the water. The man shouted and nursed his hand.

"I'm a pretty good shot," Reese said. "I could probably ace every one of you from a hundred yards with this rifle." He smiled. "On the other hand, you could just do what I asked and go away."

"If you want to damn yourselves to hell, then I won't try to save you." Jay stood and glared at Reese. "But you won't stop our holy mission." He jabbed a finger toward the glowing whirlpool of doom. "We will destroy the root of his power."

Reese snorted. "With grenades and guns?" He shrugged. "Be my guest. Now get out of here, and don't think I won't be watching you."

"Onward to God's glory!" Jay raised a fist in the air. The man driving the boat gunned it and Jay tumbled backwards with a yelp as his holy chariot bounced away toward the whirlpool.

Cheers went up from our group.

I gave Reese a thumb's up. "Nice going, man."

"My pleasure." He turned away and stopped. "By the way, I stowed the bodies I found onboard in a compartment near the engine room." A sigh. "At least they can get a decent funeral." Reese pressed his lips together, turned, and ascended to the upper deck, presumably to keep an eye on Jay and company.

We quickly helped everyone board the ship and loaded the supplies. The doctor had found a med kit and managed to awaken the pilot. Though the man was still mostly out of it, he instructed Alon how to operate the yacht and the advanced sonar.

I walked to the bow with Elyssa and looked to the east where Jay's motorboat was closing on the maelstrom, probably quarter of a mile away by now. "I wonder if they can even scratch the thing with grenades."

"That's if they don't get sucked into the whirlpool first," Elyssa said.

I magnified my vision and watched as Jay and the others tied several gray bricks on a small inflatable raft, and I realized they must have gotten their hands on something more powerful than grenades. They were also a bit craftier than I'd given them credit for being.

If they did destroy the meteor, I wondered what would happen to all the aether. Had the meteor sucked in all the aether, or was it doing something else to it? I really didn't know. Then again, I didn't want to be anywhere near that thing if it blew up.

Outboard motor fighting the violent eddies, they released the raft. It swirled away toward the gaping maw and was quickly consumed. At first I thought Captain Jackass Jay and his boatload of flunkies might not escape the swirling current around the vortex, but the small boat fought free.

"Those idiots are gonna get themselves killed," Reese said. He pulled a pair of binoculars from his eyes and shook his head. "Maybe they'd be doing the world a favor."

"Who knows?" I said. "There might be somebody in this world who'd miss them."

Reese chuckled. "Yeah, their psychiatrists." He lifted his head in an upward nod. "What's your story, man? I've been saving Q&A time for later, but I gotta admit, I'm curious about that transformation you pulled on the roof yesterday."

"Uhm…" I wasn't sure if I wanted to launch into the story I'd given Harley, or make up something on the spot. "It's complicated, and probably best kept secret unless you want people in black knocking on your door someday." I didn't really know if the Custodians made house calls on people they suspected had knowledge of the Overworld, or simply let them be until they started making waves.

"Ah." He nodded again. "Some kind of government thing."

I didn't challenge his supposition. "More or less. Let's just say that the fewer people who know, the better."

"I gotcha." Reese shrugged and put the binoculars to his eyes. "I've had to keep my share of secrets."

"Special forces?" Elyssa asked.

He nodded without lowering the binoculars. "That obvious, huh?"

"Let's just say you know how to handle a gun." She shuddered. To her and most Templars, guns were grody nom weapons.

"I can tell by the way you handled yourself on the roof, you might know a thing or two." He glanced away from the lens and winked.

By now, Jay and pals were a couple hundred yards from the whirpool. Someone was fiddling with the engine on the boat, and I wondered if they'd run out of gas. I hadn't thought to check the fuel situation on this rig and hoped we had enough.

A distant rumble told me the explosives must have gone off. A brilliant burst of light from the maelstrom confirmed the theory. A shockwave rippled through the ocean and blasted me in the face with mist. Then the real explosion happened. A massive sphere of crackling ultraviolet and white energy bubbled up from the depths of the ocean and spread at a terrifying rate.

Jay and the others with him threw up their arms. I could almost hear their screams over the deafening roar as what could only be malaether—corrupted, poisonous aether—burned them to ash.

"Holy mother!" Reese looked at the other spectators on the deck. "Get inside now! Go! Go! Go!" The look of panic in his eyes was enough to send everyone scuttling to shelter.

The giant wave preceding the malaether blast was enough to turn my insides to water.

If the tidal wave didn't kill us, the malaether blast would probably burn us all to ash.

Chapter 6

Elyssa and I raced to the control room where Alon, his arm in a makeshift sling, guided the boat.

"Are we at full speed?" I asked.

He shook his head. "I thought we should conserve fuel. What was that—"

I ran forward and jammed the throttle all the way to max. The ship lurched. "We've got to get out of here!"

During the war, both sides had used small malaether crucibles like mini-nukes. Those detonations had been relatively small. If that crystal meteor had been soaking up aether all this time, it meant the explosion would be exponentially greater.

I looked back and saw the leading wave racing toward us, the sphere of cascading death close behind. The water caught us, slammed into the stern, and the entire ship groaned as it tilted forward. Water bottles and other loose objects tumbled to the floor. Everyone grabbed onto seats or consoles to keep from crashing into the control panel or front windows.

The ship rushed down the wave, riding it like a giant surfboard, and cries of terror rose from everyone present. I looked back—rather up— since the ship was at such a precarious tilt, and saw the deadly energy wave not more than a hundred yards behind the rising ocean.

"C'mon, baby." I patted the console. "You survived the first tidal wave. You can make it through this one."

"I don't think petting the ship is going to help," Elyssa shouted over the din of rushing water, groaning metal, and the thunderous roar of malaether.

The bow shuddered as if it had hit something. I saw a cluster of small boats that must have been cast out to sea spinning before us and figured we must have hit at least one. The yacht spun sideways and gravity shifted. Alon slipped and fell hard against the wall. The ship captain, who I hadn't noticed before, was buckled into a large chair, eyes wide with terror.

I almost wished he'd shout something crazy but encouraging, like, "Argh, mateys! This here ship has sailed the seven seas and ridden the deadly waves of hurricanes. Never has she let me down, and never will she!"

Instead, he closed his eyes and whimpered.

I'm totally with you, bro. Unfortunately, I wasn't buckled in, and it was all I could do to keep my grip on the slick console. The yacht pitched, and for a moment, I thought it would completely roll over. For a split second, I saw nothing but dark waves and water through the left windows. The hull slammed into more of the small boats riding the wave before us, and the entire craft shuddered.

We crested the tidal wave and the ship wobbled to the right. I lost my grip and tumbled down the aisle, crashed through the window. My fingers barely gripped the railing in time to keep me from hurtling into the water. The ship bobbed upright and catapulted me back onto the deck just in time to see the malaether sphere rushing toward us.

We're dead.

I tried to stand, but my body was beyond tired and beaten. Even if I got inside, it would roast us alive.

"I love you Elyssa!" I shouted at the top of my lungs and futilely threw up my arms.

Death didn't come. The crackling energy faded, leaving a boiling sea behind. Dead fish floated to the surface, and the steam turned to a dense fog.

The yacht's engines cut off and for a moment, there was nothing but profound silence. I heard movement, and Elyssa appeared by my side. She hugged me, not too hard, thankfully, and peppered my face with kisses.

"Justin, are you—oh, never mind—I know you're hurt." Tears sparkled down her cheeks.

"I'm going to need another vacation after this," I groaned.

She helped me to my feet. My legs were skinned to hell, and so were my arms, for that matter. I tasted blood in my mouth and found a painful cut on my lip. Elyssa put my arm over her shoulder and helped me limp back inside the control room.

Alon lay motionless beneath the broken window I'd fallen through. Elyssa knelt, touched his neck, and shook her head slowly. "He's dead."

The captain sobbed uncontrollably, but seemed otherwise unharmed. Two other people had strapped themselves into chairs and appeared okay as well.

We went inside the upper deck cabin and found two more bodies amidst stunned and frightened people. I didn't recognize the two men, but sorrow burrowed into my chest. I found Elizabeth and several other people clustered into one of the cabins.

"There are probably a lot of people who need your help," I told her. "Can you use the lounge up here as a makeshift medic station?"

She wiped tears from her eyes and nodded. "How many did we lose?"

I shook my head. "Three so far. I'm going downstairs to check on the others."

The lower deck situation wasn't as dire as I'd feared. Many of the people were strapped onto a long leather couch in the lounge by a length of sturdy rope. Thankfully, all the furniture appeared to be bolted to the floor, though glasses had shattered, and the odor of spilt alcohol rose from liquid on the floor. Several people had bruises and cuts where their heads had knocked against their neighbor, and one person who hadn't gotten seated in time had a broken leg.

"Rope always comes in handy on a ship," Reese said, loosening the knots of the rope he'd used to secure himself to a separate chair.

"He saved our lives," Harley said, rubbing a cut above his eye, "though I still can't believe the ship didn't break apart."

"I want to give the builders a medal." Reese patted the bulkhead and looked out the window. The fog was already lifting, revealing a sea littered with dead marine life. "Wonder if those fish are cooked to order," he mumbled.

Even though they'd been boiled in the water, I didn't want to chance eating any of them. Malaether crucibles didn't leave behind radiation, but that didn't mean the meteor explosion hadn't.

"Was it a nuke?" A man asked.

"We'll let the government figure that one out." Reese turned from the window. "Does the ship still work, Justin?"

I shrugged. "Don't know yet." I turned to the others. "In the meantime, if you need treatment, the doctor set up a makeshift ward on the upper deck." As the injured filed out, I walked over to Reese. "There are three more bodies—two upstairs, and one in the control room. Can you see to them?"

He snapped a salute. "You got it."

"I'll go to the bridge and see if the captain has stopped wetting his pants," Elyssa said. "The sooner we get moving, the better."

We were underway within half an hour.

Several hours later, we docked at the port in the city of Myeik. Unlike the other coastal towns, it had been shielded from the brunt of the tsunami by the islands off its coast. Refugees flooded the harbor and stranded ships and boats clogged the port.

A flustered official directed us to a large fenced in area where a mob of miserable people waited for food and medical attention.

"I'm not going in there," I told Elyssa. "We've got to get to Bangkok."

Reese produced a cell phone. "Just so happens I have a buddy who runs a charter plane company for tourists. I might be able to call in a favor."

"That would be wonderful," Elyssa said. "How long do you think it'll take?"

He shrugged. "Let me find out."

Harley approached us. "Something tells me you two are off to save the world again."

I sighed. "No rest for the weary."

"Well, I guess this is where we say goodbye." He shook Elyssa's hand and mine. "Take care, you two. And if you're ever out this way again, I want to treat you to a beer."

"Sounds amazing." I really liked the guy.

Elyssa hugged him. "Take care, Harley."

He smiled shyly. "Don't let this princess out of your sight, Justin. She's a keeper."

I slipped an arm around her waist and kissed her cheek. "Wouldn't dream of it."

Harley nodded. "Well, until next time." He turned and walked into the refugee camp.

Elizabeth hugged each of us. "We all owe you our lives." She squeezed her eyes shut for a moment. "I can't wait to go home and put this nightmare behind me." She turned to Reese and gave him a slip of paper. "If you're ever in New York, call me."

A broad grin stretched Reese's face. "I haven't been there in a while. Sounds like I have a good reason to go now."

She smiled. "Well, then, I'll look forward to it."

After she left, several more people approached and expressed their thanks. The mother and father of the children we'd saved gave us their number and told us to come by anytime.

"We'd all be dead if not for you," the mother said.

"Demons are awesome!" The boy chimed in.

The mother rolled her eyes. "I heard a lot of rumors on that roof. I think you're angels."

When the crowd departed, Reese walked away and made a call on his cell phone. He spoke for several minutes, and returned. "My buddy said he can get us tomorrow. Until then, maybe we can find a place to eat that's better than the gruel they're serving in there." He took out his wallet and counted some bills. "This should be plenty."

Unfortunately, Elyssa had no money in her purse. "We'll pay you back."

He pshawed. "Nah, it ain't a big deal. Besides, I figure I owe you."

"You did a lot too," Elyssa said. "And we're grateful."

We found a small restaurant, ate, and located a questionable looking hotel. I crawled into bed and fell asleep before my head hit the dingy pillow.

Reese's buddy, Nathan, landed at the tiny airport the next day and flew us to Bangkok. I slept most of the ride, hoping to give my injuries a chance to heal. Once there, Reese handed us some cash to hire a taxi and gave us his number.

"Call me anytime. If you ever feel the urge to tell me more about whatever secrets you're keeping, I'm all ears." He ran a hand down his face. "I think I'm gonna go back to the States, rest, and then pay that pretty doctor a visit."

"Sounds like a smart plan," Elyssa said. "Maybe when we visit, we'll see the both of you." She hugged him. "Take care, Reese."

"You too." He saw us to the taxi and waved as we pulled away.

The Obsidian Arch was hidden deep beneath a parking deck about twenty minutes from the airport. Our footsteps echoed in the eerily empty way station. A sign on the ticket booth declared, *Closed until magic crisis resolved.*

Like most way stations, this one had a stable, and behind it a hidden door to the control room. We went inside and found an arch operator sitting in a chair and reading a book titled, *How to Be a Nom, for Dummies.*

He glanced up and frowned. "What the hell? Didn't you see the sign?" His head jerked back and recognition set in. "Wait a minute, are you Justin Slade? Elyssa Borathen?"

"That'd be us," Elyssa said dryly. "We need to get back to Queens Gate."

"But we were told not to use the arches." His forehead creased. "Do you know something I don't?"

"From what I understand, the Obsidian Arches will work." I sighed. "Can you give it a try?"

"Let me contact Queens Gate." He took out an arcphone and argued with someone for a few minutes. "Okay, they're willing to try it, but won't take the blame if you end up in the Gloom or blown all over creation."

I didn't relish the thought of being trapped in that strange place, but I'd lost my passport, and taking a plane home would create a lot of unwanted complications.

"We've got to take that chance," I said.

He shrugged. "Are you working on solving this aether problem?" He held up the book. "If you don't get things working right again, I'll have to find a stupid nom job, probably working at a fast-food restaurant or something awful like that." His shoulders slumped. "It's about all I'm qualified for without magic."

I felt his pain, though I at least had my demonic powers to fall back upon. He walked to the raised platform at the front of the room. A large world map with markings for each Obsidian Arch in the world stretched along the front wall. In the center of the platform stood a raised block of stone with a large gray orb atop it: the modulus. It allowed the operator to power on the arch and select which waystation to target.

"We'll head to the arch," I told him.

"Good luck." He managed a half smile, but it quickly faded.

Elyssa snickered when we left the control room and walked toward the towering Obsidian Arch in the center of the cavern.

"What's so funny?" I asked.

"Just imagining robed Arcanes flipping burgers." She quirked her lips. "Life without magic would be pretty depressing. Hopefully we can get to the bottom of this."

A low hum filled the cavern, building in volume and rising in pitch as the arch powered up. The expansive silver band around it flashed as it closed, trapping magical energy within it. The process usually only took a moment or so, but this time it took a lot longer than usual. After a long wait, arcs of aether flashed across the arch columns and the middle flashed. An image of another way station appeared on the other side.

"Looks clear," Elyssa said in a hopeful voice. "Let's pray we don't get zapped."

We raced forward to the massive gateway, hesitated at the threshold and looked at each other, then dashed through.

My skin flashed hot the instant we crossed over and I thought we might end up vaporized. Instead, we stepped into the Queens Gate way station deep below London and shared looks of relief.

"That kinda hurt," I said, looking at my skin for signs of burns.

Elyssa checked herself as well. "Looks like I'm all here, except—" Her eyes widened. "I'm missing a toe!"

"What?" I dropped to my knees as the hum of the arch wound down, and inspected her feet. She wore sandals so it was plain to see she still had all her toes.

Elyssa burst into laughter. "Gotcha!"

I rose and gave her a dirty look. "Not funny." I had to admit, it was a bit humorous, and god knew we both needed a laugh after what we'd been through. "Let's go talk to Shelton."

We walked across the wide space to the large pair of doors at the entrance of the pocket dimension of Queens Gate. Though I'd been through them many times, it was still somewhat wondrous stepping through into a whole new world.

We opened the doors and stepped onto a brick paved road. A wide valley stretched before us, cliffs towering on all sides. Atop the cliff to the right sat the Science Academy, a silver gleaming citadel dedicated to mad science. Out of sight on the cliff to the left, a plateau showed the towering spires of Arcane University. The city of Queens Gate nestled in the green valley between the two cliffs, and far behind it rose another mountain.

I called Shelton and had him open an omniarch portal. I didn't feel like hitching a ride on the sky car up to the university and hiking to the secret tunnel near the Dark Forest at the back of the university.

"You're here?" He whooped. "One portal coming right up."

A moment later, a nice proper portal without deadly static sliced open the air before us and we exited in a large room where the smaller sibling of an Obsidian Arch stood.

Shelton gave me a hug. "Great to see you, man." He traded hugs with Elyssa and kissed her on the cheek. "I wasn't sure you'd make it."

Bella, a petite Colombian, embraced us and kissed us on the cheeks. "We were so worried. Harry couldn't concentrate when we played Scrabble, and I won every game."

"You always win, woman." Shelton flashed a smile. "Let's go to the mansion and relax. I gotta hear what happened."

I almost broke into tears at the thought of being home among family.

It was great to be back.

Chapter 7

Over cupcakes and milk, Elyssa and I took turns telling the story.

"Holy Mary, mother of midgets." Shelton ran a hand down his face. "So destroying these things is like setting off a nuke?" He grabbed another cupcake and bit into it. "How are we supposed to counter them?"

"Perhaps we could move them and fire them into space," Bella suggested. "The only other option is disabling them somehow."

"I need to speak with my father, but the aether lines are down outside the pocket dimension." Elyssa looked doubtfully at her phone. "I have a signal here, but only get an error message when I try to call."

"We might have to go topside so you can use the nom cell towers," Shelton said. "Or, I guess we simply go to Atlanta."

"That seems our best bet," I said. "No sense hanging around here." I stood, stretched, and cracked a yawn. "I'd like to get a good night's sleep first."

Shelton slapped the table. "It's settled then. Tomorrow we head to Atlanta." He stood and rubbed his hands together. "Just when I thought things were getting boring, we're back in the saddle."

"I really thought ending Daelissa's conquest would be it for a while." My lamentation was greeted by sad nods.

"It never ends." Bella collected the cupcake platter and stacked the empty cups on it. "The Overworld government is still in shambles, and the lack of magic is making everyone grumpy."

"It definitely puts a damper on things." Shelton snatched a half-eaten cupcake from the plate and wolfed it down. "On the bright side, Ryland and Stacey had a litter of kittens or pups, or whatever you call baby lycan and felycans."

"They're called babies, Harry." Bella gave him an admonishing look. "They moved to a nice house in Atlanta, but I haven't heard much since the baby shower."

"I got the message from Stacey about their twins," I said. "I wonder what kind of morphs they'll be."

"We have a few years before discovering that." Elyssa stifled a yawn. "I'm ready for bed too. Goodnight."

"Goodnight, dear." Bella vanished into the kitchen.

Shelton clapped me on the back and elicited a groan from me. My muscles were still plenty sore.

"Oops, sorry," he said. "It's good to see you again, man. Got a second?"

I nodded.

"I'll be upstairs in our room," Elyssa said with a curious glance at Shelton. She walked upstairs and left the two of us alone.

Shelton motioned for me to follow him and went down the hall and into the war room, a large place with only a conference table and chairs. He closed the door behind us and produced a small box. "I'm gonna pop the question to Bella." He opened it to reveal a bright opal ring.

I slapped him on the shoulder. "Congrats, dude! When do you plan to do it?"

"Well, I've been looking for the proper romantic moment, you know?" He rubbed the back of his neck. "I want it to be memorable, but I'm not that great with this stuff."

"I'm sure she'll be happy no matter how you do it." I tried to think of something or somewhere he could do it, even falling back on my favorite movie of all time, *The Princess Bride*. Taking her out for a ride on white horses didn't seem to be Shelton's style, and I came up short on ideas. "Um, maybe take her for a carpet ride and have a picnic somewhere nice."

He chuckled. "Yeah, that could work, but it might be kinda cliché." He shrugged. "Maybe you could ask Elyssa for some advice."

"Sure." I looked at the ring. "Sometimes, simple is best, though. Don't go overboard."

He ran a finger over the opal. "Yeah, I definitely don't want to mess this up."

"I don't think it's possible. You know she'll say yes." Another yawn yanked open my mouth. "Let's sleep on it."

Shelton chuckled. "All right. See you in the morning."

I went upstairs and considered taking a shower, but was just too damned tired.

"What did Shelton want?" Elyssa lay atop the covers in only panties and a bra.

My mouth watered at the sight. "Huh?" My mind finally took in her question. "He wants to ask Bella to marry him."

She popped to her knees. "Really? That's great!" Elyssa clapped her hands like a little girl. "Does he have something romantic planned?"

"That's what he asked me for advice about." I shrugged. "I couldn't think of anything."

"Hmm." She tapped a finger on her chin. "I'll help you come up with something. In the meantime, I just want to cuddle and go to sleep."

I stripped down to my boxer briefs. "I am totally down for cuddling." I crawled into bed next to her and ran a hand up her smooth, muscular leg. "And maybe a little something more."

She giggled. "Sure you're up for it?"

I kissed her. "For you, always."

My phone rang. I groaned, but knew any call coming through couldn't be ignored. I didn't recognize the number but answered anyway. When I moved the phone from the nightstand, the only remaining signal bar vanished. I quickly moved it back in place and put it on speakerphone.

"Hello?" The voice was barely audible through the static on the line.

"Who is this?" I asked.

There was a long silence, and I feared I'd lost the call.

"Justin, hello? It's Nightliss." She repeated herself once more.

"Nightliss?" I jerked upright and sat on the edge of the bed. "Where are you?"

"Oh, thank goodness you can hear me." More static covered what she said next. "…don't know how but I will."

"Repeat what you said."

"I'm in India…finding way home…what's happened to the magic?"

I adjusted the phone a tiny bit to the left. It was amazing I had a nom cell signal so far underground, but it seemed to be limited to this one spot. The signal didn't grow any stronger when I moved it.

"Have you seen the meteors? They're sapping the magic." I leaned over the phone, hoping she was still there.

"I thought so," she said, her voice much clearer. "One of them caused chaos in the village I was visiting. There were men—awful men who tried to take the women. I protected them, Justin."

"Are you okay?" I asked.

"There is no use running from conflict is there?" Despair clouded Nightliss's voice. "It always finds you."

"Are you coming home?" I asked, daring to hope.

"Yes." She sighed. "I do not know how, but I will find a way."

"We'll be waiting," Elyssa said. "We love you."

"I love you too, my friends." Her voice broke.

"Try to find the nearest Obsidian Arch," I told her. "Some of them are still working."

"Let me find the nearest one," Elyssa said.

There was a crackle, and the call ended.

"Damn it." I tried calling the number, but only received an error message.

"Your call cannot be completed as dialed," a robotic voice informed me.

We waited by the phone, but Nightliss didn't call back.

Elyssa rubbed my arm. "I'm sure she'll make it home safe."

I lay back on the bed and stared at the ceiling. "I hope so. The Templars need their Clarion."

I woke up the next morning feeling much better. The soreness in my bones and muscles had faded to a dull ache. My ribs felt mostly whole again, and it seemed I was on the mend, albeit slower than usual. Elyssa and I went downstairs, the smell of pancakes and bacon wafting into our noses.

Shelton popped out of the kitchen with a heaping platter of flapjacks and a huge grin on his face. "Just in time."

Bella followed him with plates of bacon and eggs. "Good, you're up before Harry eats all the food."

"Smells heavenly." I took a chair and wolfed down a pancake. "It's good to be back."

I chowed down two helpings of pancakes, and finished with eggs and bacon then sat back and released a contented burp.

"I knew you missed my cooking." Shelton sipped his coffee, a smug grin on his face. He checked the time on his phone. "Welp, guess we should get a move on. I have a feeling Commander Borathen is on the warpath to figure out what's going on, and I sure don't want him blowing up one of those meteors before we get there."

"I doubt he'd do anything so rash." Elyssa finished off her orange juice. "He'll study them from every angle before committing to anything."

"Let's hope the nom militaries around the world are so cautious," Bella said.

I told them about the call from Nightliss.

"Goodness, I hope she makes it," Bella said. "You're already quite an inspiration to have around, Justin, but Nightliss would really help morale with the Templars."

"Hey, what about me?" Shelton said. "I'm awe-inspiring." He stood and pulled the string on an invisible bow and held the pose. "Am I right?"

We burst into laughter.

"Nobody can stop us now," Elyssa said.

"Maybe we could use your muscular butt cheeks to crush the meteors," I said with a snort.

After showering, Elyssa and I dressed in full Templar fatigues, consisting of a black unitard called Nightingale armor. The clothing started as a black belt of cloth that grew to cover a person from head to toe, if so desired. I extended it from the neck down while Elyssa did the same.

Shelton and Bella waited below, Shelton dressed in jeans, a T-shirt, and his faithful leather duster. He perched a wide-brimmed hat atop his head and holstered a staff and wand at either side.

He shrugged. "Never hurts to be prepared, even if I can't use magic."
Bella had her Arcane instruments as well, and wore a slim-fitting robe. She ran a hand along her curved pink wand and sighed. "I feel so crippled without magic. At least I have my dhampyr abilities."
Like Elyssa, she had the strengths of a vampire, but none of the weaknesses. Her violet eyes and warm blood were the telltale signs of her condition.
We went to the Queens Gate way station and had to convince the arch operator there to open a gateway to the Grotto way station beneath Phipps Plaza in Atlanta.
"Look, bud, we're on official business." Shelton jabbed a finger at the obstinate man.
The operator threw up his hands. "Fine, just don't blame me if you explode." He sighed. "I supposed I'll be the one to clean up the mess."
The gateway opened slowly as it had in Bangkok, but eventually we were able to cross through into a nearly identical way station, complete with stables. During peak business, they usually brimmed with animals of all sorts, from exotic elephants and giraffes, to more conventional beasts of burden like horses. Aside from a lonely donkey and a dejected looking lad named Oliver, the place was empty.
"G'day, guvnah!" Oliver managed a cheery smile, despite his obvious gloominess.
"Slow day, eh?" Shelton ruffled the boy's unruly mop of hair.
"It's bloody awful." He leaned against a wooden fence and kicked a small pile of hay then suddenly brightened. "I take it you're here to set things straight with the magic outage?"
I nodded. "We're on it."
"We'll have things up and running in no time," Shelton assured him.
The last time I'd seen the boy, he'd revealed that he had a connection to Underborn, the most notorious assassin in the Overworld. Despite our rough history, including a fake contract on my father, and several uneven dealings, Underborn had come through during the last phases of the war against Daelissa.
"Heard anything from Underborn?" I asked.

"He's got his contacts on high alert for information about the meteors." Oliver picked up a piece of hay and idly tossed it. "Otherwise, I don't know what he's up to."

"Well, if he wants to help, we're headed to the Ranch." The Templar headquarters were located on a horse ranch in Decatur.

"I'll tell him if I see him." His mood dampened once again. "I really miss all the animals and people that come through here."

"I'll be you miss shoveling the poop too." Shelton grinned.

Oliver stuck out his tongue. "Not so much."

I looked out at the parking lot where a lone white Lamborghini with zebra stripes sat. "I think we need to have someone pick us up."

"We'll have to walk topside so I can get a phone signal," Elyssa said. "Someone from the Ranch can come and get us."

"We keep a few cars here for emergencies," Oliver said. He motioned us to follow him to the parking lot. He went to the wall and pressed a section with a small red mark on it. The stone rumbled aside to reveal two white sedans. "I'm certain this qualifies. The keys are on the seat."

"Thanks!" Shelton gave the boy a couple of silver bills—tinsel, the Overworld currency.

Oliver tucked them away. "Mighty kind of you, sir."

"Don't spend it all in one place." Shelton and Bella hopped in the back seat.

Elyssa took the driver's seat and I climbed into the other side. She twisted the key in the ignition and the engine turned over. "Hmm, ordinary gas engine."

"Probably not a good idea to use aether powered vehicles right now," Shelton said.

"That pretty much covers most of the Templar fleet." She put the car into drive and pulled out. Once we reached the Phipps Plaza parking deck at the top of the long winding ramp, Elyssa texted her father.

"He's at the Ranch," she said. "I let him know we're coming."

When we pulled onto the long gravel drive to the Ranch, my mood lifted. It was nice to be back in familiar environs. I wondered if the pasture where we'd fought Daelissa's first Brightling army showed any signs of recovery. We'd used sogger grenades to turn it into a bog and slow the enemy advance. That had been one of many bloody battles we'd waged against the insane Brightling before temporarily relocating the Templar headquarters to Queens Gate.

We drove into the large barn across from the house and down a wide ramp into an underground garage. Large metal boxes called sliders that used illusion spells to resemble nom helicopters sat in rows to the right, while black SUVs and sedans lined the parking spaces to the left.

A note next to the levitator shaft explained that it was out of order for the time being, so we had to take several flights of stairs to enter the underground complex.

"Man, I'm getting too much exercise," Shelton complained as we finally entered the level with conference rooms.

Bella rubbed his belly and smiled. "Maybe it's for the best."

Elyssa grinned. "Give those butt cheeks a workout."

We found Thomas Borathen in the war room along with Elyssa's hulk of a brother, Michael. A man in a black suit, a young woman, and a man with handsome chiseled features stood inside with him.

Thomas's eyes lit when he saw Elyssa. "Welcome home." He gave her a brief hug, and shook my hand. "It appears we have a new crisis on our hands."

Michael gave Elyssa a firm hug. "Good to see you, Ninjette." He nodded at me. "Justin."

I returned the nod. "Good to see you, Michael."

The young woman's eyes widened. "Justin Slade?" She asked in a British accent.

I nodded. "And you are?"

"I'm Emily Glass." She pointed to the handsome man next to her. "This is Tyler Rock."

"Hey, nice to finally meet you," Tyler said and gave my hand a firm shake. "We've seen you before, but it's nice to finally meet my nephew."

"Nephew?" I pulled my hand back.

"I'm one of Baal's kids." He grinned. "I've worked with your father, David, before too."

"Emily has unique talents," Thomas said.

"They aren't much good in a situation like this," she admitted.

"They work with me," said the man in the black suit. "I'm Agent George Walker with the Custodians."

"Well, if it isn't the man of the hour," said a pleasant baritone voice behind me.

I turned to see a tall man in black Arcane robes. Though he looked pleasant enough, his dark eyebrows and thick black hair gave him something of a sinister appearance.

"Chancellor Victus Edison of Science Academy." He shook my hand, covering the grip with his other hand like a politician trolling for votes. "I'm also here as an acting member of the Arcane Council."

The faint odor of brimstone hung around the man and I wondered if he'd had recent dealings with demons. "Justin Slade," I said simply, and reclaimed my hand.

"Victus is one of the foremost scientists at the academy," Thomas said. "He's been helping me sort Overworld political issues."

"Unfortunately, this incident is a dark cloud over everything," Victus said. "We need to solve this crisis so we can move forward and reestablish law and order in the Overworld."

"Save the political speech," Shelton said. "I'm in."

I introduced everyone with me to the others.

"What a pleasure," Emily said, shaking Elyssa's hand. "We work in the background, we rarely get to meet those on the front lines."

"Wait a minute," Elyssa said. "Weren't you involved in the Demonicus Incident? I read some of the reports about it."

"Demonicus?" I asked.

"Domathus, a demon overlord, attempted to physically enter Eden," Thomas explained. "Apparently, he had designs on Eden and thought his minions could take over Eden and defeat Daelissa."

"Ain't no shortage of crazies who want to rule the world," Shelton said. "I'm glad we didn't have to deal with that."

"Commander, we should be going," Agent Walker said. "We have a few leads to investigate, including some reports from the Overworld Transportation Authority. Apparently their ASE network tracked one of the incoming meteors, and the footage could offer clues to their origin."

I wrinkled my forehead. "The tracking network is still working?"

Agent Walker shook his head. "Unfortunately, the ASE network went offline shortly after the meteors hit since they couldn't recharge their aether supply."

"Did the OTA download the data before that happened?" Thomas asked.

"Not all of it. We hope to find the actual ASEs with the raw footage for examination." Agent Walker headed for the door. "We'll keep you apprised."

Michael headed after him.

"Where are you going?" Elyssa asked.

"I'm on assignment with the Custodians for now." He kissed her forehead. "I'll see you again soon."

"Nice meeting you," Tyler said to me. "Let's get together sometime. A double date maybe."

"Sure." I had a million questions for the guy, but settled for one. "Are you Daemos?"

He shook his head. "No. It's a long story we can save for later."

"A pleasure," Emily said, shaking mine and Elyssa's hands. "I hope to see you again under better circumstances."

"That'd be nice." Elyssa seemed to like the other woman, judging from her smile. "I'd really like to hear your version of the Demonicus Incident."

"It's a doozy," Tyler assured her.

I felt a bit strange after they left. Why hadn't my father mentioned this Tyler Rock fellow to me before? I planned to grill him the next time I saw him.

"The OTA files sound like a good lead," Shelton.

The Overworld Transportation Administration used all-seeing eyes, ASEs, to record and track all magical forms of travel, primarily to make sure no one broke Overworld law. Shelton and I had once used it to track down my mother so we could rescue her from Daelissa.

If it could help us discover the origin of these meteors, I had to believe we could be well on our way to solving this thing.

Chapter 8

"Maybe we could investigate this OTA footage Agent Walker mentioned," I said.

"Wish Cinder was here," Shelton said. "He loves digging through data like a troll loves dirt."

Our golem friend, created by a Seraphim named Fjoeruss, had somehow achieved sentience after being the subject of experiments by an Arcane. He'd come through for us many times when it came to analyzing reams of data.

"Where is he now?" I asked.

"Probably learning how to smile without scaring small children," Shelton said.

"I'm ready to offer assistance wherever necessary," Victus said. "Science Academy hasn't been nearly as affected as the Arcanes."

"Are you an Arcane?" I asked.

He nodded. "I'm a level sixteen Arcane, though I far prefer scientific pursuits. My wife, Delectra is a nineteen, and is far more skilled at the Arcane arts than I."

Shelton whistled. "A nineteen? She just about tops the scale."

I almost pulled out my level forty-one rating, but it wouldn't be a fair comparison. My Seraphim side gave me a lot of raw power. Besides, we had more important things to talk about. "Do we have any ASE footage available here?" I asked Thomas.

"Not at present with the aethernet down." He put a hand on his chin. "You'll probably have to retrieve it in person."

"Bella and I can do that," Shelton said. "Better than sitting around doing nothing."

"Maybe I should brief everyone on what we know so far," I said. "I don't know what actions you're considering with regard to the meteors, but I have vital information."

Thomas nodded. "Go ahead."

I told them about the incident in Thailand. Thomas, as usual, remained stoic, though his eyes flared when I told him about the explosion.

"Amazing," Victus said. "Think of the power we could harness if we understood these meteors."

I shook my head. "This is the kind of power we don't want in Eden."

"We've tried moving the crystals," Thomas said, "but digging revealed crystal roots piercing deep into the earth."

"I wonder what would happen if any of those roots broke," Elyssa said.

"It could trigger a reaction like the one Justin described," Thomas replied. "We can't move them and we can't destroy them. We have to deactivate them."

"I'd like to see one up close if possible," I said. Another question came to me. "What happens when you touch the crystals?"

"So far we haven't risked it," Thomas said. "We've used nom construction vehicles to dig around one under our control."

"Don't even think of touching one, Justin." Elyssa gave me a pointed look. "I don't want you getting vaporized."

Shelton blasted a breath. "How are we supposed to know what'll happen if someone doesn't try?"

"Let's think about this logically," I said. "From what we know, the crystals absorb aether, or somehow distort it. I don't think they operate like interdictors and turn it into malaether." It suddenly occurred to me how we could see what was happening. "My demon vision allows me to see the aether. Maybe it would help if I looked at one of those things."

"You can see aether?" Victus raised an eyebrow. "I've never heard of such a thing."

"Yep." I didn't trust the man enough to go into details.

Thomas consulted a tablet. "The closest meteor is in Sweetwater Creek State Park. We haven't tried to access it because the National Guard cordoned off the site."

"What're we gonna officially call these things besides crystals and meteors?" Shelton asked.

"Crasteroids," I suggested. "Or how about meteocrysts?"

Elyssa groaned. "Awful. Just awful."

"Meteocryst sounds like fast food," Bella said.

"I vote for crystoids," Shelton said. "That has a nice ring to it."

Elyssa smiled. "Better."

"Fine, crystoids, whatever." I turned to Thomas. "Let's go to Sweetwater Creek and check out that crystoid."

Shelton pounded a fist into his palm. "Let's infiltrate that bad boy."

"We'll need to wait until dark." Thomas folded his arms. "Unfortunately camouflage armor and most functions of Nightingale armor won't work without aether. The built in charms should be okay, but there are no guarantees."

"A small team would be best," Elyssa said. "Justin and I can do it alone."

Shelton growled. "Why do you get to have all the fun?"

Bella put a hand on his arm. "I know something fun, Harry. We can go to the OTA and get the meteor recordings."

Shelton wasn't appeased. "Now I'm an errand boy."

Bella elbowed him. "You're the one who suggested going in the first place."

"Yeah, but busting a military perimeter sounds so much more fun." He threw up his hands. "Who am I kidding? I'm just a nom without magic. Might as well fetch those ASE files."

"Better than getting shot," Bella said brightly.

"We have a nom vehicle you can use," Thomas said. "Just ask the carpool attendant."

Shelton put a hand on my shoulder. "Don't do anything stupid, man. I have a bad feeling about this."

"Hey, you know me." I grinned. "I'm always careful."

"Yeah right." He gave me a dubious look. "We'll be back soon."

After he and Bella left, I checked the time. "We've got an hour before dark. Maybe we can head that way and recon the area."

"Do lancer darts still work?" Elyssa asked.

Thomas nodded. "You can get outfitted in the armory." He gave us a steady gaze. "No nom casualties. I want you in and out without them ever knowing you were there."

Elyssa saluted her father with a fist over her chest. "Yes, Commander."

I wasn't sure if she was being serious or not, since she didn't usually salute her father. Thomas simply nodded and handed her a paper map with a red X on it. "Here are the coordinates."

Elyssa's forehead wrinkled with confusion. "This looks archaic."

"Desperate times and all that," I said. I told Thomas about the call from Nightliss.

His eyes actually brightened and his shoulders straightened. "I wish I had the means to get her here faster."

"We hope she can reach an Obsidian Arch," Elyssa said.

A small smile curved the tips of Thomas's mouth. "I'll tell the troops. They could use the morale boost."

I nodded. "Well, we'd better get going."

"Good luck," Thomas said.

Victus put a hand on my shoulder. "I'm certain you'll do us all proud."

This dude is downright creepy. I gave him an uneasy smile then turned and followed Elyssa out of the room.

After outfitting ourselves with lancers at the armory, Elyssa and I went back to the garage and took the car across town and about twenty miles outside the perimeter to Sweetwater Creek State Park.

"It's so inconvenient having to drive everywhere," Elyssa said as we cruised down the interstate.

"I remember the days when we could infiltrate any place with an omniarch portal." I was a little nervous about trying to sneak past the nom military without magical aid. The lancers would give us the option of incapacitating anyone who got in our way, but leaving a trail of unconscious people hardly fit Thomas's command to get in and out without detection.

"This is so different than what we've faced before." Elyssa stared at the road ahead. "I just can't figure out what the endgame is here. Why would Serena destroy magic? She's an Arcane and needs magic as much as anyone else."

"Yeah, but if she's looking for revenge, she might not be thinking rationally." I thought about Serena's huge Gloom fortress and the insane experiments she'd conducted there. "Then again, she might be crazy enough not to care."

"Well, whoever it is certainly has Eden by the balls." Elyssa steered onto an exit. "Maybe she has political demands."

"If that's the case, why hasn't she given us a list?" I thought of other people that might want revenge, but the list was too long to visualize. "There are a lot of people out there who would do something like this."

"Who would benefit the most?" Elyssa asked.

"Obviously anyone who doesn't need magic."

"That includes vampires, Daemos, lycans—a lot of factions." She shook her head. "A better question would be who could actually pull this off?"

"Science Academy?" I said.

She glanced at me. "Did you get a bad feeling from Victus like I did?"

"He seems like a greasy politician, but he and his wife are Arcanes."

"True, but it would give the scientists a huge advantage." She quirked an eyebrow. "Like he said, he prefers science to magic."

"Yeah, but scientists use aether power for a lot of their inventions." I knew that from Shelton. "Of course, they could always switch to another power source."

"We might need to go to the academy and take a look around," she said. "The scientists weren't eager to help us during the war."

"Chancellor Frankenberg flat out refused." Just thinking about my meeting with him and the council made my face hot. I'd later learned that Frankenberg and his cronies held academy students hostage so they couldn't help our alliance. Underborn had resolved that situation and come through in the end.

Elyssa frowned. "I suppose we'll fit them on the list just below Serena. I can't think of many people or organizations capable of such a massive undertaking."

A cold feeling settled into my stomach. "What if it's not any of the usual suspects? What if a nom government got wind of the Overworld and this is their first strike?"

Her eyes widened. "I hadn't considered that."

"The U.S. government certainly has the resources to pull off an event like this." I shuddered. "Fighting a war against such a large, well-equipped military would be a nightmare."

Elyssa slowed and turned onto the road leading to Sweetwater Creek State Park. Troop transport trucks blocked the entrance to the park and soldiers lined the perimeter.

I frowned. "Looks like they mean business."

"It's a good thing they're keeping people out." Elyssa navigated past crowds of curious onlookers and finally reached the end of the long line of cars parked along the side of the road. She pulled off into the grass. "We might have an easier time getting in thanks to all the civilians around here."

I looked down at my black Templar uniform and wished I'd put on some street clothes over it. "I think we're gonna look out of place no matter what."

She wrinkled her nose. "Yeah, I suppose you're right."

We examined the map and determined the meteor had landed about a mile down the creek from the start of the hiking trails. We got out of the car and merged with a group of female hikers who were trying to figure out how to get into the park.

Soldiers held positions every twenty yards or so to prevent people from slipping into the woods, making the task of getting by them more difficult than it needed to be.

"Move along," one of the soldiers said in a bored voice. "Keep moving."

I looked at the gender composition of the group we walked with and came up with a brilliant idea that was oh-so wrong on many levels. I whispered into Elyssa's ear, "Get ready."

Before she could respond, I opened my incubus senses and latched onto the auras of the women. I didn't bother keeping my feelings neutral and let the sexual urges fly free. Using the women as anchors, I extended my senses into the male soldiers and let them have a taste of pure carnal lust.

The women moaned. The men groaned. Soldiers began tearing off their helmets and uniforms, tossing their gear on the ground in their haste to lock lips with the lady hikers. The women were equally eager to engage in unspeakable acts.

"God, I love men in uniform!" One of the women said, just before passionately kissing the nearest soldier.

Three more soldiers were sucked into the sexual maelstrom, leaving Elyssa and me plenty of room to slip through the perimeter and into the trees. Just as the kissing and touching started to get serious, I released the captive auras and let everyone come back to their senses.

Elyssa shuddered. "I hope none of them had cooties."

I paused behind a tree to make sure everyone recovered from their lust.

"Oh my god, I don't know what happened," one of the soldiers said as he helped a woman to her feet. "I'm sorry."

The dazed women stood up, uncertain looks on their faces.

"I don't know what came over me," one of them said. "But that guy is a pretty good kisser."

I turned and noticed Elyssa already scoping out the woods. "I think we're clear to proceed."

She nodded. "The trees aren't very thick so we'll have to be careful moving through them."

"Any sign of guards?"

"Not yet." She stepped lightly across the leaves, making almost no sound.

I moved just as noiselessly, but it wasn't because I was a stealth ninja. The noise-dampening charms on the nightingale armor were still functional. I hoped the bulletproofing worked just as well. We hiked up a steep rise and paused at the crest. Squads of soldiers patrolled the hiking trails, but none of them left the path.

71

"There's a bridge crossing the river here." Elyssa pointed to the paper map. "Because of the patrols, I think we should ford the river further downstream and cut inland."

"Exactly what I was going to say," I lied. Elyssa was the planner, not me.

"I figured." She pecked a kiss on my lips. "I know how much you hate to think though."

"Ha, ha." I folded the map and handed it to her.

We continued onward.

Darkness fell about twenty minutes later and I extended the armor over my face to use the HUD—heads up display. Unfortunately, neither the night vision nor HUD worked. I removed the mask and relied on my blue-tinted incubus night vision to make my way through the forest. Elyssa's eyes glowed as she engaged her own dhampyr night vision.

Thanks to the rocky terrain, we had to move slowly and carefully. Wobbling flashlights indicated another patrol passing below. We waited them out and then scaled down the rocky cliff next to the trail. We paused, listened. Singing insects and the rush of water over rocks drowned out almost everything else. I heard voices to our left as the patrol moved away.

Elyssa flicked a hand forward and we dashed across the trail. Even with my night vision, the turbulent river water looked black and uninviting. I took a careful step into the water. The armor kept me dry and protected from the chill. I took another step and almost lost my balance when my foot found loose, jumbled stone. Elyssa stumbled as we waded forward.

"I didn't realize it was so rocky," she whispered.

I winced as my foot found a crevice in deep water. A couple of tugs pulled my foot loose, but it highlighted the dangers of trying to make it across the river quickly. We soon resorted to using our hands to aid our balance as we navigated the rocky riverbed. Even so, it took us a good thirty minutes to make it across. Once there, we had to climb another steep grade.

Judging from the bright lights, a blackened crater, and dozens of soldiers in the woods below, we were just up the hill from the impact site.

"Let me take a peek from here," I said, and switched to demon vision. The area all around us was almost pitch black thanks to the lack of aether. The meteor shone quite literally like a spotlight, casting a beam of energy back into the night sky until it vanished in the distance.

"What do you see?" Elyssa asked.

I described the sight. "It looks like it's shooting the aether into space."

These things were leeching Eden dry.

Chapter 9

"Into space?" Elyssa peered up into the sky. "That's not good."

"Understatement of the year." I stared at the beacon until the glare began to hurt my eyes, and switched back to normal vision. "I've reached the conclusion that whoever is doing this is a real jackass."

"Well, we have what we came for." Elyssa turned to head back.

I grabbed her arm. "I want to get closer. There's got to be something more we can learn." Frustration tied my stomach into a knot. "If we let this continue much longer, it may permanently crippled Eden."

"There must be at least twenty soldiers down there." She shook her head. "There's no way we can get close enough." Her eyes narrowed. "Besides, remember what I told you about touching that thing."

"What if I tossed a squirrel at it?"

"Then I'd slap you silly." Elyssa jabbed a finger back the way we'd come. "We're going."

I stabbed a finger toward the meteor. "I'm going down there for a closer look."

She grabbed my arm. "Justin, don't be a stubborn idiot."

"I'm not being stubborn." I gripped her hand. "We have a duty to Eden to take necessary risks to keep her safe. Maybe fighting through twenty soldiers isn't the ideal way to do this, but I don't see an alternative."

She was just about to speak when I heard a faint cough-cough-cough. The soldiers below toppled like puppets with cut strings. By the time they realized what was happening, it was over. I magnified my vision and saw bloody head wounds on most of the fallen.

My stomach twisted with nausea. "What in the hell is going on?"

"Get down," Elyssa hissed.

I flopped to my stomach just as a tall figure in bulky black armor marched stiffly into view. I quickly realized from the way it moved that it wasn't human—was it a robot? People in black uniforms swarmed from the woods behind the robot, checking downed soldiers for signs of life. Two of them lowered a square metal device into the crater then stood and gave a thumbs-up to the others.

One of them removed a ski mask and grinned. Others followed suit and began to speak, but I couldn't hear what they said over the background noise of the river and chirping crickets.

"They have a robot," I whispered.

Elyssa sucked in a breath. "I think they put a bomb inside the crater."

"They don't seem to be in a hurry to leave."

"Probably because they want to make sure it goes off." Her lips peeled back in a scowl. "Now we really do have to go down there."

"What about the robot?" Neither of us had weapons capable of destroying it, and it had just smoked an entire squad of soldiers in less than five minutes.

Elyssa looked frustrated. "Are you telling me you don't want to go down there now?"

"Oh, I want to go down there." My fists tightened. "They just murdered twenty people. I don't plan to let them get away with that."

"Agreed," Elyssa said. "Let's go."

We crawled down the slope until we met our first interloper at the fringe of light. Elyssa savagely twisted the man's head and lowered the corpse to the ground. We crept around the perimeter, taking out the mystery soldiers as we went.

At last it came down to the ten well-armed men standing around the impact zone and their robot.

A thin man with white scars on his cheeks said something in a foreign language to a bearded man. The other man answered and flicked his hand forward for the others to move out. A few seconds after they left the lit area, the other soldiers began shouting, presumably as they stumbled on the bodies of their former comrades.

The bearded man shouted an order and the survivors raced back into the lit area. He took out a phone and flicked his thumb across the screen. The robot extended its arms revealing wrist-mounted guns. Its torso rotated three-hundred and sixty degrees and its eyes glowed red, scanning the environs. I hoped our Nightingale armor would camouflage us.

Elyssa crept to my side. "I think we can take them out."

"Leave that bearded man and thin man alive," I told her. "I think they might be able to disarm the bomb."

"And the robot?"

"Use the enemies as meat shields until we can get the bearded man's phone."

She nodded then counted down from three with her fingers. When she hit zero, we blurred toward the soldiers. I slammed into two of them and knocked them out before the others could train their weapons on me, then held one in front of me as the robot spun my way. It held its fire, presumably because it recognized my human shield as a friendly.

Meanwhile, Elyssa attacked from behind. She whipped out her sai swords and slew three men before they could pull the triggers on their guns.

I threw the man I held right on top of the outstretched arms of the robot. The thin man took a shot. I juked right, twisted the gun from his grasp, and swept the bearded man's feet from beneath him.

The robot's torso swung around following me, but still didn't fire. "Error, error," it said over and over again.

The bearded man took out his phone. I kicked it from his grasp. Before I could retrieve it, the thin man surprised me with a quick martial arts demonstration. Thankfully, Elyssa had taught me well. I threw up an arm to ward off one attack, and leapt over a low kick. Then it was my turn. I went for a good old-fashioned karate chop. His forearm blocked me but couldn't withstand the brute force of my supernatural strength, and broke with a loud crack. He grunted as if he'd done nothing more than stub his toe, and I knew this dude was no pushover.

Even so, I pushed him over hard and he slammed to earth.

Elyssa appeared behind the bearded man, his phone in one hand. She flicked the screen and the robot slumped, dumping its cargo on the ground. Just as the bearded man climbed to his feet, she blurred to his side and pressed her sword to his throat. "Who do you work for?"

Her captive flicked a knife from beneath his sleeve. Elyssa gripped his wrist and twisted it hard, sending the knife to the ground.

The thin man leapt up and tried to roundhouse me. He was quick for a nom, but no match for supernatural reflexes. I grabbed his ankle and held up his leg, making him hop awkwardly on one foot.

"I can do this all night," I told him. "Who's your boss?"

When neither of them answered, I decided to get the bomb. I dragged Scars toward the crater. He clawed at the ground, shouting and squirming like an angry cat caught in a mouse trap. The man apparently knew when it was time to admit defeat and head for the hills, but he wasn't getting away from me.

I looked in the deep, bowl-shaped crater and saw a large screen with a timer counting down from eleven seconds.

My heart stopped beating for an instant and my stomach tried to buy a one-way ticket to Timbuktu.

Even running at top speed, we couldn't get out of here in time.

"No!" I shouted, turned, and grabbed Elyssa's hand. "We only have ten seconds! Run!"

She didn't even pause to question me. We blurred through the woods, but dodging trees and other obstacles made top speed impossible. The explosion in Thailand had traveled nearly half a mile. I made the mistake of glancing back to see if an explosion was following us and ran into a sapling. It smacked me in the face and sucker-punched me in the groin.

My armor absorbed most of the shock, but it was enough to send me reeling.

The countdown in my head hit zero.

Elyssa jerked me off the ground. I stared back at the impact zone for a moment.

"No boom?" I said.

Elyssa frowned. "No boom." She looked at me. "Are you sure that's a bomb?"

"Well, it looks like a bomb." I offered her a sheepish grin. "I guess we need to round up our prisoners again." I listened and heard rustling leaves to our right. With our night vision and super speed, we nabbed our quarry in a couple of minutes and dragged them back to the crater.

The device still sat inside, but now I realized the screen on the outside of it was running some sort of calculations and displayed a drawing of the meteor and the impact crater.

Elyssa bound Beard and Scars. "Who do you work for?"

"I don't see any markings on this computer," I told her. "It seems to be mapping the crystoid."

"Do you hear that?" Elyssa said.

I listened and heard a faint vibration. I located Beard's phone on the ground. He had one missed call. Thankfully, he hadn't secured his phone with a pin number, so I went into his texts. Most of them were in foreign language, but some were in English.

The latest read: *Air support standing by for retrieval.*

Another thread from the day the meteors hit cast more light on the identity of these people. *You're hired. Fifty thousand transferred to your account. The robot is on the way.*

"Mercenaries." I showed the texts to Elyssa. "They planned to steal this thing."

"I wonder if their air support is a helicopter." She pointed at the screen of the computer in the crater as it illustrated the crystalline tendrils anchoring the meteor to the ground. "Look at all those roots. There's no way they could lift it out with a chopper."

"Holy crap." According to the depth graph on the screen, the roots had drilled nearly a hundred feet down. We watched for a few more minutes, but the image didn't change. "It must be done."

"We're taking this computer with us." Elyssa hopped into the wide bowl of the crater and grabbed the box from its position near the meteor. "We could probably use it to figure out how to move one of these things."

"We will find you," Scars said in broken English. "Kill you."

I jerked him to his feet. "Who wants this meteor?"

"Don't know," Beard said. "Hired independent."

"How did you plan to get it out of here?" Elyssa asked.

"Chopper," he replied.

"Yes, but it's anchored to the ground. A chopper couldn't lift it."

He bared his teeth. "Robot help."

"Where did you get the robot?" It looked advanced, but could have been built by noms.

Scars scowled and spat at me. "I kill you."

Elyssa forbid me from using a squirrel, but she hadn't said anything about homicidal maniacs. "We're going to conduct a little experiment." I untied Scars then tossed him into the crater. He tumbled across the rough crater floor and thumped against the meteor. He rolled to his knees and grabbed one of the crystal shards to pull himself up.

He glared daggers and me, but appeared otherwise unharmed by contact with the meteor. I was just about to announce the findings to my impromptu investigation when the man's back arched and a ragged moan tore from his throat. His eyes glowed and crackled with energy. His body swelled like a balloon.

Scars released the meteor and turned toward us. He lowered his head and bellowed like a bull, spewing gouts of energy from his mouth and nose. Scars charged. He leapt from the crater and landed next to Beard. The other man shouted desperately in his mother tongue. Scars jerked him off the ground and held him up. He opened his mouth and made an awful sucking sound.

Beard screamed. His eyeballs popped from his head, and his tongue swelled and turned purple. Brilliant arcs of energy poured from Scars and into him. Beard thrashed like a wildcat and went abruptly still. Scars dropped him on the ground and for a moment, I thought the other man was dead. Then Beard rose to his feet, eyes burning with the sickly yellow light of malaether.

"Houston, we have a problem." I raised an arm and fired half a dozen lancer darts at Scars and Beard. They didn't even flinch.

Elyssa scooped one of the rifles from the ground and opened fire. Beard's jaw unhinged and his mouth dropped open. A beam of yellow energy crackled toward me. I leapt from the path just in time. The tree behind me wasn't so lucky. The trunk splintered and the tree toppled. Elyssa fired until the clip ran empty. Beard and Scars jerked and shook from the impact, but didn't go down.

Scars fired a torrent of malaether at Elyssa. She ducked, rolled, and grabbed another rifle from the ground. I reached for a rifle, but Beard flashed toward me. Before I could react, he grabbed my throat and held me off the ground. A nauseating feeling ran through me and my eyes started to burn. I was about to become a malaether zombie.

"Remind me to never ever experiment on anything ever again!" I shouted.

Energy coalesced inside Beard's mouth. My feet couldn't touch the ground so I used his chest to gain leverage. I ran up his body, twisted hard to the side. For a moment, I thought my neck was going to break. Beard's fingers gave out first with a series of loud cracks. I dropped to the ground. Rising from one knee, I delivered a jaw-shattering dragon uppercut.

Beard flew about ten feet into the air and landed with a loud thud. Before he could recover, I dashed up behind him and put him in a headlock. I noticed blood pouring from numerous bullet wounds in his chest, and a bloody hole in his skull. The man was no longer alive and yet his body still fought on.

He might possess incredible strength, but his body wasn't made to contain it. I'd seen a lot of awful things during the war. I'd caused my fair share of carnage. Even so, I felt sick to my stomach fighting this new abomination. I jerked ferociously on his head and pulled it off. Beard's body went into violent spasms. I hurled the still-glowing head at a tree. The skull shattered and a cloud of malaether exploded. Elyssa, meanwhile, held Scars face down on the ground while she hogtied him with diamond fiber. Despite his newfound strength, he couldn't break free.

She unsheathed a machete from one of the nearby bodies and hacked off his head. I grabbed Scars's head by its hair and sent it to the same fate as Beard's. The bodies flailed about, struggling slower and slower until they twitched their last.

I stared with horror at the corpses. "Thank god we didn't have to fight an army of malaether squirrels."

"I don't understand." Elyssa looked toward the crater. "How could aether control a body like that?"

"I think it was malaether, judging from the color." Malformed aether usually had a nasty color to it. "As for how it turned them into zombies, I have no idea."

"It's almost like the meteor has protective spells or something."

I nodded. "I wouldn't doubt it. It certainly has all the aether it needs to power spells."

"We can't be the first people to discover this." Elyssa waved a hand toward the rest of the world. "What if someone starts an epidemic?"

The meteors hadn't been here for long, but curiosity would no doubt kill a lot of cats in the coming days. Someone somewhere had probably touched a crystoid or tried to destroy it. Either way, the casualties would be staggering if it happened in the right place.

Elyssa dropped to the ground and buried her face in her hands. She blew out a long breath and looked up at me. "How are we going to beat this, Justin?"

I sat down across from her and shook my head. "We can't destroy them, we can't touch them, we can't move them." I didn't even know what to do next. How long could Eden hold out with her aether being drained?

Ley worms—earth dragons—were in charge of distributing the aether through the realm, though I didn't know precisely how they did it. I wondered if they could survive without aether.

"We need to check on the dragons and see if they can help us figure this out," I said.

Hope sparked in Elyssa's eyes. "You think Altash and Lulu can help?"

I held out a hand and pulled her up. "I can't imagine these crystoids are pleasant for them. They also might know what they are."

"How are we supposed to get there?" Elyssa tapped a finger to her chin. "I guess we could take an arch to Bogota and take a plane from there, but I don't have a clue where we'd land."

El Dorado was one of the first cities conquered and rebuilt by the Seraphim when they'd originally crossed into to Eden thousands of years ago. The ancient city sat over a way station, but the Obsidian Arch had been destroyed long ago. "We might be able to use an omniarch. The way station sits over massive ley lines, so maybe there's enough charge to open a portal."

Shouts echoed from faraway to the north.

"I hope you're right." She picked up the cube computer. "We need to go. The soldiers probably heard all the gunfire."

I looked at the inert robot. "What about that thing?"

She opened an app on Beard's phone and pressed an icon labeled *Dismantle*. The robot stiffened. After a series of hums and clicks, it fell into a jumbled mess.

"Hmm," Elyssa said. "I suppose that'll do."

I took one last look inside the crater and opened my inner demon eye. The bright beam of energy blinded me for an instant. "I need to check one more thing."

Elyssa grabbed my arm. "Justin, don't do anything stupid."

"I'm not." I held down my middle fingers with my thumb, forming horns with my index and pinky finger. "Demon's honor, babe."

Her lips flattened. "Hurry!"

I walked to the edge of the crater and held a hand over the beam of aether. My Seraphim side instantly responded. I drew in the magical energy and channeled a thin beam of Brilliance into the sky.

Elyssa's mouth dropped open. "How did you do that?"

"The aether from the crystal is still usable." I looked up into the night sky. "Unfortunately, I'd have to stand in front of the beam to make use of it."

The shouts of soldiers drew closer. I relished the touch of magic washing over my hand for a second longer and tried not to cry when I pulled it away.

I sighed. "Let's go."

Chapter 10

Our little gun battle had caught the attention of someone in charge. Before we were a hundred yards to the west, I spotted a line of soldiers slowly and deliberately marching our way. We weren't getting to the river that way.

We turned south and found more flashlights bobbing in the dark.

Someone shouted, "They killed everyone!"

"It's a noose," Elyssa said. "And I they're going to blame us for killing those soldiers if they catch us."

"Let's climb a tree. Maybe they'll go under us." The idea was hardly out of my mouth when I noticed someone shining a portable spotlight into the branches of every tree. A startled squirrel chattered angrily at the intrusion. "Okay, bad idea."

Elyssa looked around and spotted a boulder just wide and tall enough to conceal us." Our only chance is to break through the line with speed and force." She pulled me behind the boulder with her. "When I give the go, you follow me." She gave me a stern look. "And don't trip."

My nerves twisted at the thought of plowing through a line of heavily armed soldiers. Even if they didn't have supernatural reflexes, they'd probably launch a hail of gunfire after us, and neither of us were faster than bullets, especially not in the woods.

Crunching leaves and heavy footsteps grew closer.

"Corner check," someone shouted.

Someone issued a command. "Weapons ready, spotlight on mark."

Elyssa made a face. "Damn, they're thorough." She extended the armor over her face.

I followed her lead. A bullet in the head wouldn't be very pleasant.

83

Her muscles tensed. She held up a fist, ear cocked at the approaching sounds, then motioned forward.

We burst from cover and plowed into two soldiers cautiously approaching the boulder.

"What the hell?" a man shouted.

Shots rang out. "Hold fire! Hold fire!"

We flashed through the line of soldiers.

"About face!" came another command.

We were about twenty yards away when the dreaded next command came.

"Weapons free!"

Tracers zinged through the night air like lasers. Bark exploded from trees and dirt flew up all around us. Something nailed me hard in the back and I lost my footing. Elyssa grunted, spun, and landed hard. She shook her head as if to clear it and rolled behind a thick tree.

The shooting stopped for a moment. I heard the clicks of fresh magazines being inserted into guns and a fresh salvo commenced, once again lighting the air like New Year's Eve.

A spotlight found me as I peeked around the tree and the bullets converged on my position.

"Cease fire!" The last whine of a speeding bullet faded. "You are surrounded. You have no avenue of escape. Give yourself up."

I knew this was our chance to escape, but one look at Elyssa told me something was wrong. Without the armor's HUD active I couldn't see through her mask, but her head lolled. I wondered if a bullet had hit her in the head. That had happened to me once and even though the armor blocked most of the pain, it still knocked me silly.

"Elyssa, are you okay?" I hissed.

She held up her hand and then gripped her head.

Boots crunched on leaves as the soldiers approached. I had to buy some time. "Wait, stop! I'll give up."

"Halt," the commander said. "Show yourself."

I stepped from behind the tree, hands in the air. "Don't shoot."

"Remove your mask and identify yourself," said a young man, the apparent leader of this squad. The patch on his breast read, *Glover.*

I didn't lower the mask, just in case someone had an itchy trigger finger. "My name is Justin."

"Arrest him." Glover motioned the others.

I picked up the computer and held it over my head. "This is a bomb and I will detonate it if you come another step closer."

The squad leader's eyes flared. "Step back!"

The soldiers were way ahead of his command, already backing away.

"Justin, explain why you have a bomb." Despite the concern on his face, he didn't seem overly frightened—a fact that made me respect him.

"I'm part of a team tasked with discovering how to disable these crystal meteors—"

"I haven't heard of a team tasked for that," he said.

"They're extremely dangerous." I looked to my sides, hoping I wasn't being flanked while I talked and also to check Elyssa. "I need to warn you about them."

"We're under orders not to touch them," Glover said.

"That's good, because if you do, you'll die." Murmurs went up from the other soldiers nearby, so I pressed my slight advantage. "These things soak up massive amounts of energy. Destroying them will cause an explosion similar to a nuclear bomb. Touching them will irradiate the person."

"Jesus," someone said. "I was standing next to that thing all day."

"I don't think standing near a crystal will irradiate you," I said. "Only touching it will."

"Did you intend to blow it up?" Glover asked.

I shook my head. "I sneaked in here to investigate it, but a group of mercenaries beat us to it. They planned to steal the meteor with a helicopter."

His face darkened. "Are they the ones who killed my people?"

I really didn't want to tell him. "Yes. If it makes you feel any better, I killed most of the mercenaries."

His lips peeled back from his teeth and curses rose from the other soldiers. I had a feeling they wanted to kill me right then and there, bomb or not. I felt a hand on my ankle. Pretending I was looking around for other soldiers, I glanced at Elyssa. She gave me a thumbs up.

Glover stiffened. "We'll need to take you into custody and sort this out."

"I can't let you do that," I said. "I've got to save the world."

"You're delusional," Glover said. He narrowed his eyes. "And I think you're bluffing about that being a bomb."

I still held enough aether in me to channel one spell. "Close your eyes," I whispered to Elyssa. Without waiting for confirmation from her, I held my right hand palm out toward the soldiers and willed every bit of Brilliance to flow into that hand. It coalesced into a bright white star in my hand.

Shouts of disbelief rose from the soldiers. Before they could fire on me in panic I squeezed shut my eyes and dispersed the energy in one massive flash. It was so bright my eyelids barely helped. People hollered and weapons fell to the forest floor. I opened my eyes and saw the soldiers staggering around blindly.

I grabbed Elyssa's hand and we ran.

"I guess we failed the stealth test." I lowered my mask as we finally reached a wide tract of land cleared for power pylons.

Since losing the soldiers, we hadn't seen any signs of pursuit, though I heard the whumping of a chopper somewhere in the distance.

"No, we passed that test. It was the damned mercenaries that lost it for us." She lowered her mask and rubbed the back of her head. "Can you believe they nailed me in the head twice?"

"No wonder you were out of it." I felt two large bumps on her scalp and winced. "I can't believe you recovered so quickly."

"It wasn't quick at all." She groaned. "God, I have a headache." She kissed my cheek. "Good job stalling them. I'm just glad they didn't open fire on you when you threatened them with the bomb."

"Yeah, about that—" I held up the computer box. It was riddled with bullet holes.

"Well, bring it anyway. Maybe we can recover the data."

Two helicopters zoomed over the trees and shined spotlights toward the area we'd probably be if we weren't supernaturally fast. Thanks to our speed, we'd covered a lot of ground, even with the treacherous terrain.

We headed due east then headed north to circle the state park. Several hours later, we finally reached the car. Though most of the crowd from earlier had dispersed, a few people with tinfoil hats held signs about alien intruders and marched around, demanding access to the meteor.

By the time we arrived at the Ranch, I was ready for beddy-bye night-night time since it was already midnight, but I wanted to check in with Shelton first. We took the computer to the war room. Thomas wasn't there, but Shelton and Bella huddled in front of what looked like a computer monitor.

"Honey, I'm home," I said when we walked inside.

They turned around, worried eyes filling with relief.

Shelton blew out a breath of relief. "We figured you guys were in jail or something."

"Elyssa, dear, you look awful." Bella put a hand on Elyssa's cheek. "What happened?"

Before we could answer, a third figure rose from the chair in front of the computer and turned around.

"Justin, it is good to see you again." Cinder spoke in his typical monotone voice, but the smile on his face looked genuine.

"Cinder!" I gave the golem a hug and backed away. "Your smile looks great."

"Thank you." He adjusted the smile to something a bit smug. "Though I have yet to master it, I no longer frighten children." He laughed stiffly, making it obvious he still had things to practice.

I also noticed the peach tone of his skin instead of the sickly gray that gave the gray men their name. "Did Fjoeruss teach you how to color your skin?"

He nodded. "He has also been teaching me how to create golems."

"Creepy," Shelton said. "We're gonna be overrun by the soulless things before we know it."

"That is not my intent," Cinder said. "However, it would be nice to have someone of my kind who can appreciate life with me."

Elyssa's eyes widened. "Cinder, are you going to make yourself a girlfriend?"

He tilted his head slightly. "I had not considered that, but it sounds like a good idea. It is obvious from my observations that having a kindred spirit to converse with is healthy, as is daily copulation, though I'm not certain if that is possible with my kind."

Shelton snorted. "It's so romantic when you put it like that."

The rest of us burst into laughter.

I slapped Cinder on the shoulder. "I've missed you, man."

He tried to laugh again and only succeeded in drawing grimaces from the rest of us.

"Found anything with the OTA footage?" I asked.

"Meh." Shelton went back to the computer and fiddled with the mouse. "I hate these things. It's so much easier just telling an arctablet what to do."

"Show him the hole," Bella said.

"Hole?" I wrinkled my forehead.

Shelton clicked on a video and enlarged it to fit the screen. "It ain't in three dimensions, so we had to cut out the angles we wanted. Thankfully, Cinder knows his way around these things."

For a moment, only blue sky appeared on the screen. Suddenly, a rift split open several hundred feet above the camera's perspective and a crystoid fell through. Though it was difficult to tell how large the meteor was from this distance, it swelled from the size of a watermelon to the size of a small boulder within seconds, growing larger as it plummeted past the recording ASE and toward earth. The ASE locked on and followed the meteor through a hole it punched in a cumulus cloud as it went traveled down.

The video flickered with static and the crystoid pulled away from the ASE. Still hundreds of feet from the ground, the video went black.

"Most of the recordings are like that," Shelton said. "We think the crystoid sucked the aether from the air as it traveled."

"That's probably why it grew so fast," Bella added.

Shelton nodded. "Yeah, and because the ASE was in its wake, it ran out of its aether charge."

"Makes sense." I pointed at the computer. "Do we have other angles?"

"Yeah." Shelton searched and clicked on another one. The rift was barely visible from the angle of the camera, but it was apparent from the way the crystoid seemed to appear in midair that it hadn't originated in space.

I stated the obvious theory. "Someone must have used omniarches to launch these things."

"Looks like it." Shelton closed the video and turned around. "Here's the way I figure it happened. Someone took a flying carpet, snapped some pictures, then used an omniarch or several of them and just dropped the crystoids through, let gravity do the rest."

"Devious and efficient." Elyssa quirked her mouth in a way that told me she was impressed.

"Man, I wish you guys could've grabbed a chunk of the one you went to look at." Shelton walked over to the conference table and grabbed a cookie from a plate. He took a bite and crumbs scattered down his duster. "I need to analyze—oh wait. I don't have magic so I guess I can't." He cocked his arm as if to throw the cookie on the plate, seemed to reconsider it, and gulped down the rest.

"Yeah, well breaking off a piece is risky at best." I told them about our little adventure.

"Malaether zombies and robots?" Shelton shook his head in disbelief. "Man, we can't catch a break, can we?"

"Do you think the noms could have made a robot?" I asked.

Shelton shrugged. "Sure. They've got the tech to make remote controlled ones like the one you saw."

"Science Academy makes robots too," Elyssa said.

"Yeah, but the one Justin described doesn't sound like one of theirs," Shelton said. "We don't give the noms enough credit for their abilities."

Bella didn't seem to care about robots. "If we stand in the way of a crystoid's aether beam, we can use magic?"

"Yep," Elyssa said. "Which means if we're going to examine one, we need to go to the one under Templar control."

"That could be a problem," Shelton said. "It's in western North Dakota."

89

"Why in the world would anyone drop something way up there?" I asked. "It's the middle of nowhere."

"We examined the map of impacts, and there are at least a dozen, maybe more that landed in areas nowhere near major ley lines. The vast majority seemed to hit pretty close to where they could soak up the most aether." Shelton sat back down at the computer and pulled up a map with red marks on it. "When the mastermind behind this took the pictures from the sky, they didn't take into account how a single cloud might alter the destination."

I snapped my fingers. "Yeah, you're right. If they didn't take the pictures on a perfectly clear day, then a different cloud formation might confuse the omniarch."

Omniarches could open a portal anywhere so long as the user perfectly envisioned the destination. That was why we took pictures of destinations and sent them to omniarch operators so they could open the portal in the exact spot. If someone took a flying carpet up above the clouds, it made sense that a different cloud formation might confuse whatever enchantments allowed the omniarch to do its magic.

"In other words, some of these impact zones were accidental." I looked at the spot in Atlanta. "If they were after maximal aether drainage, why didn't they drop the crystoid into Thunder Rock, or the Grotto?"

Cinder provided an answer. "Whoever did it could not also take into account all the meteorological conditions on a specific day. There was a high altitude crosscurrent of wind on the day the crystoid was dropped here. If it had dropped straight, it most likely would have landed near Thunder Rock. Instead, it drifted to the west."

"Here's another question," Elyssa said. "Why drop them from high altitudes at all? Why not plant these things on the ground and let them grow?"

"Probably because by slamming into the earth, it allowed them to root themselves more firmly in the ground." Cinder, said. He stepped next to the computer. "Pardon me, Harry." He took the mouse and opened several images of the crystoid the Templars controlled. Unlike the crater in Sweetwater, this one rested in a shallow trench. "Notice how much of the crystoid is buried in the crust. This prevented anyone from removing it before it could root itself deeper."

"I'm sure the chaos and damage from these things slamming to earth was just a bonus." I bit my lower lip and fantasized about dropping the mastermind behind this from the stratosphere.

"I guess the next order of business is getting to North Dakota and checking out the crystoid," Shelton said. "But how in the hell are we gonna get there?"

A marvelous plan occurred to me. "The omniarch portals can't materialize without aether at the other end." I grinned. "But it just so happens their aether beam provides plenty of juice."

Shelton slapped me on the back. "That's the way to use the old noodle. We get the Templars there to take a picture from over the crystoid and bam"—he slapped the back of one hand into the other—"we got a portal."

"Exactly." I was feeling pretty good about my noodle right then.

We were getting closer to answers but time wasn't on our side.

Chapter 11

First thing the next morning we took off for the Grotto and its control room full of omniarches.

Elyssa called her father who contacted the Templars on the ground in North Dakota. They sent back a picture of the crystoid from overhead and we were ready to test my theory.

We went into the control room, told the operator what we were up to. He shrugged and went back to playing games on a nom tablet. We walked down the corridor between rows of arches to the niche where the omniarches resided. Several of them were marked with green paint to indicate they had been tested and functioned.

I took a deep breath, stepped into the silver band of metal encircling an arch, and willed it to close. After a few moments, I felt the static sensation of aether build to a point I hoped could sustain a portal.

Looking at the image on my phone, I willed a portal to open. The omniarch flickered. Bands of electrical energy flickered weakly on the columns. The portal struggled to open. The air split vertically just a crack. I felt a rush of aether from the crystoid and the gateway ripped open.

"Yes!" I pumped a fist.

A platform with a railing was on the other side of the portal. I stepped through and looked down at the crystoid. The tingle of aether against my skin felt so good I stood in place and sucked in a breath of air.

Hills rose to either side of the crater, and the smell of something sweet tickled my nose.

Shelton bumped into me from behind. "You gonna move or sit here looking like a pervert in a porn store?"

I chuckled and moved aside to make room for the others. While the others came through, I ducked beneath the portal and walked down the platform's stairs to the ground.

A woman with brown hair and fair skin gave me a friendly smile. "Why, hello there! That sure is a nifty hole you have there."

I grinned and extended a hand, noting that she wore civilian clothes. "I'm Justin, and you are?"

"Viola." She greeted the others as they descended the platform. "Welcome to North Dakota."

Another woman with just as friendly a smile waved to us. "Hello you guys. I have some cookies fresh out of the oven if you want some."

"That's my mom, Ann," Viola said. "She's really excited about all the activity."

"Yeah, I tell you," Ann said, "I heard the boom when that thing landed, and it sure panicked the horses something awful." She grimaced. "I came out to take a look and found that meteor there."

"Are you with the Templars?" I asked.

She laughed. "Nope, just a farmer. I was reading a real interesting story in the *Pioneer* newspaper about Thelma Hutchins and how she likes to pluck chickens when all of a sudden my house shook like we were having an earthquake."

"Um, where—" I noticed several soldier types walking our way along with two robed Arcanes and walked over to meet them. "Hey, I guess you arranged the portal?"

The woman in the lead nodded. "Ann asked us to go get these for when you arrived." She sighed and held out a pan of cookies.

Shelton grabbed one immediately and gobbled it down. "Man, these are good. Compliments to the chef."

"Say, I have some lemonade too, if you guys are thirsty." Ann pointed to another Templar carrying a cooler and some paper cups.

"So, these guys haven't told us much about this meteor," Viola said. "They said to keep it hush, hush. What is it?"

I wasn't sure how much they knew, but since they'd seen a portal open in the air and hadn't freaked out, I figured it wouldn't hurt to explain. "We're part of a magical society called the Overworld. These meteors—we call them crystoids—are sucking up all the magical energy and shooting it into outer space."

"Ooh, I like that name," Viola said. "Crystoid has a nice ring to it."

Shelton flashed a toothy smile at me.

"Sucking up the magic?" Ann tutted. "Well, it sure makes sense why you guys are so concerned." She motioned to the plate. "Take a cookie, Justin."

I did and had to admit it was very tasty. "Does anyone besides you and Viola know about the crystoid?"

"I don't think so," Ann said. "The phone lines went out when the crystoid landed, and my cell phone wasn't charged." She chuckled. "Luckily for you guys, because I probably would have told half the town by now."

"Well, we should get to work," Shelton said with a mouthful of cookie. He grabbed a cup and gulped lemonade.

"Goodness, Harry." Bella looked at the nearly empty plate of cookies. "You need to slow down your cookie consumption."

I snorted. "We could be in the middle of a life-threatening situation and Shelton would still take a time out for cookies."

"Damned right," Shelton said. "A true life-threatening situation is being in a life-threatening situation without cookies."

"Couldn't have said it better myself," Viola said.

"Well, I'll let you guys get to work." Ann turned toward a pickup truck. "I've got to go do farm chores."

"We'll let you know what we discover," I said. "And thanks for the cookies."

"Oh, sure, you betcha," Ann said and waved goodbye then she and Viola got in the pickup and drove away.

Elyssa, Bella, Shelton, and I walked back toward the crater. The two Arcanes who'd accompanied the Templars walked with us.

"I'm Pixie and this is Boris," the woman said. She was short, petite, with a pert nose and a short pixie haircut to match her name.

Boris stood a head shorter than me. Thick unruly hair hung low on his face, framing big brown eyes like those of a puppy dog. He waved. "Howdy."

I introduced the group.

94

"I can't tell you how awesome it is to meet you guys," Boris said. "Watching the Skywraiths zip around on flying brooms and blast Daelissa's goliaths was awesome."

"Yeah, there's no way we could've won that war without the Skywraiths," Pixie said. "We're avid broom racers ourselves."

"Oh, I used to race brooms too," Bella said.

"Cool." I glanced ahead at the crystoid. "The Skywraiths worked out a lot better than I hoped. Those boomsticks aren't easy to ride at first."

"Yeah, racer brooms have a steep learning curve," Boris said. "Our buddy Rai won't stop bragging about how he trained you guys."

Pixie groaned. "I know. You'd think he saved the world himself."

"How is Rai doing these days?" I asked.

Boris gave Pixie a knowing look. "He's designing a new boomstick he calls the Skywraith Edition."

"Hah, you should've trademarked that name," Shelton said. "First decent name you come up with and it's gonna make someone else money."

"I don't know," Elyssa said. "I'm sure there's a market for the meteocryst or crasteroid names."

I huffed. "You people don't recognize genius when you hear it."

Pixie made a face. "What's a meteocryst?"

"Is a crasteroid like a hemorrhoid?" Boris asked.

Shelton snickered.

I threw up my hands and turned to Shelton. "Don't you have work to be doing?"

"Yep." He backed away. "Gonna go treat a nasty case of the crasteroids."

"It's a shame we don't have an ointment for that," Bella said.

Pixie giggled. "Just wait 'til we tell Tasha that Justin Slade was here."

"She's gonna be so jelly." Boris looked at the crystoid. "We'll be around if you need us."

"Thanks guys." I waved goodbye and our group headed for the meteor.

The offending crasteroid sat in a shallow trench of broken red clay. I kicked at the ground. "The terrain is pretty hard. I guess that's why the crystoid didn't make a deep crater."

Elyssa knelt and held a sample that looked like broken pottery. "Yeah, it's like crushed rock."

"Welp, I'm gonna go up the platform and use some magic to analyze this thing," Shelton announced. He rubbed his hands together. "This is gonna be great." He and Bella headed toward the platform.

There wasn't much I could do since Shelton was the one with the expertise in this department. I looked around at the hills. "Want to take a walk?" I asked Elyssa.

She looked at Shelton and Bella as they wove a diagnostic spell over the crystoid then turned to me. "I could use a little break."

We climbed up a hill, treading over patchy grass until we crested the rise. A few scraggly trees dotted the landscape, and in the distance, a herd of antelope grazed peacefully in the valley on the other side.

"Smells nice out here," Elyssa said. "So fresh."

"And quiet." The sounds of traffic and people were oddly absent here. Only the occasional breeze broke the silence.

"It's really nice." Elyssa picked a flower and sniffed it. "I wouldn't mind visiting when we're not fighting to save the world."

I sat on a rock and jumped up when something stung my backside. "Ouch!" I looked down and noticed cacti poking between the cracks.

Elyssa giggled. "Better watch where you sit."

"No kidding." I decided North Dakota didn't want me sitting on its hill, so I took Elyssa's hand and we walked back down through the valley to a large pasture where cows chewed their cuds and stared at us curiously.

"I've always enjoyed farms." Elyssa leaned against the fence and mooed.

Every cow that wasn't already watching us looked up from the grass and ambled toward us. One of them mooed back, and a chorus of bellows joined in.

"You really know how to work the crowd." I kissed her cheek. "You're the cow whisperer."

She elbowed me playfully in the ribs. "Guess I'm just special."

My phone rang—surprising given we were so far out in the country—but the nom cell signal showed four bars. "This is the cow whisperer's boyfriend," I said.

"Apologies," Cinder replied. "I must have the wrong number."

I barked a laugh. "Dude, it's me, Justin." I put him on speakerphone so Elyssa could hear the conversation without use of her super hearing.

"I wasn't sure, because a moment ago I phoned Shelton and somehow contacted a Joe's Pizza Parlor where the sausage is always big and hot."

That sounded like something Shelton might say just to mess with Cinder, but I decided not to tell him. "What's up?"

"Agent George Walker and his team returned with some of the powerless ASEs." Cinder made a noise as if taking a breath, despite the fact he didn't need to. "I took them inside the Grotto so they would have enough aether to operate and then watched the recordings."

I tried not to get excited. "What did you find?"

"Justin, it would appear some of the portals used to launch the crystoids are still open."

Elyssa narrowed her eyes. "But if the ASEs failed a few minutes after the crystoids landed, how could you know that?"

"Apparently, one of the ASEs fell atop a crystoid. Once the meteor began projecting aether, it powered the ASE once more." Cinder cleared his throat. "The ASE rose back into its original position and took footage until yesterday before a gust of wind blew it out of the aether beam."

I jumped on the conclusion. "In other words, it recorded the portal still being open."

"Precisely."

"Which crystoid?" I asked.

"This particular one landed in California."

I looked up and squinted, but the bright blue sky hurt my eyes. "What did it look like on the other side of the portal?"

"It was cloudy." He grunted a bit louder than necessary. "I had only a glimpse of a land mass."

Elyssa tilted her head slightly. "In other words, the portal is in the sky directly above the crystoid?"

"In most cases, yes," Cinder replied.

I thought of another question. "If wind currents pushed some crystoids around during their fall, then how could the original portal still be right above them?"

"The crystoids may have opened new portals with their aether beams," Cinder said. "If you have an ASE available, perhaps you could see if there is another portal above your location."

"That's a good idea." I ended the call and turned to Elyssa. "Do you know if we have any ASEs here?"

"I don't. We'll have to ask the other Templars." A curious cow nudged Elyssa's arm and sniffed her. She leapt back and realized it wasn't an enemy ninja on the attack. Elyssa petted the cow and smiled. "Don't you worry, my pretties. I'll be back soon."

The cow lowed in response.

I chuckled. "Your new best friend."

We were about to head back when Viola and Ann rode around the base of a nearby hill in the pickup. They gave us a friendly wave and stopped along the rutted dirt trail.

Ann peered at us through her thick glasses. "Oh, hey there, you guys. Do ya need anything?"

"We were just headed back to the crystoid," I said. "We've got to see if there's a portal in the sky above it."

"A portal?" Viola leaned out of the window and looked up. "Where do you suppose it goes?"

"That's anyone's guess right now," I replied.

"I've got a telescope you could use," Ann said. "It's back at the house."

"That would be great." I pointed back down the dirt road. "Is the house that way?"

She grinned. "Just hop in the back and we'll fetch it."

Elyssa and I climbed aboard. Viola turned around the pickup and headed back. The bumpy trail made the ride a bit uncomfortable, but I enjoyed feeling like a country boy.

I raised an eyebrow and looked at Elyssa. "Yeehaw?"

She pumped a fist. "Yeehaw."

It took a good fifteen minutes to reach the house even though it couldn't have been more than a mile away. The homestead sat in a nice flat area in the shadow of a hill. Unlike the rest of the land, several groves of hardy trees grew around the house and outbuildings, probably to serve as a windbreak during the winter. A big red barn and a rusty windmill rose about a hundred yards to the west. Chickens clucked and strutted about, and turkeys raced away with frightened gobbles as the pickup pulled into the gravel driveway.

"Come on in, you guys." Ann headed for the house and we followed her inside.

A wonderful odor greeted my nostrils.

Ann must have noticed the grin on my face. "I'm making a nice big roast for dinner. You guys are sure welcome to stay and eat."

Elyssa chuckled. "We haven't even had lunch yet."

She nodded. "Around here, dinner is lunch."

"Oh." Elyssa looked confused, but didn't argue the point.

I knew I should say no, but my stomach urged me to say yes. "Dinner sounds great. Can I borrow the telescope in the meantime?"

"Sure." She took me into a family room and pointed it out to me. "Food will be ready in an hour. Don't be late."

"Wouldn't dream of it." My mouth watered in anticipation.

I took the telescope onto the main gravel road in front of the house and aimed it skyward. I soon realized how hard it would be to locate a relatively tiny hole in the sky especially without having the crystoid nearby for a reference. I switched to demon vision and located the shimmer of the aether beam. Thanks to the crystal clear sky, I was able to follow the beam with my naked eye until it vanished from sight.

I rotated the telescope to an approximate angle and took a peek. It was still off by a few degrees. I used the finder scope on top and traced the beam with it. By alternating between the eyepiece and the finder, I was able to at last find the end of the proverbial rainbow. Even with it pinpointed, the portal was difficult to see thanks to the white clouds visible on the other side.

Nonetheless, it was a portal, perhaps to another realm, perhaps to another place in Eden.

Elyssa had remained quiet while I looked for the portal, but my expression must have told her I'd finally found it.

"What does it look like?" she asked.
I stepped away and let her use the eyepiece.
She grunted. "Definitely a portal, but no telling where it leads."
"One thing is certain," I said in a foreboding voice. "Someone isn't destroying all our aether. They're stealing it."

Chapter 12

Aether could be stored in magic batteries—that much I knew from using flying cars, sliders, and other magical gadgets. "Is there a battery big enough to hold that much aether?"

Elyssa looked up and tapped a finger on her chin. "I seriously doubt it."

"How does an aether battery work?" I asked.

"I have no idea. I've never seen or opened one."

I paced back and forth and quickly arrived at a conclusion. We needed to know all the possibilities with aether batteries. Since Shelton was busy analyzing the crystoid, I decided to call another expert who'd come through time and time again.

"Justin!" Adam Nosti sounded happy to hear from me.

"Hey, I guess you're aware of the global crisis."

He groaned. "Man, am I ever. Meghan and I are trapped up here in Oregon."

"Trapped?"

"Well, we can't use the Obsidian Arches, so you know what I mean." He huffed. "I didn't realize how reliant we are on magic. Meghan and I are practically climbing the walls we're so bored."

"Well, maybe you can help me anyway."

He chuckled. "Already on the job, eh?"

"You know me; I'm always looking for trouble." I gave him a rundown of current events all the way up to my discovery of the sky portal. "Here's the question—is there an aether battery big enough to store all that energy?"

"Yes." He sounded absolutely certain. "It's called Eden or Seraphina, or whatever other realms there are out there. The planet is like one huge battery and generator all in one."

"Sort of like a magical ecosystem," I said.

"That's exactly what it is," Adam replied. "Now, if you're asking if there's a manmade battery that could do the trick, the answer is a definite no."

"How do aether batteries work?"

"Man, I wish I could project an image, but that doesn't work in nom mode." He spoke with someone in the background, presumably Meghan. "Yeah, it's Justin. Sounds like we're back in action."

I gave him a moment to talk to her and then interrupted. "Can you describe the inner workings of an aether battery?"

"Yeah, sure," Adam said. "First, you need a silver vessel, then you seal it and use an aether generator to pump in the magical energy."

"It operates like a circle does?" I asked.

"Yep." He paused for a second. "Other substances can hold magic charges as well, but this method works the best."

A female voice spoke behind him.

"Hang on a sec," Adam said. Something scuffed against the microphone and muffled the conversation.

In the meantime, I imaged building a gargantuan silver sphere to fill with aether, and realized he was right about manmade aether batteries. Only the planet was big enough to store such a massive amount of aether.

"Okay, back," Adam said. "Meghan told me about some old-school batteries she kept at home that worked even better than silver containers."

That piqued my interest. "Really? How did they work?"

"We're not sure. These were originally owned by witches."

"Witches?" I'd never heard anyone called by that term in the Overworld. "Are they different from Arcanes?"

"Yeah, but they're into natural earth magic, blood magic, that kind of stuff." He chuckled. "You can specialize in witchcraft at Arcane University."

"Interesting. Tell me about this battery."

"The witches didn't call them batteries—they called them chalices."
He grunted. "They said their ancestors found them near Thunder Rock
hundreds of years ago."

"So they could be Seraphim in origin," I said.

He grunted. "Maybe. They could be Seraphim relics, or just
something really weird caused during the backlash when the
Alabaster Arches went nuclear." Adam cleared his throat. "Anyway,
Meghan has a couple chalices at the house. They're round and encased
in tanned squirrel hides."

"Squirrel hides?" I wasn't sure what to say about that.

"Yeah, don't ask me why." Adam chuckled. "She claims the chalices
could hold an incredibly long charge, but she lost one of them over
the side of a mountain during a mission, and it exploded when it hit a
rock."

"Whoa. So they're kind of unstable."

"Yeah. She didn't take her other one with her anymore after that."

I tapped a finger to my chin. "What's inside the squirrel skins?"

"Meghan says the witch she got them from said they used something
called xanthracite, but beyond that, she doesn't know what it is or how
it looks." He made a thoughtful noise. "If we could get back to
Atlanta, we could find out."

"The Obsidian Arch network is somewhat functional," I told him.
"We'll ask an arch operator up there to open a gateway."

"Oh, man, that would be amazing." He told the news to Meghan. "Just
let us know, okay?"

"Will do." I ended the call. "Babe, can you arrange for the arch
operator up their way to let them through?"

"You got it." Elyssa made a few calls. "The closest arch is in northern
California, a few hundred miles from them, but they'll let Adam and
Meghan through when they get there."

"I'll let them know." I texted Adam and he soon replied.

We're already packing the car. Talk soon.

Elyssa and I walked back to the crystoid and looked up at the myriad
symbols flashing above it. Shelton and Bella were engrossed with
whatever information it displayed. Behind them, the open omniarch
portal to the Grotto shimmered.

"How's it coming?" I asked.

Shelton blinked and looked down at us. "Well, the crystal is an aether sponge. Once it's full, it discharges extra energy skyward through the shards at a seventy degree angle."

"Why doesn't it discharge energy into the ground?"

"The energy takes the path of least resistance." Bella pointed up. "It's just naturally easier for it to project into the sky."

"We looked through a telescope and found a sky portal," I said. "All this aether is going somewhere else—probably right here in Eden."

Shelton's eyes flashed. "Where?"

"No idea. Maybe we could send an ASE up the aether beam and through the portal."

Shelton snapped his fingers. "Awesome, yeah. Be right back." He went into the portal behind him and vanished from sight. A few minutes later, he returned with one of the marble-sized ASEs in his hand. He flicked it into the air. It spun and hovered in front of him. Shelton tapped the ASE and it projected a holographic control screen. He programmed in a flight pattern to keep it in the aether beam.

A moment later, the ASE flitted away up into the sky.

"It'll be back in a couple of hours," he said, face eager. "I can't wait to find the jackasses behind this."

"Any idea how to disable the crystoids?" Elyssa asked.

Bella shook her head. "They constantly draw in aether which also makes them grow." She pointed to a holographic outline of the crystoid. "In the short time we've been studying this one, it's grown in diameter by two millimeters."

I groaned. "In other words, these things are constantly expanding?"

"Yup." Shelton nodded. "Within a week, this thing will be double this size."

"Imagine the explosion if a crystoid that large goes off," Elyssa said.

I didn't need to.

Ann's pickup truck pulled up a few minutes later and Viola waved to us. "Lunch is ready," she announced.

We piled into the back and rode down the bumpy trail to the house. Two Templars inside unfolded a card table and chairs. Pixie and Boris arrived a moment later with a tall willowy brunette.

"This is Tasha," Pixie said. "Tasha, this is Justin, Elyssa, Bella, and Shelton."

Tasha's eyes went wide and her hands covered her mouth. "Oh my god," she squealed. "You guys are like my biggest heroes ever."

Shelton took off his hat. "Just doing my job, ma'am."

Bella rolled her eyes.

"I'm sorry to sound like such a fangirl," Tasha said. "But after seeing the Skywraiths in action, I decided a flying broom air force is exactly what the Arcanes need."

"Yeah, the Blue Cloaks stick with flying carpets," Boris said. "I guess that's okay if you can't fly a broom."

Pixie nodded. "Boomsticks are where it's at."

"I think it's a great idea." I walked to the food, grabbed a plate, and piled on some food. "Tell me more."

The others followed and loaded their plates, then we sat down at one of the tables.

Tasha sat down across from me, her eyes bright. "There are plenty of amazing broom flyers, but not all of them are Arcanes. I think we need to implement real boomstick training into the curriculum at Arcane University."

I swallowed a mouthful. "Have you passed that by the school leaders?"

The light in Tasha's eyes faded a little. "Things are a mess at the school. I spoke with Headmaster Galfandor, but he said it would need to be cleared with the other school deans first."

"Yeah, but Victus Edison is too busy running for Arcanus Primus to give us time of day," Boris complained.

"Is Victus the Science Academy dean?" I asked.

Tasha looked at Pixie. Pixie shrugged.

Boris answered. "He's acting Chancellor, and also sits on the Deans' Council for Science Academy."

"Victus is gonna be in control of a lot if he's elected primus," Shelton muttered. "The Chancellor of Science Academy is the leader of the scientific community. If he's also the acting dean of the academy, that puts him in control of the curriculum there as well."

"Holy trifecta," I said. "So if he's elected primus, he'll control the Arcanes and the scientists."

"You got it." Shelton savagely tore into a piece of bread. "Man, this food is good."

"I'll put in a good word for instituting the Skywraiths in an official capacity," I assured Tasha. "Maybe Headmaster Galfandor will listen to me about a boomstick training course."

"That would be the most amazeballs things ever in the history of humanity," Tasha said. "Thanks, Justin!"

"Yeah, thanks," Pixie said.

Boris held up a fist. "Skywraiths, form up!" He chuckled. "I've always wanted to say that."

I grinned. "Hey, I know the feeling."

We polished off the food and leaned back in our chairs to enjoy a moment or two of rest before resuming our duties.

"Any luck out there?" Viola asked.

"We know a little more than before." Shelton told them what he'd learned.

"These things will keep growing?" Pixie asked.

"Yep." Shelton grabbed a slice of bread and began buttering it. "Things ain't looking too good."

"Golly sakes," Ann said. "Isn't there a way to cut off their power?"

"That's what we can't figure out," I said. "They're tapped deep into the earth and drawing magic straight from the source."

"Gee, sounds like a tree or something," she said. "I'd bet if you could dry up the roots that would do the trick."

"The biggest problem is reaching the roots," Shelton said. "They're dug in pretty deep."

"Breaking a root might also set off an explosion," I added. I wished there was some way I could contact Altash, or any of the ley worms to see if they could assist in digging up the crystoids. We'd have to resort to desperate measures before much longer.

"If these things are growing, it sounds like they're alive." Ann got up from the table and went toward the kitchen. "Maybe some kind of poison would do the trick."

I looked at Shelton. "I hadn't thought of it that way. Maybe these things are part organic."

He shrugged. "Could be, but what kind of poison would work on something that eats aether?"

"Certainly not malaether," Elyssa said. "That might cause a crystoid to explode."

I tapped my chin. "Yeah, you're probably right."

Ann walked from the kitchen with a big cake. "Anyone want dessert?"

Shelton whooped.

After dessert, Shelton and Bella went back to the crater. Elyssa and I sat on a hill with our trio of new best friends, Boris, Pixie, and Tasha recounting war stories of the boomstick racing variety.

"I cut around the outside corner and he cast a wind spell on me," Boris said, using his hands to illustrate the position of the brooms. "I knew it was coming and barrel-looped right over it, then hit him with a flash-blind spell." He zoomed one hand out in front of the other. "From then on out, winning was a breeze."

"They allow you to cast spells on each other during the race?" Elyssa asked.

Pixie nodded. "But only in the Arcane circuit. In the general racers' circuit, it's all about pure boomstick riding skill." She nodded at Tasha. "You're sitting next to a two-time champion."

"Congrats," I told the other woman.

She giggled. "Thanks. I've been broom riding since I was little. My biggest dream was to be a racer like my older brother."

"Does he still race?" I asked.

She looked down. "He died in the war."

My mood plummeted. "I'm so sorry, Tasha."

"Greg served with the Blue Cloaks." She put on a brave smile. "He was such a strong caster. Captain Takei promoted him to lieutenant just before the final battle."

Pixie teared up. "I lost a lot of good friends in the Battle of El Dorado."

"Brutal, just brutal," Boris added.

The conversation put me in a maudlin mood. "I thought we'd finally found peace after the battle." I looked glumly toward the crystoid. "Someone had other ideas."

"God, I really killed the mood, didn't I?" Tasha said. She stood up. "We need to check our equipment."

"What equipment?" I asked.

Boris got up. "We're measuring the aether drain in the surrounding area so we can determine the rate of absorption." He held out a hand for Pixie and pulled her upright. "I don't know how useful our studies will be, but hopefully it's not a waste of time."

"Thanks for spending time with us, Justin and Elyssa," Pixie said.

Boris nodded. "Yeah, you guys are legit cool."

Adam called around mid-afternoon to tell us they'd arrived back in Atlanta. "We'll swing by the house and then head to the Grotto," he said. "If traffic isn't bad, we'll see you guys in an hour."

After ending the call, I tried to think of something useful to do in the meantime. I called out to Shelton. "Anything new?"

"That's the third time you've asked." He waved a finger in a circle. "Why don't you go take a nice long walk?"

"What about the ASE?" Elyssa said. "It should've been back by now."

Shelton shrugged. "It's probably a long way to the sky portal. Just give it more time."

I didn't want to take another walk. I had to find something to do. I turned to Elyssa. "Let's go back through the portal to the Grotto."

She didn't object, so we climbed the platform and slipped back through the gateway.

The arch operator had moved his chair closer to the omniarch with the open portal. He seemed ecstatic to see us. "I don't know how you did it, but there's enough aether here for me to cast spells again."

Elyssa and I exchanged confused looks and glanced back at the omniarch. Apparently, the silver band around it allowed aether to filter through once it hit a high enough concentration. I switched to demon vision and had to shield my eyes from the brilliant currents floating through the air. Aether poured through the open portal, gathered in the circle, and traveled up the magical container like an invisible smokestack where it poured into the air near the ceiling of the immense room.

"It's a temporary measure," I told him, but it had given me an idea.

I used a neighboring omniarch and willed it to open at El Dorado. With so much aether available, it quickly opened a gateway into a control room nearly identical to the Grotto, except for a towering Alabaster Arch veined with black and white.

The excess aether allowed me to open a portal to the El Dorado control room. "Let's talk to Altash and Lulu."

Elyssa's eyes brightened. "Maybe they can help."

"I hope so." We jogged out of the control room and into the massive area beyond. Red scales glittered on the massive snakelike form of Altash coiled in the center of the cavern. Lulu's purple scales gleamed in the yellowish light suffusing the immense space. The two dragons had once been the guardians of reborn Seraphim, but their former wards had long since grown old enough to fend for themselves. Most, if not all had joined the Darkling army and gone back to Seraphina to wrest control of Pjurna, the Darkling nation, back from Cephus where he'd entrenched himself in the capital city of Tarissa.

"Hello?" I shouted as we approached the coiled dragons. "You probably know this already, but we have a problem."

The dragons didn't even twitch. Though Altash rarely spoke to me, he usually at least opened an eye to let me know he'd heard whatever I'd said and promptly decided to ignore it. The dragon's girth towered over Elyssa and me. I figured Altash could swallow a jumbo jet without much of an issue.

Elyssa pointed to the dragon's long lean muzzle resting on the floor. "There's his head."

We picked up the pace and ran to his closed eye.

"Altash?" I pressed a hand to the dragon's chin and nudged him. His scales felt hard as diamonds. I figured a nudge wouldn't be enough and gave him a good shove. I might as well have pushed against a mountain for all the effect it had. "Hello?" I knocked on his head, but the dragon did nothing.

The magic fails, said a female voice weakly in my head.

Elyssa's eyes widened. "Did you hear that?"

We ran around Altash's head to find Lulu likewise slumbering on the other side. Her eyelid slit open a fraction to reveal the lower third of a parietal eye.

We die with the magic. Her voice was but a whisper in my head. Atlash's voice was usually like thunder. I imagined hers was probably like that on a good day.

This was not a good day.

"We're trying to fix the magic problem," I told the dragon, but she didn't respond. I shook my head. "This isn't good at all."

Elyssa touched Lulu. "They're dying, Justin."

I realized just how bad it would be if they didn't survive. "The dragons maintain the magical ley lines in the earth." I looked at the tunnels bored into the walls of the cavern. "If they die before we remove the crystoids Eden might never recover."

Her eyes tightened. "No more magic ever?"

I shook my head slowly. "I don't know, and I don't want to find out."

We returned to the Grotto and were going to deliver the grim news to Shelton when I saw Adam and Meghan enter the control room.

"Justin!" Adam jogged over, a broad grin on his face. He bumped knuckles with me, then went in for a bro-hug. "Man, it's good to see you again." He turned to Elyssa and gave her a good squeeze.

"Hello, Justin." Meghan offered a hand, but I violated the introverted woman with a hearty hug.

"I'm glad you guys are here," I said.

Meghan stiffened and awkwardly patted me on the back until I released her from the hug. She took a deep breath to regain her composure and reached into a bag. Her hand withdrew what looked like a giant, shriveled bull testicle. "This is a chalice."

Meghan was always one to skip the small talk and get straight to business. In this instance, I didn't mind one bit. I took it in one hand and hefted it. Though the squirrel hide was oiled, it had stiffened over time. Whatever was inside it felt hard and pointy.

"Do you think it's safe to cut open?" I asked.

She shrugged. "I believe so, but perhaps we should do it in a secure environment."

"Agreed." Elyssa took it from me. "Let's take it to a gauntlet room back at Queens Gate."

"Where did you guys just come from?" Adam asked.

I told them about the dying dragons. "What happens if we don't have the earth dragons to maintain the ley lines?"

Adam and Meghan looked at each other. Adam spoke first. "The dragons are the magical equivalent of earthworms. Without them working on the aether lines, the magic might just stay balled up inside the earth, or worse, it might turn into malaether."

Meghan grimaced. "The ley worms aren't the only creatures who maintain magic. For example, the minders in the Gloom harvest our dreams and convert it into magical energy. There are millions of microorganisms that survive on magical energy and feed off it. Each one contributes something beneficial to the health of the aether." She tapped a finger on her chin. "If the free flow of aether isn't restored, the magical biology of Eden could be permanently destroyed."

"Eden would be the sole domain of noms," Adam said in a haunted voice. "We'd lose the ability to traverse the realms."

My stomach lurched at the thought. "Well, if that doesn't light a fire under our asses, I don't know what will."

"I'm motivated!" Adam said. "Let's get to work."

With the extra aether flooding the room from the portal to North Dakota, I was able to easily open a portal to the gauntlet room near the underground mansion in Queens Gate. The atmosphere within the pocket dimension felt normal compared to the static rush of magical energy flooding from the crystoid and into the Grotto.

Meghan closed her eyes and breathed in relief when she stepped through. "I feel human again."

"It's good stuff," Adam said with a smile.

Elyssa marched the chalice to a shielded pedestal and placed it there. Adam pulled out a wand, but she shook her head. "Let's open this up the old fashioned way." She pulled a practice golem from a wall rack and activated it. "Take this knife and cut open that bag." Elyssa pointed to the chalice.

The golem took the knife and walked over to the target.

I braced myself for an explosion and threw up a shield of Murk to keep us protected. The golem slashed open the leather. For a moment, nothing happened, then the leather swelled and broke open.

We gasped as a crystoid burst from within and began to grow.

Chapter 13

"Son of a bitch!" I raced across the room to the newly hatched menace. "We've got to get this thing out of here." I almost touched it before remembering the dire consequences, namely turning into a malaether zombie.

Meghan calmly walked over and plucked the squirrel hide off the crystoid. She looked inside. "Ah, that's how they did it."

Elyssa grimaced. "Please don't tell me we're going to have to go on a squirrel-killing rampage to contain these things."

Meghan turned the leather inside out to reveal the inside. "Here's your silver lining." The interior shimmered with a sterling gray substance. She tentatively touched it. "Actually, I don't know if this is silver."

"Silver wouldn't allow the chalice to charge without an opening," Adam said.

Meghan pursed her lips. "You're right."

"If it's not silver, what is it?" Elyssa asked.

"I might be able to break down a sample and analyze it." Meghan retrieved a scalpel from the satchel at her side and scraped at it. "It's extremely hard."

Adam took out his wand and traced it back and forth over the spot until the leather peeled free from a section. Meghan plucked a sample with a pair of tweezers.

I spared a wary glance for the baby crystoid. It was already noticeably larger. "Um, how are we going to contain that thing?"

"I suggest you take it through a portal for the time being so it doesn't interfere with the magic within the pocket dimension." Meghan deposited the gray substance on a piece of cloth. "Use the leather to shield your hands."

113

"Ya think?" I wasn't about to touch the thing, especially having seen what it did to the mercenaries.

"I think we should put it right next to the crystoid in North Dakota," Elyssa said. "Since the bigger crystoid is already soaking up most of the aether, the smaller one probably won't be able to grow."

Adam gave her a thumbs up. "Excellent idea."

I took the squirrel hide and gingerly cradled the crystoid inside. Elyssa walked with me back through the portal leading to the Grotto. I saw Shelton and Bella on the other side of the portal leading to North Dakota. The baby crystoid began to grow even more rapidly from the aether flooding through the gateway.

"Clear the way," I said, racing toward the portal. "Dangerous package coming through."

Shelton's eyes went wide when he saw the crystoid. "Where the hell did that thing come from?"

"No time to explain." I motioned him to move with my head. "Out of the way."

"Harry, stop asking questions and move." Bella took his arm and the pair ducked beneath the portal.

I stepped through the gateway, turned, and made my way down the stairs. The small crystoid stopped growing the second I was out of the aether beam. Shelton and Bella gave me wide berth as I navigated around the platform and to the crystoid trench. I knelt, placed the baby crystoid to the side of the big one, and stood up.

"What the hell are those?" Shelton said, pointing up in the sky.

I looked up and saw parachutes pop from three large black cubes about a hundred feet above us. Even with the parachutes, the cubes dropped quickly. I dashed out of the way as they clanked to the ground.

"This can't be good," I said.

The cubes confirmed my suspicions by immediately unfolding into robots identical to the one at Sweetwater Creek. Once I realized what they were, I didn't hesitate a second longer. I raced toward the closest robot and rammed it with my shoulder. It hurt like a bitch, but sent the robot slamming to the ground.

Elyssa took on the second one, tripping it up, and jamming a sword into the gun barrels on the robot's arm to keep it from firing.

I turned to face the last one, and a metal fist met my face. I flipped through the air and rolled against something hard. Woozy from the blow, I reached a hand back to see what I'd hit. Absolute zero cold and intense heat burned into my skin. Dazzling motes danced in my eyes. The air shimmered and burst into flame around me. Energy roared like the ocean through my very soul. My brain burned. My muscles froze, heart slamming inside my chest so hard I thought it would burst.

I'd touched the crystoid. *I'm dead!*

I tried to let go of the crystal shard, but my hand refused my commands. I was burning up.

Too much! Can't keep it in!

A ragged cry tore from my throat. The world was in flames. I had to open a pressure valve before my body exploded.

Using all my willpower, I jerked up my right arm and unleashed hell. A torrent of crimson energy exploded from my hand. It absolutely annihilated the nearest robot. The next robot aimed its weapons at me. I adjusted my aim and disintegrated it. Elyssa threw the final robot into the path of my death beam, and sent it to oblivion. The torrent of raw power blew a hole the size of a bus into the hill behind the space the robots had once occupied and burned into the baked red clay beneath, reducing it to molten stone. The beam continued to bore through the hill and slammed into a rise on the other side.

The pressure in my body abruptly abated and my muscles went slack. I jerked my hand free from the shard and stumbled forward, still holding my other hand out toward the hill. The crimson beam sputtered and died. I fell to my knees then face-planted against the red clay.

"Justin!" Elyssa gripped my arm and hauled me out of the trench.

My body felt like overcooked oatmeal. "Am I a zombie?"

She hugged me. "Not yet, babe. Not yet."

"Holy flaming goat turds!" Shelton yelled. "You just blew up three robots and a freaking mountain!"

"It was a small hill, Harry." Bella kneeled next to me. "Are you okay, Justin?"

I nodded. My insides felt hollower than a political promise. "I'm really glad I'm not a zombie."

"We all are." Shelton gripped my shoulder and pulled his hand back. "Man, you feel like you just hopped out of a microwave."

Nausea slithered up my esophagus. I pulled away from Elyssa and heaved. Black, curdled blood oozed from my mouth. I felt like a hungover alcoholic after a two-week binge, and my throat was raw and dry.

"Justin!" Elyssa grabbed my arm.

I heaved again. More blood, this time brighter red spattered on the ground. I sucked in a ragged breath and dropped to my knees. "I feel overcooked."

"Someone get Meghan," Elyssa said.

I held up a hand. "No, I feel better now." Despite vomiting a pint of overheated blood, I felt a lot better.

"I don't care how much better—"

"No." I cut off Elyssa's protest. "Give me a moment, and then I'll go see her. She needs to figure out what that gray stuff from the chalice is." I gazed at the tunnel I'd blasted through the hill. The jagged red scoria looked like a wound in the earth. A pair of smoking metal feet were all that remained of the three robots.

"Wow, that was some light show," Ann said. She and Viola stood next to the pickup truck, having arrived just in time for the Justin Laser Spectacular.

"Were those robots?" Viola asked, peering at the meager robotic remains.

"Sorry about your hill." The words caught in my raw throat.

Ann chuckled. "I think it's really neat. My grandson will probably love riding his dirt cycle through it."

I shook my head and turned to Elyssa. "I wonder why I didn't turn into a malaether zombie."

"Maybe because you were able to release the energy." Elyssa shrugged. "That's the best explanation I can think of."

"About a good as any," Shelton said. "If you'd gone rogue on us, I don't think we could've stopped you."

Bella shivered. "Thank goodness you're normal."

Elyssa gave me a worried look. "He's anything but normal."

"Where did those robots come from?" I wheezed.

Shelton looked up. "I have no idea. The sky portal, maybe?"

Bella nodded. "They didn't come from an aircraft."

"Then the robot in Sweetwater Creek couldn't have been made by noms," Elyssa said. "Whoever launched the crystoids is trying to fortify their positions."

I hacked up more blood and nodded. "I wish I hadn't completely destroyed them."

Shelton looked at the slagged metal feet. "Yeah, we ain't gonna learn much from those."

My stomach ached with the burn of a thousand spicy Indian meals, and my eyes watered. I didn't let the discomfort stop me from telling Shelton about the baby crystoid, the dying dragons, and our theory about the end of magic in Eden.

He didn't seem to appreciate finding out so much bad news all at once. "The dragons are dying?" His shoulder slumped. "Holy mutated monkey meat. We've got to save them somehow."

"Well, if anyone can figure it out, we can," Bella said. She motioned to the little crystoid I'd placed in the trench. "Where do you suppose the witches got those from?"

I thought I'd already told them but repeated myself. "Adam said the witches found them near Thunder Rock a few hundred years ago."

"It's a Seraphim relic." Shelton slapped the back of his hand into the other palm. "Someone found some of the old relics from the first war and figured out how to make them really nasty."

Bella's forehead pinched. "It would appear so."

Adam appeared through the portal at the top of the platform. His eyes widened when he noticed the hill. "What the hell happened?"

"Justin touched the crystoid," Shelton said.

"Whoa." He walked down the stairs and joined us. His forehead scrunched when he looked at me. "Is that blood on your mouth? And where did those metal feet come from?"

"Robots," Shelton said.

I groaned. "Don't touch the crystoid."

"Gee your voice sure sounds dry there, Justin." Ann held out a bottle. "Want some water?"

I took it gladly and gulped it down. I could have sworn I felt it sizzle into steam as it traveled down my throat.

"Using yourself as a test subject is pretty dangerous." Adam shuddered and spoke before I could clarify that it had been an accident. "Meghan is analyzing the gray stuff on the squirrel hide. I figured I'd come down here and see what Shelton and Bella found out about these things. Maybe some of our facts will click." He looked at the metal remains again. "And where the hell did a robot come from?"

"Now that's a good question." Shelton took out his arcphone, fully charged thanks to the aether beam, and projected a diagram of the crystoid. "Here's what we've got."

I tried to make sense of the numbers and symbols scrolling across the image, but they looked like gibberish. Despite my abilities with Seraphim magic, I'd considered going back to Arcane University for a formal education so I didn't feel like a nitwit when the subject of magical analysis and spell coding came up.

"Wow, no wonder it sucks in so much aether," Adam said.

Shelton pointed to what looked like elemental symbols. "I've never seen this combination before. Any idea what it means?"

Adam looked just as puzzled. His eyes narrowed and he gazed at the crystoid. "Remember Moore's law of aether dynamics?"

"Of course. The concentration of aether is directly proportionate to the power output." Shelton shrugged. "So?"

"Justin's experiment—"

"It was an accident," I said.

Adam nodded. "Justin's accident gave him such a high dose of concentrated aether that he almost blew up a mountain."

"It's a hill," Bella said.

"What would an ultra-dense concentration of aether look like?" Adam seemed to know the answer, but let Shelton think it out.

I thought back to basic chemistry when a gas condensed and suddenly understood what the crystoid was.

Shelton slapped the back of his hand into the other palm. "Those things are solidified aether!"

"That's the best explanation," Adam said.

I pushed myself up and went to the crater, careful to keep my distance from the ledge. In retrospect, the dark purple and white crystal shards should have been a big clue, but I'd never seen crystallized aether. *That's not true.* I'd seen something like it on Seraphina. "When I was in Tarissa, the Darkling capitol, they used magic to create furniture out of Murk."

"Interesting." Adam pursed his lips. "Did it suck in aether like the crystoids?"

I shook my head. "No, it wasn't anything like this."

Adam snapped his fingers. "I know what the gray stuff is."

"Gray stuff?" Shelton took off his hat and scratched his head.

"Inside the squirrel skin," Elyssa said. She retrieved the squirrel hide from next to the crystoid.

Shelton glanced at it and understanding lit his face. "It's Stasis."

"Makes total sense," I said. "Stasis allows aether in, but prevents the crystoid from growing."

"That thing"—Shelton jabbed a finger toward the crater—"is like a magical snowball. When the aether is crystallized, its new magical properties suck in aether and convert it to more crystal."

Adam look up. "The excess aether follows the path of least resistance and flows out of the top shards and into the sky."

"So what's the answer to stopping these things?" I asked. "Do I channel Stasis into them?"

Adam and Shelton both shrugged.

"Maybe," Shelton said. "Then again, it might blow up."

"That's no bueno." I looked to Adam. "Ideas?"

"Here's one," Elyssa interjected. "Test out your theory on the little crystoid first. At least if it explodes, it won't take out the entire countryside."

"That sure would be great if we kept the farm intact," Ann said with a cheery smile. "Though, I suppose I could retire and move to Minnesota with Viola."

Viola looked a bit unsure about that prospect. "I'd sure like to keep the farm around if that's possible."

"Ah, don't worry about it." Shelton plastered on a reassuring smile. "Justin here hardly ever blows up stuff he doesn't want to."

"I think today would be a good day to visit some friends in town," Viola said to her mother. "Let's take a ride."

"Well, if you think that's best." Ann went to the pickup and took out a large glass dish. "I made some brownies. You guys sure are welcome to help yourselves."

Viola unfolded a card table and put a pitcher of red punch on top of it. "If you guys get hungry, there are some leftovers in the refrigerator back at the house."

"And you're welcome to use the bathroom there too," Ann said. "Just be careful with the toilet in the add-on room. It clogs kind of easy."

Bella glanced at Shelton. "Maybe you should use the other toilet, Harry."

He gave her a dirty look. "Don't be jealous of my healthy digestive system."

"Thank so much for your hospitality," Elyssa said. "Please remember that all of this is strictly confidential."

"Golly sakes, it sure would make for good gossip." Ann chuckled. "But even I can keep a secret." She waved goodbye and climbed into the pickup.

Viola paused as she got into the driver's seat. "Be careful, you guys."

"We will." I hoped I wasn't lying.

Elyssa spoke to the other Templars and sent them back through the portal to the Grotto to await further instructions.

The only thing that remained was for me to retrieve the baby crystoid and test our Stasis theory.

As we walked toward the crater, Shelton did a double take. "The ASE we sent to the sky portal is back."

"I'll get it." Bella climbed the platform and used her wand to lure the recording device over to her. "Want to watch it now?"

I was extremely curious to see the footage, but decided it was crucial we conduct our experiment first. "In a moment."

Elyssa took the leather hide and carefully picked up the crystoid. "Maybe we should put it in the tunnel Justin bored through the hill. It might contain any explosions."

"Just set it where he'll have a good line of sight from the platform." Shelton traced a path through the air with his finger. "Otherwise, he won't have any aether to use."

"Sounds good." I went to the table and poured myself a glass of red punch while they set the crystoid in place. I decided to eat a brownie as well. Sure, I'd just puked up blood and probably a few vital organs, but that was no excuse to pass up a tasty snack.

Meghan stepped through the portal and onto the platform. She made her way down the stairs and gave me a concerned look. "What happened to you?" Without waiting for an answer, she took out her wand and tried to scan me—all to no avail since we were in a magic-less area.

I told her about my accident. "Aside from barfing blood, I think I'm okay."

"Justin, you need a full medical exam." She set her arms akimbo. "There could be permanent damage."

"He already has permanent brain damage," Shelton said as he and the others approached.

"I'm about to have permanent friend damage in a second." I climbed up the stairs to the platform, muscles aching with every step. "Unfortunately, I'm the only one here who can use Stasis, and we don't have any time to waste."

Elyssa followed me up and kissed my cheek. "Good luck."

I squeezed her hand. "Love you, babe."

"Love you too."

I motioned her away. "Go wait on the ground."

"I want to stay with you."

I shook my head. "You might be in the way."

Elyssa frowned. "You'd better not be saying that just to get me away from you."

"I'm not." The top of the platform wasn't very large, and I didn't know what to expect when I engaged the crystoid.

She narrowed her eyes and looked at me for a moment. "Fine, but I'm coming back up at the first sign of trouble."

Once she reached the bottom, I took a deep breath and summoned my strength. The ordeal with the crystoid had left me drained. I felt better than before, but was by no means at full capacity. Hopefully, I had enough juice to make this work.

Chapter 14

I held both hands out to my sides, drawing energy from the crystoid's aether beam. An ultraviolet orb blossomed in my left hand. A white star burst into being in my right. I let the energy build until a nimbus surrounded each hand. Sweat trickled down my forehead and into my eyes.

I need a nap.

I was all too aware that I might be taking an eternal dirt nap if I didn't concentrate.

Lifting my hands, I threaded the Murk and Brilliance into a spinning globe of foggy gray Stasis that hung about chest high. I let the energy coalesce until it grew larger than my head. My knees trembled and my stomach gurgled uneasily.

Don't throw up the brownie.

Losing control of my bodily functions during such a delicate operation wouldn't be pretty. I took a deep breath to brace myself and focused a beam of Stasis toward the small crystoid. The moment it touched the shard, it felt as though I'd just lassoed a wild goat. I stumbled forward against the platform railing.

The Stasis globe unraveled like a ball of yarn as the small crystoid consumed it.

"What happened?" Elyssa called to me.

"Not sure." My voice sounded hoarse and my throat burned. I didn't see any alternative but to stop what I was doing and declare this experiment failed.

"Look!" Shelton yelled. "It's working!"

I peered at the small crystoid. The ultraviolet and white shards were slowly shading gray. The tug on my arms gradually abated until at last

123

it was gone. The small crystoid shimmered dark gray. I released the aether threads and slumped. "Yay." My voice sounded weak and puny, and it felt like the brownie and punch wanted to rise from the dead.

Elyssa appeared at my side an instant later. "Okay, that's it. You're taking a break." She helped me up.

"Can't. I've got to save the dragons." I didn't know how much longer they had before the aether drain killed them. I also didn't know how I could disable the crystoid all the way in Colombia affecting them.

"You've done all you can right now," Shelton said. "I wish we could help, but—" he stopped talking and snapped his fingers. "I've got it!"

Adam's eyes brightened. "We portal the aether straight to the dragons."

"Exactamundo, brahmeister." Shelton looked up at me. "Get rested. We'll keep the dragons on life support 'til you've recovered."

Knowing that they'd be okay for the time being made me slump with relief. "You're the bestest," I muttered, unable to project my voice.

Elyssa dragged me through the portal into the Grotto way station control room before I passed out.

When we entered the control room, a frantic arch operator rushed over to us. "Justin Slade?" he asked.

"Yup." I was almost too tired to talk.

"Excellent, wait right here." He rushed away.

"Huh?" I mumbled.

Elyssa shrugged. "I need to get you to bed."

I didn't argue, but was curious to see what the arch operator wanted. The answer walked around the corner. A petite woman with large green eyes smiled and ran toward me.

"Nightliss!" The sight of her energized me. "You made it!"

Tears in her eyes, she flung her arms around me. "I made it," she whispered in a happy voice. "I'm back."

Elyssa wiped her eyes and laughed. "We missed you."

"I missed you too." Nightliss backed away and looked at me. "You look terrible, Justin. What's wrong?"

The burst of energy faded and I slumped. "Let Elyssa tell you. I'm about to fall over."

124

She pecked a kiss on my cheek. "We'll talk later."

"My father is going to be so excited," Elyssa said.

Nightliss raised an eyebrow. "Thomas Borathen excited?" She laughed. "That would truly be a surprise."

My knees buckled and Elyssa propped me on her shoulder. "Maybe you can help me get our hero to a bed."

Nightliss took my other side. "I would be delighted."

My mouth felt like I'd eaten dust, sand, and cat fur on shaved toast when I woke up. I didn't even know where I was. I tried to blink, but sleep funk glued shut my eyelids. Wearily, I rubbed them.

"Justin?"

Finally able to see, I looked into concerned blue eyes. "Mom?"

My mother, Alysea, smoothed back my hair. "We're finally here, honey. Elyssa tells me you overdid it—again."

I sat up and yawned. "I can't help it."

"Meghan looked you over and said you're lucky touching that crystoid didn't fry you alive. Otherwise, she thinks you'll survive." She sighed. "I thought we'd finally found peace, but I guess that was just wishful thinking."

"Maybe we never finished the job we were supposed to finish." I sat up and pushed to my feet. "This could be Serena's work."

"Oh, well, perhaps you should come with me." She took my hand. "We have a pretty good idea who's behind it."

My chest tightened. "Who?"

We left the small bedroom, walked down a hallway and went into a dining room.

"Justin!" Ivy, my little sister, raced across the room and slammed me with a hug.

I felt like I was about to cough blood from the impact.

Mom pulled her back. "Ivy, your brother is still injured."

"Oh." She looked down and toed the floor. "Sorry, bro. I'm just super excited to see you."

I embraced her gently. "I've missed you too, sis."

"Maybe I need to get you a dictionary so you can see what vacation means." My father, David, grinned from a casual leaning position

125

against the far wall where he spoke with Nightliss. He pushed upright and gave me a one-armed sideways hug.

"I know perfectly well what it means." I rubbed the back of my neck. "The universe decided I'd rested long enough."

Nightliss pressed her hands to my cheeks and looked into my eyes. "Are you feeling better?"

"I'm much better." Though her spirits seemed improved since the last time I'd seen her, her calm face couldn't veil troubled eyes. Unfortunately, we didn't have time for psychological counseling, not with the clock ticking on Eden's magic issue. I looked up. "So, who's the jackass behind this?"

"Don't spoil the surprise," Shelton said. He held up an ASE. "I want to see the look on his face."

I groaned. "Fine, just show me already." I located a chair with a nice padded leather seat and dropped into it.

"Just a moment." Meghan gave me a vial of blue fluid. "I need you to drink this."

"What is it?" I asked.

"Something to heal the hemorrhaging you suffered when you destroyed that mountain."

Bella blew out an exasperated breath. "It was a hill, people, not a mountain."

Shelton snorted, and I wondered if he'd told everyone to call it a mountain just to drive Bella crazy.

I popped the cork on the vial and drained the contents. It soothed my sore throat and made the inside of my chest feel frosty. I sighed as the aches subsided.

"You suffered magical damage," Meghan said. "That's why you're taking so long to regenerate."

"I figured as much." Or, at least I would have if I'd given it any thought. Wounds caused by magic were stubborn about healing even with supernatural recovery.

Shelton looked at Meghan impatiently. "Can I show him now?"

"Yes, go." She moved away and joined Adam on the right side of the room.

126

Elyssa put a hand on my shoulder and whispered, "You're not going to like this."

Nightliss gave me a guilty look but said nothing.

Ivy came up to the other side and leaned her head on me. "I'm so glad to see you again, Justin. I really hoped when you got done with vacation we could hang out."

Though she was only ten—or was it eleven?—she sounded much more mature than before the war. "We can totally hang out once this is over and done with."

"Yay!" She kissed my cheek.

"Ahem." Shelton pointed to a holographic image floating over the table. "Here goes."

The footage zipped through blue sky in fast forward as the ASE rose into the sky and went through the portal. Clouds on the other side blocked the view. Shelton slowed the video to normal speed once it cleared the clouds. I narrowed my eyes and tried to understand what I was seeing. It looked like a city, or what remained of it. Rubble filled a large portion, especially around a huge ultraviolet dome.

I hissed air between my teeth and would have jumped up if Elyssa hadn't pressed down on my shoulder. "That's the Ministry of Research. That's Cephus's headquarters."

Shelton nodded grimly. "It looks like Ketiss and his Darkling army didn't succeed."

The closer the ASE drew to the city of Tarissa, the clearer that assessment became. Almost no buildings remained standing near the Ministry of Research, Cephus's headquarters. The last time I'd been there, he'd shielded the building and the courtyard around it with a Murk barrier so thick I couldn't penetrate it. The shield looked much larger now, going so far as to encompass several city blocks around it. Nightliss cringed and looked away. I couldn't blame her. Cephus's people had kidnapped her and treated her like a lab rat so they could understand why feeding on humans made her far more powerful than the average Seraphim. Though I'd saved her, she hadn't been quite the same. I wondered if that had something to do with her leaving the Templars in the first place.

I refocused on the main issue. Gears spun in my mind as I tried to understand several critical items. "How did Cephus deploy the crystoids from there? He's in Seraphina, and the only way to cross into another realm is through an Alabaster Arch."

"Exactly," Adam said. "How are there sky portals that lead from Eden to Seraphina?" He shrugged. "Obviously, he somehow deployed the crystoids through those gateways directly into Eden."

I certainly couldn't think of a good answer.

"What if in Seraphina they have an Alabaster omniarch that can open portals anywhere, even other realms?" Dad said.

The room fell silent for a moment.

"As far as any of us know, Seraphina doesn't have Obsidian Arches," I said. "The builders only put Alabaster Arches there. It stands to reason they might have put other kinds of inter-dimensional arches there."

"Don't you think someone in Seraphina would have found them a long time ago?" Mom said.

Adam frowned. "There's only one way to find out."

Shelton nodded. "Field trip to Seraphina."

I closed my eyes and tried not to cry. This would be anything but a field trip. We'd be entering another war. Even before defeating Daelissa, I'd promised Ketiss that I'd help him bring peace to Seraphina. Instead, I'd run away with Elyssa and tried to forget all the horrors I'd seen while Ketiss took the Tarissan Legion back through to deal with Cephus.

By avoiding my responsibility to him, I'd let the blight fester. Cephus hadn't fallen to the newly empowered Tarissan Legion. Instead, he'd somehow managed to launch a strike against us here, no doubt to keep us busy until he solidified his rule over the Darkling nation of Pjurna.

"I abandoned my duties," Nightliss whispered. "I should have gone with Ketiss and helped him. I should have asked Thomas to take the Templars and help."

"It's my fault," I told her. "I should have gone."

"How about you stop with the pity party and take a look at this?" Shelton said. He froze the holographic image and zoomed in on something sparkling in the top quadrant. "I've got more bad news."

When the image sharpened into focus, my hands clenched into fists. The sparkling object was a crystoid. "He's using these things on his own people."

"Yeah." Shelton scowled. "And he's using the crystoids here to beam aether right into his headquarters so he has plenty of magic."

I banged a fist on the arm of the chair. "Not anymore." I pushed Elyssa's hand off my shoulder and rose. "We're going to deactivate the crystoids here, and then we're gonna go to Seraphina and kick Cephus's ass!"

"Kick some ass!" Ivy yelled.

Mom put a hand over my sister's mouth. "Language, young lady."

"One problem," Shelton said. "We need Seraphim to channel Stasis into the crystoids. The only ones here in Eden are Justin, Ivy, and Alysea, and Nightliss."

"Fjoeruss is still around," I said. "Presumably, he's still running his companies."

"I've already tried tracking him down," Mom said. "He's apparently made himself unavailable. I don't think we can count on his help."

Fjoeruss, aka, Mr. Gray, was the master of Stasis. Without his assistance, our task would be all the more difficult.

"Will the four of you be enough?" Elyssa said.

I shrugged. "Maybe we can go to Seraphina and recruit a few able bodies."

"There's a problem with that," Elyssa said. "While you were asleep, we watched the footage and figured out it was Cephus, so I called my father and asked him send someone through the Alabaster Arch at the Three Sisters in Australia."

I nodded. "And?"

"He couldn't get through," she said. "A portal won't open in the Three Sisters. Not even the Obsidian Arch there responded."

"The arch in the Three Sisters is the only one that opens near Pjurna," I said. More specifically, it opened on a skylet, a floating island of land, some distance off the shore of the Darkling nation. The capital city of Pjurna, Tarissa, was several hours away by the cloud paths called skyways.

"Given what we know," Adam said, "The skyway from the arch probably isn't working due to the crystoids on the other side. So even if we got the Alabaster Arch to work, we'd be stuck on the skylet."

"We are blocked at every angle," Nightliss said.

I tried to pace, but the room was too cramped. "Fine. We'll make do with what we have."

"You know I can help," Ivy declared.

I patted her shoulder. "You're going to be a big help." It would take everything we had to shut down the crystoids, especially with many of them in nom hands. I looked around the room. "Where are we anyway?"

"Inside a house in the Grotto," Elyssa said. "A pocket dimension seemed the best place to go since magic works here."

"Shelton, do you have a map of the crystoids?" I asked.

"Yup." He turned off the ASE, flicked the screen on his arcphone, and projected a holographic globe with glowing red and green dots. "I wish I knew the radius these things affected."

"It's uneven since some are tapped directly into ley lines," Adam said. He pointed out a green dot. "We control the green ones. The noms have the red ones." He rotated the globe and indicated a yellow one just off the coast of Iceland. "No one has direct access to that one since it's underwater."

"There's a hundred and twenty-one of these damned things," Shelton growled. "We only have direct access to eleven of them."

"How did you compile such a thorough list?" Elyssa asked.

"George Walker and his crew recovered critical ASEs and plotted all the impact sites we didn't know about." Adam pointed to the green dot in North Dakota. "I suggest we start there."

"I want to go first," Ivy proclaimed.

Mom shook her head. "I'll do the first one just in case."

I gave her an uneasy look. "I hope it's no worse than the small crystoid." I described how it jerked me forward. "For all we know, the big one will be even worse."

"She'll need anchors," Dad said. "I'll hold her in place."

I opened my mouth to volunteer, but Elyssa shook her head. "No, Justin. You need to recover."

"Fine." I puffed a breath through my lips. "Let's do this."

"I have not fed since returning," Nightliss said. "I will gladly help, but first, I should replenish myself."

I nodded. "Have you rested since your journey?"

She shook her head. "Not very well. The world is a dangerous place, especially for a woman traveling alone." Her lips peeled back from her teeth. "Many found their graves when they tried to take advantage of me."

Ivy's mouth dropped open. "Wow, Nightliss, you've changed."

The Darkling looked down. "Yes. I am quicker to violence, less forgiving, and more willing to see the evil in people." She shivered. "I feel I have lost faith."

Mom hugged her and kissed the top of her head. "You're turning back into your old self."

Nightliss flinched. "What do you mean?"

"The Desecration nearly killed you." Mom's face paled. "It took your memories and powers from you for centuries. I suspect there are parts of your personality that will never come back."

"Are you saying Nightliss wasn't always a sweet person?" I asked, shocked by my mother's assertion otherwise.

Mom touched my hand. "She was a battle-hardened warrior who despised Daelissa with an unholy passion."

Nightliss put a hand to her heart. "Goodness. I don't remember feeling that way."

I put an arm over her shoulder. "It doesn't matter. To me, you'll always be the cute little cat I rescued from a stray dog."

She laughed. "And I will always be your fallen angel."

"More like guardian angel," I said. I squeezed her. "Go feed and join us when you're rested, okay?"

Nightliss nodded. "I will."

The rest of us left the house and headed back to the pocket dimension exit. In the eerily quiet way station, we walked right and entered the control room. The portal leading to North Dakota was still open. I noticed another portal open next to it and saw the huge forms of Altash and Lulu on the other side.

The huge red dragon cracked an eyelid. *Thank you*, he said in my mind.

"Glad you're feeling better," I said, a bit concerned by how weak his voice sounded.

His eyelid closed.

"Good job with the portals," I told Shelton.

He shrugged. "It ain't no thing."

Mom stepped through the portal to North Dakota and onto the platform over the crystoid. Except for Dad, the rest of us remained behind, a few steps and over a thousand miles between Atlanta and North Dakota.

"I'm ready, David," Mom said, touching a crystal prism strapped to her hand that allowed her to channel both Murk and Brilliance almost equally. Unlike me, most Seraphim had an affinity to Murk or Brilliance and couldn't easily channel the opposite.

Dad nodded and gripped her waist. "I got you, love."

She looked down at the crystoid. Flicked open her hands. Orbs of ultraviolet Murk and white Brilliance coalesced in either palm. She threaded the elements into a globe of Stasis, took a deep breath. "Here goes."

A gray beam shot forward. I stood near the portal and peered through as it struck the crystoid. Mom's arms yanked forward. She cried out with surprise, but Dad held her in place.

"Gotcha," he said.

She nodded and leaned her head forward. Stasis slowly crept down the shards. Aether arced like electricity across the crystalline tines. Shimmering motes of magic burst from the crystoid, spreading like fairy dust.

"It's so much," Mom said in a strained voice. Her shoulders slumped, then stiffened. "Die, you infernal creation!"

Dad opened his mouth, probably to make a smart remark about the crystoid actually being an angelic creation, but gave me a wink and kept quiet.

Minutes ticked past. Once the outer shards were completely gray, the color rapidly expanded to the main body of the crystoid, as if Mom had breached a barrier. The intense flow of aether from it subsided. The crystal cracked.

I braced, ready to throw up a Murk barrier if it exploded.

Instead, it shattered like a vase and crumbled to dust.

"The little crystoid didn't do that," Shelton muttered.

"Probably didn't have much aether in it," Adam replied.

Mom slumped and breathed a sigh of relief. "It is done."

"Yay!" Ivy jumped up and clapped her hands. "We did it!"

One down. A hundred and twenty to go.

Chapter 15

Mom gave me a tired smile when she turned and came back through the portal. "I feel a bit weak, but I'll be ready to go after I rest."

"I'm up next," Ivy said.

Mom and Dad looked at each other. Dad turned to my sister. "All right, kiddo. You get the next one."

"I'll go tell Pixie and the others the good news," Shelton said. "I'm sure they're eager to come home."

"A splendid idea," Bella said. "We'll be back soon."

"Please thank Ann and Viola for the delicious food," Elyssa said.

Shelton tipped his hat. "Will do." He and Bella walked through the portal and stepped out of view.

"You know he only volunteered so he could eat more brownies," Adam said with a grin.

I chuckled. "Ain't that the truth."

Elyssa called her father and gave him the good news. She grinned and nodded as they spoke, but a frown drew down the corners of her mouth. She ended the call and gave me a grim look. "Four crystoids exploded over the past twenty four hours. One in Greenland, another two in separate parts of the Middle East, and one in Morocco."

"Yikes." Shelton grimaced. "Casualties?"

"Collectively, about a thousand noms." She shook her head. "My father says two of them exploded when the noms tried to remove them with construction equipment. The other two were destroyed with explosives in firefights against robots."

"Robots again?" The fact perplexed me. "Didn't we theorize the robots came through the sky portals?"

"Hmm, I see where you're going with this," Adam said. "Why would Cephus use technology like robots?"

My mind hit a wall. "It doesn't make sense."

Shelton and Bella returned and we told them the news about the exploding crystoids and the robots.

Shelton projected the map with the crystoid locations and put a slash through the ones in question. "At least that's four less we have to deal with."

Elyssa narrowed her gaze. "People died, Shelton. Show some respect."

He held up his hands defensively. "Hey, I wasn't dissing them. I'm sorry people died, but we've got to find the silver lining in all this too."

She nodded and took a deep breath. "Sorry. I just hate this."

"We all do," Bella said in a calm voice. "Let's try to get through this without more needless death."

"We've got to find the link between the robots and Cephus," Adam said.

Shelton took off his hat and scratched his head. "I'm beginning to think there might be a Science Academy angle to all this."

"Yeah," Adam said in a grim tone. "I agree."

Elyssa looked at her arcphone. "My father sent Templars to the crystoid in Atlanta. They were able to infiltrate the site and take pictures so we can open an omniarch there."

"First, I want to check something." I stepped past Mom and through the portal. At the bottom of the platform, I switched to demon vision and looked around. A large cloud of aether drifted lazily where the crystoid had been. I looked at the ground and saw weak glowing lines pulsing brighter with every passing second.

"What do you see?" Elyssa asked from behind.

"The ley lines are recovering." I felt a grin spread across my face. "We just returned magic to the great white north—or at least part of it."

Elyssa kissed me. "We're going to save the world."

I nodded. "One crystoid at a time."

We went back up the platform stairs and through the portal to give the good news.

Shelton whooped and slapped Adam on the back. "Nobody messes with Team Justin!"

"Team Justin?" Elyssa rolled her eyes.

Dad squeezed my shoulder. "Glad to be a part of the team."

Ivy pumped her fist. "Team Justin! Whoop!"

Mom and Elyssa groaned.

I clapped my hands together. "What do you say we disable the Atlanta crystoid next?"

"Mine, all mine," Ivy sang. "I'm gonna be your wrecking ball."

Shelton snorted. "You get 'em, Ivy."

Elyssa closed the portal to North Dakota and took out her phone. "Give me some space, please."

Everyone cleared the circle around the omniarch. Using the image sent by her father, she opened a new portal above the crystoid we'd visited. As with the first time opening the portal to North Dakota, it took a moment for the gateway to split open.

Since there was no platform on the other side, and a twenty-foot drop to the ground, Ivy had to stand in front of the portal. Elyssa stepped outside the silver band, and Dad braced Ivy around the waist.

"Ready, honey?" he asked.

She nodded eagerly. "Let's do it, Pops."

Ivy channeled Stasis in about half the time it took Mom and me and unleashed it on the crystoid. Like Mom, it tried to jerk her forward, but Dad kept her firmly anchored. It took Ivy far less time to encase the crystoid in Stasis. With a similar light show to the last one, it finally succumbed, shattering to pieces.

Shouts rose from somewhere on the other side of the portal.

"The soldiers must have heard it," I said. "Close the portal fast."

A group of camouflaged soldiers rushed into view. One of them looked up and gasped at the sight of Ivy standing at the edge of a gateway suspended in the air. Just as he pointed, Ivy waved and closed the portal.

She giggled. "I'll bet his friends are gonna think he's crazy."

"How do you feel?" Mom asked.

"I'm totally ready to do another." Ivy's eyes brightened. "Can I, can I, huh?"

I nodded. "If you're up for it."

"I was born up for it." She looked at Elyssa. "Do we have pictures of the other ones the Templars control?"

"Yes." Elyssa gave Mom a questioning look. "You sure she's not tired?"

"I'm not tired even an eensy weensy little bit," Ivy protested.

My sister was crazy strong when it came to channeling Brilliance—far stronger than even me. She'd obviously gained strength channeling Murk as well. I noticed she wasn't wearing a prism. "How did you channel Murk without a prism?"

"Well, I just practiced a lot." She shrugged. "I stopped using the prism because I didn't need it."

Considering how quickly she'd disabled the crystoid, I imagined all of her Seraphim powers probably outclassed mine. On the other hand, she didn't share the demonic abilities I'd inherited from Dad—at least as far as I knew.

"Cool," I said. "Let's go to the next one."

Within a couple of hours, Ivy disabled four more crystoids. As we closed the portal, she slumped. "I think I'm tired now."

Mom gathered my sister at her side. "Let's go rest."

Dad ruffled her hair and looked at me. "We'll see you tomorrow."

"Goodnight." I hugged them goodbye. "Great work, Ivy."

She managed a weary smile. "Thanks, bro."

After they left, I looked at the holographic map of the crystoids. Shelton marked out the last one and sighed. "Man, we've got our work cut out for us."

"Most of the targets are under heavy nom guard," Elyssa said. "I don't know how we'll get close enough to take pictures so we could open an omniarch portal, much less infiltrate the sites and disable them from there."

"Magic is still out of the question," Shelton said. "We can't use the omniarch to open portals unless the location is right over the aether beam from a crystoid."

"Not to mention, many of the military forces in control of the crystoids are going to be a lot tougher to penetrate than the National Guard troops they had at the Atlanta site." Elyssa pressed her lips together. "It could take us months to do this."

"In the meantime, the leyworms will weaken and possibly die." I blew out a breath. "There's got to be a faster way."

"My father wants to meet first thing in the morning," Elyssa said. "I'm sure he'll come up with something."

Adam nodded. "If he doesn't, Shelton and I will."

"Let's hope so." I drooped with exhaustion. "I'm ready for bed."

Shelton cracked a yawn. "Me too."

"At least the magic is back in Atlanta," Bella said with a bright grin.

I couldn't help but smile. "At least there's that."

Elyssa wasn't kidding about Thomas's meeting being the first thing in the morning. She woke me up at the ungodly hour of six a.m. and we had a quick breakfast in the mansion's kitchen. Since we'd disabled the crystoid in the Atlanta area, the ley lines there had recovered enough to allow us to use the omniarch to portal straight to Templar headquarters.

We stepped through the portal and into the underground complex beneath the barn. My joints, muscles, and bones ached. My body still hadn't recovered from touching the crystoid, and it didn't feel like I'd be able to do much heavy lifting if we found another meteor to disable. I hoped Ivy and Nightliss were up to the task.

Templars stood guard next to the closed conference room door. They snapped to attention when they saw us.

"Did they start without us?" I asked.

The one on the left answered. "Sir, I'm not authorized to answer that."

I looked at the one on the right. "How about you?"

He stared at the rock wall across from the door. "No, sir."

The door didn't have a handle and was typically sealed magically from the inside. "Can either of you open this door?"

"No, sir," they answered in unison.

Elyssa took out her phone. "Thank goodness the aether lines are working again."

I heard a voice answer on the other end.

"Commander, we're here," she said to her father.

The door slid open a moment later, and the sounds of a very heated discussion spilled into the corridor. I stepped inside and flinched at the number of people inside. Across the table from Thomas and Nightliss stood Victus Edison and Colin McCloud, the lycan Alpha. He and a tall, pale man glared at each other while another man in Arcane robes cast furious glances at Victus.

"Ah, Justin, good to see you again." Victus ignored the other Arcane and extended his hand to me. "I'd like you to meet my wife, Delectra." A handsome woman with long black hair and a haughty tilt to her head acknowledged me with the barest of nods. She extended her hand as a queen might to a subject. "A pleasure."

Her imperious British accent rankled me, but I forced a smile, gripped her hand, and shook it vigorously. "Nice to meet you."

Her eyes flared and for a moment, I thought she might yell at me.

Victus wrapped an arm around her waist. "We were hoping we might speak with you in private later."

"Absolutely not!" The other Arcane slipped in between them and me. "I must insist that any conversation regarding the Arcane Council take place with me present."

I was about to ask him who he was when a slap on my shoulder jolted me forward.

"Justin, lad!" McCloud appeared from behind me and gripped my hand. "Good to see you again." A Scottish brogue thickened his words. "We're having a lively political discussion." He shuddered.

"Justin Slade?" The tall pale man offered me a curt bow. "I am Komad Rashad, executor of the Red Syndicate—"

"The bloody vampires want back in," McCloud interrupted. "Just in case you didn't recognize him for what he is."

I blinked back confusion. This was the vampire head honcho? "What happened to Otto Strassman?"

"Our former leader was relieved of his position." Komad offered an unsettling smile.

I didn't need to guess what he meant by that.

"Doesn't matter who's in charge of the vamps," McCloud said. "You betrayed us once, and you'll do it again." He pounded a large fist against the table. "The vampires have no loyalty but to themselves."

"It comes as no surprise a lycan would say such a thing." Komad's calm words slithered around the accusation.

The other Arcane tugged on my shoulder, drawing my attention back to him. "Mr. Slade, my name is Evan Farnsworth and I'm also running for Arcanus Primus." He jabbed a finger toward Victus. "This man would have you believe he's the best qualified—"

"Farnsworth, I'm certain we could arrange for a civilized meeting, but now is not the time to hound Justin." Victus shook his head slowly. "I believe we are here to discuss an issue more pressing than politics."

"Nothing is more pressing than politics with you, sir," Evan shot back.

"You would do well to remain quiet," Delectra said in a calm tone.

"What stake do the vampires have in this discussion?" McCloud said before Evan could retort. "For all we know, they're behind these anti-magic attacks."

A sensuous, burning odor tickled my nose. I whipped around as Kassallandra Assad strode purposefully into the room. Her flaming locks hung across milky white shoulders bared by her low-cut glittering red dress. Sensuous lips curved into a small smile when our eyes met. She bowed. "A pleasure, Kohvaniss."

I'd hoped to permanently shelve all the Daemos social niceties, but it looked like I was back in the thick of things. *It's like I never left.* I bowed to her. "The pleasure is all mine, Maedras Kassallandra Assad."

She took my hands and kissed me on both cheeks. "House Assad stands ever ready to aid."

"Thank you, Maedras." I waved a hand around the room and introduced everyone, including those I'd just met.

Kassallandra simply nodded and said, "A pleasure," as they greeted her.

Delectra seemed none too pleased to have another woman in the room as snooty as her. I didn't know much about Victus's wife, but she certainly hadn't made a good first impression. Kassallandra and I had a history rougher than Colin McCloud's mutton chops, but after I'd saved her life from Aerianas, another crazy Daemas, she'd been the first to acknowledge me as Kohvaniss—supreme devourer of all souls. It wasn't something I'd put on a resume.

"It is good to see the Templar Clarion," Kassallandra said to Nightliss. "I had heard you took a leave of absence."

Nightliss offered her a small smile. "It is no small thing to fight a war, and harder still to recover from the toll on one's body and mind."

"Wise words indeed," Kassallandra replied. "I should enjoy a holiday as well, but fear the houses of Daemos would not afford me the leisure."

Thomas, who'd withdrawn into a corner to speak with Elyssa, finally took back the reins by knocking on the conference table. "Now that everyone is here, let's proceed." He turned to Elyssa. "You have the floor, Templar."

"Thank you, Commander." Elyssa gave everyone a moment to find seats before continuing. "We have disabled five crystoids."

McCloud grinned and slapped the table. "Bloody good work!"

"Remarkable," Komad said.

I watched his face for signs of disappointment, but his poker face revealed nothing. Delectra narrowed her eyes and looked at Victus. His shoulders stiffened, but he maintained his affable smile.

"I am pleased to hear this," Kassallandra said. "Is there a plan to quickly disable the rest?"

Elyssa's eyes paused on Delectra, and I wondered if she'd seen her reaction as well. "We're working on a way to bypass the various nom military forces that control the other crystoids. Unfortunately, it will be a slow process."

"Might I ask how you disabled the crystoids?" Victus asked.

"Channeled Stasis renders them inert," Elyssa replied.

"Ah, the third element of aether," Victus said. "The other two are Brilliance—destruction—and Murk—creation."

He apparently didn't know about Clarity.

If he was looking for a gold star from Elyssa, she wasn't handing them out. "Correct."

"How did you channel magic without aether?" Delectra asked.

141

"The crystoids emit a beam of aether." Elyssa said. "We intercepted the aether beam with an omniarch portal and used it to channel magic."

"Ingenious." Victus turned toward me. "It's no wonder you defeated Daelissa."

Nightliss's eyes went hard at the mention of her dead sister.

I wasn't quite ready to take his compliments, especially since they reeked of politics.

Evan glared at the other man. "I'm sure we can agree that Mr. Slade is quick on his feet without the brown-nosing."

Delectra turned a fierce gaze on Evan. "Perhaps you should learn to detect a genuine compliment when you hear one."

Evan pshawed. "Genuine? More like—"

"That's enough." Elyssa's steely voice quieted them. She displayed the crystoid map. "As you can see, we have a monumental task ahead of us." Next, Elyssa showed them the video footage from the ASE that went into Seraphina. The big reveal about Cephus brought a round of concerned looks.

I was going to remind her to tell them about the robot attacks, but everyone began to speak at once.

McCloud pounded a fist on the table. "We win a war, and yet Eden is once again besieged by the Seraphim." He leaned forward. "We need to end this threat once and for all."

"First, we have to disable the crystoids here," Elyssa said. "We have to ensure the health of Eden before embarking to another realm."

Victus raised a hand and spoke. "Might I ask how you propose to compromise nom security around the other crystoids without magic?"

"We're still working on it," she replied. "Omniarch portals would offer the easiest way, but without a clear picture of the crystoid from a position directly in its aether beam, we can't open portals."

"Nor can you send ASEs," Evan said. "I suppose using nom aircraft is out of the question."

"We'd likely be shot down on sight," Elyssa said. "We've also received news that some nom governments are enclosing the crystoids in concrete domes."

"A reaction to reports that several exploded?" Victus asked.

She nodded.

"I have other troubling news," Evan said. "According to some of my best researchers, the affected ley lines will be permanently damaged within a month." His mouth set in a grim line, he delivered the kicker. "Magic in Eden will be no more."

Chapter 16

Delectra didn't seem convinced by his dire prognosis. "Won't the ley lines simply refill with aether once the crystoids are gone?" She gave him a disbelieving look. "After all, a dry riverbed can still sustain a river once the water returns."

"Your analogy is not quite on point." Evan seemed to repress a smug smile and turned to Elyssa. "When the organisms in soil die, vegetation can no longer thrive. This is why enemies would salt the earth of the conquered."

"Are you saying these crystoids are like someone salted the earth?" I asked.

He nodded. "The lack of aether is killing the ley worms." He steepled his fingers. "No doubt many of you have at some point seen Altash and the smaller ley worms in El Dorado."

"Aye, I've seen them before." McCloud's grew troubled. "Are they dead?"

I shook my head. "No, we've managed to preserve them."

Evan raised an eyebrow. "Interesting. Unfortunately, the ley worms in El Dorado are but a small sample of the creatures that keep the magical ecosystem in Eden healthy. The vast majority are, no doubt, dying like fish out of water."

His warning sounded much like Meghan's theory. "You think this aetherial annihilation will kill the earth dragons within a month?" I asked.

He nodded. "We discovered several smaller ley worms in Thunder Rock. One of them appeared dead. The other two were alive, but slumbering."

"They should recover now that the Atlanta crystoid is gone," I said.

"There are ley worms in other realms," Delectra said. "Even if we lose many of the ones here, I'm certain we could import others."

"They're sentient creatures," Elyssa said. "I doubt they'll move here at our request."

"Let's call them what they really are," I said. "They're earth dragons, and they're far older and probably far smarter than anyone here."

Even Kassallandra didn't argue that point.

Thomas broke his silence. "The reason I called you here today is to gain cooperation for a common cause."

"It would seem to be more of an Arcane problem," Komad said. "The vampires have no stake in this."

McCloud made a spitting sound. "Spoken like a true vampire. The lycans don't use magic, but we're ready to assist in any way we can."

"As are the Daemos," Kassallandra said.

Victus tossed his hat into the ring before Evan could. "Science Academy and the Arcane Council are, of course, committed to doing whatever it takes to solve the crisis."

"Despite my disagreements with Victus over who should lead the Arcane Council, I agree with him there," Evan said. "But, I'd like to point out why the vampires have a major stake in this fight."

Komad regarded him coolly. "My interest is piqued, Mr. Farnsworth."

Evan leaned his elbows on the conference table. "When Daelissa was the Templar Divinity, she used her powers to 'bless'"—he wiggled his fingers like air quotes—"Templars. During the original reign of the Seraphim, they also used a similar method to create the original vampires." He looked at Nightliss. "As the Clarion, you now grant Templars and others the blessings of supernatural strength and longevity."

She nodded. "I plant a seed of power within a person to enhance that which they already possess."

"All very interesting," Komad said, "but vampires do not use magic."

"You don't actively use it, but at your very core is an ancient enchantment." Evan nodded toward Elyssa. "The same goes for the Templars. Picture it like concentrated magic at the core of your supernatural identity."

145

Delectra's eyes widened. "An enchantment will eventually expire if there is no aether to sustain it."

"Precisely." Evan gave that a moment to sink in. "Without magic, vampires will either die or revert to normal humans and Templars will lose their supernatural strength and other gifts."

"What about lycans?" McCloud said.

Evan shrugged. "Lycans are a natural magical product of Eden. It's possible you'd lose your ability to shapeshift." He turned to Kassallandra. "I don't know much about Daemos, but I'm certain your shifting and feeding abilities would be affected as well. Without magic, we would lose our connection to the other realms permanently." He waggled a hand in a so-so manner. "On the bright side, there would be no more demon possessions."

Kassallandra's lips peeled back from her teeth with distaste. "Mr. Farnsworth has made it quite clear that the Overworld as a whole must invest in a solution. Otherwise, we supernaturals will cease to exist and noms will rule Eden."

Her statement cast a pall over the room.

Komad's forehead furrowed—the first sign of distress he'd shown. For a long moment, he stared at the table, then finally spoke. "The Red Syndicate stands ready to serve."

No one cheered.

Though we still didn't have a plan, at least we had everyone on board. Despite converting the vampires to the cause, I knew better than to celebrate. As I turned back toward Elyssa, I caught a meaningful look from Evan. He gave me a brief nod. Victus and Delectra caught it too. Evan had just proven he could be an asset. So far, Victus hadn't done much except try to sell me snake oil.

Though I was still a baby by Overworld age standards, some people regarded me as a hero. If I endorsed someone for a particular office, they would almost certainly get the votes they needed. On the other hand, if I publicly announced that I really liked Komad, his people would probably kill him. The vampires bore me all the ill will of a conquered nation. I might have won the favor of young vampires compelled into fighting, but those in power might still despise Komad's decision to ally with me, no matter the cause.

146

I thought back to an earlier discussion about the vampires and decided now was a good time to find out. "Are the ancients back in control of the Red Syndicate?"

Komad shook his head. "They have no interest in the affairs of modern vampires. The only being they revered was Daelissa, for she gave them their powers."

"The goddess of the ancient vampires is dead," McCloud said, a troubled look on his face. "Perhaps they will be more dangerous now than ever."

Komad didn't offer an opinion. Instead, he turned to me. "As I said, the Red Syndicate will join in your cause."

"A wise decision," Kassallandra finally said, since no one else offered encouragement. She turned to Elyssa. "How should we proceed?"

"Am I right to assume your organizations have contacts within nom governments?" Elyssa asked.

"Aye, but not many," McCloud said. He nodded toward Komad. "I know for a fact the vampires have plenty."

"I'll be more than happy to use our contacts," Victus said quickly.

"As will I," Evan added.

I looked at Kassallandra and raised an eyebrow. "My father told me the Daemos do as well."

She seemed reluctant to answer, but finally relented. "Yes, but I will have to speak with the other house heads for a better assessment."

"We might be able to use those contacts to get images of the crystoids so we can open portals." Elyssa waved a hand toward the holographic map. "I can give everyone a list of the nations involved, then meet again tomorrow to discuss our potential reach."

Komad shook his head. "That doesn't give me much time."

"Agreed," Kassallandra said. "It could take several days to find the information."

"Share with the others in your organizations what we've learned here today." Elyssa gave them both stern looks. "If we don't act fast, magic in Eden is finished."

I pounded a fist on the table. "Aetherial annihilation."

My melodramatic demonstration elicited hesitant nods from Kassallandra and Komad.

"I will do what I can," Kassallandra said.

Komad sighed. "As will I."

"Let's adjourn until ten tomorrow morning," Elyssa said. "Send me whatever images or information you can in the meantime. If any of it is actionable, we'll get right on it."

The meeting broke up and I noticed Victus and Evan dithering nearby, casting furtive glances at me. They obviously wanted a word.

"Might I speak to you in private?" Kassallandra was never one to beat around the bush when she wanted something.

"Sure." I motioned toward the hallway.

"I'd also like a moment when you're done," Victus said.

"Me too," Evan added.

McCloud snorted, obviously finding the whole thing amusing. He walked around the table and slapped me on the back. "Being important is quite the bother, eh?"

I smiled and shrugged. "Thanks for coming, McCloud."

"Aye, my pleasure." He tipped his head at the others and left.

I went into the hallway with Kassallandra and walked to an adjacent conference room. Once inside, I closed the door. "How can I help you?"

"Why hasn't your father taken a more active role in house politics?" she asked bluntly.

I sensed her frustration and saw it plain on her face. "I think he's happy letting you take over. Wasn't that what you wanted?"

She frowned. "If we had married, it was to be a joint effort."

"That's not how I remember it." I pressed on without waiting for a reply. "You threatened to throw your support to Daelissa if he didn't marry you. By combining the two most powerful houses of Daemos, you planned to rule them all." I held out my hands in a *what gives?* gesture. "Isn't that what you wanted?"

Kassallandra's frown deepened, marring her beautiful face. Finally, she huffed. "Yes, it is precisely what I wanted, but now that I have it, I must admit it's very difficult controlling everything on my own. Every house has a mind of its own, and the house heads have insufferable egos I must deal with."

I tried not to laugh, really I did, but it burst out. "Coming from you, that's a rather ironic statement."

"Do not mock me," she hissed.

I stiffened. "I'm calling it like I see it, Kassallandra. As the noms say, be careful what you wish for—you just might get it."

She threw up her hands. "I would kill Yuuki Wakahisa with a blunt object if her murder brought me no consequence." Her red eyes blazed. "And Godric Salomon would be next."

"I wouldn't blame you one bit if you did." I held up a hand. "That's not permission from the Kohvaniss to start killing other Daemos leaders just because you hate them."

Kassallandra looked down, for once appearing almost humble. "Please speak with your father about helping me."

I almost felt sorry for her. Almost. "This is what you've always wanted. I'm certain my father is happy to let you lead and most likely won't interfere unless you really mess up." I shrugged. "I'll tell him, but no promises."

She nodded. "It is all I ask."

There was nothing more to say, so I slid open the door and walked outside.

Evan, Victus, and Delectra waited for me in the corridor. I repressed a heartfelt sigh. "Next."

Victus motioned toward the room. "You may go first, Farnsworth."

"No, you go first," the other man said.

"Really, now, I insist." Victus put a hand on the other man's back.

"Don't touch me!"

I suspected the two would argue all day about it, so I pointed to Evan. "Come inside, please."

Kassallandra made her way through the group, but not before giving me a slightly smug look. I suspected she enjoyed seeing my plight.

Evan scowled, but went inside the room. I followed him and closed the door behind me. "Speak." I was running out of patience.

"You can't recommend Victus for Arcanus Primus," he said bluntly. "The man is a scientist first, and an Arcane second. He'll surely use the position to undermine the Arcane Council."

"Who says I'm going to recommend him?" I said.

149

He looked relieved. "Then you realize that I offer the most for the position?"

I put my hands on the back of a chair and leaned on it. "What I see is that the Arcanes need to choose their leader for themselves. I don't want to recommend anyone."

His mouth dropped open a fraction. "But your word could easily decide the next primus."

"Yes, and I don't think it's up to me to decide." I released the chair and folded my arms. "If it were up to me, I'd go with someone I know, like Captain Takei of the Blue Cloaks." That man had shown he knew how to lead, and he'd been a vital asset in the war against Daelissa.

He nodded vigorously. "He would be an ideal choice. Unfortunately, when I spoke to him, he showed no interest in politics."

"Well, the people most qualified to lead are rarely the ones elected." I shrugged. "I think it's best to leave it up to the Arcanes."

"In that case, Victus will likely win." His shoulders slumped. "I fear for the future if that man gains more political power."

"Why do you feel that way?"

"There are rumors that he's conducting genetic splicing experiments between humans and animals."

It sounded like something out of a mad scientist movie—precisely what Science Academy was all about. "Is he using actual humans, or just human DNA?"

"Well, I'm not well versed in science, so I can't say for sure." Evan tapped his chin as if trying to jog loose a bit of scientific fact. "Are you familiar with the tragon?"

I snorted. "Probably a little more familiar than most, yes." Part Tyrannosaurus rex, and part dragon, the monstrous creature had helped me in a couple of pivotal battles, though not willingly. I suspected he'd much rather have eaten me than served as my reptilian sidekick.

"Victus created him during his schooling at Science Academy."

My arms dropped to my sides. "He's the one who made that monster?"

"My sources at Science Academy say the tragon was supposed to fight in the Grand Melee, but since it's not a golem or a robot, it wasn't allowed." He jabbed a finger toward the door. "That man is busy creating more such monstrosities."

"You have proof?"

He shook his head. "No, but I trust my sources."

That led me to another question. "Is it illegal to create monsters?"

Evan paused. "If it's not, it should be."

I couldn't argue with him there. Unfortunately, I wasn't the one in charge of Overworld rules. "Do you have any other reasons why you think Victus would be a danger if he takes power?"

"Perhaps I should put you in touch with my people at Science Academy. They went to school with the man. They know him much better than I do." His eyes shone with sincerity. "I trust their word and think it would be a horrible mistake to allow Victus to gain power."

"Why isn't his wife running for the position? Isn't she an Arcane?"

Evan's lips peeled back. "She doesn't have the personality to win. Delectra has always relied on her last name to open doors for her."

My eyebrows pinched. "I didn't realize Edison was such a good name to have."

Evan nodded. "If you're a scientist, having a name like Edison, Einstein, and so on will open a lot of doors in that community." He crossed his arms. "In the Arcane world, Delectra's maiden name is powerful."

I waited for an answer, but he was really milking the suspense. "What's her last name?"

"Her full name is Delectra Moore." He let that sink in. "She is a descendant of the very founder of the Arcane Council itself, Ezzek Moore."

Chapter 17

I couldn't believe my ears. "Ezzek Moore had children?"

Evan nodded. "He had many children over his long lifespan."

I rocked back on my feet. "Are you certain?" The first Arcane had lived thousands of years and gone by many names—Moses, Ezzek Moore, and finally Jeremiah Conroy. I'd known him only a fraction of his lengthy time on earth before Daelissa killed him. He'd never mentioned children to me, but it made sense that anyone with such a long life conceivably had whole flocks of rug rats.

"He had twenty-three children we know of over the course of a century—most by different women." A wondering look came over Evan's face. "For all we know, he had many more than that."

"I didn't know Ezzek very well, but I suppose it makes sense he probably has descendants who are alive today." An image of Daelissa burning him to death flashed into my head and I shivered. "Does she have Ezzek's gift for magic?"

He waggled his hand. "I believe so. She used to be a different person—a world class broom racer, if you can believe it. Then her entire family was murdered, and it turned her into the ice queen you met today."

I grimaced. "Yeah, I suppose I could see how that might affect someone." I paced a few steps toward the door. "Unless you have anything else to add, I think we're done here."

"I'll give you the contact information for my people at Science Academy so you can verify the unsettling truth about Victus," Evan said. "Please talk to them when you get a chance."

"In case you hadn't noticed, we're in the middle of a crisis." I put my hand on the door. "I'll talk with them when I have a chance."

"That's all I ask," he said, an almost verbatim repeat of Kassallandra's last words to me.

I didn't remind him that he'd asked for a lot more and slid open the door. Evan narrowed his eyes at Victus and Delectra, then left.

The power couple entered the room, and I closed the door. Victus must have told his wife to tone back the cold bitch look because she wore a plastic smile.

I cut to the chase. "If you're here looking for an endorsement for Arcanus Primus, you've come to the wrong place. I turned down Evan, and I'll turn you down too."

Victus shook his head. "I suspected Farnsworth would badger you about that." He gave me a helpless look. "I must admit I'm pleased to hear you've decided not to interfere in Arcane politics."

I regarded Delectra. "I hear you're related to Ezzek Moore."

Her fake smirk vanished, replaced by a proud, but genuine smile. "I am six generations removed. I also have the blood of Alexander Tiberius in my veins." As she spoke, I smelled the faintest hints of brimstone about her. I hadn't noticed it earlier with Kassallandra around.

"Do you have dealings with demons?" I asked.

Her eyes flared. "That is none of your concern."

"It's fine, dear." Victus put a hand on her arm. "Yes, Justin, we have. Ever since you proved that Daemos aren't evil just because of their demonic heritage, we recently tried opening a dialogue with the powers that be in Haedaemos."

His outright admission caught me off guard. "That's extremely dangerous."

"But long overdue, don't you agree?" His voice sounded so reasonable, it was almost as if we were talking about our favorite flavor of donuts. "Demons have visited our realm frequently, but we've never reached out to them."

A pshaw escaped my lips. "I disagree. Plenty of people have reached out to demons. They usually end up possessed."

"I meant in the political sense." Victus lifted a hand as if he wanted to place it on my shoulder, but seemed to reconsider. "Your father is the son of Baal, the king of the demons. I wanted to talk with you about arranging a meeting with him."

"My father or Baal?"

"Both, if possible."

I couldn't tell if he was being serious, or if this was all some ruse to keep me from asking why his wife reeked of demons. "Baal doesn't speak with my father, much less mortals. I can't just request a business meeting."

"Any effort would be appreciated," Victus said.

I tapped a finger on my chin. "Let's get back to why you want to talk to me. I know it's not about demons."

"It would seem our original reason is a moot point since you refuse to endorse anyone." Victus shrugged. "So long as you adhere to that decision, I have no concerns."

He looked very secure at that moment, so I decided to spring a trap on him. "How long did it take you to create the tragon?"

Two pairs of eyes flared in response to that question. *Gotcha.*

Victus's surprise quickly morphed to a proud smile. "Well, I won't ask how you discovered my little—or should I say big?—secret, but yes, I love dinosaurs and always dreamed of reviving them from the dead. Unfortunately, I needed living DNA as well, so I borrowed some from a ley worm."

My smugness quickly faded in light of his admission. Victus was slick. The moment I thought I'd pinned him with something, he turned it around as a point of pride. "How did you convince the ley worm to part with its DNA?"

"I found it in one of the tunnels beneath Thunder Rock several years ago."

I looked at him like he was crazy. "You went to Thunder Rock while it was still infested with husks?" The infantile creatures were all that remained of Seraphim caught in the backlash when the Grand Nexus went nuclear thousands of years ago. Though we'd found a way to revive most of the husked Seraphim, my skin still crawled when I thought about the light-sucking little monsters.

"It was foolish, I know, but I was young and eager to prove myself." He squeezed Delectra's hand. "My lovely wife discovered a way to

154

temporarily mask us from the presence of the husks and the shadow people."

"Do you know how useful something like that could have been during the war?" I'd nearly died countless times.

"My apologies, but by the time the war was in the open, your people had already figured out a way to contain the husks." He pulled off a very sincere look of regret. "I assure you, we did our part during the war."

There had been so many people involved in the fight against Daelissa, I had no way of ascertaining the truth behind his statement—at least not without asking around. Once again, he'd given me a very reasonable explanation that left me no room to blame him. The man clearly outclassed me as a politician, but quite frankly, I didn't give a damn.

"Since I've refused to endorse anyone, I suppose there's nothing else to talk about."

He nodded. "I want to assure you that Science Academy will do everything in its power to solve the crystoid problem, Justin."

"I will use all my Arcane intellect to assist my husband," Delectra said. "Together, nothing can stand in our way."

I caught a small wince from Victus, but he put on a convincing smile. "My wife is, as always, supremely confident in our abilities."

I nodded. "I can admire that." I just wondered how many nothings stood in the way of what she really wanted. As they turned to leave, I remembered that the subject of robot attacks hadn't been discussed at the earlier meeting. "I do have one thing you could help with right now."

Victus turned and raised an eyebrow. "Of course."

"We were attacked by three robots at the crystoid in North Dakota."

The other man's eyes twitched. "Robots?"

I nodded. "All that remains of them are a couple of metal feet."

"What happened to the rest of the robots' bodies?" Delectra asked.

I showed them my teeth. "I disintegrated them with my Seraphim powers." My boast left out the crucial detail of me inadvertently touching the crystoid, but they didn't need to know that.

Delectra backed up a step. "I see."

"I can analyze the remains and try to identify the source, if that's what you'd like," Victus said.

I nodded. "I would. Just ask Thomas and he'll give them to you."

The other man flashed a confident smile. "I'm glad to be of service."

After they left, I sat in a chair took a few minutes to collect myself. I felt stressed out and tired from getting up so early. It felt good not to think about anything, even if only for a short time.

After I had my moment, I left the room and ran into Leia, Elyssa's mother in the hallway.

She smiled and gave me a quick hug. "You look as though you haven't slept much."

"Thanks to this early morning meeting." I sighed. "Sleeping really isn't the problem. It's the recovery from all the beatings."

"Yes, Thomas told me about your encounter with the crystoid." She motioned toward the conference room. "I assume they're still inside."

"Probably." The door wasn't shut all the way, so I slid it open for her.

Leia walked in and hugged her daughter. "I see you're back in the swing of things." She turned to Nightliss. "We are very happy to have you back."

Elyssa sighed. "I feel like I went from relaxing to swimming with the sharks."

"I do not care for Victus or his wife," Nightliss said. "There is something unpleasant about them."

"Agreed," I said.

"I dislike their political posturing, but we need them." Elyssa shook her head. "This is a global effort."

"Unfortunately, there's not much we can do without solid intel," Thomas said. He turned to me. "I authorized Victus to take the robot remains as you requested. I assume he and Evan asked for endorsements?"

"Yeah." I crossed my arms and leaned against the wall. "I told them I'm not handing out political favors."

"I'm certain they won't be the last ones to ask." Thomas turned off the holographic map. "I've been asked to intervene as well." He shook his head. "As head of a neutral entity like the Templars, I can't play favorites."

"What did Kassallandra want?" Elyssa asked.

I chuckled. "The burden of leadership is weighing heavy on her shoulders. I almost pity her."

"She got what she wanted," Elyssa said with a satisfied smirk.

"If I had to deal with Yuuki Wakahisa or Godric Salomon one more time..." I shuddered.

Thomas put a hand on my shoulder. "Let's hope she can band them together for this new challenge." He took his wife's hand and headed for the door. "I'll let you know when we have actionable intel."

"What would you have me do in the meantime?" Nightliss asked him.

"Would you go to the barracks and visit them?" Thomas said. "We also have over a hundred new recruits who need to be blessed."

Her eyes widened. "Goodness, so many?"

"We're still recovering from all the losses from the war," Leia said. "Phoebe has been traveling and recruiting candidates."

"Have you heard from her since the magic outage?" Elyssa asked.

Leia nodded. "She's fine. Goodness knows she's survived worse."

Elyssa's sister, Phoebe, had once thought her parents had betrayed her and her brothers, leaving them to die during a battle with vampires. Thankfully, she'd seen the light and rejoined her family.

Nightliss turned to me. "It appears I'll be very busy blessing new Templars."

"Don't overdo it," I said. "We'll need you to conserve your strength if we get intel on more crystoids."

"Ivy seems able to handle many on her own," the Darkling replied. "But I will be ready to assist if needed."

"We'll keep everyone apprised," Thomas said. He led Leia out of the room.

Elyssa rested her head on my shoulder. "Let's get something to eat."

"I'm game." I looked at Nightliss. "Want to join us?"

She nodded. "That would be nice."

My stomach rumbled "Where to?"

"I was thinking the mess hall," Elyssa said.

I groaned. "I was hoping for something better."

"I want to stay close in case solid information comes in." She kissed my cheek. "Besides, you love the grub they serve here."

The food was actually fine, but the atmosphere felt a bit too much like a school cafeteria. "I hope they're serving square pizza and burnt French fries."

She giggled. "Reminds me of our school days."

I snorted. "Yup."

We made our way up to the mess hall and were rewarded with beef stew and a hearty side of vegetables.

"You still haven't told me about your journey back here," I told Nightliss.

She prodded a piece of broccoli, but hadn't eaten more than a bite since we sat down. "A crystoid hit the southern coast near the town I was in. Many people died from the shockwave, and lawlessness took hold." Her lower lip trembled. "The men thought the women would be easy prey, but I quickly showed them otherwise." Her eyes grew hard as jade. "Suffice it to say they will never trouble another person again."

Elyssa grimaced. "You killed them?"

Nightliss nodded. "Those were the ones I granted mercy. To the worst offenders, I made them eunuchs."

"Alrighty, then," I said. "Um, maybe we can save this for a time I'm not eating."

"I am sorry," the Darkling said. "I went south, found transport to Sri Lanka, and took an Obsidian Arch from there. The journey was long, but in the end, I made it." She stood up and took her tray in hand. "I apologize, Justin. I am not very good company at the moment."

I tried to stop her, but she backed away. "Nightliss, I understand. You remember the conversation we had after the war?"

She nodded.

"I felt the same way." I bit the inside of my lip. "You're not the only one who ran away."

Her eyes softened and she sat back down. "Shelton said you and Elyssa went on vacation."

"That's the euphemistic term for it." I felt Elyssa's hand tighten on mine. "Look, neither you nor I want to fight another war. This crystoid incident has been foisted on us and we really don't have a choice." I pinched the bridge of my nose and sighed. "The truth is, if I hadn't run away, I would have gone with Ketiss and we probably would've defeated Cephus already."

A tear trickled down Nightliss's cheek. "We absconded our duties, Justin, and the price for peace has doubled in the meantime."

"Neither of you absconded," Elyssa said. "Nobody could have predicted this."

"You're right," Nightliss said. "There is no choice but to move forward. Thank you for lunch." She flashed a sad smile and left.

I ran a hand through my hair. "I don't know if I feel better or worse."

Before Elyssa could answer, her phone buzzed. She flicked on the screen and read a message. "Looks like we have a lead."

I took her phone and scrolled down to the image of a crystoid. "I know what I'll be doing after lunch." The text above the picture said, *Impact zone Changrim, North Korea.*

Elyssa made a face. "Talk about a place I wouldn't want to visit."

"Well, with any luck we won't have to if this picture is reliable." I looked for the message sender, but it was blank. "Any idea where it came from?"

She shrugged. "I've been getting strange glitches since we have to rely on the nom cell towers." She put away her phone and rested her chin on my shoulder. "How are you feeling?"

"Much better." My muscles still felt sore, but with the return of aether to the Atlanta area, I actually felt normal again. "I just need to feed my Seraphim side, and I'm good to go."

Elyssa polished off her broccoli like a good girl. "Then let's pay the feeders a visit."

We took the levitator up to ground level and walked outside the barn toward an ancient stone church. The upper level looked newer than the rest of the building because it had been recently reconstructed. After Thomas split his legion from Synod controlled forces, they'd tried to assassinate him and blown up part of the church in the process.

Once used as a place to receive blessings from the Daelissa, aka the Templar Divinity, it was now where the Templars housed noms who volunteered other services such as feeding Seraphim. Katie, Ash, and Nyte, Elyssa's and my former high school friends, had tapped into older veterans and people with medical issues to form our volunteer corps. Templar healers provided health care unavailable to most noms, and people who'd abandoned hope once again felt healthy and valuable.

We'd moved some of the feeders to Atlanta, though many of them lived in La Casona, a pocket dimension located in Bogota, Colombia. Since most of the revived Seraphim had returned to Seraphina with Ketiss and the Tarissan Legion, there wasn't much call for their services these days.

"I wonder how Ash, Nyte, and Katie are doing in La Casona," I said.

Elyssa bit her lower lip. "I thought of them yesterday, but we've been so busy I haven't had a chance to reach out to them."

"Colombia should be a priority," I said.

"It will be if we get good intel." Elyssa tugged open the door to the church and we went inside.

An older gentleman with a scraggly beard met us inside the foyer. "It's a real pleasure to see you again, Justin."

It took a moment, but I recognized him. During our efforts to revive husked Seraphim, he was one of several nom volunteers who'd nursed the infants back to adulthood. "Abe, how've you been?"

"Mighty fine." He opened the doors to the former sanctuary, now a large open room with a few temporary partitions so Seraphim could feed in private. "We haven't seen much action since the war ended and all the Darklings left."

"Well, at least I won't have to wait in line."

He chuckled. "It'll be the other way around." Abe's smile faded. "I know you're probably busy, but while you're here, I'd like to talk to you about something."

I nodded. "Sure."

"A lot of feeder volunteers really enjoy this line of…work, I guess you'd call it." He shrugged. "If you want the gospel truth, I reckon a lot of the folks got addicted to feeding the angels. For some, I think it was like a drug—made them feel good."

Elyssa grimaced. "And now they can't get their fix?"

He nodded. "Some folks went looking for vampires, felycans, or any kind of super that needs to feed off humans. Most of 'em came back, real unsatisfied with what they found. The only ones who seemed happy were the ones who went to feed the demon spawn."

"I hope they weren't turned into sex slaves," I said. "There are unscrupulous Daemos who take advantage of noms."

"Well, the ones who stuck with the Daemos were the younger folks with a bit more steam in the engine, if you know what I mean." He winked. "While I'm being honest, I'll tell you that I miss feeding the angels about as much as the others, but not because I'm addicted."

Elyssa put a hand on his upper arm. "It gave you a sense of purpose, didn't it?"

Abe looked down, eyes sad. "Yep."

"What about joining the Templars?" I suggested. "I don't know how to do the blessing thing, but my mother could probably figure it out."

He shook his head. "Others might feel different, but I fought in a regular old human war. It was brutal, bloody, and devastating. I lost friends—hell, I nearly lost my sanity. It wasn't until your people recruited me from a veterans home that I felt like I was worth a damn again."

Elyssa put a hand on his arm. "You're always worth a damn to us, Abe. If there's anything we can do to improve things, we'll do it."

I glimpsed movement and saw people gathering at a door in the front of the sanctuary, many of them regarding me with delight. "How many feeders are there?"

Abe turned his gaze toward the crowd. "Well, just so you know, we gussied up our titles, so now we're called caregivers."

"I like that name," Elyssa said.

He looked up and tapped his chin. "At last count, probably two thousand or more spread across the world. I could contact Katie and ask her."

Katie had once been my crush. If not for bad timing on her part, she'd probably be just a not-so-fond memory of my days in high school. Instead, she'd grown from a whiney brat into a somewhat disciplined Templar. "Is she running things well?" I asked.

"Well, I got a newsletter from her last month." Abe snorted. "I think she might be getting bored too."

"Did any caregivers go with the Darklings back to Seraphina?" Elyssa asked.

Abe shook his head. "We were told to stay here for our own safety since Ketiss was gonna lead his folks into battle. Commander Borathen said he didn't think it would take Ketiss long to free Tarissa from Cephus, but seeing as how we ain't heard much for three months, I'd place bets that something didn't go according to plan."

"I assume you know about the crystoids," Elyssa said.

"You mean them crystal meteors?" he said. "We've taken to calling them crasteroids around here."

I gave Elyssa a smug smile. "See? I do come up with good names."

Abe chuckled. "Sorry to disagree, Justin, but crystoid sounds a heck of a lot better to me."

Elyssa smiled wanly but didn't seem to be in a joking mood. "We believe Cephus is the one who attacked us. Once we've gotten through this crisis, we're invading Tarissa with everything we have. That includes the caregivers."

A cheer arose from the gathering crowd at the door.

Abe grinned. "I reckon we'll be more than happy to invade with you so long as we don't have to fight." He turned toward his comrades. "Ain't that right?"

Whoops and shouts of encouragement met his statement.

"Well, with that settled," I said, "I'd like to feed."

The others stampeded toward me, and Abe shouted to slow them down. "I'd say we draw straws, but there ain't enough straws to handle this many people," he said.

"I have a number between one and a hundred," Elyssa said. "Closest one gets to feed Justin."

The number turned out to be three, and the winner was a curvy young woman who jumped up and down with glee when she won the Justin lottery. I ended up feeding from her and two others before I felt sated. By the time we left, I felt ready to take on the world.

"Let's do this!" I skipped across the yard toward the barn.

Elyssa grabbed my hand and skipped with me. "You're crazy, but I love you."

"I'm just plain crazy 'bout you, girl." I stopped and kissed her long and hard. "Man, I feel great!"

"Someone had too much sugary soul essence." She giggled. "Let's go conquer North Korea, babe."

"I'm on it."

A stoic Templar in the garage beneath the barn arranged for a portal back to the Grotto. We stepped through it and closed the omniarch gateway behind us. Shelton, Bella, and Adam stood before of the world map at the front of the control room, comparing it to the holographic map of the crystoid impact sites.

I shouted a greeting across the huge room. "Howdy, y'all!"

"Yo!' Shelton waved back. "C'mere."

"Hang on, gonna kill a crystoid," I yelled back.

"Gotcha." Shelton headed over, a confused look on his face. "You sure look chipper for some reason."

"He just fed," Elyssa explained. "We got a picture of a crystoid, so he's going to take it out."

"You'll need to anchor me when I channel," I told Elyssa.

"Just let me know when you're ready," she said, and waited outside the silver band around the omniarch so I could open the portal.

Using the image from Elyssa's arcphone, I willed the omniarch to open a portal at the crystoid in North Korea. The air shimmered and split, revealing a massive glowing crystoid on the other side. Something flashed through the gateway and wrapped around my waist. Before I could shout in alarm, it yanked me through.

Chapter 18

My hands and knees met unforgiving rocks at the edge of the impact crater. I identified what had pulled me through the portal—a thin steel cable with a weight on the end. A shiny black robot stood on the other end of the cable. It jerked it once more before I could gain solid footing.

I tumbled into the impact crater and rolled within inches of the shards. "You're gonna be sorry if I touch this thing," I shouted. I rolled to my feet and yanked the cable, but didn't catch the big fish at the other end as the slack end slid into the crater with me.

These damned robots are a real nuisance!

"Justin!"

I turned toward Elyssa's voice and saw her face for only an instant. A flatbed trailer with a sparkling gray wall raced in front of the crater, blocking my view. Elyssa's shouts abruptly stopped and I didn't have to ask why. The wall on the back of the trailer looked like diamond fiber, magic immune, and apparently a great way to block the aether beam from the crystoid. The wall toppled toward me.

The crater was a death trap, and the diamond fiber wall was the lid.

I leapt out of the pit and rolled away just as the wall crashed into place. A quick glance told me it was a thick steel slab with a coating of diamond fiber. Even with my super strength, I'd have a hell of a time lifting that thing.

Shouts echoed in the air. Soldiers garbed in dark green uniforms and the sort of warm furry hats Russians favored emerged from behind boulders, guns waving. These men were no Russians. The big red stars on their uniforms left no doubt that they were North Korean soldiers.

Without the aether beam to supply me, I couldn't magic my way out of this, and there were too many soldiers to fight even with my supernatural strength. *Why the hell didn't I put on Nightingale armor?* This quickie project had just turned into a longie. I held up my hands and looked for an escape route. In addition to the encroaching soldiers, I spotted several snipers perched on boulders. I might be super resilient, but my skin wasn't bulletproof.

It didn't take a genius to realize this crystoid had been a setup.

First, a robot was ready to lasso whoever opened the portal. Second, they had a giant steel wall coated with diamond fiber. Third, the soldiers and snipers were perfectly positioned to shanghai me.

Although it was night here, several massive glowing balls floating above illuminated the area like the sun. At first I thought they were the magical ones, but dark silhouettes barely visible through the glare revealed large blimps—airships.

I tried to channel Murk just in case there was enough aether diverted by the diamond fiber and into the air, but the barest flicker of ultraviolet vanished the moment it was born.

Meanwhile, the soldiers shouted at me in their language. Of course I couldn't understand a word. I decided to remain absolutely still in case one of them had an itchy trigger finger. Admittedly, I also thought the mastermind behind this trap might make an appearance. If Cephus himself stepped from behind a rock, I wouldn't be surprised.

Instead, a man with several medals weighing down his uniform stepped forward. "You get on knees!"

I did as asked. "How did you know I was coming?"

"You shut mouth." He took out two glittering strands of diamond fiber and gave it to another solider.

A ball of ice formed in my stomach. If these people secured me with diamond fiber, I'd never escape. My heart clawed frantically at my chest. Maximus, a rogue vampire, had kept me tied to a table for days while he fed on my blood. If the North Koreans had even an inkling of my supernatural abilities, they'd no doubt dissect me like a lab rat or brainwash me into becoming their country mascot.

Holy hell, I'm freaking out.

The soldier marched forward with the diamond fiber.

165

Heart slamming against my chest, I zoned in on the leader. Knowing what little I did about this country, I doubted they'd let me escape even if I took this guy hostage. At best, he'd be a diversion. On the other hand, there were so many guns pointing toward me from the circle of soldiers, they were more likely to kill each other if they started firing.

I waited for the soldier to reach me, then held out my hands.

He reached the filament toward my wrists.

I burst forward, slamming my shoulder into him. He flew backward, crashing into his leader and the soldiers behind him. Before anyone could put a bullet in my head, I rushed through the gap. Shots echoed. Bullets whined and pinged off rocks all around me. Despite the tall boulders nearby, the snipers on the cliff probably had a clear shot. Even if they didn't, they'd pin me down and the soldiers would recapture me.

Rough terrain and loose stone did their best to trip me. I crested a ridge and prayed I didn't find a sheer drop off on the other side. Fortune favored me with a steep wooded slope. Something slammed into my right hamstring. I flew forward and tumbled down the incline. Grasping desperately, I caught a sapling and stopped my fall. Fire blossomed in my leg. I felt a small hole in the back of my jeans and pulled back blood-covered fingers.

I'm lucky it was just my leg they hit.

The wound hurt like a bitch, but I was able to stand. Soldiers appeared at the crest and opened fire. I dodged behind a tree. Bark and dirt exploded from the impact of hundreds of bullets.

There wasn't much underbrush to use as concealment, so the moment I ran, the soldiers would see me. I waited until the gunfire stopped, and the sounds of marching boots perked my ears. I didn't need to peek around the tree to know they were on their way toward my position. I lined up my retreat vector with another large tree and ran. Pain exploded in my leg, but I refused to slow. My leg, however, had other ideas and dragged when I ran.

Gunfire shattered the air. A bullet grazed the side of my shoe. Another scorched the skin on my shoulder. I ducked behind the target tree and, without pausing, turned straight downhill, hoping the tree would grant me protection for a few more seconds. I finally reached a copse and dashed through a narrow opening between trunks. A hail of bullets peppered my newest refuge. Spasms clenched my right hamstring. Limping on my stiff leg, I continued forward.

The light from the airships flickered through the trees like a pursuing UFO, casting strange shadows and playing tricks on my eyes. I switched on my demon night vision, but the glare from the overhead lamps blinded me. I switched back to normal vision and nearly tripped as my leg locked up again.

"C'mon and heal already." I pressed a finger to the bullet wound and winced. "It's not even magic damage."

I continued forward for what felt like an eternity until I reached the bottom of the mountain slope. The rattling steel of heavy vehicles told me it was too soon to celebrate. I spotted a tank patrolling the forest perimeter. A man with binoculars protruded from a hatch in the top of the turret. In the distance, a jeep with a mounted machine gun drove back and forth.

They had me penned in tight.

A wide, muddy field outside the forest offered no concealment and would make me an easy target. Troop transport trucks stopped on a road several hundred yards away, and more soldiers piled out. The rustling sounds of pursuing troops served a stressful reminder that I couldn't dilly-dally here all night.

A thrumming noise sounded overhead. I looked up at the silhouette of another airship just before the massive globe on its underbelly flickered on. *These people don't play around.*

I heard more armored vehicles to my left, and imagined there were more somewhere to my right. I couldn't go forward or backward, and unless I learned how to dig like a troll, I couldn't go down. That left only one way to go, and it wasn't diagonally.

Drawing upon my demon side, I grew sharp black claws from my hands and feet. "There goes another perfectly good pair of shoes," I lamented as my new toenails punched holes in the leather. I found the thickest, tallest pine tree and scaled up it like a giant, furless squirrel. When I reached the top, I found a possible escape route.

Using a hand to counter the glare from the light globe, I spotted a mooring rope hanging from the side of the airship. Unfortunately, it was about twenty feet above my head. Under normal circumstances, jumping that distance wouldn't be hard, but with an injured leg and a wobbly branch beneath my feet, my chances didn't look good.

I looked around for a taller tree, but nothing nearby rose higher. The airship's cockpit wasn't visible from my vantage point, but the outline of something metallic above the light ball hinted its location. In other words, the pilots probably couldn't see me when I was directly beneath them.

A gust of wind raced through the trees. I grabbed hold of the trunk and held on tight as it swayed to the side. Something cracked, and I prayed it wasn't the branch I stood on. The turbines on the airship whined faster as it fought to maintain position. It lurched higher and the rope went hopelessly out of reach.

The wind died down and shouting soldiers caught my attention. I looked down and saw my pursuers combing the forest. The airship turbines engaged again and it began to move lower over the trees, probably to give the soldiers below better vision. *God bless the black little soul of whoever gave that order.* The rope drew to within ten feet.

I couldn't risk waiting another second.

Bracing my feet on the thin branches, I bent my knees and jumped. My left leg overpowered my injured one, and I sailed upward at a bad angle. Desperately, I flailed and barely caught the rope by the tips of my fingers.

I dangled precipitously for a moment then swung my other arm up to grasp the rope. "One day I'm grabbing ropes on a boat. A few days later I'm doing the same damned thing on a blimp." I pulled myself up hand-over-hand, keeping an eye on the area where the cockpit should be. I couldn't see anything through the glare of the light globe, leaving me little choice but to climb as quickly as possible.

Finally, I reached a point where the light from the globe cut off, revealing a large reflective dish over the top part of the lamp that directed the glare downward. It also gave me a clear view into the windows of a large cockpit. Two men stood at the opposite end from me looking out the front window. A third man stationed in front of a large microphone on the side, stared down at a pad of paper. If he glanced to his right, he'd see me. The struts supporting the turbines driving the airship angled down from the sides, hanging just over the mirrored dish for the light globe.

I clambered up the rope until I was right at the bulge in the side. Instead of ascending to the top, I looked down at the side of the cockpit. If I used one of the other mooring ropes in the middle of the blimp, I might be able to climb down to a window and burst inside.

Taking over the airship, however, wouldn't grant me a ticket to freedom. The minute I made a run for it in this lumbering whale, they'd know something was up and shoot it down. Bracing my feet on the side of the airship, I climbed all the way to the top and sat on one of the metal girders so I could consider my options.

Pitch black engulfed the land around the blimp aside from the mountain slope where the airships cast their brilliant lights. If I escaped the perimeter of tanks and soldiers, where would I go? I could probably use my phone for navigation, but how long would it take me to reach the border, and how would I cross it?

I slid out my phone and opened the maps app. Thankfully, it didn't need an internet or aethernet connection to work, and calculated a distance of nearly a hundred and seventy miles from my location to the border. Without an injured leg, it might take me three or four days. I didn't have a passport or any form of identification on me, so I doubted the South Koreans would let me cross even if I made it through the minefields with all my limbs intact.

I couldn't sneak into Pyongyang and hijack a plane or helicopter. Even if I knew how to fly, one side or the other would surely blow me out of the sky. Swimming down the coast might possibly be an option, but the chilly climate promised frigid waters. It was doable, but not preferred.

No, my safest, fastest option home would be to somehow return to the crystoid and remove the steel plate covering it. Hopefully, Elyssa could reopen a portal and rescue me before I was discovered. The best way to achieve that goal meant blimp-jacking this thing and flying it back up the mountain. Hopefully, all the soldiers were at the base of the slope searching for me, along with the snipers.

Before I enacted this daring plan, I decided to give myself a few moments so my leg could finally start to heal. I lay on the girder and looked at pictures on my phone. Without a connection to the outside world, I retreated back to the fantasy world I'd lived in for the past few months.

The first pictures of Elyssa's travels and mine were in Venice, Italy. I grinned at the image of a selfie we'd taken with a gondolier during a cruise around the canals. Another picture showed the two of us at the top of one of the tall Venetian towers we'd scaled one night, just because we could. I'd good shots of the people below, and then several of me kissing Elyssa.

The next album took me back to Switzerland where we'd toured the gorgeous countryside, hiking the Swiss Alps and skinny-dipping in azure lakes. I snorted at the pictures of us dressed in lederhosen when we'd gone to Germany. I'd jokingly told Elyssa we had to wear the local garb, and she'd surprised me by doing just that.

"God, we look ridiculous." A tear stung my eye, but the cold wind dried it up before it could journey down my cheek.

Elyssa and I had gone so many places, seen so many wonderful things, and had so much fun. Thailand hadn't been the last in the list, at least not until the meteors changed everything. Being with my true love every day had been a gift and a remedy for the brutal war against the Brightlings. It hadn't totally healed me—nothing could do that— but it had made me remember how wonderful life could be. Those who gave up their lives had sacrificed themselves so the rest of us could enjoy this life.

"I just want peace." I squeezed shut my eyes. Regret twisted its cruel fingers around my heart. I'd wanted peace so badly I'd stopped fighting at the earliest opportunity. Instead of taking an unstoppable force to wrest Tarissa from Cephus, I'd let Ketiss go with only his people and whoever volunteered to accompany them.

I'd promised him I would return and help him, but I'd liberally interpreted that to mean after I returned from vacation. Deep down inside, I knew the truth. Once I'd tasted peace, I hit the road with

Elyssa and planned to never look back. My vacation would have gone on and on while I let Ketiss take care of his own problems.

It made me realize all the more that the problems of one realm would eventually spill over into the other ones. Seraphina had to be pacified. Cephus had to fall, and the Brightlings and Darklings needed to settle their differences and finally unify.

If I kept running and ignoring the ugly truth lurking in the shadows, I'd only end up stranded on top of a blimp in North Korea.

"Ain't nobody who deserves that fate," I muttered.

The skin on my injured hamstring pinched and spasms ran through the leg. Excruciating pain burned the muscle. I gritted my teeth and held out as something hard slid through my flesh. I tried to ignore the pain by looking at more pictures and only partially succeeded. At long last, I felt something pop from the skin. I jiggled my pants leg, and a slightly dented bullet fell from the bottom.

Though I still bled, my leg felt much better. I stood up and walked along the girder, keeping a grip on a rope in case I lost my balance. My leg wasn't in perfect shape, but it was good enough to do what needed doing.

Time to commandeer a North Korean airship.

Chapter 19

I chose the middle rope on the left side of the blimp to begin my assault since the radio operator should still be facing the opposite way. With my recovering leg, it didn't take long to rappel down the side of the nacelle and reach the mission-critical phase of the operation. It was only when I saw the cockpit that I realized how difficult it would be to swing myself on the rope with enough force to break into or even reach the window. If I didn't have enough momentum, the suction from the wind turbines might draw me into their blades and shower the people below with Justin stew.

To reach the objective, I'd have to propel myself from the side, slide to the end of the rope, and then swing beneath the curve of the airship. Physics informed me that this would be pretty hard to pull off from this position. Physics then promptly chided me for my ignorance and told me exactly how I might pull this off. I didn't like it one little bit, but finally agreed it was the best way to make this happen.

Science for the win.

I climbed back to the top, tied a loop in the end of the rope, and gripped it with both hands. I looked out at the pitch black and imagined the rocky terrain far below. "This is crazy."

Crazy, yeah, but I had no choice.

Before I could chicken out, I took a long running start and leapt off the side. The rope jerked and I swung down, air whistling past my ears. As I rounded the curve of the nacelle, I realized that the rope might not be quite long enough to reach the window. My enhanced senses took over my reflexes, and time seemed to slow. The radio operator's back faced me and the two pilots were at the controls.

The rope went taut. Several feet remained between me and the window, but I saw a ledge and took a chance. Momentum carried me toward my goal. I reached out. My fingertips grasped the ledge—and slipped. I plummeted. My crotch saved the day, meeting the support bar for the propeller. Somehow, I held in a high-pitched scream of pain and my legs locked together. I spun upside down and conked my head on the light reflection dish.

The last thing I wanted to do was move. The propeller whizzed to full speed. If not for the housing around it, I probably would have gotten a free haircut. Fighting the sick feeling in my guts, I pulled myself upright and grabbed the ledge beneath the window just as the propellers went silent. I looked up and my stomach knotted. Three shocked faces looked back at me.

Adrenalin and endorphins, the cocktail of the gods, rushed through my veins. I rammed a fist through the window and sent one of the operators smacking into the bulkhead on the other side. The others turned toward the radio. I ripped out the safety glass and pulled my torso inside. One man drew a gun from a holster on the wall.

I grabbed his wrist and squeezed hard. Bones cracked. He screamed and dropped the gun. I caught it in my other hand and threw it at the man reaching for the radio mic. It smacked him on the back of the head and he went down in a boneless heap. Shoving the gunman aside, I pulled myself through the window and rolled onto the floor.

The gunman continued to scream and hold his wrist. The other two were down for the count.

"Can you fly this thing?" I zoomed my hand through the air like a plane. "Fly." I pointed toward the mountain. "There."

The pilot was too busy screaming to listen.

I picked up the pistol and chucked it out of the window then dragged the unconscious people to the aft section of the cabin where they'd be out of the way. I turned to examine the control panel. The controls looked a bit like a plane's. A joystick protruded from a panel in front of the left and right seat. Several mysterious levers and switches were on a panel between the pilot and copilot's seat.

"Looks easy enough," I told myself, but I wasn't fooling anyone. The joystick might be the answer to everything, but I might also crash us right into the mountain.

A stern voice crackled on the radio and I wondered if this airship had just received a command. Someone else answered the voice and I relaxed. The last thing I wanted was for the person in charge to get suspicious if nobody answered our radio. I didn't know how long I had before a command like that might come through, so I went to the controls and gave them a test.

Moving the joystick to the right caused the left propeller to spin and turned us in the desired direction. I oriented us toward the mountain. We were well below the crest. I pushed forward gently and the airship glided forward. Unlike a plane, or a flying broom, pulling up and down on the control stick didn't control the yaw, or the side-to-side pitch for that matter. I really didn't want to turn this into a literal crash course so I released the joystick and examined the other controls.

Two levers looked like they might do something useful, but I was afraid to touch them. I heard rustling and turned to see the injured pilot trying to open a cabinet. I grabbed him and waggled my finger.

"No." I shook my head then pointed to the controls. "Up." I pointed up.

He looked up.

I groaned and shook my head. I pointed at the controls then pointed up. "Up!"

The pilot clued into my request, but didn't look cooperative.

I pointed to his other wrist, then held up my hand and clenched my fist tight enough to crack the knuckles. His already pale face turned a shade of green. Jabbing a finger at the console, I repeated my demand. He sighed and nodded. The pilot sat at the controls and held down two buttons. I heard what sounded like air hissing out of a leaky balloon. Alarm bells went off in my head. The pilot saw my face, and fear shone in his eyes.

"Up!" he said, and pointed up.

"First thing I do when I get an internet connection is research how to fly one of these things." I looked out the window and saw with relief that we were indeed ascending. I pointed to the glowing lights on the crest. "Go."

He gulped and nodded. I then realized the giant lamp on the bottom of the cockpit might give us away. After all, I didn't see any other blimps illuminating the top of the mountain. Thankfully, a black button next to the illustration of a light bulb told me all I needed to know. I pressed it and heard a clicking hum. The light beneath us went out. I hoped extinguishing the lamp didn't raise more of a red flag than leaving it on, but it was too late to change my mind.

"Now all I have to do is lift a huge slab of steel." That was going to be quite a trick. The blimp was big, but I didn't think it had a chance of budging something so heavy. I went to the cabinet the pilot had tried to open just in case he had another gun. When I opened it, I found a tablet computer.

That's not what I was expecting.

Had he planned to wallop me on the side of the head? I pulled out the tablet and found a slick silvery gun beneath it. It looked like something out of a science fiction movie. I took it out and examined it. I wasn't a gun expert, but it didn't seem to have a clip or a place to hold bullets. I turned on the tablet and nearly dropped it when text appeared on the screen.

It's in English!

It offered instructions in English, and several other languages. I chose my native tongue and activated an introductory video. I glanced at the pilot to make sure he was still doing as instructed. He gave me a nervous glance and turned back around. The mountain slowly drew closer.

"Congratulations on your purchase of the Model Four nuclear dirigible," said a peppy female voice. "Although it looks like an ordinary airship on the outside, you'll find that it's anything but ordinary."

A nuclear dirigible?

I hadn't kept up with nom technology over the past year or so, but I knew for certain airships were more of a novelty than an actual form of travel, and there was no way most sane countries would allow something nuclear powered to fly over their cities.

The video assuaged my concerns in the next sentence. "Unlike nuclear fission, this reactor uses cold fusion to create abundant, safe energy. Although standard airship controls are available to disguise the true nature of this vehicle, you can easily switch to nuclear power by twisting the decorative sundial on the bulkhead. This will enable the advanced controls."

The video went on to demonstrate how to deploy weaponry, towing hooks, and a number of other things I'd never heard of on an airship. I knew enough about North Korea to realize there was no way they'd developed this thing on their own. In fact, no nation I knew of possessed such technology. It could have only come from one place. The robots we'd encountered only solidified my suspicions.

Science Academy.

I immediately thought of Victus. But why would he want to help the North Koreans capture me? The minute I returned home, I planned to find out who sent in the tip about this location. First, I had to make this tub work to my advantage.

The pilot shouted something and I glanced up at him. He pointed frantically behind us. When I turned, I saw three airships gliding up the mountain, their huge lamps illuminating the ground beneath them. Either they were onto us, or they were returning to search the slope since they hadn't found me. The blinking lights on the closest one revealed a transformation underway. Large wings extended from the sides and the silhouette of a turret rose from the top.

They must have twisted the damned sundial.

Things were about to get real nasty real fast.

I raced to the sundial and twisted it. A loud thrum vibrated through the cockpit and a light on the ceiling flashed. The top of the cabinet next to the radio station slid aside to reveal a monitor and joystick rising from inside.

The pilot screamed, pointing to the control panel in front of him. The normal controls were in the process of flipping upside down while a more advanced touchscreen rotated into place. Apparently, we were dead in the water while the airship transformed.

"Shut up!" I shouted. A conniption fit wasn't going to solve anything.

"Ablative armor activated," said a pleasant female voice. She repeated the message in various languages while transparent covers slid up to cover the windows, including the one I'd broken to gain entrance.

The monitor finally flickered on revealing a green-tinted night vision view of the area ahead with a white reticle in the center. To the upper right, an outline of the airship highlighted its various components in green.

I didn't have time to read the instructions, relying instead on my video game knowledge, and twisted the joystick. The view rotated to the right. I centered the reticle on the closest airship and hit the red trigger on the joystick.

A brilliant beam lanced through the air and splashed off the airship. The target fired back. I threw up my hands as the laser hit the hull. The temperature in the cockpit rose several degrees and sweat trickled into my eyes. A section of the hull outline on the monitor changed from green to yellow.

I pulled the trigger again, but a red X appeared in the reticle right next to a timer counting down from six seconds.

It's got a cooldown.

That might be good for us. The airships seemed capable of taking a beating, but how many direct hits could we take? If we had several seconds between each blast, it might give us time to get over the mountain ridge.

A loud click, like something latching into place vibrated the floor beneath my feet. The pilot spoke in a relieved voice and ran his fingers up the touchscreen controls. Turbines whined and the airship lurched forward. We finally reached the mountain. A massive laser beam exploded on the rocky slope to our right. Trees burst into flame and boulders tumbled into the forest.

I zoomed in on the closest airship. Just behind and to its right I spotted two more of them fully transformed and plowing ahead at full speed. Destroying just one of them seemed impossible. Forget knocking three of them out of the sky. I sought weakness in the airship design but came up with zilch.

Sweat drizzled into my eyes. The laser blast turned the cockpit into an oven, though it wasn't hot enough to kill anyone. Already, the heat was dissipating, thanks to whatever armor protected this thing.

I'm going to make them sweat.

Finger on the trigger, I stopped as an idea occurred to me. The armor dissipated the brunt of the heat, but what if I hit something particularly heat sensitive? I focused on the large jet turbine beneath the right wing of the closest enemy. A jet engine put off a lot of heat, but like any engine, it didn't work well past its tolerance level.

I locked on and fired. The laser struck the engine, but did no obvious damage.

"C'mon," I said. "Overheat."

The seconds on the monitor ticked down as the laser recharged. The airship fired on us. The beam splashed over the hull, and the temperature shot up again. The pilot gasped and gripped his throat. It occurred to me that the heat didn't bother me nearly as much as it did him. I jerked open a small refrigerator and took out a water bottle then opened it and gave it to the pilot. He poured some over his head and guzzled the rest.

The weapons console beeped. The laser was ready again. I wasted no time firing on the enemy airship's engine once again. Still nothing happened.

The other two airships were nearly even with their leader. In seconds, they'd open fire. Armor or not, the pilot and I would be cooked alive.

The jet turbine on the lead airship sparked. The vessel listed sharply to the right and plowed into the wing of the neighboring dirigible. Like dominoes, the middle airship collided with the third ship and they careened off to the right, the crippled vessel pushing them.

I pumped my fist. "We did it!"

The pilot gave me a frightened look—one that turned to relief when he spotted the crippled airships behind us.

I ran to the front and looked down. I spotted the bright lamps next to the crystoid and pointed toward it. "Hover," I said and hovered one hand over the other. This game of charades meant life or death, especially if the enemy airships recovered and came for us. I repeated my gestures and instructions, and the pilot seemed to get it.

Now I just had to figure out how to deploy the grappling hook on this thing. I went back to the weapons station, figuring the answer had to be nearby. A down arrow on the touchscreen seemed to provide the answer I needed. I pressed it. The turret view strafed to the side and suddenly, the monitor displayed the ground.

The down arrow hadn't activated a grappling hook—it had rotated the turret to the bottom of the nacelle. I pressed another icon beneath the arrow. The green-tinted night vision vanished, replaced by what looked like infrared. I was about to curse my inability to find the right button when I saw a cluster of human-shaped heat signatures hiding behind the nearby boulders.

Dozens of soldiers stood between me and my destination.

Chapter 20

I couldn't afford to be gentle with these people—not if I planned to survive. Killing was not something I enjoyed, but sometimes it was necessary.

I wrapped my hand around the joystick, aimed, and pulled the trigger.

The nearby boulders exploded into chunks of molten rock. Bodies scattered like leaves. I scoped out the cliffs while the laser recharged, and found only one sniper. He seemed to realize the danger and bullets pinged off the hull. The countdown hit zero and I blasted him. The rocky cliff shone bright in the infrared.

Further sweeps of the area revealed no more soldiers, so I inspected the monitor again for a way to grapple the steel. I couldn't find anything. I went back to the pilot and pantomimed what I wanted, holding a hand flat and touching my finger to it like a cable and lifting.

The pilot knew exactly what I wanted. He motioned toward the touchscreen on the copilot's side. I found an icon that looked like a cable and touched it. The monitor flicked to a view of the ground below, displaying a cable with a thick electromagnet on the end. The pilot switched his monitor to a similar view and adjusted our position right over the steel plate. He pointed to another icon shaped like a lightning bolt.

I touched it. The cable snapped taut and the end gripped to the steel plate. The vessel shuddered and groaned with the added weight.

Singing like a piano wire and sounding like it could snap at any moment, the cable vibrated the entire cabin. The pilot pushed forward a lever and finally, the airship gained momentum. Through the monitor, I watched the steel plate slide along the ground and finally uncover the hole.

The pilot shouted a command. I pressed the lightning icon. The cable snapped free of its load and the airship lurched forward before the pilot wrenched it back under control. I watched the massive steel slab rush downhill like a massive guillotine, slicing through trees until it vanished from sight.

Before I could pantomime the next order, the pilot dropped the airship lower until the rugged terrain prevented it from descending any further. He pressed a button and the door on the side sprang open. A rope ladder extended to the ground. He jumped from his seat and said something in an urgent voice, eyes pleading. He pointed out the door and spoke again. I wasn't sure if he was begging me to leave, or asking to come.

I pointed to the unconscious people in the back. He pointed to his injured wrist. I shrugged. He could do what he wanted at this point. The running lights of two airships caught my attention. They must have finally untangled themselves from the crippled vessel. The pilot grunted as he scrambled down the ladder with one hand. I grabbed the unconscious copilot and slid down the ladder, dropped him on the ground, and repeated the process with the radio operator.

Before abandoning ship, I ran to the flight control touchscreen and dragged my fingers up the speed slider, adjusting the speed to max.

The aircraft lurched forward. I blurred to the ladder, slid down it, and hit the ground rolling as the airship thrummed away into the night. Brilliant lasers from the pursuing ships hit it on the wing, but missed the engines. I hoped they'd continue to chase it until a portal opened.

The charred and smoking skeletons of my victims were scattered around the crater amidst the molten and reformed shapes of rock the laser had briefly turned to lava. I looked away from the carnage. The pilot waited for me near the crystoid, eyes brimming with fear. I retrieved the unconscious bodies and dragged them closer to the crater.

"C'mon, Elyssa. Open a portal." I tested my arcphone, but still couldn't get a signal.

The distant sky flashed with more lasers. A huge explosion thundered and bright energy cascaded across the darkness as my faithful airship finally went to the afterlife. With it gone, the pursuit was almost certain to turn back to this area. Even if they believed I'd died in the explosion, someone would notice the missing steel slab.

The radio operator groaned and pushed himself upright. His eyes went wide with confusion, and then with fear when they settled on me. The pilot spoke with him, and the other man began to cry. Was he sad because his airship blew up, or had the pilot told him something else? If Elyssa didn't open a portal soon, I'd cry too.

The running lights on the enemy dirigibles drew closer. It wouldn't be long before the pursuers were close enough to find us with infrared and blast us all to hell. Unfortunately, there was nowhere else to go unless a gateway appeared. I raced to the impact crater and judged the angle of the aether beam. A jagged boulder a few yards from the crater looked as though it might be in the right spot. I just hoped it was tall enough.

I scrambled to the top and shuffled from one side to the other until I felt the whisper of static against my face. "This might work!" I looked around and spotted a large flat rock that could boost me a little higher. I dropped to the ground and hefted it.

The pilot and radio operator gasped and broke into an argument. The copilot finally achieved consciousness again. He tried to run, but the other two men tackled him and shouted desperately in his face.

"Damn, I wish I knew what they were saying." Obviously, they weren't plotting escape, or they would've run already. I doubted they had any hope of capturing me. I hoped they simply wanted to get the hell out of North Korea like I did.

With my booster rock in place, the aether hit me in the upper chest. It wasn't perfect, but it was good enough. I focused on the airships. "Let's see how good your shields are." They were still too far off for me to hit. Their lasers would be in range long before I could hit them.

I pointed at the pilot and crew and motioned them to take cover behind my rock. Faces frightened, they huddled against it. The boulder wouldn't protect any of us—the destruction I'd wrought on the infantry with our laser was testament enough. On the other hand, I now had access to Murk.

An ultraviolet sphere blossomed in my left hand. I projected it in a wall in front of the boulder and let it thicken. The first laser splashed against it an instant later. Hot air washed past, but the shield held.

The crewmen cried out when the next blast thundered into the ground in front of the shield. The pilot looked with amazement at the shimmering energy flowing from my hand. I gave him a thumbs-up. He hesitantly returned the gesture.

I hope those lasers don't hit the crystoid or we're all cooked.

The airships closed in. Under normal circumstances, they'd need to be fairly close for my attacks to do any damage, but the aether beam was like super-concentrated fuel to my Seraphim core. I fired a thin beam of Brilliance from my right index finger. Even from a hundred yards away, it left a burn mark on the ablative armor.

My new buddies cried out at the display.

It was a promising start, but no reason to celebrate. The only hope at holding my ground was disabling the lasers on the airships. They had to get closer. Instead, the lead vessel held position while the other one circled to our right.

They're going to flank us.

In a few short moments, we'd be surrounded. I could extend my protective shield, but then what? We'd be trapped. Soldiers would soon flood the area, and surrender or death would be the only option.

Come on, Elyssa!

I aimed my right palm toward the laser turret on the bottom of the first airship and unleashed everything I had. A torrent of Brilliance sliced the air and speared into the weapon. The energy splashed over it, seeming to do no damage. I felt perspiration break on my forehead. Salt stung my eyes, and my arm began to ache from the strain of pouring so much energy through it. In my peripheral vision, I saw the other airship drift into position. Its turret swiveled toward me.

"No!" I shouted. "Blow up, you son of a bitch!"

The laser on the first vessel glowed cherry red and finally exploded. I released the energy and shifted my left hand to form another Murk shield to protect our flank. Before I could move, a red beam speared from the second airship.

I threw up my arms, as if that would save me. It didn't.

The laser slammed into another shield of Murk that appeared from nowhere.

I heard someone shouting—in English. I looked up and behind me to see the glorious sight of Ivy channeling the protective barrier from a gateway ten feet above. Elyssa appeared behind her and dropped a rope. It unfurled to the ground a few feet behind the boulder.

"Go! Go!" I motioned the crewmen toward the rope. The pilot shimmied up, but his progress was agonizingly slow. "Didn't you go through boot camp?" I yelled.

A look of puzzlement swept over Elyssa's face, but she quickly recovered and pulled up the rope. I shouted at Ivy. "Blow up the laser turret!" I jabbed a finger at the target.

Still holding the Murk shield, she balled up a crackling sphere of Brilliance and released a massive beam of energy. The turret didn't hold out long before it melted to slag. Ivy wasn't finished. Face locked in a fierce scowl, she directed the beam up the nacelle of the airship.

"Nobody messes with my brother!" she shrieked.

The deadly beam splashed off the nose of the aircraft, but within seconds the metal glowed red and Ivy's attack blew a hole through it. The vessel listed and lost altitude, plummeting down. With a loud groan and shriek of metal, the airship smashed into the ground and broke apart.

"Now, Justin!" Elyssa shouted.

I spun and saw the rope hit the ground. Shouts echoed all around me and gunfire erupted. I leapt from the boulder and grabbed the rope, shimmying up it as fast as my hands could move. Elyssa jerked the rope. I flew through the portal and skidded to a stop at her feet.

"Close the portal," I told Ivy.

Lips peeled back from her teeth, she faced me and said, "This isn't finished." Lifting both hands, she channeled Murk and Brilliance into a ball of stasis and fired a gray beam into the crystoid.

Bullets zinged somewhere on the other side of the gateway, but the soldiers apparently didn't have a good angle to fire directly into the portal. I leapt up and summoned Murk, ready to shield my sister from attack. The crystoid crackled as Stasis consumed it.

I saw a soldier run into view and take aim. A quick lance of Brilliance from my finger pierced his chest and he dropped, smoke pouring from his mouth. I saw another and cut him down. Two more burst into view, one with a rocket launcher on his shoulder. I hit the projectile on the nose and it exploded. Body parts rained across the blasted terrain.

The crystoid shattered.

"Got it!" Ivy piped.

I pulled her back from the gateway and willed it closed. The portal winked away and the only sound was our heavy breathing.

"Son of a bitch!" I dropped to my knees and breathed a sigh of relief.

Elyssa gripped me in a fierce hug. "What happened? Are you okay?"

I pulled myself up and peppered her face with kisses. "I'm wonderful now." Turning to Ivy, I smothered her with a hug. "Thanks, sis."

She giggled. "You got it."

"I was beginning to wonder if you'd open another portal," I said.

"We tried for over an hour." Elyssa wiped tears from her eyes. "How did they block us?"

"A steel plate covered with diamond fiber." I gave them the details of my encounter and looked around for the crewmen. They huddled, eyes wide, in the aisle between the omniarches and the smaller black arches. "Anyone speak Korean?"

"Uh, I suppose we can find someone." Elyssa took out her phone. "I have no idea what to do with these people."

I walked over to them and smiled. "Welcome to the Overworld."

They all spoke at once, motioning around the control room, faces screwed up in confusion.

It was great to be home, but this development pointed toward something sinister afoot in our own ranks. It seemed we had a traitor in our midst.

Chapter 21

We traveled via portal to the Ranch with our North Korean refugees and met with Thomas and the others.

"Man, I thought you were done travelling the world," Shelton said with a wry grin after I finished the story.

"The pilot and crew are in an interrogation room with a translator," Thomas said. "If they know who gave them those airships and the robot, we'll find out."

I repeated my suspicions. "It's obvious someone from Science Academy supplied them. It all points to Victus. He has first-hand knowledge about our operations."

"The evidence does seem damning," Thomas agreed. "But you still have plenty of enemies at the academy. It could have been any one of them. Our operation to nullify the crystoids is no secret."

"Why would Victus want to stop us?" Elyssa said. "He wants to be the next Arcanus Primus, so getting rid of the crystoids should be at the top of his priorities."

Their arguments make too much sense. "True. His interests should align with ours." I thought back to my failed meeting with the Science Council during the war. They'd done everything possible to prevent anyone, even students from aiding our cause. Several members had likely been in cahoots with Daelissa. That realization broadened the spectrum of possible culprits.

"None of this changes our objectives," Elyssa said. "We need to continue wiping out the crystoid menace. From now on, we'll be more careful before following anonymous tips."

"Got that right." Shelton looked at Thomas. "Speaking of which, any intel on potential targets?"

"We have images for three more," Thomas replied. He set an arctablet on the table and projected the map. "One in California and two in Canada. If we nullify them, North America will be free of crystoids."
Shelton pumped his fist. "Let's get on it."
Ivy stepped forward, an eager look on her face. "I'm good to go."
Elyssa, Shelton, Ivy and I portaled back to the Grotto and used the image of the crystoid in California. This time, I stayed at the edge of the gateway to avoid any traps and poked my head through.
Four men in lab coats stood at the crater edge, an array of various instruments nearby. None of them seemed aware of the portal open in the sky above them. They'd certainly be aware the moment Ivy started channeling and we couldn't allow that. A tall chain link fence topped with razor wire surrounded the perimeter and a pair of soldiers in camouflage guarded the only gate.
I pointed two fingers at my eyes and then held up six fingers. Elyssa nodded and joined me at the gateway. She licked a finger and held it up to gauge the wind, then carefully aimed a wrist-mounted lancer at the nearest scientist. Within seconds, four darts found their targets and dropped them. The soldiers, however, would be harder to knock out thanks to their body armor and the fence.
Elyssa strapped another lancer to her other wrist and slid down a rope with catlike grace. She stealthily approached the guards from behind and held both hands up to the holes in the chain link fence. A heartbeat later, the pair took a trip to dreamland and slumped to the ground. Shelton and I slid down the rope and moved the unconscious scientists all the way to the fence, keeping them away from the crater in case something went wrong.
Shelton looked around nervously. "Glad there aren't any robots."
I puffed a breath through my lips. "Tell me about it."
The moment we climbed the rope and returned through the gateway, Ivy took her place and channeled Stasis into the crystoid, rendering it inert within minutes while I anchored her. I closed the portal and exchanged high-fives with everyone.
Shelton grunted. "Let's hope the next one goes as smoothly."

We decided to target the crystoid at Algonquin Provincial Park north of Toronto next. The moment we opened the gateway, a very startled man on a platform on the opposite side of the crater looked back at us. Eyes, wide, he backed up a step and said, "Oh, excuse me, but are you floating in mid-air?"

I looked around and saw several more people staring up at us. Thankfully, there weren't any gun-wielding soldiers nearby.

I decided to use truth instead of force with this group. "These crystoids are a huge danger to our world, so we're disabling them."

"You're Americans?" He asked.

"Some of us are, yes."

Elyssa stepped into view. "We're an international group trying to stop the crystoid menace before it wrecks the environment."

"Oh." He nodded vigorously.

"That sure sounds good," said a woman standing near the crater edge. "Some of these things have already exploded in other parts of the world and killed thousands of people. We sure don't want it ruining our lovely park."

"If you'd like, we can neutralize this thing and be on our way," I said.

"Yeah, sure," the man on the platform said. "I'm sure sorry for asking, but are you using some sort of interdimensional gateway?"

"That's sure what it looks like, Bob," the woman said.

"Wish I could explain, but it's better if you don't know," I said. "May we proceed?"

"Sure," Bob replied. "Should we move away?"

"I'd stand back a good ways, just in case." I motioned Ivy over.

She stepped into the gateway and grinned brightly. "Hey, everyone!"

"Wow, they sure do hire young these days," Bob said.

Ivy seemed eager to perform for a crowd. "Enjoy the light show." With that, she blasted the crystoid with Stasis, and blew the Canadians' minds.

The Canadians clapped politely after Ivy finished. She bowed and waved. "You're so polite!"

"They're Canadians," Shelton huffed. He checked the crystoid off the map. "See if they have any connections at the site in British Columbia."

I relayed the question to Bob.

"Sure, I know a couple of the fellas over there." He took out a cell phone. "I'll bet they'd be real pleased if you could help them out."

"We'll get right on it," I said.

"I'll call and let them know you're, uh,"—he stared at the portal—"coming, or whatever you do."

"Tell them we'll be there in about ten minutes," I said.

"Wow, okay then."

We waved goodbye and closed the portal.

Elyssa and Ivy burst into giggles.

"They were so nice," Ivy said.

"Gotta love Canadians," Shelton mused. "If the rest of the world was like that, we'd never have to worry about war again."

"Yeah, but you'd never get through a door either," Elyssa said. "Everyone would be too busy saying, 'you first' to ever get inside."

"I'm really disappointed in all of you," I said, giving them a stern gaze. "You're stereotyping an entire nation of people just because a few of them happened to be polite."

Elyssa narrowed her eyes at me. "It's a positive stereotype."

"I'm sure there are plenty of mean Canadians," I said.

"I dunno, but the farther north you go, the friendlier they get," Shelton said. "Those people in North Dakota sure were nice, and they made some great cookies." He frowned. "I wonder if those scientists had cookies somewhere."

His statement opened a meaningless debate, which did little but give us a way to pass ten minutes. I quieted everyone down and opened a portal to the next crystoid, keeping out of sight just in case.

"Oh, hey there it is," someone said from the other side. "Hello, is anyone in there?"

I poked my head into the opening and saw a small group of people near a crater bordered by fallen trees. As with most impact zones, the crystoid had made a mess.

I waved. "Hello, I'm here to neutralize the crystoid."

"Bob told us you'd be by, but—wow." A woman in a yellow raincoat stared up at me. "That is the neatest thing I've ever seen."

I noticed a man lifting a cell phone. "No pictures, please. We can't let anyone know we're doing this."

"Put that thing away, Alan," the woman said. "We don't want to get these nice people in trouble for helping us."

"I'm sorry," Alan said. "I sure don't want that to happen."

"Okay, well, stand back from the crater, please." I motioned for Ivy and she came to my side.

"I just want to thank you for being so nice," Ivy said to the onlookers. "If everyone was so nice, we could save the world super quick. Instead, they're mostly mean and have to be blasted."

A chorus of "I'm sorry," rose from the Canadians.

Ivy smiled. "It's okay. Nice people make all the danger totally worth it, plus I like blasting baddies." With that, she did her job, much to the amazement of the Canadians.

"Holy mackerel, that's some little girl," the woman said when Ivy finished. "Thank you for saving us."

Ivy crossed her arms and grinned. "All in a day's work for a hero."

Elyssa snorted.

I pulled Ivy back. "Goodbye, everyone!"

"Goodbye!"

I closed the portal and ruffled Ivy's hair. "You're too much sometimes."

"Thanks, Justin." She hugged me.

"Well, three more down," Shelton said. "Cinder called me a minute ago and said he's got a few more leads. I'll go meet with him in the conference room to see how that pans out."

"I need to speak to my father," Elyssa said. "I want to task someone to finding out who set a trap for us in North Korea."

"Hopefully, the soldiers I brought back gave us some intel," I told her.

Ivy looked up at me. "What are you going to do, Justin?"

I was tired as hell and considered taking a much-needed nap, but caught a hopeful look in Ivy's eyes. She and I hadn't spent much one-on-one time together since the war and this seemed like a good chance to get in some sibling bonding. "How'd you like to go get some ice cream?"

Her blue eyes flashed wide. "I'd love to!"

"Hey, I want some ice cream," Shelton said.

Elyssa grabbed his arm. "Unfortunately, you don't have time for that."

"Nah, I have plenty of time—"

"Shelton, don't make me knock you out," Elyssa said calmly. "Because I will do it in a heartbeat."

He threw up his hands in surrender. "Fine." Shelton jabbed a finger at me. "Get me something to go, though, okay?"

I rolled my eyes. "You got it, pal."

"Vanilla chocolate crunch with extra sprinkles," he called out as Elyssa dragged him away. They rounded the corner and I heard him shouted. "Extra sprinkles!"

"Harry is so crazy," Ivy said. She bounced on her toes. "Where are we going?"

"I know just the place." I opened a portal right in front of the Copper Goose in Queens Gate. The restaurant looked exactly like its namesake, and boasted some really good food, but it wasn't our destination. We stepped through the portal and I closed it behind us. I took my little sister's hand and we skipped up the street to Snowman's, a huge ice cream store shaped like a castle.

"Oh, this looks so neat." Ivy rushed inside and clapped her hands with delight at what she saw inside. Snowman golems whisked around on a snowy floor, delivering frozen treats to kids and adults alike.

Ivy ordered a magic truffle cone. I ordered crusty mango with fruit on top. Our snowman server delivered it a moment later.

"It's been a long time since we had ice cream together," Ivy said after she swallowed her first bit. "I've really missed you, Justin."

"I've missed you too." I bit into the crusty ice around the creamy mango and my taste buds rejoiced. "What have you been up to while Elyssa and I were traveling?"

She frowned. "Oh, just learning stuff. Mom wants me to go back to Arcane University so I can learn normal magic." She sighed. "I hate it. School's so boring."

"I was thinking about doing the same thing," I said.

Her eyes perked. "Oh, really? Well, school is boring, but we should totally go back and learn Arcane magic."

I repressed a chuckle. *It's so cool having a sister who looks up to me.*
"Seraphim magic is powerful, but Arcane magic has a lot of utility."
"Utility?"
I nodded. "Yeah, you can do cool stuff with it."
"Oh, yeah, totally." Ivy ran her tongue around the ice cream. "Mom also said I need to socialize with kids my own age, but I don't know why. I like adults a lot better."
"She's right," I said. "It's nice making friends close to your age."
"But the kids I went to school with were so stupid." Her forehead pinched. "And mean, too. Sometimes I wanted to blast them to ashes."
I grimaced. "You wouldn't do something like that, would you?"
Ivy smiled. "Well, Bigdaddy—I mean Jeremiah—told me that just because Daelissa said something was okay didn't mean it was really okay. Otherwise, I probably would have blown up a bunch of meanies."
"Do you ever miss Jeremiah?" I asked. Ezzek Moore had posed as Jeremiah Conroy for several decades, raising my mother as his own, and continuing the charade with Ivy, telling her he was her grandfather. While he hadn't been the best role model, and had tried to kill me on a couple of occasions, he hadn't really been a bad person—just someone obsessed with revenge at any cost.
Ivy looked down. "Is it okay that I do miss him sometimes?"
I reached across the table and touched her hand. "Of course it's okay. I didn't know him very long, but I wish he was here too."
"He lied to me, but we did fun things," Ivy said in a wistful voice. "He played dolls with me sometimes. It seemed to make him happy, at least for a little while." She sighed. "Bigdaddy was a very sad man."
"Daelissa killed the woman he loved, Ivy." I shook my head slowly. "Jeremiah never recovered from it."
"Even with thousands of years to find someone else?" Her eyes flared. "Is it really that hard to find someone to love?"
I snorted. "No. I think Jeremiah stopped looking for love because he wanted to kill Daelissa so badly."
"Oh, okay." She licked her ice cream. "I suppose I can see that now."
I lifted my cone to my lips and saw something that made me stop. Victus and Delectra had just entered the shop, a little boy by their

side. They seated themselves on the opposite side of the large crowded room and ordered something.

Ivy turned and looked. "What are you looking at?"

"Victus and his family." *This can't be coincidence.*

"Oh, do you want to blast him, Justin?" Brilliance flickered at the tips of her fingers like candle flames.

I shook my head. "Not unless I find he's the traitor."

"His son looks super pale." Ivy pooched out her lips. "Poor thing."

The boy looked about Ivy's age, which made me all the more suspicious. A couple with a young girl approached Victus's table, faces beaming with smiles. I noticed the father glance my way and hurriedly avert his eyes when he saw me looking.

"Must be admirers," I said. Talking to Victus in this environment wasn't an option I planned to entertain. It might be possible he was trolling Queens Gate for votes. After all, the majority of voting Arcanes lived here. If he'd shown up here because of me, his agenda was too subtle for me to detect.

"I don't like him," Ivy said. "He reminds me of the people who came to Jeremiah begging for favors. Those people will say anything to get what they want."

I chuckled. "I have a smart sister."

"Thanks, bro." She blushed. "I want you to be proud of me."

"Ivy, I'm always proud of you, unless you start blasting people for no reason." I winked. "But I know you won't do that."

"Nope." She flashed a grin. "I'll always come up with a reason before I do that."

I remembered the first time Ivy and I had gone out for ice cream together. I'd just started attending Arcane University and was trying to find a way into my sister's heart. But my sister had grown up with Daelissa as one of her mentors and it didn't help that she thought I was evil.

We've come a long way.

My sister still had issues, but she was proving to be as resilient as she was powerful.

I ordered Shelton his ice cream cone, extra sprinkles and all, and we headed outside.

Victus stood up from his table and turned around just as we passed his table. "Justin, what a pleasant surprise."

I managed a fake smile. Though I dearly wanted to interrogate him about North Korea, I simply nodded and said, "Hello, Victus. We were just leaving."

"Ah, well, our son, Conrad, has been dying to come here." He looked at the pale boy. "Isn't that right, young man?"

"Yes, father," the boy replied in a monotone voice. "Thank you so very much for bringing me."

"He's our little treasure," Delectra said. "We're thinking of adopting war orphans so he'll have siblings to play with."

I want to throw up. These people proved that politicians would do absolutely anything for a vote. "That's great." I put my acting skills to the test, filling my voice with enthusiasm. "I'm glad to know there are good people out there." I pointed to the ice cream in my hand. "Unfortunately, I really must go. I got this for a friend and don't want it to melt."

"Of course," Victus said. "We'll stop by Templar headquarters later for a progress report."

"Please do."

Ivy waved at the boy. "Would Conrad like to come back with us? I'd like someone to play with."

"I'm afraid he isn't feeling well," Delectra said. "We brought him for ice cream to make him feel better."

Ivy walked around the table and put a hand on the boy's forehead. He hardly reacted, staring almost blankly at her. "He feels fine to me."

I felt an embarrassed blush creep up my face. "It's okay, Ivy. Maybe another time."

"Until next time," Victus said.

When we got outside, I turned to Ivy. "Was it really necessary to do that?"

Ivy nodded. "Yep. Don't you think it's strange?"

I furrowed my brow. "What do you mean?"

She huffed. "That boy smells like a demon."

Chapter 22

I didn't know what to say at first, but my mouth tried to talk anyway. "A demon?" I hadn't gone close enough to smell a demonic influence, and I certainly wasn't going to go back inside for a sniff. "How do you know that's what he smells like?"

Ivy shrugged. "It's the same thing I smell when you, Dad, or one of his people are around." She put a finger to her chin and furrowed her forehead. "You know, I only recently started noticing that odor."

"Maybe you got a little bit of Dad in you after all." It made sense. I hadn't developed my demon abilities until well into puberty.

Her nose wrinkled. "Ew. You mean I might be a stinky demon someday too?" Her eyes flared. "Oh, I'm sorry, Justin. I shouldn't have said that." Ivy came closer to me and sniffed. "You don't smell that bad."

I laughed and ruffled her blonde locks. "Thanks. I'll wear extra deodorant from now on."

"I don't think it'll help." Ivy touched my arm. "Don't worry, I still love you even if you stink." She grinned.

"Aww." I hugged her. "I love you too, Ivy." *I'm so glad we did this.*

We returned to the Ranch. Shelton's ice cream, thankfully, was charmed to prevent it from prematurely melting. His eyes lit up when I held it out to him.

"Man, extra sprinkles and everything." He licked it. "Thanks, bud."

"No problem."

Bella patted Shelton's belly. "Harry, you really need to stop eating so much junk food."

He gave her a defensive look. "Hey, food this good ain't junk." He licked the ice cream again and got sprinkles on his nose.

Bella burst into laughter.

We went to the conference room and found Elyssa there with her father. She turned to us. "Good, you're back."

"Any news from our North Korean guests?" I asked.

"They didn't know much, which isn't surprising." Elyssa looked at her phone and read from the screen. "They claimed that a western man showed them how to operate the airships."

"What did he look like?" I asked.

"I'm getting to that." She continued reading. "They were supposed to guard the crystoid at all costs because it was supposedly a weapon of great power." She lowered the arcphone to her side. "I showed them pictures of people at Science Academy, and they positively ID'd Chancellor Frankenberg and two of his assistants."

"Frankenberg." I smacked a fist into my palm. "He must have seen this as a chance to make Science Academy number one in the Overworld."

"Yes, well, we made inquiries with the academy, but Frankenberg retreated to one of his secret labs after the war and hasn't been heard from until now." She shook her head slowly. "Let's just hope he hasn't handed out his toys to any other governments or mercenaries."

"David and Kassallandra supplied additional intel," Thomas said. "Their contacts in several European governments have paved the way for us to disable the crystoids there."

"Good news," I said. "I'm ready to get started."

"I've got the images we need," Elyssa said. "Alysea is on the way to help us and should be here soon."

I nudged Ivy. "How are you feeling? Think you can disable any more crystoids today?"

She nodded. "I need to feed first. I'm a little tired."

"I could use a bit more soul essence myself," I told her. "What's the Colombia situation?" Katie, Ash, and Nyte usually worked from La Casona in Bogota, Colombia, and I wanted to see how they were holding up during the current crisis.

"Commander Salazar and I spoke using normal phone lines earlier," Thomas said. "His legion has had great difficulty infiltrating the impact site south of Medellin."

"Can we travel there yet?" I asked.

He shook his head. "Since the La Casona way station is aboveground, it's been more severely affected by the aether shortage than the others."

"What about opening a portal inside the La Casona pocket dimension itself?" I asked.

He pursed his lips. "Since we cleared Atlanta of crystoids, it might work, but our earlier efforts to do just that failed."

"Can't hurt to try," I said. "If we make it, we can feed at La Casona and maybe help clear the crystoid in Medellin."

"I think it'd be better to take the safer alternative and feed here at the compound," Elyssa said. "It doesn't make sense to risk traveling there." She showed me a map on her phone plotting a route from Bogota to Medellin. "Plus, it'd take us over seven hours to travel to the crystoid."

I sighed. "Yeah, you're right." Seeing my friends again would have to wait.

We left the room and took a levitator back to ground level, left the big barn and made our way to the church. Mom showed up not long after, and she, Ivy, and I filled our tanks.

"Where's Dad?" I asked on the way out of the church.

"He's personally coordinating with operatives from Eastern European governments," Mom said. "They're being very stubborn, especially Russia."

I feigned a gasp. "You mean, he's being responsible?"

She smiled. "Yes, it's rather unsettling, isn't it?"

Ivy yawned and rubbed her eyes.

Mom stepped in front of my sister and put a hand to her forehead. "Are you sure you're up to disabling more crystoids?"

"I'm fine," Ivy said. "I probably shouldn't have eaten so much chocolate ice cream though."

I chuckled. "Feeling chocolate wasted?"

"I hope that's all it is," Mom said. "How's your leg, Justin?"

"How did you know—"

"Elyssa told me." Mom raised an eyebrow. "I know we've been through a war, but I still worry about you."

197

"My leg is fine." I rubbed the hamstring in question. "Not even a little bit sore."

We walked over to the underground garage. Elyssa, Shelton, Adam, and Bella waited for us there along with a small group of Templars.

"I figured having a rescue squad available might be a good idea," Elyssa said.

Shelton grunted. "Especially knowing we have a crazy scientist hell-bent on stopping us."

The levitator doors slid open and Nightliss ran out. She saw us and smiled. "I heard you were going after more crystoids and would like to help."

"Sure." I waved her over. "Have you blessed many new recruits?"

"So many I lost count." She sighed. "It will be nice to do something else for a change."

"Can you channel Stasis good?" Ivy asked.

Nightliss nodded. "I even practiced to make sure."

Ivy grinned. "Okay, well, someone's gonna have to hold you down or the crystoid might yank you off your feet." She hugged Nightliss. "I wouldn't want anything to happen to you."

"That's very sweet," Nightliss said.

Ivy backed away and nodded. "You're totally my favorite Darkling."

Shelton snorted. "How about we get moving?"

"Good idea." I led the group across the garage to the portal zone.

The Templar portal coordinator saluted when our group approached.

"A portal to the Grotto, please," Elyssa said.

"Right away." The Templar tapped on an arcphone and looked up a moment later. "ETA one minute."

The portal appeared precisely one minute later right inside the yellow zone.

"I think you missed a sprinkle," Adam said to Shelton as they stepped through ahead of me.

"I never miss a sprinkle," Shelton replied.

Adam snorted. "You still have one on your nose."

Shelton rubbed the tip of his nose, dislodging the refugee sprinkle onto his finger. "Man, I hate to waste it."

Elyssa gagged. "Please, dear god, don't tell me you plan to eat a nose sprinkle."

Bella knocked the sprinkle off Shelton's fingertip. "Harry, no nose sprinkles."

"Hey, that was a perfectly good sprinkle!" Shelton protested.

Ivy giggled. "Nose sprinkles sound so gross!"

I threw in my two cents. "We're off to a fine start, folks. Maybe we can just use Shelton's nose sprinkles to defeat the crystoid menace."

That sent a ripple of laughter through the group, though our Templar comrades maintained a stoic demeanor.

Thankfully, our precautions were unneeded. Neutralizing the crystoids threatening Western Europe went flawlessly. Mom and Nightliss handled two each; Ivy and I finished off the rest.

Shelton took great joy in updating the map. We now had a larger beachhead to work with, but Asia still had the complexion of a pimply-faced teen, and Africa looked only marginally better.

"We're down to seventy-three crystoids," Shelton announced. "We've come a long way."

"Still have more than half left," I grumbled.

Nightliss massaged her temples. "I feel so drained."

Eyelids drooping, Ivy leaned against Mom. "I'm ready for sleepy time, Mommy."

Mom kissed me on the cheek and hugged Elyssa and Nightliss goodbye. "I'm going to take her home." She squeezed my hand. "You need to rest too, okay?"

I held up my hands. "No argument from me." It had been an incredibly long day, and it was nearly one in the morning already.

"I will see you tomorrow," Nightliss said, and took a portal back to the Ranch.

Elyssa and I went back to the mansion with Shelton and Bella.

Shelton pulled me aside after the women went upstairs. "All right, so I got some ideas for asking Bella to marry me."

I hadn't given his request much thought and instantly felt guilty. "I haven't come up with anything yet."

"That's okay." He joined the tips of his thumbs together as if framing the view. "Picture this. I take Bella on a walk, then other people who are pretending to be on a walk themselves just burst into song and start dancing. I figure we could get a lot of Templars to do that. By the time we get to this cliff overlooking the valley, you, Elyssa, and all our friends jump out of hiding, dance and sing while I drop to my knees and pop the question. I call it the flash mob wedding proposal."

I blinked several times, before realizing he was serious. "Uh, that's probably the worst idea I've ever heard. Can you imagine getting Templars to perform song and dance?"

"I thought it would be kinda neat." He shrugged. "Okay, so another idea I had was we commandeer one of those old battle golems from the war—"

"You mean a goliath?"

He nodded eagerly. "Yeah, exactly. Me, you, Bella, and Elyssa go on a picnic. We make the goliath attack. You pretend that you sprained a back muscle or something, so I come to the rescue and pow! I knock it over. On the bottom of its foot it says, "Bella, you're a real knockout. Will you marry me?"

My initial snort of mirth turned to uncontrolled laughter. "Shelton, where in the hell are you getting these ideas?"

He frowned. "Cinder researched them for me. He said the noms have all sorts of neato ideas for proposals."

I groaned. "If I didn't know better, I'd say Cinder is totally playing you." I gave him a pointed look. "And you'd deserve it after the rotten advice you've given him about acting more human."

"My advice is straight from the heart, man."

"Yeah, like telling him to grunt every few minutes because that's what real people do?" I rolled my eyes. "Look, you don't need to impress Bella with all that crap. She loves you—heaven help that poor confused woman—and that's the only thing you need to know. Take her out for a fun date, and ask her to marry you beneath the full moon."

"Oh, I could ask Ryland and his buds to fake a lycan attack." He clawed at his neck. "I'll have blood pouring from a wound, and then when she thinks I'm dead, I'll pull a ring from the blood and propose."

"Now I know you're just making stuff up."

He laughed. "Yeah, but the look on her face would be priceless."

"Right before she punched you." I put a hand on his shoulder. "Look, I'm exhausted, and I'm dying to brush my teeth after the ice cream today. Let's sleep on it, okay?"

"Sure thing." He looked toward the kitchen. "I'm gonna get a snack first."

"Are you sure you need something else to eat?" I set my arms akimbo like Elyssa did when she challenged me. "I think you're stress munching."

He shrugged. "Yeah, I suppose the stress of proposing is getting to me."

"All the more reason to get it done and over with." I stifled a yawn. "Goodnight."

"Night, man."

I headed up to my room and got ready. Elyssa was already in bed reading something on her arctablet.

"Whatcha reading?" I asked when I snuggled up next to her.

"Invasion plans." She turned off the tablet and set it on the nightstand. "Once we finish off the crystoids, my father wants to enter Seraphina in force and finish off Cephus."

"I was thinking the same thing." I squeezed shut my eyes and groaned. "It feels like we're never going to have a lasting peace."

Elyssa stroked my head. "I know, baby."

I rolled onto my back and stared at the ceiling. "Why didn't we just invade right away? All I had to do was redirect the army to an Alabaster Arch, and we could've ended this months ago. Instead of chasing crystoids all over the world, we'd still be sitting on the beach."

"Maybe." She tapped a finger on her chin. "Or we might still be embroiled in a war. Once we defeated Cephus, I imagine we'd have moved on to fix the conflict between the Darklings and Brightlings."

"Yeah, you're probably right." I nuzzled my nose against hers and kissed her forehead. "We still should've skipped vacation and taken the long road to peace. Instead, I chose short term pleasure, and now we're paying the price."

"You've got to stop beating yourself up over that, Justin." She leaned against me. "We'll beat this like we've beaten everything else."

"Yeah." I knew we'd eventually prevail, but cleaning up the crystoids looked to be a long-lasting project if we didn't gain access to all the impact sites.

Thomas met Elyssa and me with a grim face the next morning in the conference room. "Commander Salazar requested help in Medellin." He projected a video from his arctablet showing at least a dozen transformed airships circling the impact zone. "His forces have taken casualties from camouflaged robot forces hiding in the jungle."

"How are we supposed to travel there?" Elyssa asked.

Thomas switched to a map and zoomed to Central America. "Our people were able to open a portal as far south as Panama. I've rented two troop transport planes that we'll take from there to the international airport in Medellin. From there, it's a three hour drive south."

"How are we supposed to fight robots and laser-equipped airships without magic?" I asked. "Granted, we might do okay against the robots if our Nightingale armor holds up, but the airships are another matter."

Thomas switched back to the airship footage. "I tried to purchase combat helicopters from a black arms dealer in Panama, but they couldn't supply the ammunition we needed. Commander Salazar employed the use of anti-aircraft missiles, but the airships are equipped with flares that divert the projectiles."

I paused the video and zoomed in on one of the airships. "With their armor active, we can't hijack them like I did in North Korea." I tried to rotate the holograph, but it was two-dimensional. "How old is this recording?"

"It's actually recent. Commander Salazar is utilizing a satellite phone and relay system." Thomas folded his arms. "We purchased enough bandwidth to allow a live video feed if we want it."

"Who'd have thought we'd be using nom technology for a Templar mission?" I stared at the frozen image of the airship and noticed it had a turret on the top and bottom instead of just one. It also sported a missile launcher. "Did anyone else notice these things are upgraded?"

"This is going to be a nightmare," Elyssa said. "How far away is the crystoid from populated areas?"

Thomas switched to a map and zoomed to a three-dimensional view. "It's located in a valley, miles away from any habitats." He narrowed his eyes. "Why?"

Elyssa walked up to the holographic image and surveyed the area. "The terrain is treacherous, guarded by robots in the forest and heavily armed airships above. A ground assault would yield heavy casualties on our part, with very little risk to the defenders."

"Where are you going with this?" I asked.

"There's an alternative." She sighed. "I think our best hope is destroying the crystoid."

Chapter 23

My eyes went wide. "You want to blow it up?"

Elyssa nodded. "I hate to say it, but that might be the easiest way."

"Do you suggest we bomb it using a plane?" Thomas said. "I might possibly procure the ordinance, but it would likely be an unguided drop. Our chances of hitting the target would be slim."

Inspiration struck. "You know the portals in the sky above the crystoids?"

They nodded.

"Did the ones above the neutralized crystoids close?" I asked.

Thomas nodded. "Apparently the aether from the crystoids was the only thing keeping them open."

"Damn." I pinch-zoomed the map for a worldwide view and looked at the remaining crystoids. "Do we have images of anymore impact sites?"

He pointed to one off the coast of Iceland. "That's the only one, but it's several hundred feet underwater."

I scrolled to the location. "Is it visible from the surface?"

"Yes, but it's created a maelstrom like the one off Thailand." Thomas flicked to an image of a great foaming vortex in the water.

Elyssa frowned. "You want to travel through the sky portal above the crystoid and find the corresponding one over Colombia, don't you?"

I nodded. "Think about this. We could fly a broom down the aether beam to every other crystoid site and take pictures, then open a portal and neutralize them." I slapped the back of a hand into my palm. "I don't know why I didn't think of this before."

"That won't solve the Colombian issue though," Elyssa said. "They'll probably anticipate a portal opening over the crystoid, and you have to be fairly close to channel into it."

"Right, but if I fly a broom close enough, I might be able to drop a timed explosive into the crater." I made a diving motion with my hand, then swooped it back up. "I fly back through the sky portal, the timer goes off, and boom."

"I have a better idea," Elyssa said. "Didn't Cinder learn how to make golems from Fjoeruss?"

"Genius!" I hugged her and pulled back. "We could have a golem fly an explosive right into the crater."

Elyssa beamed. "Let's call Cinder."

"I'll tell Commander Salazar to pull back his troops," Thomas said. "If this works, they'll need to be miles away to escape the blast radius."

I called Cinder, but his reply to my request dampened my mood.

"Justin, I'm afraid I can't make a golem coordinated enough to fly a broom," he said. "So far, my creations have been rather rudimentary. I can offer an alternative."

"Fjoeruss?" I said.

"Perhaps, though Victus Edison might provide you with a robot that could perform the task."

I scowled at the thought of asking Victus, but he might actually prove useful. Plus, unless he was in league with Frankenberg, he hadn't actually done anything to hinder our efforts. "Thanks, Cinder."

"I wish I could be more useful, Justin, though I may have come up with a way to safely neutralize the crystoids from afar."

My grim mood brightened. "Really?"

"Indeed. I studied our past encounters with the malaether crucibles," he said. "Theoretically, it should be possible to fill a crucible with Stasis and detonate it on a crystoid."

I whooped. "Cinder, that's brilliant!"

"Ha, ha, ha," he responded with a somewhat manic laugh. "I am glad you think so. Though I lack the ability to infuse a crucible, you should find all the materials you need at the Templar compound."

"Cinder, you might have just found the magic bullet." I almost hopped in place like Ivy when she was overjoyed. "I'll test one right away."

I ended the call.

"Wow." Elyssa gave me a wondering look. "Did Cinder pull through?"

"He more than pulled through." I told them about his crucible theory.

"We have dozens of empty crucibles in the armory," Thomas said.

I turned for the door. "I'm on the way."

"Wait." Elyssa grabbed my arm. "A crucible can't be guided. We'll still need a delivery system."

It seemed Victus might still have a part to play. "I think it's time to ask Science Academy for help."

Thomas took out his phone. "I'll contact Victus."

"Let's be careful who we tell about this." An uneasy feeling squirmed in my stomach. "Frankenberg might be acting alone, or he might have help."

Thomas lowered the phone. "Are you suggesting I contact someone else at the academy?"

"Maybe. I think we need to play it safe." Unfortunately, I didn't know who else to contact.

Commander Borathen folded his arms across his chest. "I've dealt with plenty of similar situations. Let me handle it. What I need to know is if the crucible idea will be feasible."

Thomas Borathen had a few centuries' worth of dealing with scumbags and fighting wars. Knowing he was in charge of the Science Academy issue made me feel a lot better. "In that case, we'll be in the armory." I grabbed Elyssa's hand and we made our way down to the weapons room.

A Templar behind a window let us into the back room at Elyssa's command. We walked past racks of swords, past shelves filled with crates, and to the back wall where pads held the spherical glass crucibles. They varied in size from small melon-shaped globes to the largest that came up past my waist. They looked incredibly fragile, but were strong enough to be launched from catapults. Arcanes usually filled them with destructive magical spells, which reminded me—I didn't know how to charge one.

"How do I get Stasis inside one of these things?" I asked.

Elyssa pointed to a large bronze contraption shaped like a box. A wide vice with suction cups on the clamps protruded from the center. "Arcanes put the crucible on the sealer and tighten the arm so a suction cup touches the top and bottom. Then they cast spells at the crucible." She pretended to wave a wand. "Once they're done charging the crucible, you spin the handle on the sealer and it charges the outside of the glass to keep the spell from leaking out."

"Sounds easy enough." I picked up a large crucible and set it on the lower suction cup then twisted the wheel on the side of the arm until the top suction cup made contact.

"Not too tight," Elyssa said. She inspected the top. "It's not all the way down."

I eased the vice tighter until Elyssa told me to stop.

"Good enough." She backed up. "Do your magic, hot stuff."

I kissed her on the cheek. "As you wish." I summoned spheres of Murk and Brilliance in either hand, then wove them into a ball of Stasis. I channeled a gray beam into the crucible and it began to fill with fog. "How much can this thing hold?" I asked.

"I have no idea." Elyssa backed up a few steps.

I gave her an alarmed look. "Will it shatter if it gets too full?"

She shrugged and backed up again.

Discerning the correct amount of Stasis was something I hadn't considered. It typically took me a solid minute or two of channeling to disable a crystoid, so I counted the seconds and let the Stasis flow. When I reached the two-minute mark, I breathed a sigh of relief and released the weave. "I hope that's enough."

Elyssa pointed to the lever on the side of the machine. "Don't forget to seal it."

I spun the handle on the side and the sealer hummed.

"Keep spinning it until it crackles," Elyssa said.

I did as instructed. A few seconds later, magical energy arced across the surface of the glass sphere, crackling like electricity. I stopped rotating the handle and the crucible emitted a dim glow.

I stepped back and admired my handiwork. "Looking good."

Elyssa stepped to my side. "Now we have to test it."

I pumped a fist. "Colombia, here we come."

After carefully loosening the vice, I lifted the sphere and noted it felt only slightly heavier than before. Even so, it was cumbersome to walk with such a large glass ball in my arms.

Elyssa snorted as I waddled toward her. "We have levitator carts for those things." She walked behind the sealing machine and returned, pulling the handle of a floating platform with four pads lined up in a row on top.

I placed the crucible on it. *One might not be enough.* "I'm going to fill four crucibles just in case."

She nodded. "Yeah, good idea."

About a half hour later, I breathed a sigh of relief and loaded the cart with the fourth and final crucible. The process had drained me, but hopefully it would be worth it.

I towed the cart out of the armory. At Elyssa's suggestion, we rode the levitator at the end of the corridor all the way up to the underground parking garage and tucked the cart with the Stasis crucibles in a corner.

Practically the whole gang except for Nightliss was waiting for us when we reached the conference room.

Shelton went for a high-five when he saw me, and I didn't leave him hanging. "You ready to kick some ass?"

I slapped his hand. "You know it."

A hopeful gleam shone in Mom's eyes. "If this works, it could be the turning point."

"It's got to work," I said. "We just need a way to land them to the crystoids."

"Do you need me to fill some crucibles?" Ivy asked.

"Not yet," I told her. "First, we need to test them."

Thomas appeared in the doorway and motioned me into the hall.

"What did you find out?" I asked.

"I spoke with Victus," he said. "Before I could talk to him about our new idea, he told me that he'd heard about Frankenberg's betrayal, and had assembled a small army of battle bots to assist us."

I felt my eyebrows rise. "Interesting."

"I invited him here so we could discuss logistics." Thomas's phone beeped and he checked it. "In fact, he just arrived in the hangar."

"What do you want me to do?" I asked.

"I'll speak to him about specifics and make it very clear he's not to tell anyone, not even his wife, about our plans."

"Let's hope he agrees to it."

Thomas nodded his head toward the levitator at the end of the corridor. "I'll go meet him and join the rest of you after our discussion." He turned and left without another word.

Shelton was arguing with Adam when I entered the room. "Are you kidding me? Rocket sticks would be perfect."

"You can't guide the stupid things," Adam said. "Plus, how in the world would you secure a big honking crucible to the stick?"

"Duct tape." Shelton circled his arm through the air as if taping a crucible to a rocket stick.

"Doesn't Science Academy have guided rockets?" I asked.

"Yeah," Adam said. "But even if you could strap a crucible to them, their aerodynamic profile would be so far off, the missile would probably fly in loops or crash."

"There must be some way to guide the crucibles to the crystoids." I ran a hand through my hair. "What about strapping a crucible to the back of a robot and command it to fly a rocket stick into the crater?"

"Sure, that could work," Shelton said.

Adam nodded. "It'd work, but robots are expensive and time-consuming to build. I doubt we'd have enough to spare."

"Man, you guys really know how to spoil the mood." I puffed out a breath. "And here I thought we had the answer."

"We do have the answer," Adam said. "It's just not going to be as easy to use it as we'd hoped."

Thomas marched past us and to the front of the room with Victus Edison behind him. The conversations faded.

"As I'm sure you're all aware, we've had some recent developments that may speed the conclusion of the crystoid incident," Thomas said. "Victus also has something he'd like to share."

"Thank you, Commander Borathen." Victus's lips curved into a politician's smile. "Science Academy wholeheartedly condemns the actions of former Chancellor Frankenberg. We don't know if he's a key player in the crystoid incident, or simply an opportunist, but we will do whatever possible to bring him to justice."

"Sounds like a stump speech," Shelton murmured.

"To that end, we're donating twenty-five new battle-bots to help combat Frankenberg's troops." He paused as if waiting for applause, but Ivy was the only one who clapped.

"Oh, I love robots!" she exclaimed. "Do they make beep-beep boop-boop noises, or can they talk?"

Victus's smile faded. "Uh, these talk." He cleared his throat and continued. "Commander Borathen also asked if we could provide a reliable delivery method for crucibles."

"Rocket sticks and duct tape," Shelton said.

Adam face-palmed.

Victus nodded as if it were an idea worthy of consideration. "I thought about rockets or missiles, but the size of the crucibles would be a hindrance to navigation."

"What about flying robots?" Ivy said.

"The current generation of flying robots suffers from too many deficiencies to do the job," he replied. "Robots are also not very good at flying rocket sticks or that might also be a consideration."

Shelton frowned. "Dash all our hopes and dreams, why don't ya?"

Victus frowned. "The situation might seem rather hopeless." His frown turned upside down. "Fortunately, we do have a solution."

"Of course he does," Adam muttered.

"Delivery drones." Victus's statement didn't exactly arouse a big cheer, primarily because we were trading confused looks.

"You mean like those remote-controlled planes the noms use?" Elyssa said.

He shook his head. "No. It's better if I show you." Victus took out an arcphone, set it on the table, and projected a video from it. "This is a promotional video, so please excuse any hyperbole."

A somber voice spoke. "Getting a time-sensitive package to a recipient is a challenge." The video showed a frustrated man trying to fly a rocket stick with a big box under one arm, and crashing into the water. "Until now, you've always had to rely on others to do it for you." The image switched to a kid tossing a package onto someone's doorstep and the sound of glass shattering inside.

The voice grew excited. "Now there's an easier way. Introducing the UFO Three-K personal delivery drone." The image switched to show a flying saucer the size of a dinner plate lifting a large box off the ground and carrying it from a man with a huge grin on his face, to a woman who squealed with joy as she pulled fragile glass statues from the delivered box.

Victus paused the video. "I think you get the idea."

"Yeah, I get the idea," Shelton said. "That thing will get shot out of the sky faster than a buck-toothed fairy on a flying corncob."

"Uh…" Victus gave him an uncertain look. "We can fit the drones with camouflage. If we only activate the camouflage during the crucial transition through enemy forces, the battery should last long enough to see it safely to the ground."

Adam raised a hand. "The crucible actually needs to smash on the ground to be effective."

"We can program the drones for a low altitude airdrop." Victus forwarded the video to show one of the flying saucers drop a box with a parachute attached. "Instead of putting a parachute on the package, we allow it to freefall."

"How soon can we get these drones?" Elyssa asked.

Victus splayed his hands. "Right now if you want."

"I'll go with him," Shelton said.

Adam waved a hand. "Me too."

"Can I have a flying saucer?" Ivy asked Mom.

Mom rubbed her shoulder. "Maybe after the war, darling."

Ivy sagged. "Aw, but I want one now."

"You can fill crucibles for the flying saucers," I told her.

She brightened. "Sure. Where do we go?"

"I'll take you." I turned to Elyssa. "We'll be in the armory."

"Sounds good." She motioned toward the holographic map. "I'll be up here discussing logistics. If the test in Colombia goes well, we could launch dozens of attacks at once."

Victus stopped in front of me on his way out the door. "Let us hope this will be the blow that brings us peace."

Well, it'll give you something to brag about on the campaign trail. I planted a smile on my face. "If it works, it'll bring us a step closer to victory."

He nodded. "I suppose the next logical step would be invading Seraphina."

"Maybe." I didn't want to give him anything else for the campaign trail.

"I'm certain Science Academy will donate more battle-bots to the cause." He leaned closer and whispered, "Unfortunately, right after the war, hundreds of our top of the line units went missing from our warehouse. It appears Frankenberg must have absconded with them while everyone was busy celebrating."

"Just what we need," I said. "A well-armed madman on the loose."

"Hey, we're burning daylight," Shelton said. "We need to get those drones."

Victus stiffened and his jaw went tight. He obviously didn't like anyone telling him what to do. He quickly recovered with an affable smile. "Of course. Let's go."

"What about Nightliss?" Ivy asked.

"Blessing Templar recruits has tired her," Thomas said. "She's resting."

I turned to Ivy and Mom. "Let's go charge some crucibles."

We were about to turn this battle around.

Chapter 24

Ivy sagged after charging her sixth crucible.

"I think you might have overcharged that first one," I told her, looking uneasily at the webbed cracks in the glass. I hadn't paid close enough attention to the time she took to fill it.

"Can we get more ice cream now?" Ivy asked, a hopeful gleam in her eyes. "I'm so hungry."

"Let's get some real food after I'm done," Mom said. She looked at me with a radiant smile. "I hear you two had a good time going out together."

I grinned back. "It was a blast."

Ivy let out a long sigh. "Ice cream would be tops right now."

I kissed her forehead. "Maybe later."

Mom pulled back the sleeves on her dress. "I suppose it's my turn."

I placed a crucible on the sealer and reset the timer on my arcphone. "Ready when you are."

She took a deep breath and channeled. By the time she was done, we had four more crucibles ready to go.

I loaded the last globe on a levitation cart. "That's fourteen including mine," I said. "Good start."

We each grabbed the handle of a cart and loaded them onto the levitator. Only two fit in at a time, so I took them up to the garage and parked them next to the ones I'd filled, then returned and brought up the last one. I met everyone in the conference room where Victus demonstrated one of the drones.

He held up a shiny chrome disc shaped like a flying saucer from a vintage movie. It measured perhaps three feet in diameter and four inches thick at the base with a curved hump in the middle complete

213

with little lighted windows. "The UFO delivery drone can be programmed or controlled remotely from an app on your arcphone or arctablet devices." He held up a tablet and touched an icon shaped like the drone. When the program started, he demonstrated how to use a map to assign coordinates where the drone would automatically travel.

"Simply zoom into the map and touch the precise location or put in an address." Victus switched to another screen with a first-person view from the camera on the drone. "Alternatively, you can fly the drone using these simple controls."

"Looks easy enough," Adam said. "How will the drones carry crucibles?"

Victus flicked the controls on the screen and the drone lifted off. A small hook extended from the bottom. "You'll need to harness the crucibles in some sort of net so the hook has something to hold onto."

Shelton grunted. "I expected something fancier."

Victus stiffened. "Sometimes, simpler is better."

"What about the camouflage?" Elyssa asked.

"Simply affix this module"—he held up a thin coin-sized device—"to the side of the drone. It holds about a three minute charge, so you won't want to activate it until absolutely necessary."

Adam took the camouflage module and turned it over in his fingers. "Remotely activated, I hope?"

"Yes, yes," Victus replied, a note of impatience in his voice. He cleared his throat and was once again Mr. Friendly. "Once the package is in the desired position, press the release icon." He landed the drone back on the table and deactivated it.

"Let's test it," I said. I motioned toward the drone on the table. "May I?"

Victus was all smiles again. "Of course, Justin." He affixed the camouflage module to the underside of the saucer. "First, you'll need to download the app and register it with the drone."

"Already done." I'd followed along when he'd registered the drone on his phone, even though he hadn't given us a step-by-step tutorial.

"Oh, excellent." He pocketed his phone. "I'm ready when you are."

I turned to Thomas. "Is everything set?"

He nodded. "The ASE we sent to scout for the correct portal to Colombia returned with the information."

"Use my cracked crucible first," Ivy said. "I want to see what happens."

"Cracked one?" Shelton gave Ivy a troubled look. "How did it get cracked?"

"I accidentally channeled too much Stasis inside." She giggled. "I'll bet it's gonna look neato when it hits the ground."

"Uh, yeah." Shelton shook his head. "Man, I didn't even know it was possible to fill a crucible so full you cracked it."

Adam nudged me in the ribs and spoke in a low voice. "Your sister is kinda scary powerful."

"Thanks, Adam!" Ivy blushed. "That's so sweet."

I snorted. "Let's go." I tucked the UFO drone under an arm and headed toward the levitator while the crowd followed behind.

Victus kept pace with me, but seemed content to remain silent. I didn't really feel like engaging him in small talk, so I kept quiet and thought about the mission. We packed into the levitator and rode it up to the garage.

Ivy clasped her hands as if in prayer. "The cracked one, Justin, please."

I handed Shelton the drone. "Hold onto that one for me, please."

He took it and looked warily at the damaged crucible on the cart. "That thing makes me a little nervous."

"Yeah, well Stasis doesn't usually kill—it just freezes things for a while." I shrugged. "At least that's the theory."

He shuddered. "Just make sure you don't drop it."

I chuckled and grabbed the cart handle. "I'll be extra careful."

Elyssa spoke with the Templar in charge of scheduling portals, and requested one for the Grotto control room, then she and her father each grabbed the handle of the remaining two carts and pulled them up to the yellow line around the portal zone. Another Templar jogged over and handed Thomas several black nets to harness the crucibles.

A portal opened a few minutes later, and we stepped through it to the Grotto control room. After everyone filed through, I closed the portal and turned to Elyssa.

"Do you have the image for the ocean portal?" I asked.

"Yep." She stepped into the silver ring around the omniarch, sealed it, and concentrated on the image on her phone. The air within the arch split open a moment later to reveal a massive maelstrom roaring about twenty feet below. Despite how often I'd used portals, it was still strange to be looking straight ahead at something that was technically below me. If I stepped through the gateway, I'd plummet into the foaming salt water.

A shiver ran through my back.

Elyssa touched my arm. "You okay?"

I nodded. "Yeah. Just looking at that thing reminds me of Thailand."

"Gives me the chills," Elyssa said. "Just don't think of going for a swim."

"I didn't bring my water wings." I turned around and took the drone from Shelton, setting it on the floor in front of the portal.

"One cracked crucible coming right up," Adam said, as he helped Thomas secure the glass sphere with one of the nets.

A bead of sweat trickled down Shelton's face as he watched them outfit the Stasis bomb.

"Whoops!" Adam shouted.

Shelton leapt back and nearly tripped over his own feet. He scowled. "Not funny, man."

Ivy giggle-snorted. "That was hilarious."

Adam chuckled. "Go clean your pants, Shelton."

I flicked to the drone app on my phone and levitated the UFO off the floor using the remote controls. Thomas and Adam lifted the cracked crucible by the net harness and brought it over to me. I flew the drone over the net, lowered the grappling hook, and latched on.

Shelton recovered some of his dignity and walked closer. "Man, I feel like a straight up alien invader."

"Aliens versus robots," Adam added. "This would make a great movie."

"It would be pretty sick," I agreed.

Bella sighed. "I suppose anything with robots, aliens, and explosions would make you boys happy."

Shelton nodded. "Yeah, pretty much."

"Totally," Adam agreed.

I flew the drone through the portal. It flipped to adjust to the change in gravitational orientation. "Let's hope this explosion does the job."

"Yeah, well first you gotta reach the target," Adam said. "Remember, every single crystoid on the planet is holding open a sky portal to Seraphina. Once you get through the sky portal above this crystoid, you'll be directly over Cephus's fortress. There will be dozens of sky portals there, and you'll need to go through the correct one to reach the target crystoid."

"You make it sound so easy," Shelton grumbled. He nudged my arm. "Oh and don't forget every one of those portals is sucking Eden dry. Every second you waste brings us another step closer to annihilation."

"Will you two shut up?" I glared at them. "I know what's at stake here."

Adam grinned. "We just want to make sure you're on top of your game."

"Yeah, no pressure." I sat on the floor, set the phone in front of me, and projected a holographic image of the controls. From this perspective, I could rotate the camera three hundred and sixty degrees around the drone. The perspective shifted up from the drone's perspective and I saw myself seemingly sitting in the sky with the group huddled behind me.

"Whoah, that's weird," Shelton said.

"Can I fly it?" Ivy asked.

I shook my head. "Sorry, sis. I'm gonna drop this bomb." I made the drone climb higher and higher until finally it reached the crystoid portal to Seraphina. Since this gateway faced the ground in the other realm, the drone and its cargo flipped in response to the reversal in gravity.

I released a relieved breath after the drone made the transition. Even though the grappling hook looked secure, I feared it might lose its cargo. The next part of the journey might have taken hours if Thomas hadn't sent ASEs to scout the way. Just as Adam said, dozens of portals, one for each remaining crystoid in Eden, shimmered in the air above the drone. Every single one of them was like an open drain hole sucking away Eden's magic.

Thomas consulted his arcphone and held it up next to the holographic camera view from the drone. "I believe it's this one." He circled a gateway with his finger.

Elyssa looked from Thomas's phone to the view from the drone. "Yep, that's it."

I sent the drone up and through the portal. Once again, the view spun as gravity flip-flopped. Dark clouds formed a gray landscape far below the portal.

I sent the drone into a sharp descent. It cleared the clouds moments later and revealed verdant mountains covered with trees. The winged shapes of modified airships circled far below, confirming we were in the right location.

"Thar they blow," Shelton said.

Ivy giggled. "Thar they blow up!"

A gust of wind sent the drone off course, so I adjusted its flight path, taking it lower and lower. "How far of a drop will the crucible need to break?" I asked.

"At least a hundred feet," Shelton said.

Adam nodded. "Yeah, that'll do it."

The altimeter on the drone read five-thousand feet. The airships hovered far below. If they were at the same altitude as the ones in North Korea, that would put them at only a few hundred feet.

It wasn't until the drone reached five-hundred feet that a laser beam flashed past. I hit the camouflage button and took evasive action.

Five more airships opened fire on the UFO's previous coordinates. Brilliant energy crackled past. A timer in the lower right corner of the holographic control panel told me how much time remained on the camouflage module's charge. Despite my best efforts, the drone was descending too slowly to make it.

Another stiff wind took the drone farther away from the target. "Damn it." I drove it back against the current and finally got back on course.

"C'mon, Justin," Shelton said. "You got this."

"Go, bro, go!" Ivy shouted.

One minute remained on the timer. The airships dove lower until they barely skimmed the trees, firing blindly all around the UFO. One laser nearly engulfed the drone, missing by inches. I shifted the camera angle directly at the ground. The altimeter read two hundred feet. Thirty seconds of camouflage remained. Seconds ticked past. A hundred and fifty feet remained.

"Drop it," Elyssa said. "They won't be able to hit it in time."

I trusted her instincts and released the crucible. The glass sphere lost its camouflage the moment it separated from the drone. I flew the drone with the prevailing wind and spun the camera behind it just as the crucible hit home.

For a long moment, nothing happened. Suddenly a huge cloud of Stasis exploded from the crater like a thundercloud, rushing across the landscape and engulfing the airships. I pulled the drone into a steep climb and barely managed to keep out of the blast zone. Over the course of several seconds, the energy sparkled and slowly dissipated.

Airships drifted aimlessly, spiraling toward the forest below. Some shattered on impact; others crumpled like paper. Trees smashed apart like glass. The landscape below resembled a gray petrified wasteland.

"Whoa, that was awesome," Ivy breathed.

"The crystoid." Thomas said.

I took the drone over the crater and zoomed in. The last pockets of Stasis faded away, revealing shattered crystal below.

"Yes!" I pumped a fist and turned to meet fist bumps from Shelton and Adam.

Ivy jumped and hugged Mom. "Did you see what my crucible did? It was so cool!"

Elyssa smothered me with a hug and a long hot kiss. She pulled away. "You did it, babe. We're going to wipe out these things."

Victus wore a smug smile and extended a hand. "Excellent work, Justin."

I shook his hand and shrugged. "You can thank my family."

Shelton slapped my shoulder. "Brothers from another mother."

"You got it!" I squeezed him in a hug then pulled back. "Let's finish this."

Chapter 25

The next week seemed like an endless cycle of feeding on soul essence, filling crucibles, and falling exhausted into bed. Shelton, Adam, Bella, Elyssa, and even Thomas took turns flying drones over impact craters and dropping the crucibles onto crystoids. Mom, Ivy, Nightliss, and I were careful not to overfill the crucibles, and kept collateral damage to a minimum.

With Colombia enjoying magic once again, Christian Salazar and his Templar legion were able to help us, and the rest of the gang finally joined us in Atlanta.

Elyssa and I went to the underground hangar to meet the new arrivals.

"Justin!" Katie Johnson gripped me in a tight hug the moment she came through a portal from La Casona.

"What's up, man?" Ash and Nyte, two friends from my high school days, dashed through the portal after her.

We fist-bumped and bro-hugged like there was no tomorrow.

"You and Elyssa practically vanished after the war," Katie said. "Where did you go?"

"We traveled the world," I replied.

Ash ran a hand through his thick black hair. "We wondered if you were ever coming back."

Nyte shrugged his huge shoulders. He'd gone from gangly ginger to muscled hulk during his time in the Templars. "I wouldn't blame you if you took a year to relax. The war was brutal." He shuddered. "I still have nightmares."

Guilt weighed heavy in my chest. "I shouldn't have left. Taking out Cephus and bringing peace to Seraphina should have been the priority."

"Cephus is the one behind all this?" Katie asked.

Elyssa nodded. "No question about it, though he might have help from Frankenberg, the former chancellor of Science Academy."

Ash put a hand on my shoulder. "Don't be so hard on yourself. Like Nyte said, you deserved a good long break. Nobody could have predicted Cephus would be able to pull off something so massive."

"A worldwide magic outage." Katie bit her lower lip. "How does that help him? He's a Darkling. He and his followers rely on magic as much as the rest of us."

"Probably wanted to keep us out of Seraphina," Elyssa said. "He had to know we'd come for him eventually."

I heard footsteps behind me and turned around to see Nightliss exit the levitator.

"Nightliss!" Katie said. She ran over and hugged the Darkling. "It's so good to see you again."

"It is good to see you too," Nightliss said.

"I thought we were done with war," Katie said sadly. "Haven't we been through enough horrors already?"

Elyssa leaned against me. "We've all seen terrible things," she said. "What's important is that we have each other, and that we rely on each other for strength to get through the difficult times."

"That's what family is for," Katie said, wrapping an arm around Nightliss's shoulders.

"I think the universe is trying to tell us that our work isn't done until we get Seraphina set right," Nyte said. "I'm ready to follow you again, Justin."

Ash nodded. "Me too."

"You can add me to the list," Katie added enthusiastically.

Someone cleared their throat behind me. I turned and saw Shelton and Bella there.

Shelton grunted. "Man, you guys really know how to get mushy."

"Harry, you just ruined a beautiful moment," Bella said. She came forward and hugged Katie. "It's so good to see you again."

"I'm so happy to be back with everyone," Katie said.

"It's good to be back," Nightliss said. "With family."

Shelton slapped me on the back. "I'm just glad the gang's all here."

It felt good to see everyone again. "Me too."

The feel-good moment was interrupted again by a text on my phone from Thomas. *Everyone get to the war room.* Elyssa's phone went off at the same time with the anxiety-inducing message.

"Looks like trouble's brewing again," Shelton said.

I nodded. "Let's get below to the conference room."

People packed the war room. I spotted Christian Salazar and an entourage of his Templars, along with Kassallandra, my parents, and even Captain Takei of the Blue Cloaks—the Arcane elite army. Victus Edison and his political opponent Evan Farnsworth stood near Thomas, actively avoiding looking at each other. Even Komad Rashad, the head vampire, was present.

Colin McCloud entered the room, followed by a hulking felycan everyone called Saber, since his preferred feline form was that of a massive smilodon—better known as a saber-toothed cat.

Mom came over to speak with Nightliss. "How are you holding up with all the work you've been doing?" she asked.

Nightliss clasped Mom's hand in her own. "The work is hard, but I feel once again like I'm making a difference."

"It appears we have a new challenge ahead of us," Thomas announced. He strode to the front of the room. "I call this meeting to order."

Conversations died away and all eyes turned to Thomas.

"While I'm sure many of you have some knowledge of the events leading to this day, you may not know everything." Thomas projected holographic footage of the crystoids streaking through the atmosphere and crashing to earth. "Two weeks ago, crystal meteors entered Eden through portals from Seraphina. Dubbed 'crystoids', these objects embedded themselves in the Earth's crust and began draining aether and redirecting it back through sky portals to the compound of a man named Cephus."

Shelton nudged me. "Hah, I knew my name for those things would catch on."

I put a finger to my lips to shush him.

Thomas flicked to an image of the great Murk dome around Cephus's fortress. "Cephus was once a member of the Trivectus, the ruling council of the Darklings. He murdered the other two members of the governmental body and then walled himself off in the Ministry of Research."

"Oh, my," Captain Takei said. "Isn't this is the man Ketiss took his Darkling army back to Seraphina to fight?"

"Yes," Thomas said. "Unfortunately, it appears he's had little luck." The video shifted to show the destruction around the compound, and the crystoid to the east. "With that crystoid in place, the skyway from the nearest Alabaster Arch is inoperable."

Christian Salazar spoke. "Australia is still suffering the effects of the crystoids. I spoke to Commander Taylor of the Australian Legion using nom phone lines. Apparently, one of the meteors landed close to the Three Sisters."

Murmurs rose as people absorbed the bad news.

In the realm of Seraphina, Pjurna was the geographical equivalent of Australia. The Alabaster Arch in the Three Sisters way station was the most direct way to reach it.

"So, even if we could use the Alabaster Arch in the Three Sisters, we still couldn't reach Pjurna," Captain Takei said. "That's quite troubling, to put it mildly."

"Agreed." Thomas switched to a recording of the airships guarding the crystoid we'd destroyed in Colombia. "Meanwhile, on this side, a former chancellor of the Science Academy, Charles Frankenberg, has been doing everything in his power to prevent us from disabling the crystoids."

"We confirmed that the robots and airship fleet guarding the crystoid near Medellin were all destroyed," Christian said.

Thomas frowned. "Unfortunately, it appears that was not his entire fleet."

"Son of a—is he in Australia?" Shelton asked.

"Not yet." Thomas switched to an image that caused gasps around the room.

In the video, nearly a dozen airships glided over the ocean, many of them towing large cargo containers.

"Where was this footage taken?" I asked.

"Over the Indian Ocean." Thomas switched to a map view with a mark just off the tip of Antarctica. A red line extended from the mark, crossing Tasmania, curving around the coast of Australia and terminating at the Three Sisters. "This is the likeliest route they'll take." Three more markers formed a triangle in northern Antarctica. "Given the location of the enemy fleet, we believe Frankenberg's secret base is located somewhere in this area."

"Should've known that sneaky bastard would hide down there," Shelton said.

"How did you get this footage?" Elyssa asked.

"As the crystoids have been cleared and aether restored to the affected areas, the ASEs which were part of the Overworld Transportation Authority's monitoring system have recharged and resumed recording." He touched an icon on the holographic image, and most of the map shaded green. Australia and other isolated areas remained red. "The green indicates the restored areas. Red indicates the influence of crystoids."

"How are we supposed to stop Frankenberg if we can't portal to Australia?" I asked.

"We hit his base," Thomas replied.

Shelton blew out a breath. "That's an awfully large chunk of land to search."

"I already have people on the ground," Thomas said. "Once we locate the base, we'll attack with everything we have. That should draw his forces back to defend it."

"Can't we use the ASEs to locate it?" Captain Takei asked.

Thomas shook his head. "Frankenberg is likely using camouflage or other means to block the ASEs within this area." He traced a finger along the lines of the triangle marked on the map.

"I can send robots in to aid the search," Victus said. "They have advanced scanning equipment that may help."

"The Arcane Council also stands ready to help," Evan added, "as you can tell by Captain Takei's presence here."

Captain Takei raised an eyebrow. "The Blue Cloaks are always ready to serve the Overworld in times of need."

"Pshht," Shelton muttered." I don't think Takei trusts the council after Cyphanis Rax ordered him to fight with Daelissa. Takei don't play politics."

I nodded. "He's a good man who doesn't blindly follow orders."

Colin McCloud walked forward and inspected the map. "I think this is a job best done by Lycans." He turned and looked at Saber. "And of course our brother felycans."

Saber nodded grimly, but said nothing.

McCloud tapped his nose. "You can't hide from our excellent sense of smell, and with four legs, we can cross rugged terrain in no time."

"Excellent suggestion," Thomas said. "How soon can you deploy?"

"The lycan packs are assembled and ready." He nodded toward Saber. "My large friend here has his people primed for action as well."

Saber circled a finger around the search zone and spoke in a low voice. "We will come from all sides and circle the prey." He flashed sharp fangs. "Their blood will festoon the frozen land."

Shelton gulped. "Remind me to never piss off that guy."

I raised my hand. "I think it's time for the Skywraiths to fly back into action."

Ivy cheered. "Yeah!"

Mom quickly quieted my overly excited sister, then nodded at me. "I'm ready to fly again."

"As am I," Nightliss proclaimed.

I turned to Thomas. "We'll provide air support and aid in the search."

Mom, Ivy, Nightliss, and I were the only Skywraiths left in Eden. The rest had gone with Ketiss back to Seraphina. I thought about Pixie and her crew and wondered if it might be wise to increase our ranks.

Commander Borathen pursed his lips and looked at the map for a moment while everyone watched in silence.

Everyone except for Ivy. "Why is he so quiet?" Ivy whispered loudly to Mom. "Doesn't he know we're all waiting for him to talk?"

"Shh," Mom told her.

Dad snorted and quickly covered his mouth.

"He's thinking real hard," Shelton whispered across the room to Ivy.

"Oh," she hissed back. "Okay."

Thomas, the seasoned professional, didn't acknowledge the banter. Using his finger, he traced several markers on the map and drew curved lines that appeared to be plans of attack. Elyssa shook her head and whispered in his ear. He nodded, wiped away one line, and replaced it with another. When he looked back at his daughter, pride shone in his eyes. Elyssa was too busy double-checking her father's work to notice.

"McCloud and Saber, you will be responsible for finding the base." He indicated blue markers around the triangulated area. "Divide your forces as you see fit, and each group will be portaled to one of these markers."

"Aye," McCloud said. "We'll sweep the area and report back."

Thomas nodded. "Please report to the main hangar for portal assignments."

McCloud and Saber left the room.

Thomas turned to me. "The Skywraiths will portal behind the airship fleet."

"Behind the fleet?" Shelton said. "Out in the middle of the ocean?"

"Your job will be to harass and slow their advance," Thomas told me. "Attack their flanks, but retreat back through the portal if they turn to attack."

"By slowing them down, you'll give us more time to launch the attack on Frankenberg's secret base," Elyssa said. Her violet eyes met mine. "Harassment only, Justin. No heroics."

I saluted. "Yes, Commander."

Her lips spread into a smile. Apparently, she liked the title.

"Once the base is located, we'll launch a full-scale attack." Thomas slashed a line through the triangle. "Templars, Daemos, and Blue Cloaks will take the front line. Support crews with crucible catapults and healers will come behind."

"House Assad and House Slade are ready to serve," Kassallandra said. "I may not have enough time to rally the other houses."

"Do what you can, please, Maedras Kassallandra." Thomas directed a look at my father. "We will likely need everyone if Frankenberg's fortress has heavy defenses."

226

"I'm certain it will," Victus said. "We took a full inventory of missing assets from Science Academy. It amounts to two hundred battle-bots, three mega-bots—"

"Mega-bots?" I asked.

"Yes, they stand several stories high and are equipped with all manner of weaponry." Victus pressed his lips together and shook his head. "I'm afraid he's amassed quite an arsenal."

"Christ Almighty," Shelton said. "He's got a full-fledged robot army."

Chapter 26

The room went deathly quiet.

Kassallandra ended the silence. "I will rally the other houses." Her eyes flashed red. "They will submit, and we will defeat Frankenberg's army."

Thomas nodded and braced a hand on his chin. "Is there any way we can take control of the battle-bots or mega-bots?"

"Yes, but it requires infiltrating the fortress and finding the command and control center," Victus replied. "It's unlikely we'll discover the secret base before it discovers us. With his defenses online, we'll have to fight through his main force."

"Not if we act quickly," Bella said. "Once Frankenberg activates his defenses, the battle-bots will have to emerge from wherever they are. This would give an infiltration team the ideal opportunity to slip inside."

"I'm putting you in charge of that operation," Thomas told her. "Gather a team and meet with me after this meeting."

Shelton gave Bella a wide-eyed look and opened his mouth to speak. She tapped a finger on his lips and shook her head. He frowned.

Thomas pointed to Victus and flicked his finger toward Bella. "Chancellor Edison, please speak with Bella and give her all the intel she'll need for success."

A smug smile appeared on Victus's lips. "Yes, sir."

Despite Victus's helpful attitude, I still couldn't make myself like him. His usefulness obviously played right into his political ambitions. Judging from the downcast look on Evan's face, it was obvious he felt a bit useless.

I didn't want Victus to feel too comfortable. "Councilor Farnsworth, do you know three Arcanes by the names of Pixie, Boris, and Tasha? They were assigned to the North Dakota crystoid. I'm afraid the Skywraiths are a bit shorthanded and they expressed interest in helping us."

Evan's face brightened. "Absolutely. I know the people in question."

Victus's gaze darted my way, and just as quickly flicked away.

"I see what you did there," Shelton whispered, an evil grin on his face. "Better watch out, or you'll be endorsing candidates next."

I matched his grin. "Yeah, maybe I'll endorse you as a write-in candidate."

His eyes flared. "I swear on my grandfather's three-legged porcupine that I'd beat your ass if you did."

"How may the Red Syndicate serve?" Komad asked. He'd remained quiet until now, and I had to wonder if he really wanted a part in this battle, or was simply playing along.

"How many vampires will fight?" Thomas asked.

"Three-hundred Red Cell soldiers are standing by."

I was a bit surprised to hear him volunteer the troop of elite vampire warriors to the cause, but chose to accept it as a positive development.

"They can help bolster our front lines," Thomas said. "Please report to the hangar for a portal assignment."

Komad bowed. "It shall be done."

"Any questions?" Thomas asked. When there were none, he dismissed the meeting.

Elyssa took my hand and pulled me to the side while the others filed out of the room. "As your commander, I'm ordering you to use common sense and not over-engage the airships."

I tucked a lock of dark hair behind her ear and kissed her soft, wonderful lips. "You're so beautiful when you're bossy."

She raised an eyebrow. "I'm not being bossy, Justin."

"I know." I looked at her and sighed. "I never get tired of looking at you. Spending every single day with you during our travels was the most fun I've ever had in my life."

She blushed and looked away. "How do you make me feel so giggly inside when I'm trying to be stern?"

I nuzzled my nose against hers. "I think it's called being hopelessly in love."

Her violet eyes gazed deep into mine. "I never want it to end."

"Neither do I."

She kissed me. "Then be careful so we can have our forever."

I squeezed her tight, savoring the feel of her soft cheek pressed to mine. "I will, babe." I pulled back. "I assume you'll be on the command platform with your father?"

"Yep." She bounced on her toes. "He really listens to my suggestions now. Did you see how he changed the approach patterns on the map?"

I chuckled. "I think you live for planning."

She giggled. "I was a little controlling on our vacation, wasn't I?"

"You plotted out everything, woman." I sighed contentedly. "I loved every minute of it."

"Well, that's good." She pecked a kiss on my nose. "I'd better go." She glanced toward the door. "I think the Skywraiths are anxiously awaiting their glorious leader."

I walked her out the door and met my illustrious crew. "I hope you all remember how to fly a boomstick."

"I could use a little practice," Nightliss said.

Mom nodded. "Me too."

"Okay, we'll grab boomsticks, Nightingale armor, and go back to Queens Gate for a quick refresher course." I motioned toward the levitator at the end of the hallway.

Evan Farnsworth approached. "I have the requested personnel for your Skywraiths."

"Excellent," I told him.

He nodded. "They're all expert fliers and excellent spell casters."

"You can add another to them," Victus said. "Delectra would like to join your crew."

A strangled growl rose in Evan's throat. "You'd really risk your wife?"

"She was the reigning boomstick champion for four years running." Victus's lip nearly rose into a sneer, but he pressed his lips tight together. "Delectra is also a powerful caster. After all, she's descended from the first Arcane himself, Moses."

Somehow, Evan maintained a firm upper lip, though it was evident he wanted to either murder Victus where he stood, or burst into tears. "My people will meet you in the hangar," he said at last. "They already have their equipment."

"They'll need Nightingale armor to combat the cold," I said.

He nodded. "As I said, they have everything they'll need."

"Sounds good." I turned to Victus. "Will Delectra meet us in the hangar?"

Victus observed Evan for a split second, then turned to me. "Yes, she's already on her way."

"Why wasn't she at the meeting?" Evan asked.

"She's been busy helping an orphanage built for war orphans," Victus replied. "The Second Seraphim War destroyed many families, and it's our responsibility to help the suffering children."

Evan's jaw went so tight I thought his muscles might burst through the skin. "How very kind, Victus." He offered me a curt bow. "I must be going to organize the other Arcane forces. Good luck, Justin."

"Same to you." I turned to Victus. "Are you certain your wife has the temperament to take orders?"

He stiffened, but nodded. "She is a proud woman, Justin, but she will be a great asset in the battle."

"You realize that she'll be in real danger, I hope." I folded my arms across my chest. "She could die."

He swallowed hard and nodded. "She is willing to risk everything as we both did during the war." Victus mirrored my stance. "I was a bystander during your speech to the Science Council. I was furious when Frankenberg refused to enter the war."

"I don't remember seeing you there."

"I was there." He dropped his arms. "When Underborn was looking for a solution to the hostage crisis, I gave him valuable information and helped him free the students." Victus sighed. "I know this will sound like more bragging, Justin, but I played a major role in the Science Academy forces coming to your aid at the last battle. I'm just as firmly committed now as I was then."

I hadn't spoken to Underborn since the last battle, but I planned to ask him if what Victus told me was true. Until then, I needed to concentrate on this battle. "I'm glad." I nodded toward the levitator. "I need to get my people ready."

"Of course." He stepped back. "Best of luck, Justin."

"Same to you." I took the levitator down to the armory level just in time to meet my team returning with brooms and armor.

Mom handed me my armor and broom. "I assumed you might be a while with Evan and Victus so eager to speak with you."

"As usual, you were right." I lifted my shirt and fastened the strip of cloth around my waist, then pinched the hems and tugged on them until the armor grew to cover my body beneath my clothes.

"Whatever happened to Lanaeia?" Ivy asked. "She was a Skywraith too."

"She went with Ketiss to Pjurna," Nightliss said.

Mom nodded. "We're all that's left of the originals. I hope the Arcanes Justin asked for can perform."

I grunted. "Delectra will join us as well."

Ivy made a face. "Eww. She's a bitch."

Mom groaned. "Dear, I would really appreciate it if you'd wait a decade before cursing like that."

Ivy shrugged. "The truth's the truth, Mom."

"They grow up so fast," Nightliss mused.

"I might be a kid, but I've been in more battles than most adults," Ivy said. "I should be allowed to smoke, drink, and vote too."

Mom looked ready to cry.

"Voting, totally," I said. "Just please don't ever smoke. It's gross."

Ivy nodded. "I totes agree." She hugged Mom. "It's okay, Mommy. I'll always be your little girl."

With a great look of relief, Mom kissed the top of her daughter's head, completely missing the mischievous grin Ivy directed toward me.

I chuckled. Ivy might be a little messed up in the head, but she was still a good kid.

We piled into the levitator and took it up to the main hangar. The place was already empty of other troops. Our new squad mates, eager smiles on their faces, stood near the portal along with someone I didn't recognize. Delectra stood apart from the others, wrapping her long black hair into a tight bun.

The person I didn't know, a woman with a jagged scar running from her forehead to her upper lip approached me and held out her hand. "Hello Justin, I'm Pri."

"This is awesome, Justin," Boris said. "We thought it'd be okay if we asked another expert flier to join us."

"Nice to meet you," I said to Pri, trying hard not to notice the scar and failing. Even with the scar, she was an attractive woman. "Did you get that during the war?" I asked.

"She got it saving me," said Tasha. "You can count on her in battle."

Pixie waved. "It's an honor to be a part of the skywraiths." She giggled. "I can't believe it's really happening!"

Pri chuckled. "We've all competed in boomstick racing or at the Arcane Tourney, so we know each other as opponents, colleagues, and after the war, as friends. All we could talk about after the war was how amazing the Skywraiths were."

"Well, we're glad to have you with us," Ivy said. "Blasting baddies from a boomstick is my specialty."

"This banter is a waste of time," Delectra said. "I suggest we—"

I marched right up to her and got in her face. "Getting to know the people you're about to enter a battle with is not a waste of time." I narrowed my eyes. "If that's what you think, then maybe you need to stop wasting our time and leave."

Her eyes flared, and for a moment, I glimpsed something far more vulnerable than the ice queen. This close to her, the unmistakable odor of brimstone prickled my nose.

Her eyes blinked rapidly and she backed up a step. "Please, no—" She shook her head, and the cold façade slammed back into place. "I will do as you ask."

I switched to demon vision and looked at her aura. Though it wasn't the brightest I'd ever seen, it bore a slight yellowish tint. She didn't seem to be possessed.

I returned to the subject at hand. "Please introduce yourself to the others."

Her chin rose a notch as she faced the group. "I am Delectra Moore, wife of Victus Edison."

The others waved and said, "Hello, Delectra."

I caught an approving look from Mom and repressed a smug smile. *Delectra is going to follow orders or I'll send her packing.*

"I'm Alysea," Mom said.

My sister jabbed a thumb to her chest. "And I'm Ivy! Great to meet you."

"Great to meet you too," Pri said.

The others echoed her reply.

I turned to the portal scheduler. "Templar, please schedule an omniarch portal for Queens Gate."

He saluted and made a phone call. A moment later, a portal to the Queens Gate way station opened and I led the group through it. Once everyone was in the room, I closed the portal and opened one straight to the large grassy meadow behind Arcane University, and led everyone through. Since we'd need to return soon, I left the portal open.

I turned to the Arcanes. "We use several squadron formations, depending on our attack pattern." I demonstrated the signs for each formation, and described them. "Let's hover in place and practice."

Delectra sighed.

I ignored her passive-aggressive outburst and climbed onto the broom. It took a few seconds to reacquaint myself with the controls, and Nightliss actually rolled over once before regaining control. The Arcanes had no issues at all.

I held up two fingers, and we shifted into a V formation with me at the lead. I twirled the two fingers in a circle and we spread out into a reverse V. Nightliss and Mom took a bit longer to get into position, while the Arcanes and Ivy easily glided into place. I went through the other formations, each one going more smoothly than the last, then said, "Let's practice staying in formation while moving."

Delectra grimaced, but said nothing.

We swooped over the Dark Forest, and looped around Colossus Stadium while switching through formations. The stadium still looked like a warzone from a previous battle against Daelissa's forces. Boulders from destroyed goliaths littered the ground, and parts of the seating areas lay in ruins. I decided to have our people do target practice on the boulders below.

"Just tag the targets with light," I said. "Conserve your strength for the battle."

Delectra's first attack annihilated a boulder, turning it to dust.

My hand tightened on the boomstick handle, but I held my tongue. After an hour of practice, I felt we were good enough to report for duty, and called Thomas.

"When can you portal into position?" he asked.

"About fifteen minutes," I told him. "I'll text you when we go through."

"Good luck, Justin."

"Same to you, sir." I ended the call and rounded up the group on the ground in the middle of Colossus Stadium. "We leave in fifteen minutes. Head back to the portal we came through and I'll meet you there in a moment." I pointed to Delectra. "I'd like a word with you first."

"A woo-woo!" Ivy jabbed a finger at Delectra. "Someone's in big trouble."

"Ivy, get on your broom and follow me," Mom said in a stern voice.

My sister looked down. "Aw, okay."

Despite the curious looks on the others' faces, everyone left, leaving me and Delectra standing on the muddy war-torn earth.

"I have done all you asked," Delectra said. "What more do you want of me?"

I shook my head slowly. "You're obviously an excellent boomstick pilot, and judging from the boulder you destroyed, you have plenty of power." I stepped closer and gave her a pitying look. "But you're arrogant, pompous, and just unpleasant to be around."

Her pale face shaded pink.

I held up a finger. "I'm not finished yet, so kindly keep your mouth shut."

The pink turned to crimson.

"I've heard you weren't always this way." I shrugged. "Maybe you were once a nice person. The worst part is I can't really be mad at you."

She raised an eyebrow, but kept silent.

235

"The reason I can't is because all your misbehavior boils down to one thing." I sighed. "You're insecure."

Her eyes flared. "I am not."

"Yes you are."

Her wand flicked toward me. Not knowing if she intended to hit me with a spell, I blurred forward, gripped her shoulders, and pinned her against a boulder. Her wand clattered to the ground.

Delectra's eyes softened. "Please no—I can take no more."

Her sudden change reminded me of what I'd witnessed earlier. "Can't take what?"

Her lips curled into a snarl. "Why did you attack me?"

"You aimed your wand at me."

She took a deep breath. "I only meant to point it. I was not casting a spell."

I released her and backed away. "I just don't think you're a good fit, Delectra."

"But I'm the best at this. I can prove it."

I shook my head. "That's not my point. I don't care if you're the best, I just care if you're part of the team." I threw up my hands. "Don't you get it?"

For a moment, she looked genuinely troubled, and I wondered if maybe she couldn't comprehend what I was telling her. Delectra nodded slowly. "I will follow your orders precisely. I will not deviate."

I almost turned her down and told her to go away, but the Skywraiths needed every ounce of firepower we could muster. "Do you swear it?"

She knelt on one knee and bowed. "I swear it, my liege."

I jerked back, completely caught off-guard by this display. "A simply 'yes' would have been fine."

Delectra rose, her lips a flat line, but she looked somehow less defiant. *She'd give Kassallandra a run for her money in an ice queen competition.*

"May we go?" Delectra asked.

I hopped on my broom. "Yup." We returned to the portal and took it back to the Queens Gate way station.

The Skywraiths were ready for action.

Chapter 27

Concentrating on an image of the airship fleet given to me by Thomas, I opened a window into the great blue yonder. The Skywraiths lined up behind me, brooms at the ready. I activated a stealth charm to hide us from radar, mounted my broom, and glided through the rift, going from North America all the way to the bottom of the world in the space of a heartbeat.

No matter how many times I used a portal, it still seemed like the coolest thing in the world.

The southern reaches of the Indian Ocean glittered far below. I flashed the signal for single file formation. So long as everyone remained directly behind me, the stealth charm should keep them hidden.

The flotilla of airships hung in the distance in two neat rows of six like a still portrait, fluffy white clouds forming a deceptively serene backdrop. It was a magnificent sight, despite their deadly intent. I counted seven robot pods swaying beneath the vessels, each one capable of carrying at least twenty battle-bots. Frankenberg had to be throwing everything he had at Australia.

Freezing cold air whistled across my face and burned my lungs. I hurriedly extended the Nightingale armor over my head, and the temperature became bearable. Though the mask completely covered my face, I could easily see through the material as if it weren't even there. I looked back and saw the others had already extended theirs. The internal HUD—heads-up-display—flickered on. It was nice having fully functional armor again.

I left off most of the features except for the FFI—friend or foe identifier. When I looked at the others in my group, a green bracket highlighted them along with their name. Even though they had on their hoods, the HUD allowed me to see their faces as clearly as if they weren't concealed and the communication system allowed us to speak freely.

We were still about a half-mile out from the flotilla, and I needed to figure out the best place to attack them. Unfortunately, there were no airships lagging behind that we could easily harass. Attacking from above might be safest, but we were already at such an altitude that even the Nightingale armor was having trouble supplying extra oxygen to support our lungs.

That left us with one option—attack the lowest airships. Each of those on the bottom tier towed the massive robot pods, making them high-value targets.

"We'll swing wide and attack the airship on the lower left of the formation," I told the others through the comm system. "Aim for the cables supporting the cargo container. Maybe we can make it fall."

"May I make a suggestion?" Delectra asked.

"Go ahead," I replied.

"The cables are likely diamond fiber," she said. "I suggest we target the cable module attached to the bottom of the cockpit."

I magnified my view using the HUD and spotted the hump containing the winch. The cables themselves glittered like black ice—a clear indicator they were indestructible diamond fiber. "The winch might be just as hard to destroy due to the ablative armor," I replied after a moment of contemplation. I turned my view to the cargo container itself. It looked like plain metal with a handle on the outside. "Will seawater destroy the robots, Delectra?"

"Not immediately no," she replied. "But if the ocean is deep enough here, the pressure might crush them. Most battle-bots are waterproof, but not seaworthy."

"New plan," I announced. "Go for the doors on the crates. Let's see if we can dump at least one load."

Ivy giggled. "Dump a load. I like the sound of that."

We still faced the problem of remaining undetected, especially if we went for the outmost airship since there'd only been one stealth charm available. I held up a fist and the formation halted. Twisting my wrist gave everyone the order to rotate in place. The following hand forward signal told them to proceed in the current formation. We were still far enough away that moving laterally in a row should keep us out of radar longer.

"Justin, I have a suggestion," Pri said through the squadron comm link. "As we move farther to the left of the airship flotilla, we should angle our formation to keep it behind the stealth charm."

"Sounds good," I said. "Adjust your positions accordingly."

I imagined the charm like a wall several feet long to my side, and the radar like a light trying to peek around the edge. For several tense minutes we flew in an arc, those furthest in the back adjusting their angle until we finally reached the side of the airship formation. We spun in place, realigning again, and headed for the lowest airship.

"What if we opened the container in the blimp above the other one?" Ivy said, pointing to the single upper-tier airship towing a pod. "Then all the robots would fall on top of the bottom one."

"I don't think it would damage the airship," Mom said. "And then the robots might stand on the airship and fire at us."

Ivy sighed. "Oh, okay."

We closed to within a couple hundred yards, our formation as tight as possible. Still no reaction from the airships to indicate they knew about our presence.

I called a halt. "They'll probably detect us soon, so let's swoop in at full speed. Use the target as a shield from the laser fire from the other airships."

"Affirmative," came the replies.

I flicked my hand forward and we were off. The boomsticks were made for speed, and we closed on the target quickly. The laser turrets on the airship swiveled our way and opened fire once we closed to within a hundred yards. I channeled a thick beam of Murk to intercept. The laser beam exploded against it. A volley of five missiles burst from the launcher on the belly of the airship.

I signaled for V formation, and we spread out. Ivy blasted a missile with a beam of Brilliance. Mom and Nightliss met two more missiles with attacks of their own. The last two missiles zipped straight for the Arcanes.

Pri barrel rolled to the side, and the missile flew past, trailing thick smoke. Delectra thrust out her staff. Brilliant red light erupted from the end and ensnared the last rocket. With another flick of the staff, the missile flipped around and launched back at the airship above our target. It slammed into the cargo container beneath it with a tremendous boom. Fire exploded and silvery battle-bots poured from a large breach in the metal, tumbling across the nacelle of the target and toward the ocean far below.

"Wow," Pri said. "That was awesome."

The missile she dodged had turned around and was coming from our rear. Ivy pulled into a steep climb and zipped over the rocket. Brilliance burst from her fist and detonated the projectile before it could reach us.

Seconds later, we reached the target container.

Mom and Nightliss unleashed torrents of Brilliance into the door as we zipped past. It melted to slag. I channeled a beam of Murk and hammered it into the end of the container, sending it swaying forward. It tilted lazily, and bots spilled from the opening and fell toward the water.

I glanced up and saw the entire flotilla rotating toward us. "I think we got their attention. Retreat!"

Delectra fired another beam of translucent red into the turbine on the side of the target airship. The energy fizzed and popped. Propeller blades burst from the housing. Black smoke filled the air, and the airship listed to the side. She rotated toward the opposite side of the airship.

She's going to get someone killed. "I said retreat, Delectra!"

She slid to a halt, spun and returned to formation. "As you command." Laser fire exploded from the other airships. "Dive!" I commanded.

Still in a V formation, we dove to put the crippled airship between us and the incoming fire. A laser narrowly missed Pri, and Tasha rolled sideways to avoid being toasted by another deadly spear of light. We were several hundred yards out when more missiles burst into flight. I lost count of the smoke trails winding their way toward us.

"Oh, crap," Ivy said. "I think they're mad."

Think, Justin, think! I willed the HUD to highlight the incoming missiles. Red brackets appeared all over the place, indicators steadily counting down the distance before impact. The brooms were fast, but the missiles were steadily gaining and we'd never reach the safety of the portal in time. We had less than a minute to do something.

I reached a decision. "We're going to stop and throw up a barrier of Murk. I want the Arcanes behind me. Ivy, Alysea, and Nightliss help me with the shield. Hopefully we can make it thick enough."

"Justin, there are far too many missiles," Mom said. "We can't possibly shield against them all."

"I agree," Nightliss said. "A shield might not work, but what about Stasis?"

I slapped my forehead. "Of course!" I looked back at the missiles and calculated how quickly they'd reach us once we stopped. "Start channeling now. When I give the word, spin around and channel the biggest cloud you can."

The others summoned spheres of Murk and Brilliance and threaded them into orbs of Stasis. I followed suit, fighting to maintain the energy, while keeping my broom straight with my knees.

"Uh, Justin, how are we supposed to turn around while holding the channel?" Ivy asked. "I can steer with my legs, but I can't stop or steer the broom."

"Boris, Pixie, Tasha, do an inverted roll and steer their brooms from below," Pri shouted. "I'll take Justin."

"You would choose the cute guy," Pixie said with a laugh.

Pri drifted close, rolled upside down, and hung beneath me, her broom pacing mine. With a free hand, she reached up and gripped the throttle of my broom. Boris, Pixie, and Tasha did the same with Ivy, Nightliss, and Mom.

"Neato!" Ivy shouted.

"Everyone ready?" I said.

"Ready," came the replies.

"Stop and turn!"

Pri pulled back on my throttle and pulled my broom handle to the side, performing the same action simultaneously on her broom. Like mirror images, we spun in place and hung before the frightening volley of missiles.

"Channel!" I shouted.

We projected clouds of Stasis into the air. Ivy's thread dwarfed ours, like a great gray snake, coiling into the air before her. Our clouds merged, growing into a thick dark fog bank blotting out the sky on the other side.

"Will this stop the forward momentum of the missiles?" Delectra asked.

"I don't know," I muttered between clenched teeth as the strain began to take a toll.

Delectra spun her staff in a wide circle, chanting. The air itself seemed to coalesce into a shimmering wall. Seconds later, dozens of inert missiles clanked against the barrier and tumbled like giant matchsticks toward the ocean.

"Apparently, the Stasis didn't completely stop them," Delectra said in a satisfied voice.

"Good work." I released the channel as more rockets clanged harmlessly off the barrier and fell away. "Now fall back."

Delectra released the shield and we spun around, putting distance between us and the Stasis cloud. In the distance, I saw the airships slowly coming after us. We'd done our job, but the main battle lay ahead.

"Let's return through the portal and recharge," I said. "We'll need all our energy for the next fight."

"Excellent work, Delectra," Boris said. "That was a really solid shield."

"Yeah, I don't think I could cast one that large on my best day," Pri added.

"I am a descendant of Ezzek Moore," Delectra replied plainly, no hint of condescension in her voice for once.

"Whoa," Pixie said. "Now that's badass."

"Yeah, it is," Tasha said. "Wish I had that much juice."

We reached the portal. I motioned the others through and looked back at the airships still trundling our way. I flew through the portal to the

Queens Gate way station and closed it. My backside thanked me for standing and stretching after the long flight on the broom.

I fired off a text to Elyssa. *Mission accomplished.*

She replied. *Still haven't found the base. Need your help.*

We're going to feed, then join you. I motioned the others close and laid out our next steps. "Nightliss, Ivy, Alysea, and I need to go to the Templar compound so we can feed." I motioned to the aisle next to the omniarches. "The rest of you can wait here. We won't be long."

"I am going to stretch my legs," Delectra said. "I will meet you back here in thirty minutes."

I didn't think we'd be back before then, so I nodded. "Sounds good."

"I could use some food," Boris said.

Pri yawned. "It's so late, at least by the time here. My brain needs coffee if I'm going to function."

Pixie quirked her lips and looked up as if trying to decide what she wanted. "Food sounds good."

"Maybe you could grab something from the mess hall while we're feeding," I said. "We don't have much time before we need to join the search for the secret base."

Boris nodded enthusiastically. "Yeah, I'm down with that."

My stomach grumbled to let me know it wanted grub as well. *Now is not the time.* It rumbled again. *Fine, you greedy bastard.* I opened a portal just outside the big barn at the Ranch and led my entourage to the other side and into the darkness. There was a fourteen-hour difference between Atlanta and the other side of the world.

"But did you like what we did?" Ivy said to Boris and Pri as we walked outside. "We could have blown up that ship if Justin let us."

I tuned in to the conversation, curious to hear what they were talking about.

"I mean, yeah, it's awesome how powerful you Seraphim dudes are," Boris said. "But we'll never be able to do that."

"Delectra is an Arcane like us," Pri explained. "She's really powerful, but we can identify with her, and maybe even aspire to be that good."

"But she's not *that* strong," Ivy protested. "Let me blast something. I'll show you what power is."

"Ivy, you're starting to talk like Daelissa again," Mom said. "Please leave the nice people alone."

Ivy stomped her foot. "But, Mom, I just want to show them something."

I took my sister's hand. "Someone's sounding grumpy. I think you need a little soul essence."

She looked down and toed the dirt. "Fine."

Pri looked relieved. Boris wiped sweat from his forehead.

My sister could be a little scary sometimes.

"We'll see you in a few," Tasha said.

I waved bye and headed for the church.

"I don't get what the big deal is with Delectra," Ivy said in a pouting voice. "I could blow her to smithereens."

"Ivy, what has gotten into you?" Mom said.

"I don't like that woman. She stinks like rotten eggs all the time." Ivy's gaze darted to me. "You smell like good rotten eggs, though, Justin. You and Dad and even Kassallandra smell better."

"Good demons smell great," I theorized. I really didn't know if some demons had worse body odor or not, though the brimstone from Delectra smelled a bit sour. It was just one of those things I really didn't think much about. "But her bad smell is no reason to dislike her." I wondered what sort of demons she and Victus had consorted with.

"Ivy, I don't want you talking about blowing up anyone, not even Delectra," Mom said in a stern voice.

"I just want to show I'm better," Ivy said.

"You don't have to prove anything," Mom said. "You've proven yourself time and time again, daughter."

I squeezed Ivy's shoulder. "Just remember that brute force isn't always the answer." I tapped my temple. "If you really want people to think you're cool, just outthink them."

She pursed her lips. "Hmm, Jeremiah used to say, 'Don't use a sledgehammer when you can make them walk off a cliff.'"

I wished Jeremiah had been a better influence, but in his blind lust for revenge, he'd been only marginally better than Daelissa. "Umm, I guess that's close enough." I lifted her chin. "There's more than one way to approach a problem, Ivy. I think you're smart enough to think of alternate tactics."

"I guess I am kind of smart." Ivy grinned, her insecurities hopefully forgotten for the time being. "Thanks, bro."

Mom gave me a worried look. We'd hoped Ivy would stabilize now that our family was whole again, but she still exhibited flashes of anger and even narcissism—ample evidence that Daelissa's influence still clouded her mind.

It'll just take time. The reassurance felt hollow, especially after an outburst like this one.

Ivy never had a childhood. She'd been groomed for power by Daelissa, and thrust into war by the time she hit the age of ten. Though she was a powerful asset, she was also my little sister, not some grown adult who truly understood consequences.

As much as I hated the idea, it might be best to keep Ivy out of the fight.

Chapter 28

Mom and I finished feeding before Ivy, so I took Mom aside and told her my concerns.

"I've tried to keep her from fighting," she said. "But it's not like your father and I could actually make Ivy do something she doesn't want to do."

I grimaced. "She's used her powers against you?"

"No, but she's threatened." Mom sighed. "I didn't see any harm in Ivy helping with the crystoids, but I told her she couldn't fight in the battle."

"What did she say to that?"

"It was the scariest thing, Justin." Mom's eyes clouded with worry. "Her face went absolutely expressionless just like Daelissa's used to when someone told her she couldn't do something."

My heart constricted. "Oh, crap."

"I won't lie to you," she said. "Sometimes, I'm afraid of my own daughter."

Ivy skipped out of the feeding room, a bright smile on her face. "I'm all powered up and ready to kill some baddies."

I almost knelt down and tried to give her a little talk about how killing people shouldn't be something to look forward to, but we really didn't have time for it. We'd already used thirty-five minutes for feeding, and I was still starving for normal food. I swung by the mess hall to gather the other Skywraiths, and grabbed a couple of sloppy joes to go. I polished them off by the time we reached the portal I'd left open next to the barn.

Delectra sat with her back against an arch when we returned to the arch control room. She put away an arcphone and stood. "Is it time?"

I nodded. "Hoods on, people, it's time to hit the cold again."

I texted Elyssa. *We're ready. Need an image for a portal.*

She sent a picture of frozen tundra with a red X painted on the snow. I extended the armor's hood and mask over my face, and opened the portal. Wind howled through the gateway, dusting the floor with snow. The HUD in my suit flashed on and lit the snow-clouded air.

"Lovely vacation spot," Pri said. "I'm glad I brought my bikini."

"Dude, this Nightingale armor is the bomb," Boris said.

"That place looks awful," Ivy groaned. "How are we supposed to find a secret base in this?"

I walked through, holding my boomstick under one arm. Sunlight filtered through a cloud of snow. The armor cut down on the glare, but it was still difficult to see more than a few feet in any direction.

I spotted the command platform hovering nearby and flew my broom up to it. The HUD allowed me to spot Elyssa even with her hood on. I walked up behind her and pinched her on the bottom.

She spun, hands at the ready, then saw it was me. "Justin, I just about socked you in the face."

"I'm used to it." I looked at the arctablet on the console in front of her. "How's the search going?"

She pointed out dozens of green blips and the shaded area around them. "This is where they've searched. It'll probably take them another hour or more to cover the remaining miles."

"I don't know how much help we can provide from the air." I shivered, though the armor kept me comfortable. "The weather here is nasty."

"This windstorm should die down soon, according to the forecast." She leaned against me. "How did the Skywraiths do against the airships?"

"Great." I told her the details. "They're returning to base."

"Well, you slowed them down." She looked into the distance. "I hope we find the base before they decide to turn around and head back toward Australia."

"Me too." I looked back toward my group. "I guess we'll hop on our brooms and help with the search. Maybe we'll get lucky."

"Don't count on it." She blew me a kiss. "See you soon."

247

I flew back down to ground level and circled my finger in the air. "Saddle up. It's time to go." I led the group a few feet above the frozen tundra and headed in the direction of the search parties. About twenty minutes later, the wind died down and visibility went from zero to as far as the eye could see.

A huge white wolf and spotted snow leopard bounded through about a foot of snow on the ground. A hundred yards to either side, other lycans and felycans plowed across the rugged terrain. I took our formation higher so we could see better and farther. The land below looked deceptively flat from here, but the slow progress of those on the ground showed just how challenging the terrain really was.

"Do you think the base is underground?" Nightliss asked.

"Could be," I replied. "Even if it is, there should be vents or something on the surface."

"Might be camouflaged," Pri suggested.

"It could be underground and camouflaged," I said. "For all I know, it's flying above us." I looked up on the off chance I might be right, but saw nothing except a lone cloud.

A while later, we crested a small rise and entered a bowl-shaped valley. At least a hundred black and white shapes clustered below.

"Wow that's a big penguin nest," Boris said. "I wonder what they're doing so far inland."

I magnified my vision on the birds. Something looked different about them. *This valley looks like the perfect place for a secret base.* No sooner had the though crossed my mind than my trouble sense tingled. The penguins waddled about, looking cute as could be, when suddenly they turned our way and tucked their wings. Eyes glowing red, they stared at us in a very unpenguinlike manner. Flames lit beneath a dozen of the birds, and they soared straight up before curving toward us.

"That's no penguin nest," I shouted. "It's a secret base!"

"Shoot the penguins," Boris cried.

Beams of deadly energy speared out from everyone in the squadron. Penguins exploded. Shrapnel flew in all directions and black smoke filled the air. The last explosion echoed in the distance, and the smoke cleared to reveal a bowel-wrenching sight: every last penguin missile roaring into the air and arcing toward us.

"I don't think Stasis is going to help with this," Mom said in a horrified voice.

I spun around the broom. "Fly from the penguins! Fly for your lives!"

For the second time that day, the Skywraiths ran like little bitches. There were so many penguin rockets behind us, the red brackets on the HUD melded together into one big mass.

I switched communications channels to the command platform frequency. "Elyssa, are you there?"

"I'm here. Justin, is that you?"

"It's me." I glanced back and wished I hadn't. The missiles were far behind, but closing. "The good news is we found the enemy base."

"Ok. You sound really stressed." Her breath caught in her throat. "What happened?"

"The bad news is, about a hundred or so rocket penguins are about to blow us sky high and we need some help, pronto."

"Rocket penguins?" Her voice rose a couple of octaves. "We don't have our main forces in position yet. There's no way to shoot them down from here."

"Son of a—okay, we'll figure out something." I switched back to the squadron channel. "There's a mountain range ahead. Maybe we can lose the missiles in there."

"How do the missiles lock onto us?" Nightliss asked. "Do they use a spell?"

"These are science-based, so it's probably something like body heat," I said.

"And we're by far the hottest things out here." Mom said.

Ivy raised a fist and fired a beam of destruction at a distant hunk of black rock. By the time we whooshed past, the rock glowed bright red and began to melt into slag. Ivy continued firing on it even after we passed. The penguins streaked over the rock, completely ignoring it.

"Well, it's definitely not heat," Pixie said. "Any more ideas?"

"I believe I know," Delectra said. "I spoke to Victus just now, and he told me Frankenberg favors an image lock system. Their eyes are scanners, so even if we were to jump off the brooms, they would follow us."

"How in the hell are we supposed to get away then?" Pri said.

The twin peaks of mountains rose before us. "Maybe we can dodge them."

"I may have a better idea," Delectra replied. "Do as I say, and we may have a chance."

She told us her plan, and I prayed to the bird god almighty she could pull it off.

We threaded the eye of the mountain pass and hoped for the best

A volley of missiles slammed into the valley wall right next to Pixie and a fireball engulfed her. Ivy zipped down toward the ground, but dozens of penguin rockets found their mark exploding in spectacular fashion, and left nothing behind. One by one, the missiles slammed into their targets. The last group of ten found me. The blast sent snow and ice tumbling onto the valley floor.

"I think that's all of them," I said, finally daring to breathe.

"Man, I must have had twenty missiles on my ass," Boris said. "Did you see how many hit my illusion?"

"I counted thirty-one for me," Ivy said.

I sighed. "Well, apparently I wasn't that important, because only ten wanted me dead."

Pri laughed. "Aw, don't feel bad. We'll make sure more rocket penguins come after you the next time."

Delectra put away her staff. "It's been some time since I conjured so many complex illusions. I'm glad I was able to perform adequately."

"If you decide to run for Arcanus Primus, you've got my vote," Pixie said.

Boris raised his hand. "Same here, dudette. You're awesome."

Delectra looked utterly surprised. "My husband is running for the post."

Pri made a raspberry noise. "Don't let him run. Men are awful leaders. We need a strong woman in that position."

"I will consider asking him," Delectra said in an oddly humble voice.

"I can do illusions too," Ivy said. "I just haven't done them in, like, forever."

I clapped my hands together. "Let's get back to the command platform. I have a feeling the other shoe is about to drop."

We reached the deployment zone about twenty minutes later. Portals ripped open all around base camp, and hundreds of troops poured through. Daemos and Templars spread out in long lines while Blue Cloaks whooshed overhead on flying carpets. Red Cell, the elite vampire forces, raced forward in their crimson armor. Another rift opened and dozens of shiny robots dashed onto the snowy tundra.

Within minutes, the army had arrived.

The command unit, a large round platform, rose into the air. I spotted Thomas in the center. Other Templars manned the consoles all around him, each one responsible for relaying orders to different squads.

Elyssa's voice spoke into my ear. "Justin, I'll be relaying commands to you for the Skywraiths."

A grin spread across my face. "My guardian angel."

"You know it, babe." She paused. "Hang back behind the front lines. We're about to advance."

Several levitating catapults emerged from a gateway, and spread out behind the assortment of supernatural warriors. Support crews with cargo platforms laden with crucibles took positions behind their respective siege engines.

Images of our last battle with Daelissa flickered through my mind. I shuddered. *Feels like it just happened yesterday.*

I looked at Boris. "Would you like to say what you've always wanted to say?"

His eyes widened. "Are you serious?"

I nodded. "Go for it."

He shivered. "Sweet!" Boris pumped a fist in the air. "Skywraiths, form up!"

I signaled for the V formation and everyone assumed their positions.

Pixie giggled. "Guess you'll be putting this in your diary, Boris."

"Oh man, you know it!" His voice sounded loopy with excitement.

I spotted Evan Farnsworth accompanied by a large group of Arcanes exit a portal, his face visible through the Nightingale armor, thanks to the HUD. He looked up at us and waved. I waved back.

Guess he wants to make sure I know he's here.

251

Victus rode a large flat platform with tank treads. Turrets, manned by Science Academy people, swiveled forward. He offered us a salute, then pressed a button. The unit unfolded and the middle of the metal treads rose to form a large triangle while the top of the platform extended higher.

"Cool," Boris said.

Thomas broadcast over the comm system. "Move out."

The army marched forward.

Despite the size of our forces, we moved forward at a rapid pace, eating up the distance between us and the secret base. We were perhaps halfway there when I spotted the flotilla of airships speeding inland. Humanoid forms of enemy robots appeared in the distance, the sun gleaming off their chrome armor. Behind them towered three mega-bots—two bipedal units, and one with four giant legs ending in sharp points. Every lumbering step threw up clouds of snow and ice.

"Prepare to engage," Thomas said.

The airships dropped their cargo containers and more battle-bots spilled onto the battlefield, swelling the ranks of the oncoming army while the aircraft themselves spread out above the enemy lines.

"Whoa, man, that's a lot of robots," Boris said.

"A whole heaping mess of them," Pixie added.

The quarter mile between our forces shrank to several hundred yards. Airship cannons swiveled down toward our front line.

Our support crews slid carts with aether generators into position in front of our people and shields shimmered in the air.

The airships opened fire. Ice and snow exploded. Deadly beams of light splashed against the shields, and the robot army surged forward, lasers firing from their eyes and arms.

The battle had begun.

Chapter 29

"Skywraiths, priority target airships," Elyssa said through the comm link. "I suggest flanking from the north."

"We're on it." I relayed the message to the squadron.

"How are we supposed to get close to them with all that ground fire?" Boris asked.

We really had only one option. "We fly high, and flank them." I spun around and led the squadron to our back lines, then pulled back on the broomstick, entering a nearly vertical climb. We climbed far above the battle, until even the airships were hundreds of feet beneath us. Lasers flashed. Crucibles smashed into the attacking robots. Within moments, the frontlines would be fully engaged.

From this vantage, it was clear the airships were spreading out to attack the flanks of our ground troops. We couldn't allow that to happen.

"Remember these things have heavy armor, so it'll take a lot of firepower to disable them." I pointed to the airship on the northern edge of the flotilla. "Target the laser cannon on the top then hit the left engine. Use the bulk of the airship to shield you from the others."

A chorus of assents echoed from the comm link and everyone slid into V formation.

I pumped a fist in the air. "Let's kick ass!"

"Kick ass!" everyone, even Mom, shouted back.

I pushed down on the broomstick and fell into a steep dive. The HUD's red bracket around the airship counted down the distance. The top turret turned toward us and fired a brilliant red laser. Our formation split apart just in time for the laser to miss, then rejoined. I counted down the seconds it took for the laser to recharge.

Since the missile turret was on the bottom of the ship, it seemed incapable of firing on us—an oversight Frankenberg would be sure to correct if we gave him the chance.

My mental timer hit zero. "Split!"

The formation broke apart just as the cannon aimed and fired.

"Now I see why they need so many blimps," Ivy said. "They can't hit us with just one laser."

The airship weapons probably weren't designed to take on small nimble broom fliers, but slower ground targets. A laser flashed from the lower turret and slammed against the top of the shield protecting our ground forces. If the airship drifted any closer to our lines, it would be able to fire over the shield and into our people. We had only seconds to stop it.

We reached firing range before the top cannon could take another shot at us. Ivy, with her superior range, encased the laser in a block of Murk. With a deafening roar and brilliant flash, the turret blew itself apart.

Pri whooped. "Brilliant move, Ivy!"

I was so proud of my little sister, I nearly forgot to give the order to take out the engine. Thankfully, Delectra was a step ahead. She flung a coil of the same disruptive energy she'd used on the one over the ocean, and the turbine smoked and blew apart while the crew inside the cockpit looked on with horror.

Nightliss shielded our group from shrapnel as another explosion rocked the crippled engine.

"Take out the bottom turrets," I said. We swung beneath the airship. Mom and I followed Ivy's example and cocooned the missile and laser turrets with Murk.

The airship crew apparently couldn't see what we'd done. The man at the weapons control glared furiously at us and slammed a fist on the console.

"Shield yourselves!" I shouted.

The missile turret blew a massive hole in the bottom of the cockpit and the airship's reactor exploded a split second later. I threw up a wall of Murk just in time, but the blast sent me spinning away. The rest of our formation scattered like leaves in the wind. I spotted an armor-clad body in freefall and dove after it. I caught the body by the arm and saw it was Pri.

I tried to pull her up, but the broom didn't like the extra weight and began to lose altitude. "Someone help me!"

Mom and Nightliss were the first responders, zipping in and grabbing Pri's other arm, and a leg. The redistributed weight took the pressure off my broom. The hulking airship groaned and plummeted toward the ground. The remaining wing caused it to veer right toward us.

"The airship!" I shouted.

The nose of the aircraft would slam into us in seconds.

A blast of sparkling ultraviolet wind shoved us forward. The nose of the vessel grazed my arm. I glanced back and saw Ivy release the Murk that saved us and dive away from the crippled airship.

She swooped up from beneath and drew level. "Is everyone okay?"

"I think so." I steered away from the battle so we could check on Pri. "You really saved our hides, Ivy. Great work."

She beamed a smile. "Thanks."

The rest of the Skywraiths joined the formation. I realized with a jolt that someone was missing. "Where's Tasha?"

"I lost her after the blast," Boris said. "I don't know where she is."

"I haven't seen her either," Delectra said.

"Oh, no." Nightliss pointed back toward the ground far below where a body lay still in the snow.

I couldn't see the person's features from here, but knew it was our missing comrade. My heart ached.

"Oh god, no." Pixie sobbed. "I need to check on her."

"No. She's dead." It hurt to say it, but even Nightingale armor couldn't have saved her from such a fall. Robots marched past Tasha's body, making any attempt to check on her extremely dangerous.

"Bastards." Boris ran a hand over his face. "We'll make them pay."

We reached a safe distance from the robot army and set down to check on Pri. Before I even lowered the hood on her armor, my armor's HUD revealed her lifeless eyes staring into space.

Mom ran a hand down Pri's neck. "It's broken."

Pixie burst into fresh sobs. "She's dead too?"

Mom nodded sadly. "She's gone."

I got off my broom and stormed back and forth in the snow. *It's war. Death happens.* I heard my knuckles crack and looked down at clenched fists. *Shake it off. The fight isn't over.*

"We need to finish the job." I climbed back on my broom. "If anyone wants out, now is the time to say so."

Tears soaked into Boris's armored mask. He shook his head. "I'm not leaving until this is over, or I'm dead."

"Me neither," Pixie whispered in a strained voice. "I'm in 'til the end."

Delectra stiffened. "I intend to finish this as well."

"We're all in, bro." Ivy took my hand in hers. "We can win."

"I will stand by you," Nightliss said.

Mom nodded. "I'm ready."

Boris knelt next to Pri and held her hand. "Rest well, Pri. We won't forget your sacrifice."

Pixie wiped her face despite the armored hood absorbing her tears. "Promise me we'll find Tasha's body after the battle. She deserves a proper burial."

I nodded. "I promise."

We left the body of our fallen companion lying in the snow and lifted off into the sky.

We lost two people for one damned airship. There had to be a better way.

Elyssa's voice interrupted my silent contemplation. "Justin, I lost sight of you. What's your status?"

"Pri and Tasha are dead." Anger burned deep in my chest. "We're going to finish the job."

"I'm so sorry, but the airships are hitting our left flank. The Blue Cloaks are engaging, but we need the Skywraiths." She blew out a breath. "The mega-bots are almost in range. If the airships aren't stopped, our ground forces will get hammered."

"We'll handle them." I stared at the flying warships in the distance. We had no magic bullet to take them all out at once. It would take a series of concerted attacks to render them useless. The explosion taught me that we were vulnerable in a close formation.

"Pixie and Boris, you're with me." I turned toward the others. "Alysea, pair with Delectra. Nightliss you're with Ivy."

"We're splitting up?" Boris asked.

"We're going to be mosquitoes," I explained. "Starting from the right side of the flotilla, each team will take on an airship. Encase the laser and missile turrets with Murk, and take out an engine just like the last one and watch each other's backs."

"We can't channel Murk," Pixie said. "What are we supposed to do?"

"I have a good electro-magnetic pulse spell I can use on the engines," Boris said.

"Do you know any heat spells Pixie?" I asked.

"Sure," she said. "I'll help Boris on the engine."

I handed out airship assignments. "We approach from the north and split at the first airship, okay?"

The team signaled their readiness.

"Let's go." I aimed the broom north and led them in a wide circling arc.

The airships were too busy firing on ground troops to see us until we were nearly upon them.

"Skywraiths, attack!" I commanded.

Mom and Delectra dove for the first airship. Nightliss and Ivy took the next. My team attacked the third. I hit the laser and missile turrets with a wide beam of Murk. It crystallized around them in a solid shield. The gunner seemed to realize something was wrong and didn't fire. Boris and Pixie thrust forward their staffs. Lightning erupted from Boris's staff. The energy crackled and slithered into the engine like a glowing snake.

Pixie unleashed a volley of small fireballs. The turbine sputtered, smoked, and burst into flames. Through the cockpit windows, I saw the airship pilot fighting for control as the airship listed to the side. He regained control, and the vessel leveled off. The gunner still didn't fire, and I realized my Murk shield would wear off and allow him to open fire again within minutes.

"Hit the other engine," I told my team.

We swooped beneath the cockpit to the other side. Pixie and Boris destroyed the other engine with their spells. Despite the lack of maneuverability, the airship was still very much a danger once my Murk shield wore off.

We flew back beneath the aircraft in time to witness the turrets on the second airship explode with a deafening roar. The hull buckled, rippling like water, and the remains of the cockpit fell away in a trail of flames. I considered hitting my target's turrets with more Murk, but knew the gunner would hold fire.

I had to take it out with brute force. Summoning Brilliance, I waited until the ultraviolet shield around the turrets dissipated and then blasted a torrent of white energy at them. My inner demon surged at the thrill of destruction. I fought it back and slammed it into its cage.

I gritted my teeth and sent the unruly half of my soul a message. *I'm the master here.*

Smoldering resentment was the only answer I felt from the trapped beast.

"Back off," I told Pixie and Boris.

They flitted back just as the turrets detonated. I threw up a shield to ward off the blast. The last thing I saw of the airship crew were their horrified faces before the flames took them.

"Skywraiths, regroup." I flew up and north. The others joined me seconds later, and we watched with satisfaction as our three targets spiraled into the robot army below, crumpling and hopefully crushing battle-bots beneath their bulk.

"Explosions on impact would've been nice," Boris said. "But that felt damned good."

I turned around to face the remaining airships. Bodies of the dead and the silvery forms of robots littered the ground below. Crucibles soared through the air from behind our frontlines, exploding in the midst of the enemy. Some flew high enough to hit the airships. I noted several destroyed aircraft on the opposite side of the battle from us.

Bits and pieces of battle-bots flew in all directions. Lycans and felycans fought in packs, tearing the robots to pieces while Daemos in their half-demon forms commanded packs of hellhounds against the metal hordes.

Then the mega-bots reached firing range, and massive lasers and missiles fired into the melee, heedless of friend or foe.

"We've got to stop the big bots," Ivy cried out. "They're killing everyone!"

"I still count six airships," Boris said. "We've got to take them out first."

I looked back and forth between the two targets. *What do I do?*

"Justin," Elyssa said. "Prioritize the mega-bots. Victus's robots are in range of the airships."

A formation of Victus's battle-bots raced behind our front lines and arranged themselves in neat rows before the looming airships. Volleys of missiles streamed forth from them while airship lasers blasted into their ranks.

"Attack the mega-bots," I said. "Hit them the same way we hit the airships. Target their weapons." I pointed out the closest towering humanoid robot. The thing rivalled the size of the goliath golems we'd fought during the war, standing several stories tall. I flicked my hand forward and our formation made a beeline toward the target.

Multiple turrets on the monstrous robot's shoulders turned our way and fired quick short blasts, filling the air with deadly light.

"Watch out," Delectra said. "They have anti-air weapons."

"Evasive maneuvers!" I took my own advice and dove beneath the sizzling energy. A turret tracked me, rapid firing, keeping me constantly ducking, dodging, and weaving.

I heard a scream and saw a smoking body fall from a broom.

"Pixie!" Boris shouted. "No!"

He narrowly dodged a volley of laser fire and swooped back up, then thrust forward his staff and fired lightning at the closest turret. Ivy slagged three turrets with a tremendous blast of Brilliance while Mom and Nightliss engulfed the large laser cannon on the mega-bot's chest with Murk.

I destroyed the small anti-air turrets on the robot's other shoulder and swooped behind its back to avoid fire from the quadruped mega-bot to its right. I looked in vain for a panel or other access to the robot's energy core, but the smooth metal surface betrayed no weaknesses.

"There are people inside the robot!" Ivy shouted. "In the front!"

I swooped around the head and found a polarized window I'd mistaken for a large eye. Barely visible behind the glass, two men sat before a control panel. *We just found our weakness.*

My lips peeled back in a snarl. "Give it everything you've got."

"Look out," Mom said.

I heard a whoosh of wind and saw a giant arm swiping at us. We scattered. The downdraft sent my broom into a spin. I recovered and turned back to the mega-bot. Ivy and Delectra flew past the window and raked it with attacks. I fired a bolt of Brilliance into the center, and the armored glass glowed a sullen red. I broke off the attack to dodge the robot's other massive arm.

Mom and Nightliss swooped in behind and hit the glass with one massive coordinated blast. It melted like wax.

"Die, you sons of bitches!" Boris cast his lightning spell right into the cockpit.

The crewmen screamed and danced like puppets as the electricity coursed through them. Their smoking bodies slumped at the controls.

The robot's arms dropped to the side, and it stood still in the middle of the battle.

Boris flew his broom up to the window.

"What are you doing?" I asked.

He slid through the window and twisted one of two joysticks on the left console. The robot lifted a leg. He tested the right joystick on the other console and the right arm rose and fell back down.

"I'm going to give them hell," Boris said. "Go without me."

"This isn't the plan," I yelled back. "Get back on your broom."

"No," he growled. "This is for the others."

"You can't control that thing on your own," I said. "It takes two people."

I saw the quadruped mega-bot rotating toward us, its anti-air lasers aiming for our position.

"Get behind the robot," Boris said. "I'll shield you." He grabbed the two joysticks controlling the legs and rotated them. Lumbering awkwardly, the mega-bot turned to face its four-legged companion.

"Behind the robot," I commanded.

We flew behind its bulk as anti-air lasers filled the sky. The captured mega-bot walked toward its former ally slowly at first, then gathering speed. It slammed into the quadruped. The earth below shook. Enemy robots tumbled and fell. Boris's robot lifted both arms and hammered them into the other mega-bot with a deafening clang. The arms rose and slammed down again.

All the lasers on the other robot fired on its new enemy while Boris maneuvered the arms of his monster lower and slammed them against the belly of the other metal beast. The humanoid mega-bot pushed forward. Metal groaned and cracks appeared in the hull. The quadruped toppled to the side, falling in slow motion and slammed to earth. A tremendous cloud of snow rose into the air.

The other bipedal mega-bot opened fire on Boris.

"Boris, get out of there!" I shouted. "Get out!"

"It was an honor serving with you," Boris said. "Skywraiths, form up!"

Chapter 30

Boris's mega-bot exploded. A wave of energy flashed through the air. "Evasive maneuvers!" I shouted.

My command came too late. The shockwave slammed into us, casting us through the air like dandelion seeds in a storm. I heard a cry and saw Delectra tumble from her broom. I shot out a strand of Murk and barely managed to snare her.

Doing my best to hold the channel while I spun, I fought to regain control. Panting with exertion, I wrestled the broom back into level flight.

Ivy zipped over, Delectra's broom in tow with a strand of Murk. She slid it beneath the woman and Delectra desperately grabbed it and seated herself.

I released the Murk and looked around. Mom and Nightliss hovered a distance away, but they seemed okay.

"Thank you, Justin," Delectra said. "You saved my life." She turned to Ivy. "And thank you for my broom."

"Any time," Ivy said brightly.

I surveyed the battlefield. The third mega-bot lay on its side in a smoking heap. The explosion of the other two bots must have taken it out. The airship flotilla likewise lay in ruins, aside from two fleeing units. The remains of the enemy robot army fled to the west toward the secret base while hellhounds, Daemos, vampires, and lycans hounded their flanks.

I wanted to think it was over, but we still had Frankenberg's base to contend with.

"Justin," Elyssa said, "I need the Skywraiths to pursue fleeing enemies and take them out before they reach the base."

Everyone, even Ivy, looked as exhausted as I felt. We'd fought with everything we had and lost people I'd come to know as friends. If I'd learned anything from the crystoid incident, it was that you don't give enemies a chance to recover. If I'd crushed Cephus right after the war, none of this would have happened. We couldn't allow Frankenberg's troops the chance to reinforce his home base.

I squared my shoulders. "I know you're tired, but we've still got work to do."

Mom put a hand on my shoulder. "I'm ready."

Ivy lowered her hood and wiped tears from her eyes. "I can't believe Pixie and the others are gone." Her lower lip trembled and look of pure rage shaded her face crimson. "Let's kill them all."

Nightliss, eyes wide, simply nodded.

"You have proven yourself a leader," Delectra said. "I am ready to follow."

It felt like one of those moments where everyone should put their fists into the middle of a circle before throwing them up in the air and shouting something like "Go, Skywraiths!"

My mood was too somber for such things. "Skywraiths, form up and move out."

Our small formation arced around the destroyed mega-bots and swooped after the fleeing battle-bots. A group of them were just a hundred yards from us, but running so fast, a trail of snowy dust rose behind them.

Ivy projected a wall of Murk in front of the fleeing bots. The collision sounded like a truck full of pots and pans rolling down a hill. My sister sliced the robots to bits with a razor-thin beam of Brilliance.

We passed over a pack of wolves and huge felines tearing apart another squad of bots, crested a small rise, and found twenty more battle-bots fleeing. The small hills around the secret base lay a quarter mile in the distance.

Flying at top speed, we reached the next group of targets. Delectra cast a crackling net of electricity over one group. Sparks flew and the robots tumbled to the ground. Nightliss channeled a huge hammer of Murk and smashed more robots like aluminum cans. I followed Ivy's example and sliced the legs off robots with an ultra-concentrated needle of Brilliance. Within seconds, the remnants of the robot army lay in smoking ruin.

"What about them?" Ivy pointed to the two surviving airships headed south, away from the base.

I spotted a swarm of Blue Cloaks on flying carpets in hot pursuit. "I don't think we need to worry about them." Once again, we were the first of the allied forces to the secret base. "Elyssa, all robots accounted for. We're going to scout the enemy base perimeter."

"Affirmative." She made a kissing noise. "Be careful."

I chuckled. "Is blowing kisses standard Templar procedure?"

"From me to you, yes."

"Muah, babe."

I noticed the others looking at me and cleared my throat. "Um, we're going to take a look around." I flashed the signal to drop low, and took the squadron down to just a few feet off the ground. We crept up the hill then got off our brooms and peeked over the crest.

"No more penguins," Nightliss said in a relieved voice.

Mom sighed. "Thank goodness."

"I guess the building is underground," Ivy said. "The only thing I see now is a big boulder."

"Probably an entrance," I said.

"Let's go, then." Ivy tried to get up, but I held her down.

"Hang on." I noticed other small humps in the snow and pointed them out. "Those could be weapons."

Ivy frowned. "One way to find out." She pressed fingers to her temples and blinked her eyes. A replica of her flickered into existence. "I'm projecting," she said. "Just like I did the first time we met, Justin."

I remembered the day I'd seen my sister wandering among the graves at the funeral of Elyssa's brother, Jack. "Let's see what happens."

The illusion stood up and ran down the hill. Snow exploded from the humps, and turrets appeared all around the perimeter of the bowl-shaped valley. A brilliant laser show blasted the illusion.

"Take them out!" I shouted.

We rose to our knees and blasted the turrets to slag while they focus-fired on Ivy's illusion. The only turrets we couldn't reach were on the other side of the bowl.

"Let's shield and go." I channeled Murk, ready to protect us at any minute so we could rush the boulder and look for a way into the base. Before we took a step, the entire valley floor quaked. Ice shattered, and the suspicious boulder began to crumble. A thundering roar sent a blast of hot air washing over us.

The boulder collapsed to reveal a large windowed dome. I saw a dozen people inside, and in a big leather captain's chair sat Frankenberg himself.

"Holy alien aardvarks," I said, "we have a problem."

"What is that thing?" Ivy asked.

A flying saucer large enough to be an office building exploded from the ground in a shower of earth, ice, and snow. The hot exhaust rising from beneath the saucer melted the ice, showering us with sheets of water.

"Get to your brooms," I said.

We flew to a safer distance and watched the huge thing slowly rise. The platter portion of the saucer measured two stories high, and was probably the diameter of a city block. Massive landing legs folded into the bottom of the craft.

"Leave it to a mad scientist to make his secret base a flying saucer," I said in awe.

"Look at the turrets on the platter," Delectra said. "They're already destroyed."

"Those were the same turrets hidden by the snow," Mom said.

I magnified the view in my HUD and scanned for other weapons. It bracketed in red another dozen undamaged turrets on the other side, but indicated no other obvious weapons. "People, we've got to take that thing down."

We zipped toward the flying base. I braced for more attacks, but it seemed that Frankenberg had invested everything in offensive weaponry, and very little in terms of base defense. He'd probably thought he could rely on his robots and airships for protection.

He thought wrong.

Superheated air washed over us and threatened to send us tumbling out of control.

"Careful for the exhaust," Mom said.

I led the formation straight up, away from the bright blue flames shooting from the bottom of the saucer. We crested the edge of the platter and headed straight for the dome in the middle. The turrets on the opposite side of the platter couldn't target us without hitting the command center.

"That window is probably armored," Delectra said.

I grinned. "With all of us, it really doesn't matter."

The dome rose about twenty feet high and spanned probably a hundred feet in diameter. I saw Frankenberg inside and waved. Face beet red, he shouted orders at the crewmen. The saucer spun independently of the dome, swiveling the undamaged turrets toward our position.

"We've got to blow this thing open now!" I held up my hand and summoned Brilliance. Ivy pulled up beside me, right fist glowing white. Mom and Nightliss appeared to my other side.

I aimed at the Frankenberg's ugly face. "Fire."

Gouts of destruction blasted into the armored glass. A cherry red glow began at the center of our attack and radiated outward. Frankenberg and his people ran to the sides just as our attack blasted a massive hole through the dome.

The platter stopped turning, keeping the laser turrets safely away from us.

"Hold fire." Before I entered the dome, I shouted a warning. "If you fire on me, I'll simply shield myself and then incinerate you. Is that clear? Give up now and get on your knees."

Crewmen in drab gray military uniforms came out with their hands up and dropped to their knees. After a long pause, Frankenberg finally stepped from behind a large console and with some difficulty, lowered his generously rounded frame to his knees.

"Wait out here," I told the others. "Watch my back." I flew into the dome and landed. "Who can pilot this thing?"

Two women raised their hands.

"Land it now."

They shuffled to the controls, careful to keep their hands raised, then sat down and started pressing buttons and shifting levers.

Frankenberg looked down at the floor. His entire body trembled with fear. My body trembled too—with rage. I wanted so badly to kill this man for what he'd done. My demon half wanted to spill his blood a drop at a time and torture him for eternity. His actions had killed thousands of normal and supers. He'd nearly destroyed magic in Eden. Everything he'd done severely pissed me off.

I took a deep breath and closed off those emotions. Lowering the hood of my armor, I spoke. "Frankenberg, look at me."

He slowly raised his head and looked at me like a wounded dog.

"Are you working with Cephus?" I asked.

Teeth chattering, he said nothing.

"Answer me!"

He shook his head. "They'll kill me if I say anything."

I roared and lifted him off the ground by his neck. Body flailing, he gasped and choked. I dropped him on his feet. "You'd better tell me, or by god, I'll devour your soul and leave you nothing."

He sobbed, and dropped to his knees. "They made me do it. They gave me this army and told me what to do." Frankenberg clasped his hands together. "Please, believe me. I didn't want to do any of this."

I dropped my voice to a hiss and leaned forward. "Who?"

"Serena and—"

In a blur of motion, one of the crewmen next to him drew a weapon, put it to Frankenberg's temple and blew a hole through his skull. I grabbed for the gun, but the man turned the weapon on himself and left a smoking ruin of his own head. It was then I smelled something very familiar. Putrid yellow smoke rose from the body and vanished in a flash.

"A demon," I growled.

The saucer jolted as it touched down. A klaxon shrieked, and a silver case the size of a coffin rose from the floor behind the captain's chair. A display flickered on and a calm female voice spoke. "Nuclear self-destruct activated. You have two minutes to abandon ship. Good luck."

I spotted a man behind a console offer me a cruel grin. I blurred to him and slammed him against the bulkhead. His body also reeked of brimstone.

"What did you do?"

He burst into maniacal laughter. "We're going to make a pretty explosion." Insane giggles shook his body. "Pretty, pretty, pretty!"

"Son of a bitch! How do I shut it off?

"No escape." He burst into laughter. I slammed his head on the console until he stopped laughing.

The remaining crew people screamed and ran for their lives down a corridor.

Two minutes until boom. "Dear god. We're all gonna die."

"Please restate request," the computer replied.

"Shut down self-destruct."

"Command not recognized," It said. "One minute and forty-five seconds remaining."

I heard a series of roars and saw escape pods flying off into the air.

I was desperate. "How do I stop the self-destruct?"

"The failsafe has been activated," it replied calmly. "The nuclear destruct sequence cannot be aborted. For your safety, a distance of one mile from ground zero is recommended. One minute and thirty five seconds remaining."

I radioed Elyssa. "How close are the troops?"

"We're a few hundred yards away and closing," she replied.

"You need to go into a full retreat." I checked the timer. "In a minute forty, this thing is going up in a nuclear explosion with a one-mile radius."

"There's no way we can get clear in time!"

"Use the aether generator shields if you have to." I switched to the Skywraith channel. "Get the hell out of here." I told them what I'd told Elyssa. "I'm going to try to shut this thing down."

"Justin, no!" Ivy said. "Get out of there!"

"If I don't stop the bomb, it'll take out everyone."

"We're not leaving you, son," Mom said.

The rest of the Skywraiths flew inside.

"I must go find Victus," Delectra said. "Perhaps he knows how to disable it, but I can't reach him over the radio."

I nodded. "Go find him, but we don't have much longer to spare."

"One minute twenty-five seconds remaining," the computer said.

Nightliss examined the silver coffin on the floor. "This is the bomb?"

"I think so." I looked for a way to open it, but couldn't find anything.

"It's bolted to the floor," Ivy said. She dual channeled Murk and Brilliance. "Hit the bolts with Stasis."

The four of us each shattered a bolt with Stasis.

"One minute fifteen remaining," the computer said. "Please clear the area immediately or you will be obliterated."

"Politest damned bomb I ever heard," I muttered. I gripped the front of the case and lifted it off the floor. "There's got to be a way to get it out of here."

"The escape pods," Mom said. "Hurry!"

Mom lifted the back of the bomb and we hurried toward the corridor the crew had used to escape. Only one pod remained. We positioned the bomb inside and realized a problem.

"I don't see an automatic pilot button." I examined the controls—a large red liftoff button and a joystick. "Someone will have to fly it."

"One minute," the bomb computer said.

We went back into the corridor to talk options.

"Maybe it'll fly straight up if we hit the button," Ivy said.

I shook my head. "Can't take the chance. I'll fly it as high as possible and—"

The pod door slid shut. With a roar, it blasted off, straight up into the air. I looked at the group and realized someone was missing.

Nightliss.

Chapter 31

"Nightliss!" I shouted into the comm link. "What are you doing?"

She replied calmly. "Justin, you and all my friends are my family." Her voice broke. "But you have your real family—Alysea, Ivy, David, and Elyssa. I knew if I didn't take this bomb, you would. I couldn't allow that to happen. You are the hero everyone needs, and I have played my part."

Tears stung my eyes. "Nightliss, you can't do this! We need you."

"Nightliss, I love you!" Ivy pleaded. "Please come back."

Mom slumped against the bulkhead and lowered the hood of the armor. Tears glistened on her cheeks. "I love you, my friend."

"I love you all," Nightliss said in a broken voice. "I have managed to keep the pod going straight up. I pray it is far enough away."

In the background, I heard the bomb computer speak. "Thirty seconds. If you can still hear this, you will likely die. Please put your affairs in order."

Victus's voice came over the comm link. "Nightliss, there's an unlabeled green switch to the left of the takeoff button. Hit it and the autopilot will take the escape pod straight up and out of the atmosphere. Underneath the pilot seat is a rocket stick. Jump out of the hatch and freefall as long as you can, then use the rocket stick. Do you read me?"

Static crackled over the comm link, but Nightliss didn't reply.

"Nightliss, did you hear him?" I shouted. "Are you there?"

We ran back down the corridor and into the command center. I looked up in the sky, but only a thin white contrail showed the path the escape pod had taken. The pod itself was a tiny dot almost too far away to discern even with my supernatural sight.

An orange ring of fire spread across the sky, annihilating the pod. Thunder rumbled, as if a distant storm loomed on the horizon.

My voice was so choked with emotion, I could hardly speak. "Nightliss?" I grabbed my broom and flew straight up. I spotted a black-clad figure tumbling through the air and raced toward it. My heart soared. "Nightliss!"

Her body tumbled like a rag doll, blasted armor trailing smoke. I realized I couldn't simply catch her—I'd have to match her speed. I went into a dive, slowing just enough so her body caught up with me, and wrapped an arm around her torso.

The ground approached frighteningly fast. I pulled up hard and gravity seemed to redouble its efforts to crush me. The broom handle cracked and splintered. The arm holding Nightliss felt as though it would tear from the socket. But I couldn't let go. I *wouldn't*.

"Pull up, damn you!" I shouted as the ground grew closer and closer. The broom evened out, but it was too late.

Earth slammed into me in a blur of white. I lost my grip on Nightliss and tumbled blindly until I slid to a stop. Every muscle in my body ached and a sharp pain raced up my right arm. Groaning, I pushed myself up and staggered to my feet. I saw Nightliss's still form face down in the snow and stumbled over to her.

I knelt next, rolled her over. Barely anything remained of the protective mask and parts of it looked as though they'd burnt into her flesh. A gentle breath from her cracked and swollen lips fogged the air. Tears blurred my vision. Shaking with sobs, I rocked my dear friend back and forth.

"I've got you, Nightliss," I whispered. "Help is coming." I switched my comm link to Elyssa's channel. "Nightliss is down. I need help now."

"Where are you, Justin?" Elyssa asked.

My throat was so constricted with emotion I could hardly speak. "I'll fire a flare." I raised a hand and sent up a volley of Murk to light the way.

"I saw it," Elyssa said.

"Hurry," I begged her. "Please!"

"They're coming." I heard her shout orders. "Justin, how bad is it?"

I removed my hood, heedless of the cold. My tears froze to my cheeks as I lowered an ear to Nightliss's mouth and listened for a breath.

"Justin?" she said in a harsh whisper.

I cradled her head in my lap to keep it out of the wind. "I'm here, sweetie. Help is on the way."

"Everyone out of danger?"

I burst into fresh sobs and nodded. "You saved us all, Nightliss. Now you've got to hang on so we can save you."

Her hand reached up and touched my face. "It's okay, Justin." She sucked in a wheezing breath.

I held her hand in mine, leaned down and kissed her cheek. "No, it's not." I switched back to the comms link. "Elyssa, how far? I need help now. Please, tell me they're close!" I pulled Nightliss close. "Hang on, Nightliss. Your family needs you. The Templars need you. We all need you!"

Nightliss shivered and her green eyes went wide. "Tell my family I love them." She looked at me. "I love you, Justin, my sweet hero." Her body slumped and the light faded from her eyes.

"No." I pressed my ear to her mouth. Nothing. "Don't do this, Nightliss. Please, come back," I croaked. "Come back!" I reared back my head and screamed. "No!"

Flying carpets arrived, and healers rushed over. Meghan was the one who pulled Nightliss from my limp arms and helped put her on a carpet.

Meghan turned to me moments later, tears in her eyes. "Justin—" her voice broke and she knelt in the snow next to me. "I couldn't do anything for her. The burns and damage from the explosion were too much."

"The Clarion is dead," another healer whispered in a ragged voice. "The light of the Templars has been extinguished."

Mom arrived and leapt from her broom. She ran to the carpet and stared, horrified. Tears streaked her face. She turned to me. "Did she say anything before—" She choked on her last words.

"She wanted me to say that she loves her family." I forced myself to stand and helped Meghan to her feet. I walked to Mom and hugged her. "She can't be dead. She just can't."

272

Mom trembled. "My dear friend."

"She's the best hero that ever was," Ivy said. "I wish I could tell her that I love her for saving us."

I took a deep breath and straightened despite the crippling heartache stealing my breath. "I'm *furious* at her for doing this."

Mom shook her head. "Don't be, son. Be grateful that she loved you so much she sacrificed herself to keep you from doing the same thing." She brushed away tears. "True love has many forms, Justin. Nightliss's selflessness should be celebrated, not mourned."

More tears wanted to come, but I had no more to give. *I'm in shock.* The last time I'd felt anywhere close to this awful was when I thought Elyssa would die after a Seraphim burned a hole through her chest. Nightliss had gone with me to Seraphina in search of a healer. She'd helped me rescue Elyssa from the cusp of death.

I dropped to the ground and buried my face in my hands. The day I found a stray black cat being attacked by a dog replayed in my mind. Before I even knew she was Seraphim, Nightliss had helped me save my father from a vampire stronghold. She'd healed the damage to Elyssa's memories after Daelissa tried to wipe me from her mind and destroy our relationship. She'd touched all of our lives and kept me alive long enough to defeat her evil sister.

I can't believe it. How can she be dead?

Cephus, Serena, and anyone else involved in this would pay dearly.

Several days passed as we cleaned up the mess in Antarctica and disabled every crystoid but for one in northern Australia. With the Three Sisters once again operational, we tried to send an expedition through the Alabaster Arch, but the arch in Seraphina didn't respond. Crystoids on the other side were most likely to blame. Though the other Alabaster Arches worked, they all led to Brightling controlled territory. Without Ketiss and his Darkling army, we couldn't hope to take on the enemy forces.

We devised a plan to use the sky portal above the lone remaining crystoid to scout Tarissa and find a way through. From there, we could destroy the crystoids on the other side and activate the skyway.

When at last we had gathered the dead, many in our army gathered in the horse pasture at the Templar compound to commemorate the fallen heroes of the Battle of Antarctica. I sat on the platform in front of the crowd with the other leaders, Commander Borathen, Captain Takei, Colin McCloud, Kassallandra, and even Komad Rashad. I tried to keep thoughts of Nightliss from my mind as each leader delivered a eulogy.

I went last.

As I stood behind the podium, stomach twisting, throat tight, my gaze wandered to the caskets of our comrades and tears blurred my vision. I took a deep breath and spoke. "We stand here today thanks to the selfless sacrifices of those we honor today." My voice sounded weak and hollow. "Many of us lost comrades and family." I paused to clear the knot in my throat. "I lost my dear friend, Nightliss." I squeezed shut my eyes and gathered strength to speak. "Unfortunately, one war and thousands of lost lives were not enough to win peace."

"Nightliss was more than my friend. When Daelissa abandoned the Templars who stood against her, Nightliss came to our rescue." I wiped at my eyes. "She was proud—so proud to become the Clarion. She was a beacon of hope in a world threatened by darkness. In every sense of the word, Nightliss was our guardian angel."

"Bless the Clarion!" The Templars roared as one.

I looked up and pointed a finger into the distance. "Out there lies another threat, another war to be won. This latest conflict proves that until we complete the task ahead of us, Eden will not have her peace. We must bring order to another realm. We must risk our lives." I bared my teeth. "We will prove our fallen did *not* die in vain."

I looked at the neat rows of coffins and summoned all my strength when I saw the one with the symbol of the Templar Clarion. Nightliss's coffin. "Once again we will unite against a great threat. Once again we will prove our dedication to freedom. No army will break our spirits and no realm will subjugate our people." Thoughts of Nightliss's sacrifice gave strength to my voice. "Together we fight for Eden. Together we fight for peace." I pumped my fist in the air and shouted, "Seraphina awaits!"

The assemblage burst into roars. Templars pounded their fists against their chests, chanting, "To Seraphina! To victory!"

Lycans burst into animal forms and howled. The massive felycan, Saber, shook the air with a massive roar. Even the Red Cell vampires raised a cheer.

The strength left my body, and I sagged. *Goodbye, my dear sweet Nightliss. I'll miss you so much.* I left the stage and walked past the throngs, seeking the solace of the only one who could give it to me.

Elyssa rushed from the Templars and hugged me fiercely. The tight dam of sorrow broke and my heart poured out. I sensed others gathering around me and looked up into the teary eyes of my loved ones. Shelton wiped at his red eyes and offered a weak smile. Bella wrapped her arms around him and buried her face in his chest. Mom and Ivy huddled nearby. Even my father's eyes were wet.

Our heroes would not be forgotten.

As the days passed, the Templars gathered their ranks. Houses Assad and Slade sent word to all Daemos to join the fight. The Arcanes brought forth their battle mages and Blue Cloaks. The lycans and felycans readied their claws and fangs. Our army swelled with other supernaturals, all ready to fight for the peace we so desperately wanted.

Onward to Seraphina.

Onward to war.

Onward to victory.

The sleeping giant had awakened. It was time for the mortal realm to put the angels in their place.

I hope you enjoyed reading this book. Reviews are very important in helping other readers decide what to read next. Would you please take a few seconds to rate this book?

For the latest on new releases, free ebooks, and more, join John Corwin's Newsletter at www.johncorwin.net!

Meet the Author

John Corwin is the bestselling author of the Overworld Chronicles. He enjoys long walks on the beach and is a firm believer in puppies and kittens.

After years of getting into trouble thanks to his overactive imagination, John abandoned his male modeling career to write books.

He resides in Atlanta.

Connect with John Corwin online:
Facebook: http://www.facebook.com/johnhcorwinauthor
Website: http://www.johncorwin.net
Twitter: http://twitter.com/#!/John_Corwin